KUPERMAN'S FIRE

KUPERMAN'S FIRE

JOHN J. CLAYTON

THE PERMANENT PRESS
Sag Harbor, New York 11963

Library of Congress Cataloging-in-Publication Data

Clayton, John Jacob.
    Kuperman's fire / John J. Clayton.
        p.   cm.

    ISBN-13: 978-1-57962-152-0
    ISBN-10: 1-57962-152-X

    1. Jewish families—Fiction. 2. Jewish fiction. 3. Domestic fiction.
    I. Title.

PS3553.L388K87 2007
813'.54—dc22   2007004282

Printed in the United States of America.

The Permanent Press
4170 Noyac Road
Sag Harbor, NY 11963
www.thepermanentpress.com

For my son Joshua
Of Blessed Memory

CHAPTER ONE

Adonoi, *open my lips, and let my mouth declare your praise.*

Again this morning in his study, as Michael begins davening the Amidah, the standing prayer, he senses that he is living within Jacob Goldstein, or that Jacob Goldstein is living within him. Michael needs his dead grandfather Jacob this morning to help him handle the French documentary on television last night; the pictures from Rwanda, unbidden, come back to him. A one-story building; inside, one room, part of the roof gone, corpses, over a hundred, no space to die without being crushed by others, charred, clothes on skeletons, a sea of matted cloth on bones, so much like the tangle of once-Jews being bulldozed by Americans liberating Buchenwald, tumbled like dead fish into a mass grave.

They both inhabit the one flesh, Jacob and Michael.

- ✦ It's the month of Tishri, 5664 (1903) in Kishinev, Bessarabia— Russia then, now Moldava.
- ✦ It's September 23, 1994, the middle of Tishri (5755) in Brookline, Massachusetts.

We're in the New Year, inscribed, somehow, in the Book of Life.

Michael Kuperman is fused somehow with an imagined, imaginary grandfather. But it's his *historical* grandfather who rides his bones.

Michael folds away the tallis and yarmulke into a tallis bag, packs bag into the overnight case. Going into the bathroom to shave, separate from Jacob now, he talks to his grandfather about the pogrom in Rwanda. Because Jacob Goldstein, his mother's father, who died just before Michael was born—he knows pogroms.

The stories from Rwanda (dear God) have become unbearable. As if Bosnia weren't enough, as if the siege of Sarajevo weren't enough. To make sure that Tutsi and Hutu could never again live side by side in peace, fanatics in the Rwandan government made sure, when the slaughter began, that neighbors were assigned to kill neighbors, kill neighbors' children—or be killed themselves. A photograph: clothed skeletons hugging infant bones. And the numbers, the numbers keep growing, growing. Three-quarters of a million? A million? Militia members bragged that one band could kill "two thousand Tutsis in twenty minutes." You hear that figure again and again. Two thousand in twenty minutes. They slice at the Achilles tendon, the people go down, and they can butcher at their leisure. And now, Tutsi "reprisals." Half a million Hutus are running in terror to the borders.

What do you do with these stories? Michael tells them to his mother's father.

He talks to Jacob, but hears no Jacob answer—as you'd expect, since Jacob is long dead, dead before Michael was born—we're not talking crazy here. So Michael answers for him in wise, *alte-jude*, grandpa voice, sighs *Aach . . . I know, I know.* But really, what can this Jacob know? What Michael needs him to know. Still, sometimes, when he's sure he can't be overheard, in the bathroom with the water running, Michael speaks for his grandfather.

Daddy's Talking To Somebody

You shouldn't be ashamed, Jacob tells him, *that this is your life course, to make money, even a great deal of money, in a world full of suffering. "Why you?" Why not you? Does it mean you have to be a sweatshop operator?*

"Who said *ashamed*? I'm not ashamed. I give people a livelihood."

"*Nu?* Then?" And Jacob, this invented, patched-together Yiddishkeit Jacob, sighs . . .

. . . While Ari, eight years old, listens at the bathroom door.

Because Daddy is *really* talking to himself this time. Shaving and talking. Loud, easy to hear over the water, except not the words. But that's not what's so weird (Ari's used to that). It's that somebody's in there with him.

And this other person is *answering*.

So Ari goes to Señor Pedro's cage and lets the parakeet hop from his cage to his finger, then carries him down the hall to his mother's study.

Freeze-frame: you need to understand this house of theirs. It's substantial, one of a number of imposing houses in Brookline, part of greater Boston, built early in the century but in a mid-nineteenth century style, with brick façade, classical portico, long, multi-paned windows downstairs in high-ceilinged rooms with mahogany trim and deep Victorian moldings. In the spacious entrance hall, a broad carpeted staircase. To the right, a large living room; to the left, a dining room and paneled library. Deborah has modernized the big kitchen with new cherry cabinetry, a twenty thousand dollar island of wood and technology in the center, and French doors onto the rock garden at the rear. There are bright-oiled wood floors covered with Orientals downstairs; upstairs, thick, taupe, wall-to-wall carpeting.

Ari, in socks, slides along this carpet to his mother's study. Señor Pedro's clipped wings flap.

Ari knocks, "Mo-mm?" (Two syllables, descending.)

"Mmm?"

"Hi." Ari isn't supposed to be in here, he knows that. But he's so sleepy this morning. He needs her. And Dad is being *so* weird. Ari plays it casual. Tentatively, he cuddles into his mom's big leather reading chair, old leather cold against his skin, bird against his cheek, and listens to the click of her keyboard. One look at her shoulders tells him she isn't in the mood. She half-turns, keeps typing. "Good morning, Ari, I'm really busy, I'm sorry. But I've got to go so soon." He just sits. She turns a little more. "*Yes*, honey?"

He thinks about how to say it. "I thought . . . maybe you were in the bathroom with Daddy."

"Uh huh. . . ?" She's typing again.

"Because Daddy's talking to somebody."

"Well, *that's* nothing new, for godsakes. He talks to himself, you know that."

"But somebody's *there*—"

"—*Nobody's* there. Your daddy is just a little peculiar sometimes."

"—With a *different voice*."

"Oh, you know, sometimes. . . ." She stops typing, swivels. "What kind of voice?"

"With an *accent*."

"An accent?"

"And *old*, and, you know, like from another country. Like the *shammes* at synagogue?—except older, even."

"Oh, well, you know your dad, he's kidding around, that's all it is. I see you're all dressed. Well *you* look nice. Margaret will be here any minute to take you to school. You know your mom's leaving for the airport in like five minutes."

"Mom? You promised you wouldn't talk about yourself in third person."

"*I'm* leaving for the airport in five minutes. Okay?"

"Maybe I'll ask Daddy."

"Oh, I wouldn't. You'll just embarrass him."

"Daddy? Daddy doesn't get embarrassed."

"Anyway, it's nothing." Coming up for air, she asks, "Has Karen gone?"

She *has* gone; the private bus service has picked Karen up for Buckingham. Deborah's chest feels suddenly heavier—she won't be seeing them for two days, and Karen didn't even stop in to say goodbye? Well, *that's* a statement, *that's* certainly a gesture. Her face tenses up like a soldier: grim. *Life.* All right. Packed, ready for battle in Dallas. But really—*talk*ing to himself, for godsakes! In another *voice*? They're going to lock him up and throw away the key.

"Give me a kiss goodbye, you sweet, sweet boy." And he does. She kisses his forehead. Is he hot? He's probably fine. Unlike Karen, whom Deborah thinks of as earthy, full of juice, living at the edges of her skin (and not in some imitative, vulgar, Victoria's Secret way), Ari looks to his mother like a black-haired angel; about Ari she's sentimental and unashamed. It's as if God had sculpted his delicate face into being, and just before letting him go from heaven, had put forefinger to nose: *there,* and pressed lightly. She saves to disk, shuts down the computer, fusses with papers, picks up the laptop and suitcase by the door to her study. And, right on time for a change, taxi's at the front door. "Michael? MICHAEL? Got to *go,* Michael."

She's on her way down when he comes to the staircase in boxers, shirt off, hair uncombed, and waves. "So. You're leaving?"

"Of *course* I'm leaving. Barely time as it is if there's traffic in the tunnel. Goodbye." Making sure Ari's not around, she says, "Oh, by the way, Ari heard you talking to yourself."

"When was that?"

"And he doesn't look so hot. Make sure he's not getting sick, will you, Michael? Have Margaret bring him home after school; I think he's coming down with something." She sets her bag on a newel post. "What does Jonathan say about this peculiarity of yours?" When he doesn't answer, she shrugs him off. "So. Have a great week talking to yourself."

"Have a great meeting."

Margaret Corcoran has let herself in and is fixing breakfast for Ari. Deborah gives him a kiss, takes a hug, and she's off. She hears Ari telling Margaret, "Daddy *loves* to talk to himself when he's shaving."

"Well, it reminds me, sweetheart, I had an old uncle, when he first came over. . . ." Margaret begins—one of Margaret's Irish-immigrant stories. Deborah's comforted: that Ari will have a comic frame to contain his father's . . . whatever-it-is. And Deborah's out the door. A consultant. A soldier for Thayer, Fletcher, and Gringold.

The old man Jacob, hand to a cheek, has to fade out. Michael has an important day ahead. Becoming a modern businessman, he buttons his shirt of fine, pale blue cotton, while his eyes narrow onto a patch of sunlit motes in the middle of the air where he can scroll through a mental hologram of his schedule. He used to like this shift to firm practical focus, nothing better than having a clear plan to carry out. He should be joyous today. After months of negotiations, months of listening to Ken McNair's "concerns"—meant to express, like a dance in words, his canniness—here's a victory: a merger which will take their system-software company into a safe harbor. It's not a buy-out; it's a true merger of strengths, though McNair's InterCom is the bigger partner. It's Jonathan—his partner Jonathan Greene, who charmed McNair, who made McNair want to marry this contemporary high-energy company, young company going places. "We can be," Jonathan said at one meeting, "your interface with the future." But it's Michael who gave McNair the assurance: we're solid; merging with us is a shrewd move. Narrowing his eyes, Michael nodded across the table at McNair's shrewdness. And why not? Let McNair be as canny as he dreams; Michael reflects back to him his dream of himself—and closes the deal.

He and Deborah both have to be out of the house this week. It can't be helped, and at least *he'll* be back tomorrow night. He puts on a shirt, a tie from Hermès, and one of his better suits, dove-gray. He's not the dresser Jonathan is, but when he tries, he looks pretty good. His hair, like his father's, curls at the sides; unlike his father, he keeps it cut. Adjusting the tie in the mirror, he begins to feel more alive, his old business-self, like a dancer in mourning who brightens as he gets into his costume. Suitcase in one hand, laptop in the other, he goes downstairs in time to fool around with Ari, take comfort from Mrs. Corcoran. He lets her make him toast and pour coffee. "Margaret? Margaret, I wish you'd kind of . . ." (he wraps himself in his own arms) ". . . you know, *take care of* Karen tonight. We forget—because she's so competent. But she needs a little. . . ." He makes a hugging gesture but doesn't say *mothering*. "And before you leave tonight—do make sure she practices piano. That they *both* practice. Okay?"

He muscles up Ari, digs his knuckles into his curly hair. "Honey, you look absolutely woozy—you get enough sleep?"

Ari mumbles something and Michael kisses him. Warm—from sleep? Ari kisses back, fervently, for real. Oh, Michael thinks, I'm worried from guilt—that we we're both going away.

Jacob in Kishinev

Kuperman has a car and driver to pick him up—not a sign of his vanity or of corporate pomp: he works on laptop, on phone and fax, while Dennis slogs through dense morning traffic that Kuperman tunes out. It's a rolling office. His laptop gives him his day's schedule, but Michael Kuperman has a methodical mind and forgets little.

His grandfather Jacob groans. Michael is not having auditory hallucinations—but to say *imagines* is too weak. At any moment he can turn his attention that way, and his grandfather's life is *happening*, a parallel reality. His grandfather, a grandfather Michael knows only through pictures, breathes through him. He finds his own big frame shrinking. Michael's well over six feet tall, he's got thick black hair, receding where Michelangelo gave Moses horns, giving him a long, high forehead; he's long-boned, a tennis player;

in photographs, Jacob Goldstein is squat, bearded, balding. It's oddly comforting, this metamorphosis, Grandfather's presence, or Michael's presence in this other life.

Michael imagines Bearded Grandfather in a Shtetl. *This* Jacob, *his* Jacob, dances through the street on Simchat Torah in an ecstatic line of black-coated Hasidim. Michael can't see the actual, the *historical*, shrewd Jacob Goldstein leave the house of study in an expensive gabardine black suit and walk out into the streets of Kishinev. The cobblestone streets are noisy with wagons, as if this were London in Dickens' time. But it's Kishinev, and Kishinev, turn of the century, is no shtetl, is many shtetls, a small city, lots of business goes on there, and there are discussion groups and concerts. Some of the young, both men and women, not permitted to attend universities, are becoming radicalized. Beardless, in cap and open shirt, they look like people from the new century.

The cobblestones form and transform, pattern into pattern of elegant curves. Prayer (he's coming from morning prayers in the new shul) often makes Jacob Goldstein see in this way. The windows of the shops have been replaced—those shops that remained in business. It's a gray, wet-gray day. His own shop has survived, has revived—dry goods, combined peculiarly but profitably with the business of buying and selling lambs, raising lambs to sell. Whatever was in the shop was stolen or dragged in the mud. But most of the business is on paper. It is this business that his parents, and his brother Avrom and his family, can live on when Jacob leaves Kishinev.

For of course he has to take his family away. *This, this is insane.* He thinks of the poems of Chaim Bialik that have come to him recently. Bialik is angry at the Jews of Kishinev for having stood helplessly by while their wives were shamed.

There are two choices: to join the Jewish defense league being formed—or to leave.

Every winter the hot blood rises against us, and when the streets are passable, Easter and agents of the Czar come to remind the muzhiki *of the death of their messiah, and vodka burns in the blood, and a man you might do business with, might ask to have him repair your roof, might even have a schnappes with, meets another and the two meet with others and all of a sudden it's a mob. But last Easter came the pogrom the whole world talks about.* Cossacks in their red shirts, brand-new shirts provided by—provided by whom? You tell me! Who provided these brand-new shirts so the Cossacks could recognize one another right away?—Cossacks came into town to do the business right.

And thanks be to God, General Ostrov came to him, not waiting to be asked: "You gather your whole family and come to us; we have a place waiting in the cellar. It's going to be terrible this time. Never mind how I know. I know."

The Jews were going home after Passover services. A sunny day. Well-dressed Jews passed through the market square on their way home. It began there.

General Ostrov's house is on the main street. The cellar windows, high up in the wall, Ostrov's wife covered with curtains, but between the curtains *you could see the boots, the heavy legs, running, you could hear the drunken yells, the screaming. And when the servants came with food, three times a day, Sarah made them taste it first, afraid they'd poison us.*

General Ostrov has done business with Jacob, with Jacob's father, for many years. They're invited to his house for cards. Ostrov, twenty-five years his senior, has watched Jacob grow up; now, he likes mentoring him: partly, it's the seriousness of Jacob's secular reading. They talk about books that arrive, pages uncut, from Moscow, from Paris. Ostrov lends the books so they can talk together. And *argue*. Ostrov loves to argue.

We heard the screaming outside, and we shuttered the windows and said prayers—a week to live that way!

In New York there was a rally at a great hall, thousands; money came to Kishinev. Money, letters. In Paris, in London, in Berlin. Kishinev has lost its reality as a large provincial town in which many Jews live; it has become a symbol of Russian barbarism.

Jacob doesn't know that in two years, 1905, in Odessa, eight hundred Jews will be killed, shops looted, houses burned, hundreds of women violated. He doesn't know how mild the pogrom in Kishinev will seem in just a few years, during the Great War and just after—a hundred thousand will die; he doesn't know that a fourteen-year-old boy from Branau in Austria is already sick with nightmares he will try to purge by the magic trick of turning Jews into ashes.

*He doesn't know that by deciding to leave he has saved not only
wife and children but his grandson, Michael Kuperman.*
All of us are here by a miracle. A grandfather who paid off a
border guard, a gift of bread to a great-grandmother, a neighbor
who nursed a great-great grandfather through a fever. We are here
because maybe a hundred years ago someone hid or someone fled
or made a decision and his unborn children's children weren't
buried in a killing pit, weren't forced into a shower. Each of us, a
miracle.

Now, the Goldsteins have their passports (with General
Ostrov's help); their plans are made. They look at one another,
Sarah and Jacob, and every night, when the children are in bed, she
weeps, while he, too, weeps, but inside. Melodrama from Yiddish
theater?—here's the root of those melodramas. Never will they see
their parents again. And brothers, sisters, friends?

It's as if Michael Kuperman were forced to leave the planet, to
take his family and live without gravity in a space station. Jacob was
a reader but not an urban intellectual, not avant-garde. He was a
businessman who went to shul. It's impossible for Michael to enter
his bones, to walk in his rhythm, to feel with his feet the leather on
cobblestones, to feel with his flesh the heavy, stiff gabardines. Still,
the dark gray jackets with wide lapels and large buttons—Michael
remembers them in the YIVO photograph on his wall. The thirty,
forty men are standing in their best clothes, their broad-brimmed
hats (though also a few fedoras, top hats, bowlers, caps), others cut
out by the picture frame. They are burying five Torah scrolls: in
caskets, tented over by cloth with Hebrew writing—are these tallises sewn together? Are they kittels, shrouds for burial? Were they
specially sewn for this funeral? The scrolls had been desecrated
that spring by the mob in Kishinev, and so they must be put in
the earth as if they were human victims, like those laid out on a
wooden floor in the second photo. Thousands of Jews, every Jewish
family that survived, took part in the funeral procession across
the city.

Jacob Goldstein is one of the men on the far right of the picture, black-bearded, well-dressed for a poor community.

Now, through Michael Kuperman, he looks out the window of
a Chrysler sedan slogging through Boston traffic.

Zeides and Bubbes

But of course, in *Michael's* version he's a Jacob with all the rough edges rubbed off. Michael turns him into an old Jew with Yiddish lilt—although the historical Jacob sounded more Russian and tried hard to sound American. Why does he need him so much? Sometimes Michael himself wonders: *Do I have it too good, do I need a little pogrom to make me feel like a mensch?* Some Jews he knows wear the Holocaust and the history of our oppression like a costume. But that's not it. One, Jacob, he is sure, would have understood what's been happening in Bosnia, in Rwanda. Understood and been able to take it in. By himself, Michael feels overwhelmed. Michael can't stand seeing. Sometimes he wonders, *How can I bless this life?* Jacob has training in bearing, in bearing up. Two, Jacob lived a comfortable life but knew to grieve. He's an antidote to the meretricious. Life is *not* a Range Rover filled with shopping bags. And three, this grandfather was smart and tough, he got his family out, he came here and made a fortune. His other grandfather—his father's father, Nathan—Michael remembers as the cranky old man in the basement apartment who used headlines from the *New York Post* to fuel his sourness. Nathan was Michael's first socialist. He died, Nathan, when Michael was six or seven. So it's hard for Michael to invent *him*. It's his *mother's* father, Jacob Goldstein, who inhabits Michael.

Jews nowadays are crazy about grandfathers and grandmothers. Maybe always, but especially now, we need them so deeply, and they're gone, the elders, and it's just *us* left at the controls of our lives. *How do I run this thing?* Books and books have been written, like prayers, to invoke them, *zeides* and *bubbes,* because our parents often refused to carry the spark, to pass the spark that joined us to our common life of awe. We try to rekindle. We change our names back. Cohon whose father became "Colton" becomes again Cohon—or goes one more generation back to become Kohane or Kagan. Just as Michael Kuperman, whose father's father in Chicago became "Cooper," reclaims Kuperman: these past eight years, since the week Ari was born, he's been Michael *Kuperman*.

That change made his wife Deborah furious. Not that Deborah had to change *her* name. It had never been Cooper; she remained

Deborah Schiff. Still—people often thought of her as Mrs. Cooper—now, as Mrs. Kuperman. Eight years later, whenever she needs ammunition, she still brings it up. "You changed your name without even asking me."

"I *did* ask. We talked about it."

"You mean you *told* me."

"Why is it your concern? You're still Deborah Schiff."

"I'm called *Mrs. Kuperman.*"

"Deborah, are you really so ashamed to be a Jew?"

At this she turned and walked out. And he, coated in Right, retreated to his study.

He changed his name from Cooper to his *father's* father's name, Kuperman. But it's his *mother's* father who has entered his soul. When Michael Kuperman ties his shoelaces, it's with his *father's* wiry fingers; with his father's grim set of mouth and brow he writes checks. Even his handwriting is the same as his father's. But it's his *mother's* father, Jacob Goldstein, whose breath fills Michael Kuperman now.

Is he cloaking himself in the embroideries of grief—in stories of genocide, in the heavy sighs filled with the *kch* sounds from the chest? Grief that separates from your self like a Platonic idea and crystallizes the diffuse pains of one's own life. *Pain? All right, let's keep it in perspective.* What's your confusion set against the transcendent horror of the child who saw his mother's arms and legs chopped off by machete and held her, containing her spasms and listening to her screams till she bled to death? You think of this and it doesn't matter so much that your wife has seriously discussed separating, that your teen-aged daughter has no interest in spending time with you anymore, that friends you once saw daily you now see maybe once a month (except of course for your partner Jonathan).

So there's no center to your life, and it doesn't pay to look too closely at the work. What are you but a businessman?—good at what you do, but does it really matter in the world?

What am I to do? Michael asks his grandfather. Travel to Rwanda or the Bronx and help organize communities? Once, that was exactly what he'd wanted to do. After getting his MBA, he received leadership training in community organizing from the

Industrial Areas Foundation, the Saul Alinsky organization. Then, when Jonathan Greene called him, at a time when community organizing had seemed particularly futile, when he found himself not trusted as a white, as a Jew, and victories seemed to dissolve like sand castles, he'd gone along with Jonathan. It was ironic—not trusted as a white man in the black community, he joined forces with Jonathan, who's African-American. And he turned his talents towards starting a business. He blurred out the general griefs. Even now: he lets *Jacob* grieve.

Fusion

Synagogue music, one of the melodies for the *Nishmat* prayer, *Nishmat—the breath/soul—of every living things shall bless Your Name. . . .* goes through his head as Dennis turns onto Arlington Street and gets jammed up in traffic. Golden-leafed trees along the street, gold and red in the Public Garden.

At Two Beacon he shares the elevator with Dave Posner. He smiles warmly but not *too* warmly—not wanting Dave to think it's a saccharine smile, a phony smile of sympathy, and so nothing real goes on in that elevator, and the real grief Michael feels whenever he sees the poor bastard (oh, the poor bastard) has to be squeezed behind this just-appropriate-level smile.

Dave was with them from almost the beginning, when Fusion began ten years back. At first it was just Michael, Jonathan Greene, Steve Planck, and a couple of experienced programmers working part time. It was really Steve's technical ideas. Steve had shmoozed with Jonathan, Jonathan had talked to Michael. What did Michael know about software? He knew how to find venture capital, how to position a new company for growth. And Jonathan Greene has been their spectacular promoter, strategist, salesman. The software for systems integration was Steve's. And when Dave Posner came in six months later to set up customer support and run tech writing, in-house writing, packaging, all their publications, Dave was a strong young man with a lot of charm, thirty years old, confident, a *macher*.

Smile at the guy.

Dave gave them a lot. Then he got rheumatoid arthritis. Then he started getting fat, fatter, until now he can barely drag his weight around and he's half out of it from painkillers. Every time Michael sees Dave, he wants to weep with him. Or wipe him out of the world—there's that impulse too. Awful. Like seeing a big pet dog in chronic pain.

"So how you doin'?"

"Good, Mike. Pretty good. You see the brochure we laid out for presenting the company after the merger?"

"I saw it. Let's talk after our chickens hatch."

They both laugh. When they get to Fusion's floor, Michael goes through a complex decision tree in less than a second: *I get out first and it's rude. I'm bang out of the starting gate and you, you're dragging ass with 300 pounds and every step is torture. The further I get ahead, the worse it is for you. So I let Dave get out first? But then Dave feels me back there watching him, holding back out of sympathy, and maybe contempt. And Dave will feel me impatient even if I'm not, he'll make himself hurry, and hurrying hurts him. So okay, I get out first. But then I'll turn and stretch, as if time didn't mean a whole lot, and wait to stroll with him through the big glass doors.*

All that in less than a second. And that's what he does. They stroll in together, while Michael thinks, *We're going to have to let him go. Soon.*

To clear his heart he smiles hugely at Sam Winston, a tall kid with a swinging walk, one of the new crop of interns Jonathan has brought in. Jonathan has been putting all his extra time (and since Jonathan *has* no extra time it means he doesn't have time for Jessica, for Marcus) into creating, funding, building a training program for minority young people who want careers in hi-tech fields. And out of that program Fusion has been drawing talent. It takes away the sour taste from the scene with Dave Posner. *We're good guys here.*

Michael has a corner window that overlooks Boston Harbor, the Charles, gulls cruising the thermals above the office buildings, above Science Park. In twenty minutes, a conference; in three hours, his plane for Chicago. Martine has laid out seven neat piles of paper on the table by his desk, each pile prioritized. The table was a legacy from the firm of bankers that used to be in this wonderful, lofty space; the irony makes him smile: under all that paper, he's rarely able to see the beautiful dreamlike grain of the rosewood.

He skims the top layer of messages, notes, faxes, without touching, dowsing with his fingers for what's most urgent, afraid to get sucked down into minor crises. A note from Jonathan Greene congratulating him on the merger. *It's ours, Michael. And who'd have thought, ten years ago, huh? Send McNair my best. . . . And don't let him get away with a* thing.

The conference, with his in-house legal staff, nails down a few changes to the merger document. They pick away at sentences for an hour. Back in his office, as he organizes his papers, Martine buzzes him. "Sorry. But it's your wife, Mr. Kuperman."

Deborah on cell from Atlanta, changing planes for Dallas. The background noises, her breathing, tell him she's walking fast, gate to gate. He knows it's urgent. "Deborah. What's the matter?"

"It's Ari. Mrs. Corcoran got him to school and was just about to leave, but she took one more look at him and felt his forehead and he was *burning up.*"

"So she's keeping him home? Oh, the poor kid."

"*No.* She took him to the *doctor*—it was Dr. Stavros this morning—he listened to his lungs, and sent him straight to the hospital for tests."

"To the hospital! Why didn't she call *me?*"

"Please. She called my cell. Don't worry. Ari's all right. They say he has a touch of pneumonia."

"Pneumonia—a *touch*—"

"They may keep him overnight. The point is, I simply *can't* turn around and come home. We're on the edge with this client. But I will if I have to. I'll get the next flight back. Now Michael, the point is, *can* you postpone your flight until day after tomorrow?"

"Absolutely. Don't come home. Really. I can handle things."

"You're sure?"

"Absolutely." At this moment he hates his wife—doesn't even *want* her to come back. He sees her bony blonde elegance as coldness, selfishness—fantasizes she's relaxing at a spa or museum. It's as if she planned to run off and leave Ari when he was getting pneumonia—and on this week of all weeks, when he has to close the deal with McNair in Chicago. After six months of negotiations with InterCom. *We're talking millions, a huge step for Fusion,* he rehearses, but doesn't say.

Because he has nothing whatever to blame her for—who could have predicted?—though he scans the spaces of his mind for *some*-thing. Still, in the drama of this moment, in this three-second awkward pause between them, bad connection full of static, she becomes a mother who cares nothing for Ari, is somehow responsible for his getting sick. Then, instantly—*no*, no, it's *both* of them, they're both faking it as parents, trying to *pay their way* through the growing-up of their children, seeing them for a few minutes here and there, on the fly. How often do they even *eat* together, for godsakes? As a foursome?—Shabbat dinner—if that. And now look! He fantasizes Karen caught up, next week or next year, in some terrible drug scene. Sees! Everything collapsing.

"Mrs. Corcoran is staying with him at the hospital. But Michael, what about tonight? She has her own child. I won't be home till Thursday night at ten."

"I thought tomorrow—"

"—Oh, she's not going to *desert* him, don't worry, even if she has to bring Laurie to sleep at our house, but we can't do this to her."

"To *her*! What about *Ari*? What hospital?"

"Children's. Michael, why don't you call your mother?"

"My mother? I'm going to drag her up here?"

"Oh, you know she'd love it."

"I'll take care of things," he says grimly and hangs up.

So Michael makes the calls—to his staff in Chicago that worked so hard to make this happen, to McNair's staff. Finally, to McNair himself, at home, just about to drive in. The chemistry is good between them, good between their organizations. No question—the deal won't be sabotaged. Of course not. But it's embarrassing, especially with final maneuvering still to be done.

A call from Margaret. Ari's been released; they'll be at home. Thank God.

And all this time, Michael's grandfather, Jacob Goldstein, who lost his firstborn daughter at nine months, his little sister to tuberculosis years before that, sits stroking his beard for comfort. It seems to Michael that the old man is present as a separate, intact being, that he knows about Ari, knows what will happen to him, and is saying prayers. Michael almost smells his old man's breath, old man's wrinkled gabardines that he rubbed with a rag soaked in benzene. Who told him this? How can he know? It's peculiar. There are times he doesn't just dream an *alte jude* into being; he almost sees Jacob Goldstein.

As now he sees Ari. In his mind's eye, Ari, in a white johnny, long legs dangling from a gurney, is squeezing Mrs. Corcoran's hand. Michael, collecting papers to take home, mumbles a prayer for recovery along with the old man.

In the middle of his prayer, he gets buzzed by his secretary. "What! It's my wife again?"

But no, it's Steve Planck, head of Research and Support. When a company installs one of their software systems, Steve's the one who adapts the design to make sure it dovetails with existing systems; that data can be moved easily from operation to operation. Assigns the work or—on big jobs—does it himself.

"I just need a minute."

"Steve, I have one foot out the door. Ari's sick."

"Sorry. How sick?"

"Just kid-sick."

"Isn't this your day with McNair?"

"Don't remind me."

"Please. Michael, a couple minutes. We've got a problem. Maybe it's nothing."

"I'll give you five minutes."

Kuperman sits down again, checks his watch, calls, "Come in, come in," waves Steve to a seat. He can smell the garlic already. It emanates from Steve's pores. Steve *believes* in garlic, believes the garlic helps him metabolize protein or keep down the production of lactic acid.

Steve's a rower, single scull. He's small for a rower, lean, but when Michael has accompanied him to the Cambridge Boat Club and seen Steve in his scull, it's a different matter. The man has less than ten percent body fat. His body is powerful, efficient, with long arm and leg muscles. He's not a racer, though he'll compete in his club. He just loves to row. "Some of my best ideas I find on the river," he's told Michael.

Steve and Tony Kim are in charge of Fusion's training personnel, who work in classrooms and labs in a remodeled factory outside Bloomington, Indiana. Companies send their communications people out to Bloomington. And Steve or some of his people visit the company sites, go into their systems and integrate them with the new software. That's Fusion, right?—that's the *point*, that's the whole deal. Steve and Tony are the technical brains. While Tony heads R&D in Bloomington, Steve is the guy who matters most. Fusion Software could do without Michael Kuperman and Jonathan Greene a lot longer than it could without Steve Planck. So even now, one foot out the door, he'll listen to Steve.

His brows are arched high in wonder. When Steve's surprised—and it seems as if everything surprises him; he's so uncool!—his black brows lift up like a cartoon of surprise—the way kids learn to stylize birds in flight. And his eyes grow big under the wings, and he darts off to return an hour later with a solution for your problem, an elegant, playful adaptation of whatever surprised him in the first place.

Nothing playful today.

"You wait. Jesus, Mike. It's about Chemicorp, so it's about the merger, too. I mean, the deal with Chemicorp just about made the merger happen—InterCom saw we were playing major league ball. Isn't that right?" Steve hunches forward on the high-backed leather chair, as if he has to discard amenities, make this room a bare cell for thought and work, before he can get down to cases. His hands clasped, elbows on his knees, Steve looks like he belongs in a chess club. He's skinny, elbows and knees jutting up. But he's hard as a rock. His straight, blond hair lies scattered; his skin still breaks out, as if he were fifteen instead of thirty, and Michael, amused—he likes the guy a lot and so what if he looks a mess?—wonders if he washes his face enough. This is how he is on any ordinary day. His suit—one of two he wears alternately—is not wrinkled, but that's only because it's polyester. It's like he's saying, *Okay, when I'm in Boston, I have to wear a suit; this is a "suit," okay? Now can I fuckin' get to work?*

Most mornings, before work, Steve Planck stops at the MIT boathouse on the Charles and takes his one-man scull out on the river. Even this morning, cold as hell in insulated training pants, he rowed an hour, talking to himself about the possibility of depositing his printouts in the mud at the bottom of the Charles. Then he changed into a suit and came to work.

Steve hates to dump this on Michael. Michael, whom he respects, even loves. Good guy, Michael. Jonathan, too, but Jonathan intimidates him, Steve looks up to Jonathan like the top-gun cousin you see at family picnics, always smoother, stronger, smarter. Michael has always been more approachable: a brother fifteen years older. He takes advice from Michael whenever he gets involved with a woman. He and Michael took Ari and Karen to the Big Apple Circus last spring and the spring before that. (His wife Deborah hates circuses.) Sometimes after work they stop for a beer at Fanueil Hall and shop for oil, garlic, and cheese in the North End. On the Charles this morning, he imagined he was rowing the information across the river to Michael Kuperman. Like a spy, a soldier.

"All right. It's a valuable contract with Chemicorp," Michael says. "Go on."

"*Val*uable."

"Indispensable. *Please.* I've got a sick boy at home. I've got to get out of here."

"I'm sorry. Well. You're not gonna like this. Chemicorp? I'm using the software to integrate systems, I discover a couple of things. Mike? Jesus. They ought to change the name to Chemi-*corpse.* They're bad news, Mike. They're rotten news, Mike. Somebody is. I've been inside the system, inside the encrypted data—yeah, yeah, yeah, yeah, they didn't know it but I *had* to go in—no, really, I *did.* To protect their encryption system and link it up to all their data retrieval systems. I got into their own encryption files and used them. If I'd had to do it blind, some executive sitting at my side, it would have taken all week. But then I started fooling around, snooping—I mean, I got curious. Why'd they have to encrypt *so much*? Okay, trade secrets. You know me; I'm a sucker for secrets. Well, that's what it is, Mike. Trade secrets."

"Please. Just *say* it, Steve."

"They're selling—legal, illegal, I don't know. *Il*legal, I guess. Or maybe the chemicals are legal but the compounds aren't. Legal, not legal isn't the point. They're selling bad shit to God-knows-who. I don't know much chemistry, Mike, but even I could piece it together from letters, queries, orders. Especially queries and replies. I'm finding files headed 'Orion.' A sub-group at Chemicorp.

Orion. Listen. Here's the kind of things being asked: *If you mix X amount of thionyl chloride with Y amount of thiodiglycol, how long is the compound stable?* Mike?—Mike, *that's mustard gas."*

"You're saying they're selling chemical weapons?"

"Mustard gas. *When* you put the chemicals together. Again, I'm no expert, but the questions they ask, the answers they give, that's where they lead me. I know the same chemicals can be used for lots of processes. Like for toothpaste. Sure. But the *questions.* They're going to a corporation in London and France. I can't read the French. But there are references to Africa. My guess is governments. But what do I know? I do know we're talking lots of money, millions."

"Millions? Makes no sense. For chemicals? Steve—will they know you got in?"

"No. Guaranteed. I left no traces, coming in, getting out. Millions, Mike. I don't think it's the corporation exactly. It's this group—Orion. I don't know what Orion is. A code word for a kind of operation? A small group of people? Look. I'm not talking legal liability, Mike. Nobody will know I got in. Not Chemicorp, not an investigation later on. So we can say we knew nothing. I'm talking about . . . *the thing itself,* aiding and abetting, the thing itself. Mass killing."

"If we open this up—"

"That's right. Exactly. It impacts on the merger with InterCom. I know that. That's what I'm saying."

"Not necessarily. What does Jonathan say?"

"Jonathan's in Tokyo."

"All right. Let me sit with this. I've got to get home. Thanks, Steve."

"Yeah, 'thanks.' I bet, 'Thanks.'"

Mothering

He sits by the side of Ari's bed, holding his hand—still hot—while Ari dozes. Ari's books lie scattered on the bed, and, not knowing he's doing it, Michael places them in a neat pile on the bedside table next to the pills. He picks through the papers on Orion at his feet. Chemicorp. What's he supposed to tell McNair? *Your friends at Chemicorp may be selling chemicals for munitions?* And McNair: *You're talking about Myron Rosenthal? A man with his reputation? An important international corporation? And what's your evidence? What will he say? My genius systems guy, who knows nothing about chemistry, his guesswork?*

Chemicorp? It's an old, straight firm. A large publicly traded corporation. Like accusing Monsanto! Hell—Albert Braithwaite is its CEO. And Rosenthal is boring, pompous, but . . . absolutely a legitimate businessman. And he's right under Max Ferguson, and Ferguson and Braithwaite are on the boards of some of the biggest corporations in America. And then there's this: three months back, Michael remembers, Steve Planck was sure that Fusion was being "snooped on by industrial spies"—he meant one maintenance man who looked too smart—and he set traps in the computer to catch hackers: it wouldn't tell Steve who was trying to get in, but it would tell him someone was. And . . . well, *nothing.* The "spies" turned out to be a young writer, working office buildings so he could write screenplays during the day.

One way or the other, he'll have to inform Jonathan Greene— though he's sure Jonathan will tell him it's just crazy Steve again, and none of their business. And tomorrow, he has to get to Chicago, whatever the truth is about Chemicorp. He thinks of asking a favor from his assistant, Martine—to stay with Ari. She housesat for them once. Then, there's Karen—she could stay home from school. But she's barely fifteen. And as for a visiting nurse—they made do with one when Ari had the chicken pox a couple of years back—the thought of Ari, sick, left with a stranger, makes Michael weep silently, in his chest.

At once he sees his mother sitting by *his* bed, sleeping by his bed when he had whooping cough. When was this? She was bent double, lugging the mattress backwards, like one of Breugel's peasants dragging a sack of wheat. He sees her in a blue-flowered housedress and Chinese slippers: it's a permanent moment, *This is who my mother is.* In that moment, or at least in the moment as it exists for him now, she'd forgotten herself, gave herself no airs, she was who she was, period. She read to him, she kept a Vicks inhaler hissing pungent steam and kept him supplied with Kleenex. She told him stories of *her* mother. Always the story of cleaning the house for Pesach, on hands and knees at the back of the pantry, getting rid of the last flecks of *hametz*. So when was this? He must have been Ari's age, to remember it so well. He can smell her face cream, the cigarette smoke on her dress.

He reaches for the phone and calls New York.

It's his father who answers. "Ahh, I'm fine," Ira Cooper says. "I suppose it's your mother you want to speak to. Your mother's off on some goddamn committee. What else is new? She's some companion. How's everybody?"

"We're fine. Busy. Ari's a little sick. Listen, Dad, as soon as she comes in—"

"—I'll have her call you. Certainly."

But Michael knows his father won't remember, and so after a decent interval, he calls again, and sure enough, Ira has forgotten to tell her.

"For godsakes, Michael, why didn't you call right away? I'll be up in a couple of hours. You know me, darling. I throw a few things into an overnight bag. Your father will just have to fend for himself. If I could get him off his *tuchas*, we could both come up and see you. We never see you."

"Ari will be glad to see you, Mom. Now listen. I don't want him to wear you out."

"Oh, for godsakes, wear *me* out? Go back to Ari and kiss him for me. I'll be up on the next shuttle."

That was the pretense between them. Never mind the little heart condition, never mind the aches and pains of the morning. Expensive make-up and a strong determination covered anything up: she's "as strong as a horse." Michael admires this: her courage.

Courage

It's just after Sukkot, 1904, when Jacob and Sarah Goldstein leave Kishinev with the children. A few days before, Shira, the woman next door, not a close friend, comes to Sarah, and they sit by the samovar and drink tea. Her family is leaving, too. But they have no passports. A guide was to bring the other woman and her family over the Carpathians into Romania. But Sarah sees without being asked: how can Shira walk over the mountains in her condition?

Seven months pregnant is bad enough, but her chest, her bronchia clogged with fluid, always, the wheezing—consumption, but nobody whispers the word. It's impossible. "Can your friend help us, too?" Jacob is uneasy, asking Ostrov in behalf of others. And it turns out he's right. "When will it stop?" Ostrov asks. "*Your* passports, that was one thing. Please. There's only so much I can do."

And so Sarah gives Shira her own passport. And Jacob permits this. In cloak and babushka, traveling with Jacob, Shira will be all right. And Sarah takes the train with the others up to the mountains; then, hugging quickly and not looking back, she walks through the woods into the mountains with Shira's family.

Imagine their meeting in Romania: what joy! Then the train to Genoa, the ship. They "didn't travel steerage," Belle often says. They brought crates, trunks, suitcases. Over Michael's fireplace is a brass samovar, big-bellied, big as a small child to hold against the chest, slightly crumpled, no longer useable to heat water—that Sarah couldn't bear to leave behind. Belle gave it to Michael when he married.

"Think what it was like for my mother, a simple woman, to hand over that passport and follow a stranger and another family up a mountain trail. Think!"

Belle

By dinner time, her overnight bag unpacked, she's already there, filling the space as she always does, noisy, smelling of Chanel and powder, laughing with Ari, patting his hand, kissing his hand, singing "April in Paris," though it's October—and Ari, he's not so droopy, he's grinning, and Michael feels safer, he can breathe, not just because Ari's fever is a little better and certainly not that he'll be able to leave in the morning; it's his mother's raucous voice, meant to be café-elegant, Julie Wilson at the Pierre perhaps, but coming off more like Ethel Merman with a cold. He calls out from the kitchen, "Tell Ari about the time they asked you to sing at La Scala." Old joke between them.

"*Laugh*," she calls back.

He carries in tea for the three of them, then gets a cup for Karen when she comes in. He kisses her, and because her grandmother is there she lets him. "Basketball is incredibly exhausting," she drawls, and not for the first time he hears the affinity between them: his daughter, his mother. Ethel Merman—*yes!*—he likes the comparison, though Belle Cooper looks nothing like her. She's lean as a greyhound, though her belly droops. Her ankles are slim as a girl's. "My dear," she used to say as she inhaled (the Pall Malls she used to smoke before the doctor made her stop), cigarette held jauntily between index and middle fingers, fingers held straight, pinky askew, gesture of sophistication, "it takes seven generations to make ankles like these."

Belle Cooper takes Karen's hand and pulls her down for a kiss. "I've never seen anyone so gorgeous. Especially to be so gorgeous and just out of the shower. Would you look at that hair!" It *is* beautiful hair, long, reddish brown (she uses henna but he doesn't know this), corkscrewing into natural curls as if electricity were pulsing from her head. And Karen falls for Belle's compliment, and Michael thinks, *Why can't I do that?*

"But listen," Belle says to Michael, "you laugh, my singing?— did you know my grandfather, your great-grandfather on my father's side, was chief cantor in Kishinev?"

"So what went wrong with those musical genes of his?"

"*Ha, Ha.* So. Do you want me to make dinner? What's in the freezer?"

"Oh, Mother. I've ordered Chinese. It'll be here soon."

"*These days. . . ,*" Belle says, nodding her head to finish the sentence. "All right! But when you come home, Friday night, Shabbat, we're eating my brisket. First thing tomorrow morning, before Deborah comes home, I'm going to get started. By Friday my darling," she says to Ari, stroking his forehead, "you'll be hungry as a lion." And to Karen, "You remember my brisket, sweetheart?"

Later, she comes into his study. He's murmuring evening prayers.

"Do you mind if I join you?"

"I'm *happy* you're here," he says, pointing her towards a leather chair. She's wearing a blue, velour house robe, and he sees it as a kind of prayer shawl. Suppose, he thinks, Steve is right. How holy can your life be if, while you are praying, they are flying low, dropping canisters of gas? But listen—what does Steve Planck know about chemical weapons? *Orion.* Steve's voice comes into his head.

Not words, just the rhythms of that crude speech of his, as if he hadn't come out of MIT a star, as if he were really just a kid from New Jersey. Nothing like a little poison gas to ruin your prayers.

"I'm so surprised you pray like this. Listen. I had to get down on my knees to get you to go to Hebrew school."

"Well, it's because of you I had a place to start. You carried the spark."

"Me! Oh! If only you had known my *father*. Sweetheart, he was some man."

And at once, Jacob Goldstein is present to Michael—but dim, a photo from his childhood, hardly more than a beard and gentle eyes.

And as if in response to this evocation, she says, "I have a couple of pictures for you, sweetheart. You always ask about my parents. You'll remember the pictures—we kept them next to the breakfront in the living room."

She reaches into her giant white leather bag. A photo in its old wooden frame. "Here. You remember?"

"*Sure* I remember." A studio portrait of Jacob, Sarah, and children. His mother isn't born yet. Michael has always loved the patina of this photo. "Oh, Mom. *Thank* you for bringing this."

"You keep it. I have others. Not framed but nice. Next time you come down. I've been putting together things for you to see. We'll wait to talk till you come down. It's a kind of legacy."

He doesn't ask. He dreams himself down into the photograph in his hands. Jacob has close-cropped hair, a graying short beard, no hat, heavy black jacket. This must have been when they first arrived from Kishinev. Solemn-faced Russian Jews with several unusually beautiful children. All in black except for Michael's grandmother, who wears some striped, light-colored, shapeless cotton dress and a pale babushka on her head, her hands folded across her stomach, her shoulders hunched so that her neck has disappeared—like a Russian wooden doll—as if to minimize her presence. There's no indication in this photo that she would have left her family, given up her passport, for a sick woman friend. Jacob's strength is clear. He has beautifully shaped thick eyebrows; his eyes are narrowed in a smile. Of pride, amusement, success? That he's brought them safely to America? This must have been the picture they sent back to Kishinev. *He's younger by ten years than I am but looks more like a full mensch.*

"Mom, I've got a ten AM plane to catch. I'm going to kiss Ari goodbye and be gone first thing in the morning. Now, my dear mother, you listen to me: you can spoil him all you want, but don't let him wear you out, don't let him get bossy. Ari's a big, smart boy. He has books—and under these circumstances, I don't care if he watches movies or even TV."

"You act, my dear, as if I never brought up children." She lifts her chin and crosses her legs, knobby now, those legs, too skinny, he worries she'll break a bone, cold with her poor circulation, but she still thinks of them as beautiful, part of her arsenal, her high-horse, hifalutin charm. This mother, with her vanities, her brown-dyed hair cut severely short ("Don't you think this makes me appear more *au courant*?") her long red nails and theatrical charm, he can handle.

"You know how grateful I am that you could come."

"Oh, please. These gorgeous children? I can pretend I'm still useful and not an old crone," she says in her throaty vibrato; he knows that when she sounds like this she's most pleased with herself.

"So? So I repeat my last offer," he says formally.

"That's very sweet of you. I only wish that their mother saw fit to be with them."

"*Mom.*"

"All right. I'll say nothing."

"I keep thinking," he says. "It would be so good for Ari if you could move up here. And for Karen. Why not? We *built* the apartment for you and Dad. It's what I want."

"My dear, *I can't be their mother.*" She says this with quavering resonance, a stage line.

"I'm not suggesting that," he said, knowing that in a way it was what he meant. "Deborah's a good mother. She has work, I have work—we do what we can. But at your age, why should you be there and we be here? You could be with your grandchildren."

"We have a fine apartment, thanks to you and your sister. And your father?—he would drive me absolutely crazy without his New York cronies. You know—he has his life and I have mine. Anyway, *vat vuld I do in Boston in my declining years?"* Her voice quivers, parody of an *alte bubbe*. He laughs, takes off his yarmulke, folds up his tallis, and gives her a kiss goodnight. He puts in a call to Deborah at the hotel to let her know everything's under control.

Work

Deborah, who rarely has trouble sleeping, can't get to sleep. She was the one who made the suggestion; but now she feels as if she's been supplanted, her place invaded; the two of them must be talking about her, the Bad Mother. She tries to attend to her breath, as she's been taught in yoga classes; but the words creep in, the face of Belle Cooper smiles at Ari, and she, Deborah, is pushed out. Well. She asked for it! She should be thanking God, if there were a God to thank: her son is going to be fine; he's being well taken care of. *So sleep.* But now she itches—one place, another, the first again. And her breath won't work on its own; her breath is keeping her awake.

Angry at her uncooperative body (eight AM breakfast meeting she has to be alert for) she swallows a pill, another. There.

After awhile, she sleeps, but too early, she wakes, drooping from the pills, too early to call Michael, and calls room service for a pot of coffee. While she's waiting, she goes through her floor exercises with soft weights wrapped around ankles and wrists. This is a woman who does her morning routine religiously. First the floor exercises, then, at home, her treadmill; at a hotel, a rowing machine, or Nautilus. By seven, sweating, ready for the shower, she looks at herself in the mirror wall of the hotel's gym: her lean thighs made to look like satin sculpture in the Lycra, thighs she's proud and critical of. And her long face, glinting in the flattering lights of the changing room—she sees no new lines. "*Hollow of cheek as though she drank the wind,*" her friend Martha recited the other day. Martha was telling her not to *starve* herself. Really— wasn't she being *envious?* Deborah puts her hands in the hollows of her cheeks and looks at herself. *Terrible mother*, she says out of nowhere, surprising herself.

Now she laughs. God, she hates being so serious, so sour. Her friends see her as formidable—but awfully funny. Michael, she thinks, Michael has made her grim.

By 7:15, showered and dressed, she calls home. Everything is going fine. Is it only in her own imagination that he's saying, *You don't even need to come back. Stay away, make money, feel important. We're fine.*

But once outside the door, she feels good again. Deborah loves going inside a company, listening to the chief operating officer, chief financial officer, big chiefs, almost all men, trying to impress her with their efficiency, their company's efficiency—like a patient who makes an appointment with a specialist, then tries to impress the doctor with his health—it's really funny!—while she, she listens down into the gaps, into what's underneath the surface, blurring that shows on their every spread sheet, hears the way company metaphors fail. She likes the respect of men who earn five times what she earns. Still more satisfying is to sit—offstage—say in a carrel at an airlines club between planes, uncovering the strong text under company fictions, pulling strands together to compose her analysis.

Dennis drives Michael straight to Logan. From the car he puts a call in to Jonathan Greene. *It's a problem with the Chemicorp deal.* But Jonathan is still en route. By eleven Chicago time, when Michael's at InterCom, he hasn't got Jonathan's call. So what can he do? He puts Chemicorp aside. Pesticide? Or just toothpaste? This is a legitimate firm. It's too big to jeopardize its position that way. Braithwaite, Ferguson, Rosenthal: the names soothe him. They're too solidly positioned to take such a risk; even if they wanted to it wouldn't be worth it. Still . . . he places a call to Myron Rosenthal at Chemicorp. "Please tell him Michael Kuperman wants to talk to him. He can reach me on my cell the next half hour. Or I'll get back to him from the air."

He's checked in and waiting to board when the call from Rosenthal comes.

It's nothing, it's no big deal, that's what he wants to convey to Rosenthal. In the most casual way possible, he says, "Look, Myron, we came across something, this has nothing to do with our work for you, nothing direct, but one of my tech people handed me a query, and I wanted to reassure him. May I ask you a peculiar question?"

The only reason he can get away with such a question is that he'd gotten two tickets to a Celtics game for Myron Rosenthal, and in turn Rosenthal had invited him to his daughter's Bat Mitzvah last year. He couldn't go, but there had been that invitation, and Michael sent something.

"Please. Don't hesitate."

The announcement on boarding first-class echoes through the lounge. "All right. This won't take a minute. We came upon something unusual. Look. Chemicorp would never sell precursor chemicals for chemical munitions? Am I right?"

"Mike, what do you mean 'came across'?"

"Oh, my man was integrating systems, and he saw something and—asked about it. I'm sure it's nothing. But since we're involved—"

"Well, personally, I don't concern myself with such details."

"Of course, of course. But as far as you know—"

"Precursor chemicals? Michael, *water* is a 'precursor chemical.' The chemicals could be for anything."

"Of course. Of course. I'll tell him that."

"How close are you to finishing the work?"

"We're about ready to train your people. Very close."

"Good. That's good. Well, you can tell him, I guarantee this is absolutely nothing."

And they laugh together about teen-aged daughters, and Michael puts the problem aside. Soon he's sitting in a boardroom that might as well be in New York or Dallas or San Francisco, same paneling, thick gray carpet—no legal staff, just Michael Kuperman and Kenneth McNair, and Doug Shaughnessy, who will be national sales manager for the combined firm. Michael's grandfather is not present; Michael wonders what he himself is doing here. *Just last month I was collecting baseball cards and sledding in Central Park.*

The feeling disappears when the dance of the boardroom begins. He's met Doug Shaughnessy before, but he's talking to him for the first time. Big man in a crumpled beige suit. Oh, it's a dance they're doing, making their moves not with feet and not even with negotiating postures but with jokes, with reassuring tones of voice—when what's really on the table is how duplications of staff and research will shake down: whose jobs will be lost, which consulting firm will be kept on board.

Michael's good at this dance. He talks of Ari, and while he conveys the impression that things are under control—and well, *aren't they? They are!*—privately, he eases his heart. Using truth as a con: *I'm open, I'm comfortable enough with you to speak like this, I'm not protecting my bailiwick, this isn't a negotiation but a discussion of shared interests*—while in fact he's uneasy about the consolidation of their offices in the West. We're talking just under a hundred positions. McNair grows expansive, and they reveal their seriousness, their good humor. We work together well—that's how the song goes. By lunchtime, they're ready for the lawyers to join them.

Mid-afternoon in the boardroom—eight men and women working together, point by point—the call comes from Mass General. "It's your daughter, Mr. Kuperman, she's calling from the *hospital*, she says it's urgent." He takes it in the adjoining room. *Oh, my God. Oh, my God.*

"Karen, what? It's Ari? What's happened to him?"

"*No*, Ari's fine, he's *better*, it's not Ari, Dad. It's *Grandma*. It's something they call an *aneurysm*. I'm here at Mass General. I'm just waiting. She's still in Intensive Care, but they're moving her to a private room. Mrs. Corcoran's staying with Ari till Mom gets home. . . . It doesn't look so good, Dad."

"Oh, Karen. Oh, sweetie." Hanging up, he turns to McNair's assistant.

"Would you ask Mr. McNair to come out here for me? *And* Joe Bates?" Because the assistant is young, maybe just out of college, with warm, unguarded eyes, he adds, "It's my mother, a kind of stroke, my mother's in the hospital."

CHAPTER TWO

It's long past visiting hours, but he's made a couple of calls from the limo on the way out to O'Hare. Karen's still there, reading, and there's a doctor to meet him at the nurse's station. It's a bad sign that they'd let him come at this hour. She's asleep, with tubes taped to her arm, tubes in her nose; but at least he can talk face-to-face with the doctor, who touches the shoulder of his white coat to the shoulder of Michael's suit jacket as he shows him a chart Michael can't understand. But he understands the touch, he understands the doctor's words.

He squeezes Karen around the shoulders and she *lets* him. Her face is blurry, as if its complicated adult architecture that she's been slowly creating has dissolved, leaving her face pudgy, unformed, a child's blotched face. She's been crying, feeling alone, but there's something she's not telling him, and he holds her all the way to the taxi, all the way to Brookline, and she's still not saying, to a street lined with great beech and maple trees and the oversized turn-of-the-century houses like his, classical portico and brick facing, stone lions on each side of the steps leading to the brick walk, up to the solemn front door. It's a house in a neighborhood where no Jew would have been permitted to buy until not very many years ago. "Thank you, honey," he keeps saying to her. "I'm sorry you had to go through that."

She says, "It's okay, Dad." That's all. But now, just as he's about to use his key, she squeezes his arm and speaks quickly. "She said her stomach was hurting, she'd just turned off the brisket and she said her stomach was hurting and she doubled over. And then she fell down, right on the kitchen floor. Dad? It was *awful.* Grandma *messed herself.* She didn't even know. And I couldn't get her up, and I knew I shouldn't anyway, so I called. I used a towel. Then the men who came took care of it. And Margaret."

"Oh, honey. Did Ari see this?"

"I wish Mom had been home. But imagine Mom with a mess like that to clean."

"She'll be home very soon, Karen. Her plane gets in at nine something."

But when he opens the door, there's Deborah, still in tailored suit, fine blue wool, a pearl choker to accentuate her long neck. She reaches for his hand and draws him towards her, and, lifting herself, she puts her cheek next to his. And at once, all the tension that has been accumulating—his mother, of course, and Ari, but also Chemicorp, and the negotiations, and . . . so much unsaid between him and Deborah, his daily anger—anger he's known and not known, not known how *thick* until, at this moment, it comes to him in its temporary dissolution. For months, now, or for years, each of them too busy to take in the other's burdens, they've been keeping score of injuries: Who's at fault? Who has disregarded the other's schedule more? Each of them is accumulating grievances in a secret account; enough and they can be "fed up" and walk out. Or perhaps not walk out; but give up on the marriage. Nourished by these grievances, they speak continually in ironies (*I notice, my dear, you're rubbing salt into the cuts you've given me, but don't think I'll give you the satisfaction of complaining; it's what I expect from you*).

Now, letting it all drop, he feels what a weight it's been, as he sinks into her, and she says, "I'm so, so sorry."

"You caught an earlier plane."

She takes the bag he's been holding, and the laptop, and sets them down for him, and he puts his arms around her, bewildered by this release. Why, it's all simple now. For him, for her. There's just the *real* suffering to live through. He simply loves her; and he feels—almost loved. Her beauty comes back to him, her high forehead, wide-set eyes, high cheekbones. Her prominent but thin nose gives her, she has been told, the look of an Italian countess. Doesn't this nose make her look Jewish? Not anymore. Deborah is too proud ever to have had a "nose job." But over the years she has, through a process of psychic engineering, of psycho-surgery, sculpted this aristocratic, un-Jewish look. Just under six feet, she never, even as an adolescent, slumped to minimize her height; if anything, her walk accentuates it. She moves crisply, in command; when she enters a room, people stare. Her straight, honey-blonde hair is cut short these past five years. No nonsense. It seems she has no soft edges at all—except at times like these.

They sit in the kitchen with Karen so she can go through it again. "You sleep late tomorrow," Deborah says. She shakes her head, and Michael gives Deborah the slightest furrow of his brows as a sign: maybe it's better for Karen to go to school?

She feels for him. She knows without his saying, knows by his eyes, what the doctor must have said.

"Grandma's tough," Deborah says, "so who knows what will happen?" Michael, who has seen his mother, has talked to the doctor, *he* knows. "Time for bed," Deborah says to Karen.

"A few minutes. I've got to practice."

"*Now*?"

"I feel like it."

So, a sonatina by Mozart in the background, they go into Ari's room to kiss him. His forehead's cool, though he's wet with perspiration. Well, it's the middle of the night. He goes back to their bedroom while Deborah tucks Ari in.

Michael's on the bed, head bent to one side, squeezing lower lip between thumb and forefinger. He sat like this, she remembers, the night they last considered whether to stay together.

She stoops and unlaces his Italian calfskin shoes—power shoes, he joked when she happened to see the MasterCard receipt one day—and places them neatly under the bed. Whenever he's in trouble, when he's vulnerable, she's able to get like this, it's easy all of a sudden. Now, sitting next to him, she molds her body to his, holds him around the shoulder of his suit jacket. "What did the doctor say?"

"He couldn't operate. Her vascular system wouldn't hold up. Sometimes they can patch the aorta, splice in a tube—not with my mother. He said it could blow . . . any time. She's on some mix of anti-coagulants and medicine to reduce her blood pressure. It's a balancing act."

"And your father?"

"Not yet. What's the good?"

"Well, but if she's dying . . ." Deborah says.

"You think?"

"Of *course*. Michael. Call him in the morning. We can have a car bring him up to Boston."

He nods. "I called Susan from the hospital, in case she has to fly out."

"So there'll be *one* nurturing woman at least."

"Please. Don't start."

Deborah is distressed at her own meanness, especially now. To his credit, Michael never holds up his sister against Deborah as an example of true womanhood, motherhood; but Deborah feels the comparison. There's nothing acerbic about Susan; she's a gentle, nurturing woman. Her voice is soft; it creates a love space for her kids. Susan's an herbalist and acupuncturist—a caretaker, not a tough business consultant.

Deborah sighs; she helps Michael off with his jacket and hangs it up on his side of the walk-in closet. It's not *love* Deborah's feeling. Something else. *Things dissolving; now this. Belle has never liked me, no matter what I've done, I could stand on my head. I think of those fatty little cookies I made with Ari last time she was up—see what a good mother?—and all Belle could say was, "Since when are boys supposed to bake cookies?"*

Still, she grieves. She feels acutely the irony that with a child sick and Belle perhaps dying in the hospital, she and Michael stand next to one another at adjoining sinks and brush their teeth. She feels weighed down but not sleepy, not even after a glass of sherry. In mind's eye she sees an old woman, breasts sagging and belly puffed, lying on a gurney, half in a dream; something has failed, a body that others have to handle: it's herself she sees. Not all that many years.

If I can't sleep, there's the report to be written. This is the way she threatens her self. Sleep or I'll make you work. But she can't face work. It seems less meaningful than brushing her teeth. Without a word they undress and turn off the lights; she lets Michael curl up to her in bed, taking comfort by giving comfort, holds him until his breathing changes, then she slips away and wanders the house, not seeing, making lists in her head. But after awhile she sees the complex catalogue of odds and ends, Ari's woodworking projects, mail-order catalogues, videos to be returned in the morning. Suffering doesn't come naturally to Deborah. Michael's "gifted at suffering," she thinks. Meaning it works for him, quiets him, makes him go deeper. She sees suffering as an irritant. In her mind she scans the many books she's in the middle of—books on management, on the French Revolution, on Mme. de Staël, a novel by Wharton, a detective novel. She's not used to feeling this way. As if this complicated architecture of their life together were starting to tumble. But finally, the words inside quiet; like a leaf when the wind dies down. She comes to rest in Ari's room, touches Ari's forehead, and silently as she can, pulls out his trundle bed and lies down. She can hear his breathing, heavy, scratchy.

After awhile it becomes part of her dream. The wheezing, raspy breathing becomes a rocky hill to climb; she recognizes the place, though in waking life she's never been there, it's above Lake Lucerne, Switzerland, and there's a flat sward she's climbing toward, a party, women in summer dresses, and the princess is in the center of a crowd of women holding glasses of champagne, their dresses float with the wind rising from the lake, but does the path take her there or is this the wrong road? She stops to ask a postman in a peaked cap but she can't speak German or French, though in waking life she does speak French, and he scowls and passes her. She's alone, and she's afraid he has a terrible letter meant for her.

Michael dreams architecture, dreams of rooms from which his mother is absent.

A Legacy

Belle is awake, she's asleep; at times Michael can't tell. When she seems asleep he keeps checking the color monitor above her bed. Through tubes linked to IV needles, she's tied to a tower; hooked onto this rolling tower, this carousel of life, are heavy plastic bags with an intravenous dextrose solution, sedatives and medications dripping, dripping. Then there are the wires, electrodes taped to his mother's flesh; the color monitor above records her heart, her blood pressure, God knows what else, six lines of rhythmic peaks and valleys, numbers in various colors. Amazing, so amazing, he thinks. He's mesmerized by the lines and numbers. Then he looks at his mother's chest rising, falling. Until, after watching for half an hour, he has a kind of illumination: It's spectacular enough, sure, all this hi-tech stuff, but all it can do is make visible or mimic clumsily the homeostatic functions of the elegant body itself, so beautifully simple, no bells or whistles, no wires or tubes. But he prays down into the landscapes and numbers on the screen, as if he were employing spiritual power to change them or keep them steady.

And the landscape becomes the kitchen before it was renovated, his mother preparing a roast chicken for Pesach. He's chopping onions for the soup; tears come. Threading a basting needle, she prepares to sew up the matzah stuffing. He remembers something jarring in the room. He thinks it's his father, jeering, "So— you two checked for *chametz* with a feather? Me, I'm going out for a ham and cheese on rye." But she ignores him. She says to Michael, "It's the strangest thing. My dear mother, may she rest in peace, is in my fingers as I sew up this chicken."

Now he sits by his mother's bedside, and when she wakes up, he reads her a story by I. B. Singer, an early story he knows she knows. Maybe she can't follow, but she nods, as if to say, *There, what did I tell you? You see?* In throaty whisper, she says, "He knows, that man." Knows what? Knows life. She closes her eyes; he closes the book. Now, opening her eyes again and lifting her brows, she gestures him closer. "My handbag, you brought it? Crank up the bed, will you?"

He does, then holds open the bag. The leather has the smell of all his mother's bags; expensive leather mixed with the special cream she rubs in. Oh, but she's tough on purses and bags. This white one, which he's seen forever, has an abraded patch; deep lines score the sides. Last night, after Deborah slipped out of bed, he couldn't sleep for thinking of this bag, and he went to the guest bedroom. He felt like a detective; it was going to tell him something.

And yes, it *did*. There was of course a copy of one of the Ecco Press volumes of Chekhov's stories: always with her. A recent *New Yorker.* Makeup. Tums. A pocket mirror and her small, black Mason hairbrush. And so on. *Then:* she'd told him she was taking "a little preventive medication," and made nothing of it. But what he saw was pill bottles, more pill bottles—a beta blocker, a tranquilizer, Cardizem for chest pains and blood pressure, Tenormin—

use at first sign of discomfort—and Nitrostat. He knew Nitrostat from Deborah's uncle, a doctor and heart patient: it was a brand of nitroglycerine, and nitroglycerine was a "preventative" all right— but of last resort. He'd never imagined. It was like discovering his mother had a secret life. This morning he'd spoken to her doctor in ICU: Did he know about the medications? He knew—and knew more: Michael's mother was wearing a nitro patch.

"Mom, why didn't you tell me?" he asks when she seems awake this morning.

"Tell you? What? So you could worry?" she says. Ethel Merman is gone this morning; he can hear the Yiddish lilt in her voice. This is a woman who graduated from Barnard. True, Yiddish was the language she spoke as a child. But this lilt is something else—it's from listening to Molly Picon, from listening to Molly Goldberg on the radio, attending Yiddish theater on the Lower East Side as a young woman. *Still*, it's closer to the bone, saved for emergencies, this voice. Now she gathers her force, while he shushes her, *Rest, rest.* "Tell *you*? You've always been a Worrier." She closes her eyes. "Anyway, it wasn't my heart, the doctor said."

Which is in a sense true. It was her vascular system that broke down. But one way or another, Dr. McCartin said this morning, "it was just a question of time."

"It's always that," Michael said curtly.

It was Time he was looking into last night. He'd shaken her bag out onto the bed. Falling like brown snow, over pills and photos and wallet and loose credit cards, were dried brown flakes. Well, she used to smoke two packs a day; the tobacco the detritus of four, five years ago, before her "slight" heart attack that shamed her into giving it up.

Time. Here was an envelope with six, seven photos, mostly black and white, culled from her albums. The biggest, 5 x 7, was a second picture of his grandparents, this one from a number of years later, when Jacob had become a success in Rochester, New York. But it's the other pictures that drew him: his mother on a lounge chair on the deck of a ship, so pretty and swank in late-forties' style, her mid-twenties. And this one with the wiggly edge on the glossy paper: she wears a one-piece bathing suit; it's a hotel pool. *My mother, this young!* She looks a lot like Karen—and not like her at all; for there's a cultural style to expressions, and her campy charm dates her as much as the black-and-white graininess of the snapshot.

"What can I get you?" he asks, holding her bag open on his lap.

It's hard for her to turn her head. Intravenous line taped to a spike in her arm; tube in her nose. The wires. He has never, never seen her weak. A cold, maybe. A cigarette cough. Even with the heart attack—by the time he saw her the next day, she was ready to discuss Sondheim's music, question the politics of high-tech business—*his* business.

He feels the high-pitched vapor of panic press up against his diaphragm. Yet even now, she looks like the girl in the snapshot—younger than she's ever looked to him. It's the faint flush to her cheeks, the skin criss-crossed by fine lines, but so soft under the tough-old-bird face she'd worked hard all these years to fabricate.

And though he says, *It's the drugs making her face so tender*—it's *now*, seeing this innocence, that he knows she's dying. "Do you want something? The pictures?"

"You found the pictures. Weren't you *something*?"

She means the snapshots of himself and his sister as children.

"Weren't *you* something!" he says.

"Yes! That's right! *Exactement!* I was." She smiles, sleeps, and never again is she this clearheaded. When she wakes, she's a little befuddled. She asks, "How are we going to feed all these nurses? Michael, it isn't nice. But how can I shop in my condition?"

"Mom, you know where this is? Where are we?"

"The hospital. You think I don't know that?"

"And where do we live?"

"*Downstairs.* Michael, you shouldn't be so afraid. If I'm going to die, I'm going to die. You think that's peculiar? I'm not afraid. Except . . . what will he do without me, your poor father?"

"You just get better. Meantime, I'll take care of Dad."

"Don't be a fool, sweetheart."

"Let me say a prayer with you?"

"Of course. But *you* do it. I've forgotten."

It's as if, putting on the skullcap, he's shedding garments, integuments; he takes her hand and says the *Shema*. She nods to the words, and he half-sees a streak of sun on the granite and brick foundation of an apartment building they pass. They're walking along West End Avenue the few blocks to shul, as they used to walk on High Holy Days, of course, but also Saturday mornings at seemingly random times that now he believes were anniversaries of her mother's death, her father's, her older brother's. She was always secretive about death. Friday nights she would light, instead of Shabbat candles, Yortzeit candles in glasses that became their everyday glassware when the wax had burned away.

Her hands are so cool.

"The bag. . . ." she says, remembering. "Lately, all you ask about is your grandfather. Well, why not?" She takes out the 5 × 7. Now her eyes close. He sits with her several minutes and is about to take away the photograph when she's with him again. "Let me tell you a story about your grandfather, may he rest in peace."

"Better rest."

"I'll rest soon enough. . . . When the pogrom. . . ."

"1903."

"Long before I was born . . . yes, the pogrom, 1903, and my father hid the family, you've heard the story a million times, a rich man's house, a Russian general, a good friend, so they lived in the basement while the Cossacks . . . I don't have to tell you." Belle Cooper looks around. "Where's your father?"

"He's coming, Mom."

"How long does it take him to make coffee? All right, so they lived through it, my parents, Miriam, Aaron, all of them. And all around, above them, in the streets, they could hear terrible things. . . . And the synagogue, the Torah scrolls, you know about the scrolls? And so many, many people. He'd had enough. Thank God . . . passports. Well . . . important people."

More and more, her talk wanders. *My brisket. Will he remember to put on clean underwear? When can we go home, Michael?* And now she's back.

"He had money, my father. Real money. He called to him everyone who lost someone, lost one way or another, you understand? *Fershtaste?* Some things can happen to a woman, afterwards she can't find a husband, you understand? So—*lost.* To this one he gave so much, to that one he gave so much, enough to get them out, the ones who wanted to leave. Maybe twenty, thirty people, more, a little here, a little there. Especially seven families. He talked to the right people. So little by little he got them out of town. And then they too left."

"You never told me about the gifts."

"My dear, my dear, when were you ever interested? Only lately. Please. Listen. This is all written down, you'll find it in my desk. This is serious. This was a *mitzvah* that doesn't end. Your rabbi ever tell you? The reward of a mitzvah is another mitzvah. Plenty. Sure. Those people went to Paris, Buenos Aires, New York, Palestine, wherever—but mostly America, mostly, and so they were saved. You understand? From the Holocaust. And not *them*, well, they're gone a long time, may their souls rest in peace. Their *children*, their *grandchildre*n. That's your legacy. You see?"

"Mom, this is true?"

"As true as you see me before you. Who knows how many Jewish people are alive and doing big things . . . at least living good lives . . . because of what my father did."

Now he looks at the photograph she has in her hands.

"The legacy," she says, "is *you*."

"What does that mean?"

But Belle Cooper's eyes flutter, close. "You'll help me with the nurses? They'll expect their coffee, and where *is* your poor father. . . ." She seems asleep. He glances up at the monitor; her heart mountains rise and fall, rise and fall. Sometimes in dreams he trudges through a landscape like this, peak after peak; this time they're in the dream together.

Big Shot

Ira Cooper steps from the hired car at the front entrance to the hospital; he waves away his son's hand, but after a few final words to the driver, a dark man, Iranian maybe, while he shakes the man's hand—*Thanks, thanks, and to you, too*—he holds out his arms to Michael. Theatrically. Embracing ceremoniously, they pat each other's backs. His gray hair is slicked down. Michael smells the after-shave. "That driver of yours has an autistic child and a wife who's been in and out of the hospital for years. A guy like that. . . ." He shakes his head.

"Mom's been waiting for you." How dapper his father looks. His big, crooked Indian nose looks almost distinguished. There's hair growing peculiarly from his ears; the curly gray hair above his ears gives him an unkempt but *distingué* look, even with the bristles poking from his cheeks. Michael can feel with his inner fingers his father's rough skin. He wears his usual denim shirt but with the gray wool suit Michael bought for his last birthday. *Would I feel less irritated if he'd come looking like a slob, unshaven, in old pants?* Michael sighs, takes his father's small suitcase, takes his father's arm, tells him, "There's no change. Mom's been asking about you— when you're going to bring the coffee."

"The coffee?" He laughs. "Sure. I bring her coffee in the morning. That's my job. So she's a little confused—the drugs, I bet. What a lot of traffic getting downtown! It's as bad as New York. "So is she in pain? How long the doctor say she's got to stay here?"

"This way, Dad. . . ," shepherding him through the automatic doors to the bank of elevators. They watch the indicator light drop.

For the first time, his father is suspicious. "She's going to be okay, isn't she?"

He shrugs. "Come on, Dad." Into the elevator, down the corridor to the nurse's station. Karen: reading—for a moment Michael doesn't recognize her. Then, with his eyebrows, he asks. *Anything?* She shakes her head. She hugs her grandpa. Now she's in tears, she's been in tears on and off since last night; these tears relieve Michael somehow: that she's not callow, spoiled, as he sometimes sees her; that she's able to feel so strongly reassures him.

Her grandfather strokes her shiny black hair. "She's got some nerve, that grandma of yours, making you miss school."

Michael can't take this phony charm.

"Only since lunch," Karen says.

Now the nurse tells them she's awake and asking for them. A bad sign, Michael thinks, that they're letting us see her together. His father leads the way, just behind the nurse; he droops slightly to one side, looks small as Karen now. But he's talking to the nurse about "the old Boston," about Scully Square during World

War Two, when he was with the Navy. And she's taken in by his charm, and feels for him, Michael guesses, because she thinks he's being brave.

And maybe, maybe he *is*. Belle, Ira, each in their own way, puts on the dog and each has always criticized the other for it. So what, so what?

Belle Cooper is having a hard time keeping things in focus. Her look wanders. Karen takes her hand. Now, she looks at Michael. "Don't forget my brisket."

"Of course, Mom."

"Don't forget. It's in the refrigerator . . . you won't let it go to waste? You promise? Nu? What is it, Big Shot, who asked you to get so dressed up?"

"Don't pretend to be so *femisht*." Ira takes Karen's place; he holds Belle's hand.

"You see?" she says to Michael. "And he pretends he doesn't know a word of Yiddish. He does. Exactly one! And *such pronunciation*. So, finally, you decide to come see me. It's about time."

"Sweetie, will you please stop being so smart? Rest, you want to get out of here."

"Sure, rest. How long have you known me, Ira?"

"What is it? They got her on some kind of drugs?"

"Mom. We're going to have to go if you can't calm down."

"I've got *all the time in the world* to be calm." But she takes in what he recognizes is supposed to be a deep abdominal breath. Her years of yoga practice, on the bedroom carpet. Michael sees her: yoga in the afternoon—and then a cigarette, a cup of tea, and a heavy chest sigh to *really* relax. But this breath is thickly asthmatic, a struggle; he can't stand to listen.

When he turns back, his father is squeezing her hand, patting and squeezing; her eyes are closed. The heart monitor is composing the same dream landscape. Michael sits in the corner and takes from the silk bag by the chair his yarmulke. Avoiding his father's eyes, he says, in English because he can't remember the Hebrew, a prayer for healing. Karen sits cross-legged on the floor beside him and closes her eyes to affirm his prayers. He thinks, *How kind of her*. For she refused to go through training for a Bat Mitzvah. She went to Hebrew school as long as her best friend went; then they stopped together. She likes ritual; takes part in Shabbat at home; loves the rigamarole of a Seder. But to join him in prayer is without precedent.

Keening

Coming out of prayer, he finds the need to call Deborah, at home with Ari handling business by phone and Fax. Halfway down the hall he realizes he's still wearing his yarmulke. He doesn't remove it.

In the waiting room, the television carries CNN, news of the American incursion into Panama. But Michael isn't watching. He goes to the phone.

Now he hears a high-pitched howling, not a shriek but an animal-howling, and feet are running; the ICU is near the waiting room, and the cries are from there. "Jesús, Jesús, oh, *Jesús!*" A woman's high keening—there are glass doors, closed, between him and that woman, but the howling pierces him. The doors hiss open. And now a man's, "Oh Jesus, Oh, Lord Jesus, oh Jesus." *I've never heard death before. This is death. Oh my God.* Michael puts down the phone and peers through the doors into the ICU. Nurses, doctors, whoever, running in different directions, and again, that howling. It's not bounded, not "considerate," it's wild, wild. The pneumatic doors open and a nurse hurries out past him, and for a moment the howling is unbearable; it sends a shudder through his body. The woman, the mother, "*Mi Mija . . . No, no, no, Jesús, no, m'hijita!*" and the man, "Oh Je-sus!"

He goes back to the phone, shaken. The voices from behind the ICU doors, he can still hear them.

Deborah answers. "Ari's fine. No fever."

"There's no change here. . . . My father's getting on my nerves."

"Mmm. . . . What else is new?"

"You? How about you? Are you managing?—what about your client in Dallas?"

"Michael: of *course* this takes precedence."

"Thanks, thanks," he says. Then Ari's on the phone—"I love you, Ari. I love you, sweetheart. Grandma's very sick, but now you're almost all better, Mommy tells me. Good. Of *course* you can, if Mommy says it's okay. . . .Well let me talk to her . . . Deborah?"

Sudden footsteps running, voices echoing off the walls of the corridor, and Karen's there, squeezing his arm. "*Deborah*—I've got to hang up."

His mother's face is the face of a child. Hovering over her, he feels *her* hovering over *him*, young mother over sick child. But he's the parent now, and she's the child, he knows her both as little girl and gone. Jacob Goldstein is rocking, rocking, over this his youngest child.

Michael has pushed his way into his mother's room as doctors, nurses work on her. Too busy to fight him, they let him stay near the door, murmuring for Belle Cooper the Shema. They bend over Belle Cooper, Belle Goldstein Cooper, enclosing her. Now they stand, Dr. McCartin and another doctor, the two nurses. "My *mother*," Michael says.

"Mr. Kuperman? I'm sorry," Dr. McCartin says. "Please, would you please step outside just one moment?"

It's quiet down the hall, no keening, but that sound is with him under this more respectable grief. An inner howling in his chest, so that he sucks in air, as if he's been under water too long, then lets it out in a long, long, silent keening. He sucks in air again and rides the letting-go.

Now the nurses have cleaned her body and let the family return. His father stands by the bed and, nodding, pats Belle's hand, as if in reassurance. Karen's crying, or maybe trying to cry; she's not looking at her grandmother but at her father. Michael feels the need to be in charge, to father his daughter, father his father. As Jacob Goldstein, Michael shuts his eyes and whispers, "Blessed are You, Lord Our God, Ruler of the universe—the true judge." His eyes squeeze shut as if he's being tortured, as if he's giving birth.

"I had no idea," his father says. "You didn't tell me. So goddamn fast!"

Years before, he and his sister purchased a plot for his parents in Queens, and it is there that Belle will be buried. Ira will have nothing to do with Michael's congregation, their burial society. A funeral home handles her body, sending it to Riverside, the funeral home on 76th and Amsterdam in New York City, for a service. "A low-key service, tell them," Ira says. Michael doesn't look at his father. Taking control of his breath, taking control, he goes out to the hall phone, calls his sister Susan in Seattle, calls Ben Frankel, the head of the Burial Society.

On the way home that afternoon, in the station wagon—Michael's driving, Karen in the back—Ira Cooper is angry—at what?—at her dying, at her coming up to take care of the children? It comes out as anger at religion, at ritual, "all that crap you've gotten into." He turns to Karen. "Excuse my French." He clears his sinuses into a paper towel he took from Belle's room. "All that crap! *She* wouldn't expect it. Anyway, she won't know it. What's it going to help? If it makes you feel better, go ahead, say some prayers, do the whole thing, cover your mirrors, rip your clothes, but you count me out. Don't think she wasn't important to me, your mother. I got a lot of love for her, I got a lot of love now. She's my baby, I'll tell you, Michael. We fought, sure, but fifty years she was my wife. And I'll tell you something—I was a very decent husband to her. Well, for the most part. Who the hell are you to come along with your strangers saying prayers?"

"Look, Dad—After the funeral, we'll sit Shiva, three, four days up here. If you don't like it . . . that's too bad. Ignore it. It matters to me. I know she'd have wanted it. I happen to think it matters to her soul. But no one's forcing this opinion on you. You come back home with us from New York, I promise you won't have to take part."

"You think I'm going to sit around pulling a long face with a bunch of people I don't know? I'm sure they're very nice people, but no thanks. Ahh—I've got things to clear up in New York. Then maybe I'll come up to Boston for a few days."

"A few days? You know we've got an apartment for you." Michael turns to Karen in the back seat, and she puts her hand on her grandfather's shoulder.

"You're being a good son. I think this is foolish, but I know you mean well. Don't think I'm not grateful. But I've got my routine, I've got my friends, we play cards, we sit around at this place on Broadway. I do my photography. You, you'd run me ragged. You'd ship me down to your health club, you'd shlepp me to doctors. I want some peace. My whole life. She ran me ragged, your wonderful grandfather Jacob Goldstein ran me ragged. I shouldn't have been selling for somebody else. I kissed ass all my working life. Did you know I begged my father to set me up with a photographic studio, even a photographic supplies store, something along those lines? That kind of business, I knew something, y'see? He gave your Uncle Sidney money for a little business and look what Sidney did. He became something. But me he never trusted."

"What about asking Jacob Goldstein?" Michael asked.

"I mentioned it to him. Many times. I wasn't going to humiliate myself. So to hell with Jacob Goldstein. But what did he know from photography?—*You*—you've got some funny ideas about your mother's father. Where did his money go? In trust for you—he wanted to make damn sure I wouldn't get my hands on it. Jake Goldstein. Sentimental crap. He was a selfish bastard, you want to know. After all the years I worked for the guy, I could tell you a lot about Jake Goldstein. Lately, you kept bugging your mother to tell you about her father, she liked being asked. She kept telling me. *Sure . . . I get it.*" He pointed his finger to point a lesson.

"What do you get, Dad?"

"*That it's easier for you—*" He caught Michael's eye in the rearview mirror. "—Having a make-believe grandfather, somebody you never knew—that's *easier* than to work out things with your father."

"What's to work out?"

"See? That's exactly what I mean," Ira Cooper says. Then— "Hey—didn't you miss your turn? Wasn't that your turn?"

Chapter Three

The night his mother dies, it seems to Michael-the-dreamer she is being poisoned by gas hissing from a vent in the ceiling of a white room. The dreamer labors to plug the leak. But during the day these things separate; the talk with Myron Rosenthal seems distant. Steve Planck's worries come back to Michael—but only as something he has taken care of.

The funeral is in New York, at Riverside—Deborah avoids it by staying outside on Amsterdam Avenue with Ari—except for a few minutes, when Karen walks around with Ari, and Deborah goes in to pay her respects to a closed coffin.

Belle was the last of the Goldstein children—she was born fifteen years after they came to America. Her nieces and nephews, the four who could come, were at the funeral and in the small cortege to the cemetery. These children of her older siblings are twenty, thirty years older than Michael and Deborah. All are wealthy and, except for Morris Goldstein, all in bad health; Morris, in his late sixties, bikes or works out every day. He puffs out his chest and wears his yarmulke pinned far back on his head so as not to disturb his puffed-up graying hair. But the others—Henny Schulman shuffles inside a walker. And What's-her-name is strapped to a tank of oxygen. Deborah can hardly look. She remembers Belle's pride: she was more athletic than the *children* of her siblings. Ira's younger brother Dave flew up alone from Atlanta; Dave's wife is too fragile. Then, Michael's sister, big-hearted, New-Agey Susan from Seattle, and Ira's Broadway friends, four of them, all men. And maybe two dozen older people, mostly women, Belle's friends. Ira Cooper sits red-eyed, alone. Michael, she sees, isn't talking to his father.

They stay with Ira for the night, and she and Michael straighten up, organize papers for the accountant. The apartment is neat, but filled with the sad smell of old people. Dave flies home to Atlanta. Susan suggests they sit in a circle with the kids and remember Belle. This, Deborah can do without. Ira is willing enough. Sitting in his worn easy chair he tells about meeting Belle. "Washington Square Park, I think it was a Sunday. We sang folk songs. It was a great place for picking up liberal ladies." Now, for the first time, Ira starts to weep, and Susan comforts. Why is it that the more Michael's sister comforts, the more uncomfortable Deborah feels— *even when she's comforting me!*

Ira, his hands clasped between his knees, says, "That woman had a battleship full of guts. I have to hand it to her. Compared to her, I've been a coward."

Deborah says, "She was an amazing woman. I wish she'd liked me better. I *do*. Belle always brought out the worst in me."

No one says anything.

Michael lights a Yahrtzeit candle that he found in the pantry. Deborah sees this makes him uneasy. He isn't sure whether it's correct, and this irritates her much more than the candle.

Karen looked through a portfolio of photos. "Dad, did Grandpa take these?"

In the dark that isn't ever dark, New York dark, in this apartment he'd lived in all through his growing up, Michael keeps waking, remembering where he is, slipping out of bed to walk through this solid apartment on West End Avenue with its crown moldings, pebbly, thick plaster walls, smell of steam and the heated paint of the radiators. Photographs, framed, on every wall. His father's "art." Well, it is an art—these walls express for Michael his father's art—and his father's failure. Because these walls and the walls of his friends are his only galleries.

The furniture of his childhood, wonderful, heavy, bourgeois furniture from Sloan's; the bathroom of his childhood, faintly ruinous and chemical, its tiny white octagonal tile and giant, rust-stained tub. Sitting on the edge of the tub, he thinks about her face and cries silently. Yet even as he heaves and cries, he knows that this is a supportable blow from God rather than one he couldn't have borne. As if he'd made a trade.

Sitting Shiva

Monday night, when they return from New York, the house fills up. Deborah can't imagine grieving in front of other people—most of them not even friends. When her father died—and she was only sixteen—she cried in front of no one. Tonight, the rabbi, a woman rabbi, will be coming, there's Ben Frankel, there's somebody else from the Burial Society. Deborah refuses to be a hypocrite; she busies herself on the phone; when she comes into the living room, she looks at them as if they're from another planet. She sees a few people from their world, couples they visit or invite to dinner— Max and Ella, Jan and Roy. Jewish and Christian, they're a relief. But the others—members of Michael's congregation, people she barely knows except to nod to on High Holy Days, when Michael guilt-trips her into coming to services—sit on cushions and pillows spread on the carpet. Ben Frankel's wife chants a niggun, a modal Hebrew melody. A strip of black cloth is pinned to Michael's expensive shirt. A memorial candle on the mantle will keep burning for a week. Mirrors have been covered; her home has been taken over. Women are busy in her kitchen bringing out the food they brought.

Deborah's father, who quickly shrank, then died, of cancer, was a celebrated neurologist and surgeon; her mother, now retired near Santa Cruz, was an anthropologist at Berkeley. When Deborah called to tell her of Belle's death, her mother sighed, "I do wish I had the time. I feel terrible not being there. I know you don't believe that." No, Deborah certainly doesn't believe that. Her mother hasn't "had the time" to visit her grandchildren for several years. And for anything as irrational as a funeral! Roberta Schiff herself has told Deborah, "When I go, please, my dear, no funeral. Bury me at sea— from my friend Robert's sailboat—so my ashes don't take up any room." Nonsense. It's so she doesn't get dirt on her.

Though when Deborah's father, Stephen Schiff, died, oh my God, Roberta Schiff mourned flamboyantly. Dr. Schiff had been a central figure in the San Francisco medical community. Deborah felt it was her position in society her mother mourned. She'd be invited to fewer dinner parties. Her mother was a lovely looking, big woman, a successful academic, publishing papers of structuralist anthropology. Deborah was sure she'd be married in a year. But it took her ten—and then the marriage didn't last. She's alone again.

Deborah's father died when Deborah was sixteen; her father's father, Bernard Schiff, brought from Frankfort one, a chemical process for compounding aniline dyes, and two, revulsion against the neo-Orthodox Judaism he was born into, seeking the America of economic opportunity, because being a Jew in Germany simply limited his ambitions. Grandfather Bernard is alive in Deborah's exalted carriage, her horsewoman walk that so infuriates Michael, the elegant lift of her head. Deborah was brought up a secular Jew, living among wealthy, worldly, intelligent Jews and Christians, brought up to see and accept—at a distance—the anthropological strangeness of others.

Tonight she has to live on their planet. She wishes his sister Susan had come to Boston with them after the funeral. *She'd* know how to hug these people. Susan is a big hugger. Susan has a big bosom and a large heart, both real. Deborah envies.

She notices the strange regular bobbing motions some of the men go through while davening. Some sit cross-legged on the floor. These aren't Hasidim; they're modern intellectuals, professionals, executives; *feminists*, for heaven sakes. What *is* this? This is a newly minted, a reinvented Judaism, she thinks; a *self*-Chosen, People. Too many prayers, too many candles. The room smells of hot wax and Hebrew.

She remembers stopping at a turnpike Burger King: a van-load of Hasidim in black got out: ear locks, fur hats, medieval dress. They walked as if they were aliens to our atmosphere. Stiff. Not looking beyond their footsteps. I'm a Jew and these are Jews, but we have nothing in common. They might as well be from Borneo.

Ben's wife begins another *niggun, di d'di, di d'di. . . .* The others join in. Deborah hardens herself against the mournful wordless song. In her mind's eye she sees her father shaking his head. "Those minor keys and modal melodies—why," he used to say, "does a religion have to indulge itself in such sadness? It really is self-indulgence. After the Holocaust?" "Life," he'd say, "is sad enough."

Under the influence of this music that she resists, she says, *Belle. Belle*, she says, and stops. *Belle took over my kitchen.* But so *what? The kitchen isn't my field of battle. Why did I care? Why such animosity between us?* Deborah closes her eyes.

Service in a House of Mourning

Michael is ragged. *Michael, you forgot to shave.—I'm not supposed to shave.—Really? For how long?* As if it's a secret vice, whenever he's alone for five minutes, he weeps. But only when Jacob comes unbidden, when he feels Jacob's presence, can he fully mourn.

From behind he notices an overweight man in a pin-striped suit. Not from the synagogue. Who dresses like this? Then he knows him: Myron Rosenthal. Rosenthal is standing at a bookcase, head tilted, looking at titles. Michael recognizes the position—it's just what he himself does—permitting him to stay in his own bookish space in strange houses. Rosenthal knows no one else here. Now he nods and Michael joins him. "I'm *so* sorry, Michael. When you canceled our meeting, I called your secretary. She told me you'd be sitting Shiva. I'm very sorry. I know how much my own mother means to me."

This intimacy is surprising. "Thank you for coming." Michael tries to formulate what he feels. "My questions the other day, I'm sure they must have seemed intrusive, so it's particularly kind of you."

"Not at all. Nonsense. You had an unresolved issue, I'm glad we resolved it. And tonight," he says, lifting forefinger, voice shimmering with vibrato, "being with you when you're sitting Shiva—this may be an important connection for us. *Two Jews. This is real.*"

Real? His saying this makes it feel less real to Michael, less a bond, more a *demonstration* of a bond. A shrewd piece of Michael winces and judges, while an innocent piece really does feel close to Rosenthal, admires him for saying something so foolish and intense.

"Business," Rosenthal says. "Two Jewish businessmen. *Merchants, fershtaste?* For hundreds of years, all we were permitted to be was merchants—merchants, doctors. And then the *goyim* are surprised when we act like merchants. You know, Michael, in some ways, as businessmen, we can't control everything we do. We're limited. The *needs* that the market economy puts on us all. I'm glad we understand each other."

Michael nods, nods. But he suddenly *doesn't* understand, is afraid to understand, understands perfectly but keeps his eyes mournful, cast down, and doesn't ask. He says, "The rabbi will be here soon, we'll have a service."

"Ma'ariv—I can't think the last time I was at evening services, except once in a great while on a Friday night. I can't stay, my friend. I wish I could, believe me. For you, especially. But I've been out of the house since seven this morning. My wife—"

"Of course, of course. Let me introduce you to Deborah before you go. . . ."

"This week you're sitting Shiva. But in about a week, we're having a little party at my house. If you're feeling up to it. A party for Hanukkah, a few weeks early. You don't have to answer now. We'll call and leave details on the machine. All right?"

The living room fills and spills over into the dining room. Rosenthal goes, the rabbi comes, Rabbi Bamberger, and takes Michael's hand, and won't let go of his hand until he really looks at her. "We'll start soon, Michael?"

Now Jonathan comes in, alone, without Jessica, who stayed home with Marcus; and Michael, knowing that his friend won't know how to act among Jewish mourners, takes his arm, makes some patter about the strips of cloth pinned to the clothing, the mirrors covered. They embrace and hold on to one another and Michael is better able to breathe.

"Michael, hey, I'm so sorry, man. I'm so sorry. I really loved your mom. Hell. I'd be a big fool if I didn't. She was always so sweet to me."

They stand together in silence, a congregation of two.

He's known Jonathan since their first year at Harvard. They've lived together, first at Harvard, then as young men in Boston. And there's something else: somehow the fact that Jonathan is African-American makes Michael feel his friend can understand. All right, he says to himself, it's a stereotype, but there are centuries of pain to back it up—pain *and* an assumption that pain is something to be shared. Last year, when Jonathan lost his father, he'd come into Michael's office and just sit. Sit ten, fifteen minutes while Michael worked. Then he'd clear his throat, and Michael would look up, and Jonathan would maybe tell a story about his dad.

As he leads Jonathan into the living room, out of the corner of his eye he notices the other mourners looking at them, not wanting to be seen looking. Not that they're hostile; more likely they tend to be unusually friendly, just because Jonathan is a black man. But it's never simple, is it? No way around it. Race enters.

Jonathan's a large man with a strong, calm presence. When he walks into a room, eyes follow. It's the *way* he walks, unhurried, gracious, like a king, an African king, a president. Well, he *is* a president—of Fusion—but Michael means *presidential*, thinks *Kennedy*. He wears tailored suits over those big shoulders. No longer a problem paying, but even when it *was* a problem—when he was getting his MBA at Harvard—he had his one suit tailored by hand, though it cost him a hundred hours of work-study to pay for it. He'd wear jeans—or else an elegant suit.

Now Jonathan tugs at Michael's arm and whispers, "Can I see you a minute?"

"Sure. Sure." Michael leads the way to his study and closes the door behind them.

"I wouldn't if I didn't have to."

"I guess you've been listening to Steve?—Steve's concerns?"

"We do need to go over the letters, Michael."

"Steve's got letters? He printed them out?"

"After he spoke to you. He felt stupid walking in to see you with no evidence."

"But *letters*. That's theft; that worries the hell out of me, Jonathan—we do have to talk. Not tonight."

"No, Mike. Of course not."

But Michael continues. "You missed Myron Rosenthal by ten minutes. Maybe we could have all sat down and cleared it up"— not telling Jonathan that Rosenthal's visit actually had the *opposite* effect on him. "Look. Jonathan. We've signed a contract expressly forbidding us to copy company documents without permission. We're in dangerous waters here. I mean—*Chemicorp*, Jonathan? Their CEO—Al Braithwaite. Vice-President for their international business—Max Ferguson. Guys like that. This is no fly-by-night company." And when Jonathan nods but doesn't shrug it off, Michael sighs, surprised. "All right. Tomorrow morning, your office about ten? "

"Is that all right?"

"No. I shouldn't leave the house. But it's not for business. . . . Well, I suppose it *is*. But yes, yes, I'll be there."

"Good. Steve'll be there. He's coming back from Bloomington late tonight."

Back downstairs, Rabbi Bamberger takes Michael aside and talks to him about the Kaddish. "Will you come to see me?" she asks. He nods. So much he doesn't know about being a Jew. Many members of this congregation come from observant households, went to Jewish summer camps, lived in Israel awhile. They know the same songs—songs in Yiddish, in Hebrew—they know the blessings, the prayers, by heart. There are converts in the congregation; sometimes Michael feels like one of *them*. His mother—if it weren't for his mother, the beautiful thread of life extending over three thousand years would have been cut. He would have been cut off from this nurturance. His jaw tight with sudden anger, he remembers Ira at the grave site. Big cynic, big atheist cynic. That man would have disinherited me.

The rabbi calls them together for a brief evening service for a house of mourning.

Genocide Weapons

Jonathan's office is more expansive, grander, than his own. Because it matters more to Jonathan. And because he's the front man. It's on a corner, windows looking out at Boston Harbor in two directions. Jonathan said once that he *uses* the boats crossing the harbor, *thinks* with the boats, following a line of argument, a plan, as if they were his doodles on a sheet of paper. Michael was impressed at someone conceiving such a vast scratch pad. But then, Jonathan has always impressed him. When they first met, first semester at Harvard, Jonathan didn't trust him. "I thought you were pressing for us to be friends *because* I was black. So it took a while." Michael laughed, last time this was brought up. "I wanted to be your friend because you were a terrific guy. So cool. We had a class together, you remember?"

"Humanities. A seminar."

"I don't know what it was you said—right at the start of that semester. But I felt, This guy is the real thing." Well? And he is. Michael still feels this. A *mensch*.

At Harvard, because whites felt comfortable around him, Jonathan was informally designated by whites a spokesman for Black Power—and rejected the role. He sat in, picketed, took part in the strike in 1969. But he stayed away from meetings. Senior year he did a column for *The Crimson;* they'd wanted a column on race; he refused. He gave them a weekly column on music—classical as well as jazz. Sometimes he'd write about Cambridge politics or cycles of impoverization, and once a long essay, "Fantasies of Progress, Fantasies of Revolution," that got him in trouble with everybody—white radicals, black radicals, campus conservatives. No matter how he twisted and turned, it was impossible to escape other people's fantasies; finally he gave up—and learned to make use of them.

But that's not the whole story. First he got irritated, then he laughed, then grew furious; then went through all of it again. He learned to use fantasies of fools for his own benefit—then wanted out, wanted to keep away from all those sons of bitches, from anybody except a few friends. He said, "Hell, I'm black"—and gave up everyone white, including Michael. But that was no good. He was stuck with the contradictions. No way to escape being the object of other people's need to stereotype. After graduation he worked for a year for the Dean of Students at Harvard, and one day he was pulling the file of a Tony Grey—and couldn't resist thumbing back to *Greene*—his own file. He discovered that though he'd scored better than 700s on all his College Board tests, he was listed as a "high-risk admission"—a "minority candidate." This he's never told anyone but Jessica and Michael. The impudence of those smug bastards! He's buried it, but every time he gets correspondence from the college, this knowledge comes up again as a taint, a bad odor.

No way to be black at prep school, then Harvard, and not pay, not have to negotiate among the lines of force pulling at him. Especially because he was brilliant, because he picked up ideas fast, retained everything he read, and could spin out multiple vector analyses—had the ability to see the same sets of data in two, three, several ways. And so everyone needed him to be something—a leader, an example of a successful black man, a sign of the possibility for a black man to make it in white society.

Then there were his own needs, which were secret, elaborate, and extensive. Jonathan has always wanted to be wealthy, as if money could sheathe him—like his expensive suits. The suits don't matter—they aren't necessary to his success. He knows that. Because he's always had a sweetness and grace, not a put-on. Others gravitate towards him, bathe in his glow. It's false only in the sense that he *knows* it, so he can't help but use it, turn it on—but it's always there to tap into. Most of the time, when he's with a man or woman, white, black, he feels their softest part and for the moment wants to protect them.

It doesn't stop him from being pragmatic.

It's an odd kind of narcissism, Jessie tells him when she's fed up by the amount of time he gives people he barely knows. "It's as if you're saying, 'I'm so cool, so strong, I don't have to be guarded or selfish; I've got plenty to go around.' *Noblesse oblige*, Jonathan. You know—you get to be a pain sometimes." He laughs and kisses her, and this just frustrates her more.

But all the time he's working the room, the project group, the business lunch, the golf game. Five years out of college, before taking his MBA, he was national sales manager for Delta Computer. And with the MBA he found venture capital, talked Michael into coming in with him, and got Fusion off the ground.

You think he's easy—then look again. You think he's successful, complete, but what he's after is so big he can't see over its top, around its sides. Though he'd never be so foolish to admit it, what he wants is to be so powerful a figure that he can turn the whole system around. Not complain about it. Turn it around.

He works now with young people who are from minority groups, African-American, Hispanic, in a program to help them develop skills that will enable them to begin careers in high-tech industries. He imagined the project, got initial funding, and connected it to a larger, similar project developed by the Urban League. And that was supposed to be it. But he can't stop. He helps keep the program on course; he teaches management skills and helps place young interns and candidates for positions. He's stopped going to the gym, stopped running along Memorial Drive. Jessica's worried. He's on too many boards of directors for non-profits.

This morning, Jonathan's in shirt sleeves, suit jacket draped over the back of a side chair. Saying nothing, he hands Michael three pages, each part of a separate letter, and goes to the window and looks out. On almost nothing. No boats down in the harbor. Low-lying clouds, hard to see even wisps of harbor. Reading the three pages, extracts from letters, private company documents he has no right to see, Michael shakes his head.

They look at one another, deeply. It's this mutual quiet searching, as if the other's eyes had answers, that ten years ago—even earlier—made Michael feel he could work with this man, could trust his whole career to this relationship. "So?" Jonathan asks.

"It's not as unambiguous as Steve said. You think?"

"Michael, how do *you* read—" Jonathan takes the pages—"here: '. . . estimate for effectiveness of dispersal downwind of the site.'"

"That could be pesticides. Isn't that true?"

"Could be, Michael."

"But you don't think so."

"Neither do you. The company is based in London. Pell Trading—right? But the names are African or Arabic and have military titles. What about the references to 'field conditions'? And the chemicals—Mike, I don't have to be a chemist—I looked them up on the Internet."

"We have no right to these documents. And we sure as *hell* have no right to hand them to anyone else."

"No, we don't. So you tell *me*, Mike."

"I suppose we pull in Fred Waller."

"He'll be here."

"Good. Let Fred tell us our rights. But I still don't believe it. Imagine Monsanto, imagine Dupont selling weapons."

"In fact, Dupont—"

"—All right, that's true—with I. G. Farben. Jonathan, if that's what's happening, we extract ourselves from the damned contract. We do damage control."

Jonathan doesn't answer. He gets a couple of cans of cold soda from a bar fridge behind built-in cabinetry, a fridge like the one they used to lease at college. "You're trying to make it simple. *Michael*. What do you think's going to happen if we back out? What reason could we give Chemicorp—to back out of a lucrative contract? I can't think of any. We're 'reorganizing after the merger?' Chemicorp will get in touch with McNair—InterCom *works* for Chemicorp, McNair is Braithwaite's buddy, you know that. McNair will be totally bewildered. What do we tell *him*? 'We've uncovered some irregularities, unethical behavior, we had to drop the contract?' It'll be goodbye to this merger. *Think* a minute."

It's the way Jonathan says *Think* that tips Michael over into understanding. Understanding comes out of walks by the Charles at two AM as suite mates, undergraduates at Harvard. Michael quiets down to the exact timbre of Jonathan's voice, to the rhythm of late-night talk. He looks out at the rags of cloud. He can hardly see the roofs of nearby office buildings. "Sure. I see. But we're speculating. Let's get Steve in on this."

Jonathan nods, dials. "Steve? Okay. We're ready to talk. You want to come in here?"—Turning to Michael, "Five minutes." He sits in silence. Michael watches his face work. A big head, high forehead with close-cropped hair starting to recede, strong jaw—you seemed to see his thoughts churn. "Genocide weapon," Jonathan says. "Perfect genocide weapon. Better than nuclear. I read the letters, I think *Rwanda*."

"I know."

"Maybe a million people hacked to death, burned to death. They herded them into the churches and burned the churches—like Jews in their synagogues. And that was just machetes. What's going to happen when governments use chemical weapons, biological agents? They don't even require sophisticated delivery systems. When you've got control over the media, you can call it a 'typhoid epidemic.' *Or you don't call it anything.*"

"You don't have to convince me, Jonathan. I hear *poison gas*, I think *showers*."

"Sure. Remember, long time ago, we used to kid, how we were *lucky*, we always knew who our ancestors were: the ones on the left side of the picture, the ones getting beaten and robbed."

Michael nods. "Jonathan" he says, "Maybe we should go above Rosenthal's head—let's call Max Ferguson. See what he knows about Orion. And Pell Trading."

"That's possible. If Orion exists, it's got to be a small group. Not the corporation. Maybe Ferguson.—But you think we can trust Ferguson?" They're silent, looking into mid air. "I think about Rwanda all the time," Jonathan says.

Silent, they look at each other. It changes things, mourning with your friend the death of a father, a mother. They've known one another half their lives. But now, especially after last night, they can sit like this and grieve without embarrassment.

They've both read the reports, seen the films. Rwanda makes *Heart of Darkness* seem like a fairy tale. There are interviews with "survivors" who have survived their entire extended families. No one is left.

They sit, Jonathan, Michael, nursing cheeks with the palms of their hands.

Finally, Steve Planck comes in and half-sits on the edge of Jonathan's desk; the three of them turn it around and around. Michael finds himself irritated at Planck. The guy gets too enthusiastic. Michael looks at Steve biting his cuticles—always he bites his cuticles and wipes the wetness on his jacket.

Now Steve gets up and gives Michael a hug, full body. "Sorry, man. I can imagine—I mean, if my mother . . ." he says, shrugs, squeezes again.

Frederick Waller joins them. He's not from the company's legal staff—he's the lawyer Jonathan brings in for special consultations, "best guy in Boston." Looking over the letters, Waller, a man with the mane of graying hair associated with great conductors, a perfectly groomed mane, who speaks down to you from the podium of his six-four height, speaks as if every word is worth the dollar or two it individually costs, loving, oh, you could tell, the ring of those words—Waller assures them they have nothing to worry about. It's quite straightforward. He raises another finger for each point: (1) "You have no obligation to report Chemicorp. You don't even know that what they're doing is illegal. (2) Breaking through their encryption and reading documents? You've signed a contract—I've just read through it—expressly forbidding you to reveal what comes across your desk in the process of doing your work. It's to protect corporate policies, trade secrets, it's a pretty standard clause. Well, this information was found *outside* the purview of your work.

It's precisely *not your business.* (3) If you report criminal activity, if you're a witness in a criminal case, Chemicorp can't sue you. But if you make it public, they certainly *can.* I know a fellow in Commerce you might see. He can fill you in on export restrictions—interdicted materials, countries under sanctions or embargo. What they're doing might be perfectly legal."

"Legal!" Steve says. "You're missing the point, Fred. The point is how to nail them without blowing ourselves up."

Michael raises his eyes to the ceiling.

Waller puts his whole hand up like a traffic policeman. "Let's assume there *are* no export restrictions here. Let's assume they have licenses. After all—you're supposed to be *working for* these people, helping them. What will it look like if this gets out? Who else's going to trust you with their corporate secrets?"

"That's true," Michael says.

Jonathan says, "Chemicorp—we're talking Myron Rosenthal, and above him, Max Ferguson, and above him, Braithwaite. They're sure to know it's us. Steve—how many people in Chemicorp are authorized for access to this trade group's files—to Orion?"

Steve bristles. What that means for Steve is he cracks his knuckles, scratches at his chest like a dog with fleas. "It's hard to say. That's not in my purview. You look at the text—it seems like a small group. I'd say definitely a small group. Listen, this has *got* to be reported. Michael, I'll do it on my own if I have to."

"These companies," Waller says. "These companies! Back in the eighties, how do you think Saddam got his chemical weapons? Half the countries in Europe were involved." He lists on his fingers: "Germany. Switzerland. Belgium. France. They were willing, these companies, to build nuclear facilities for him, too—French firms got that contract—but Israel, you remember, blew them up in the early eighties."

"But Fred—aren't you suggesting we drop the whole thing?" Michael asks.

"*Drop* it!" Steve says. He scratches at himself.

"I'm just laying out your options, Michael. Look—they get caught selling chemical weapons systems to, let's say, Saddam—well, then *great*—it's like reporting child molesters. The Office of Export Enforcement—it runs out of Commerce—will take over.

And nobody's going to bother you about your corporate ethics. Otherwise . . ."

"I'm sorry I know about this," Jonathan says. "I wish I didn't know. Let's start making calls."

Tender Brisket

In skullcap, Michael sits in his living room reading psalms.

The loss of a loved mother is not a Holocaust. It's obscene to feel so, even for the mourner. It's just extraordinary, ordinary death. But tonight Michael feels more sharply what it was like for his unknown cousins in Europe to lose mother, sister, child, not as six million but one by one.

Wednesday—his father hasn't come up from New York or even called. Though he isn't permitted to work, Michael makes calls. Always to Jonathan and McNair—he has an hour-long talk with McNair. There's something about death, about a mother's death, that changes things, changes the space along the wires between two men who know one another only as business colleagues/ adversaries. A generosity happens. Encrypted at a level beneath his ability to say, he feels his mother is in on this business deal, has improved its climate. But he can't speak to McNair about Chemicorp. So they talk as if there were no problems.

He keeps calling his father and getting the answering machine, the old message, *Please leave a message for Belle or Ira Cooper. . . .* He should have *insisted* his father come up to Boston. It's not right. He thinks of calling hospitals; he calls an old couple, the Loebs, he's known since he was a child—but they've moved to Florida, recently enough that the phone company reports their new number on the old line. Marilyn Loeb says, "Oh, my dear, how sorry I am, look how out of touch, I didn't even know . . ." Crying, she gives him the names of two of his father's Broadway friends.

These he already knew from the funeral home. They signed the Visitors' Book at Riverside. One he can't reach. The other, the man who read a prayer at the service, says he doesn't know, but if he sees Ira, well of course . . .

Michael doesn't believe him.

Belle had friends. He knows a couple of names, but Belle and Ira lived so separately; the women he reaches know nothing about his father.

He considers calling the police. But somehow he's sure it isn't a police matter.

Now it's Shabbat. The people who came to mourn are gone. He should stop mourning, go to shul to say Kaddish, but he can't face it; he says Kaddish alone, though Kaddish must be said in a community. But Jacob is there; he hears him intoning a *niggun* in delirious minor key. Deborah has been away since Tuesday morning, but when she gets back, she tells him, "Michael? We've got Belle's cooked brisket. I hope that's all right with you. I put it in the freezer before we left for New York."

"Her brisket?" Immediately, tears. "Oh, my God, *her brisket!*" He promises himself not to weep when he eats her food. He should give this to his family as a celebration. That's his job. But his eyes cloud up. So he blows his nose and laughs. "Your grandmother!—she always loved to cook low-calorie like this." It's wonderful brisket; the gravy—defrosted, the fat skimmed off—makes the brisket spectacularly good. He thinks, *This is proper mourning. This, more than the service, more even than sitting* Shiva, *is what my mother would have wanted.* "Can I pour you more gravy?" he asks Karen. "My mother, didn't she make wonderful tender brisket, didn't she make wonderful gravy?"

"Well, so do you," Deborah says. "It's a family legacy."

The kids both love this. It's magic, communion with Grandma who's dead. He, too, loves it—though uneasily, as if there's something primitive about it, an ingestion of his mother's heart.

He wonders if this rich pungent sauce makes Deborah jealous. It's a sauce that she could never—would never want to—match; it's not, like Deborah's own cooking, a dish where you wonder, What is that herb?—but a dark, rich, back-of-the-tongue tang that comes from roasting beef bones and duck bones and cooking them with vegetables for a day and a half, reducing and pouring the demi-glacé into small containers for later use. That's the secret. You can't make a sauce like that and be in charge of the "products"—the reports—of half a dozen other consultants. Plus handle one's own clients.

He asks himself, Is that what I want from her, a sauce like this? If so, I'm a fool.

He married Deborah—why? Partly because she seemed cool, aristocratic to him—"aristocratic" a code word for restraint, taste, and grace; a code word, perhaps, for not-expressively-Jewish. She made their time together exciting with unstated ironies. That's exactly right. Deborah's special excitement comes from with-holding. There's a slight smile that tells you she has a wry take on the world. There's a terrific charge behind the smile. It's amused and it's erotic. Her immobility conveys terrific energy in check. And she seemed to him something he himself had never been: hip, suave, graceful. He married her because she never made him wince with a cliché. She's the only woman he ever went out with who he knew to be much smarter than he was himself. He might now say to her, Of course, this isn't sophisticated cooking; it's just what I grew up on. Yours—when you have the time—is extraordinary, restaurant-quality. But she's too smart for that con.

The fact is, it's not flattering to Deborah Schiff, not pleasant for either of them, and sooner or later he's going to have to deal with it or she'll stuff it down his throat and make him choke on it.

Deborah looks across the table and feels Michael's sadness. Cooking a brisket of beef is of utterly no consequence to her; she's not jealous. Eating it tonight, she remembers Belle Cooper in an apron, cutting onions, tears in her eyes. As she cuts the meat there are tears in her own eyes. . . . And she notices the gray in Michael's hair, his new, scruffy beard, the diagonal lines scored into his face outwards from his nose to the sides of his mouth, and she feels weighed down, wants to run from grief and age. But she suffers for him, too, so she smiles and says, "Well, Michael? Are we going to sing your 'Shalom Aleichem' tonight?"

CHAPTER FOUR

At odd times it hits Michael all over again—Mom, Mom! He sees her working in the kitchen, sees her sitting on a bench along Riverside Drive or playing with Ari. Even worse are the times he can't see her at all, no matter how his inner eyes search. When he finds her, his chest is suffused with tears. He hides in a men's room; if he's driving, he pulls the car over and, windows rolled up, weeps. He breathes darkness, slumps into the leather upholstery and silently howls. He thinks about the Hispanic family at the hospital—*Jesus, Oh, Lord Jesus, oh Jesus.*

In mind's eye he sees his father, dapper, in the hospital room. It rankles him, as if his father's charm were connected somehow to his mother's death. And where did the man go? He scans a mind-map of New York for where he might be hiding (because hiding is what it seems like)—the Village, where he has old cronies, Brooklyn, that painter—what's his name—Hochman? He takes time out at work, calls the hospitals, the police. Before his mother died, sometimes a month went by without a conversation with his father. Strange that now it's become urgent. . . .

Kaddish

Michael needs a minyan so he can say Kaddish for his mother's soul. In his shul there are no daily services; even the big Conservative and Reform synagogues nearby have no morning minyan, only services on Shabbat. An Orthodox shul in Brookline holds services every morning; it's there he goes on his way to work. He drives himself, embarrassed to have Dennis sitting in a big Lexus outside while he prays.

When he joined his Reconstructionist congregation, Ben Frankel laid out the terms: "Here's the deal at this shul: You cater two *onegs* a year; women count in a minyan; God doesn't physically intervene in the universe; and we're not the chosen people."

That's not how it is here.

In this little shul, tiny, old brownstone shul, with its sanctuary in a converted basement, are only men; behind the curtain meant to separate them off, no women. It's men, in skullcap or fedora or both, who come in with tallis bag under their arm; they murmur the barucha for putting on the tallis, stand covered in tallis, wrap tefillin precisely, as they say the blessing, around arm and on forehead. Now they look strange, ancient, medieval; no, older, the black straps taut over the pale flesh of their arms: they look as if they belonged to the time of Moses, as if the straps hooked them up to holy power. They nod to Michael and go about their praying business. He sneaks looks: they know their stuff.

It takes time for a minyan to collect; a scattered few, they go through the preliminary service. The morning service, led by a member of the congregation, isn't long; but as fast as they pray, he knows he can't spare this much time every day. Most of the men are old, retired. Most, he's sure, are foreign—Russians? Israelis? Their eyes, their gestures tell him: not American. For a moment he sees them naked, head shaved, tattoo numbers on their arms.

What he wants is to say the Mourner's Kaddish. But he knows he has to wait. For forty-five minutes he murmurs Hebrew words of praise, rocks, chants with the others. Up on the little bima the prayer leader murmurs the first words of a prayer, the last words; between times, everyone murmurs. There are passages familiar to him, but the intonations are different, the text is different; he loses his place. What place? Even psalms or prayers that Michael is used to singing in unison, he catches first to his left, in a croaky tenor, then to his right in a murmured baritone. The guttural, lilting Hebrew takes one voice, echoes across the room, echoes again. He's surprised at the beauty that issues forth from this chaos. This jumble of sound, what should be a cacophony, is not. Has sweetness, harmony, a harmonious jumble.

Each Jew is on his own, even facing in different directions, standing when he's sitting, sitting when he's standing. Some rock side to side, some stiffly forward from heel to toe, others are still. Some of the prayers his lips sham. During the Amidah, the oldest and most essential prayer, which an observant Jew says three times a day, he speaks in silence to his mother, *Mother, soul of my mother, be at peace. May your soul be at peace.* He sees her now with glasses on her nose and a querulous, shrewd look on her face. She's in the kitchen, looks up from the papers at him. Not bitter, as she sometimes became. But not at peace. And it has something to do with him.

He stands to say the Mourner's Kaddish. The prayer is murmured so fast by three, four of the men that at first, though he knows it well, he's unable to keep up.

But now in his chest, vibration deepens, as the voice of Jacob Goldstein mourns for him; the Kaddish reverberates in Jacob's voice through the low-ceilinged room. As if he's brought a pro with him, a ringer, he's suddenly a praying fool. And his mother comes to him no longer disturbed but sanctified, carrying her death in dignity. This is new for him. In this—oh, not *vision*, that's too strong a word, but *imagining* too weak—*seeing*, in this seeing then, death, her death, his death-to-come, seems . . . majestic, part of the whole megillah, filled with splendor. In this moment, these few moments, in this musty dark room with cheap ceiling filigree panels, it isn't a question of Belle Goldstein Cooper *dead*, he *alive*. He is *centuries* dead; his grandfather's grandfather is as alive as he is. This is simply present to him. He doesn't think: *The light from a star began its journey to our eyes a thousand years ago. Or began let's say when Moses stood at Sinai, we don't see the star now but as it burned then. Or then is now. The light in the present is from many pasts.* It's not that there is no time, but that this moment is *thickened* by time—how to say this?—There is no gap between himself and the past, he is suffused with past. He understands Belle Goldstein Cooper at this moment: she's right; he *is* the legacy.

So why is he in tears? For whom? How can this *seeing* provoke tears?

Head lowered, he says good morning, good morning, to the other men in the sanctuary, in the little shul in Brookline.

"You should come back," the prayer leader, a lean, bearded man in black suit, says. "Any weekday morning." He speaks with no foreign accent, and this surprises Michael.

"I will," he says, and means it—but he knows he can't take this much time in the morning. It's that, and maybe a certain fear that lifts when he climbs the stairs and walks out into a perfect October day. Centuries have passed. His Lexus waits for him at the curb outside. Michael Kuperman presses the remote control unit on his key chain, and the Lexus opens. He sinks into its soft leather seat.

A Question of Time

New York. West End Avenue. He lets himself in; well, it's his apartment, really—bought when it went co-op by Susan and himself years ago, the apartment where they grew up. Belle and Ira could have paid for it, but he wanted their retirement money untouched. And it's true what his father said: Jacob, who didn't trust his son-in-law, left the bulk of his money in trust for Michael and for Susan. The apartment is on the tenth floor. It's a gray day. Dark in the apartment until he turns on the lights. Fantasy: his father dead in his armchair. But the apartment is empty, nothing touched since they left on Monday morning. One coffee cup in the sink. He looks around for clues.

The first clue is what *isn't* there:

The photographs. Not all gone—but there are big gaps on the walls like missing teeth, gaps like frames, unfaded on the faded walls. In the living room, in the bedroom, in the study. Blank spaces. It was always a joke: "Why paint the apartment?" his mother would say. "There's hardly any wall left between the pictures."

His father's desk: there's no address book. No checkbook. His father's closet has a number of empty hangers; the drawers, too, seem to have odd, empty places.

So his father has gone off. And doesn't want to be found right now.

The old, sour smells. Furniture polish, God-knows-what, over the scent of Belle's perfume. He feels suddenly dizzy. Needs something. In almost a fugue state he wanders. The medicine cabinet. In the kitchen, the cupboard. Wine, liquor. He opens an almost-full bottle of cognac and sips, breathes deep. Maybe some seltzer? But the fridge is nearly empty. It smells terrible; he finds an open bottle of milk that's turned bad, and pours it out in the sink. Now he stands at a window, looks out at the narrow slice of the Hudson

River, Riverside Park. He used to play in that park, looking up at this window. He hears his father's harsh, treble yelling. Some fight about him, Michael. *You spoil the goddamn kid. What is he, a prince?*

His father's desk is in the "study"—what used to be Michael's bedroom; his mother's desk, in Susan's room. *This is all written down, you'll find it in my desk.*

Scotch-taped to one wall of the top drawer of her desk are three sealed envelopes:

For my Son Michael, in Case Anything Should Happen to Me
For my daughter Susan, in Case Anything Should Happen to Me
For Ira

He puts the envelope for Susan into his jacket pocket, the envelope for his father on top of the desk. He expected photos, he anticipated a loving letter. He could see her—oh, he knew how theatrical she was—slipping out of bed one night to write them letters of goodbye. She knew how bad: her heart, her blood pressure. A question of time. She knew.

Carefully, he cuts his envelope open with her letter opener.

No pictures. A letter and a typed list of addresses and telephone numbers.

If you're reading this, something has happened to me, as sooner or later my darling it must. I'm sorry for your sake and for Susan's sake. But don't be too upset, my son. All right—I'll permit you to be a little upset, you might even want to say Kaddish for me. But seriously, now listen: I've had a good, complete life. I know how often you saw your father and I snapping at each other, but that's nothing. At times, he and I were loving companions. I know you don't believe that. I could wish we had done things differently, but it was the fault of both of us. Both. And you and your sister always made my life beautiful, even when it wasn't so beautiful in other ways.

You should know that I'm not afraid to die. I don't know why. It's very peculiar. My father would say, "May you have a share in the world to come." But that's not it.

This letter is to tell you things. I hope I've had a chance to tell you in person. If not, so at least you'll have this letter.

There are things I couldn't say until you were ready to hear them. I'm giving you a legacy. I don't know how you'll use it. My darling, you've become a Jewish man. I know you go to synagogue and say Yiskor for my father. You can't know what that means to me. So. I'm giving you this legacy—a legacy of mitzvot.

Of course, Susan needs to hear. I've told her about it, too.

On the phone you've begun to ask about my father. Well, let me tell you.

When the terrible pogrom came to Kishinev, my father had saved a good deal of money, he owned thousands of lambs, a slaughterhouse, which is amazing to me, since a Jew wasn't allowed to own land. His own father had no money to speak of. But he'd built a little business. And my father had money from his mother's family. And he was smart. Like you. He made and made. Thank God, he had good Christian friends in high places. The mob came, drunken peasants, muzhiki, *and from out of town, Cossacks—they say the Russian secret police incited and paid them—there were lies about blood of a Christian child, the usual, I never got the details, but the blood that ran in the streets let me tell you was Jewish blood. Well, this general hid my father and my mother and my grandparents and the three little children in the cellar. This is of course many years before I was born. Then, when it was safe to come out, like animals blinking in the light, they went back to their home. Imagine what they saw. But their home was there—maybe the general had said something to the police? And my grandparents were all safe. It was a miracle.*

At that moment, my father told his father we were going to the United States. And he begged his parents and my mother's mother to join them. He could try to get passports. But they said, "No, but you go." Well, he gave his parents, my mother's mother—her father was dead—a great deal of his savings. And then, what would most people have done?—taken the rest for their own family. After all, they were going to a new country. But he kept giving. A distant cousin, two girls who had been shamed, a musician, a friend, and then . . . people. Seven families came to America or South America or Palestine this way.

Now, let me give you an example, how a mitzvah accumulates interest. This is what I want to tell you. This is where you come in. There was this one young couple he helped to leave Kishinev for America. They had three children. So. One son became a famous surgeon—he's retired now, but for years he taught surgery at Albert Einstein. So, you think of how the one small gift of my father changed so many, many lives! That man's students, his patients. And those lives changed others, which changed others. Of course, not everyone was decent. There was a gambler. There are some I won't mention. But for the most part, my father saved good people who brought other good people into the world.

Often, my darling, when I remember the millions who were starved or gassed or machine-gunned, I don't think so much about how they suffered. There was of course the suffering, there was the loss of their children, often taken away before the end. And simply loss of the chance to live a full life in this world. And there was the terror. But what I mourn is everything that was lost to us. To all of us. How some of them might have become wonderful, marvelous, might have given so much. Imagine!—a geneticist grandson, a composer or a writer. Or their children's children's children—what they might have given. We might have a very different world.

My father never felt he had done something remarkable. Oh, he liked the feeling of doing good. Don't get me wrong—he was no saint, without vanity. In many ways he was a vain man. He liked writing checks. He signed checks for helping with a flourish. Always, we kept a box—money for the poor. He loved when he heard us drop coins in the box. He would say, "for the blessing of Shabbat" or "for your wonderful marks in school," and he would drop in coins. But when I asked him about the families, the gifts, he shrugged off what he'd accomplished: "Look, Belle" he said, "our name, Goldstein, is not originally from Eastern Europe. It means that hundreds of years ago we ran east, probably from the Rhine valley. You know the suffering. So someone must have helped our family get away, travel to the East." "That," he'd say, "that is a legacy passed on to me. So I pass it on."

And now I am passing it on to you. . . .

It goes on. Appended to the letter is a list of names and at the top, a handwritten note:

See steel file in my closet.

Michael takes from the back of his mother's closet an olive green steel file holder, with heavy cardboard partitions inside held together by cloth sides, and in each folder one of the original seven families—plus one for "Others."

He wishes he had time to read through the folders. He hears in his mother's voice *made my life beautiful,* and hears *all kinds of connections.* He hears the rhythms of her voice, its courageous comedy. He has no time to look through the files now. He pockets the letter, walks up to Broadway to look for Ira Cooper.

My Dad, the Photographer

His father's haunts. It hits him how little he knows about his father's routine, where he spends his time. Once he took Michael around the corner to a restaurant and introduced him to friends. So that's the first stop. When Michael was a kid, there were a lot of big cafeterias, lots of tables, you take a ticket and they punch it when you order. Good places for old men to shmooze. Now, there's none around here. This is just a breakfast and lunch place with booths and a counter, a kind of "deli."

Looking in the window, he can see his father's not there, his father's friends aren't there. The counterman is an old Jew himself, but he doesn't know Ira Cooper—at least by name. His white apron is a little *shmutzik*—meat stains, maybe fish oil. He hardly looks up; he's slicing smoked salmon for a sandwich.

"My dad's a photographer, an affable guy," Michael says brightly, trying to win the man's attention. "He's got a full head of hair. He's very vigorous for seventy-eight. He wears a Yankees cap a lot."

"The pho*tog*rapher. Sure. Yeah, everybody knows him. Look," he says; he glances up and points.

Over a booth, a framed black and white photograph: a minor smash-up of two taxicabs; the drivers are standing by the damage with arms spread, hands open. It looks like they're dancing or about to embrace, but their jaws are wide open, so they're probably each shouting their innocence.

"That's a good picture—I'm sure it's my Dad's. I never saw that one."

"He's got them up all along Broadway," the man says. "You take a look. He gives them away, framed."

"If he comes in. . . ," Michael says—and hands the man a card.

So Michael walks store to store to store, Starbucks to a bakery to a Chinese restaurant, leaving his card. And sure enough, he finds two more photographs.

The photographer. All these years, he never thought of it that way.

His cell phone rings. He walks down Broadway, elegant black plastic sculpture to his ear, arguing like a crazy person—if you didn't know better—with himself. But no one looks his way. And he walks past Barnes & Noble's giant bookstore on 82nd, past the deli and bagel place, putting it to his purchasing manager that no, he damn well *won't* take Murray Schlegel's bid. *To hell with Schlegel, you tell him this is the time we're cutting loose the guys who can't play ball . . . no . . . no, absolutely . . . Right . . . Right . . . Well, tell him he'll have to swallow his increased costs. Tell him to think of the increased volume. . . .*

A bus hisses a noxious exhaust, and Michael holds his breath without having to think. He walks past the immense Apthorp on 79th, grand apartment house built around a courtyard—vintage c.1908, a few years after the Dakota was built. Michael glances up, walks on by, punching in numbers, and checks in with Martine, tells her, *Yes. Get Sidney onto that. . . . All right, yes. I'll get back to him as soon as I can.*

But the call to Jonathan, who'd remind him of Chemicorp—that he doesn't make.

Jacob the Patriarch

As he crosses 78th, he finds his breathing changed, he's thickened, slower, calmer, his eyebrows lift, and as Jacob Goldstein he sighs. *What do you need that schnorrer for?*

This is almost auditory hallucination, and it thrusts Michael back, dizzy at the sudden change, like a plane's sudden drop within an air pocket and your stomach has to catch up. For an instant, his own body feels as if it doesn't belong to him.

Jacob's voice is rougher than the one Michael is accustomed to imagining. Raspy. The old man used to smoke cigars, Michael remembers. In America, when he became rich, his mother told him, he learned to roll a cigar between thumb and forefinger, sniff the aroma, cut the tip with a little clippers, and lean back and puff in self-satisfaction. *I liked to sit next to my father and breathe in the smoke after dinner,* Belle told him. *But his voice grew rough.* It's not only the timbre. There's a harsh, tough, American quality he doesn't recognize.

But the actual Jacob was not always a man of honey. And Michael knows this. He's heard so many stories.

How proud Jacob was of living in the Beresford, on Central Park West and 81ˢᵗ Street. How enraged he became when he found this Ira sitting on the sidewalk in front of the entrance. In *work clothes! That the doorman should see, that the neighbors should see! That kupfson.*

Even during the depression his business prospered. In 1905 he came here with barely enough to start a little business, buy an abattoir—and then partly on money from his cousin in Rochester, who owned a junk business. Yet by 1927, when Belle was a little girl, he was able to come to New York to live. And why New York? He didn't dislike Rochester, he was part of a congregation there, but the money was in New York, and he had an opportunity to purchase a meat packing plant. He came to direct it. When the Beresford was completed in (the worst possible time!) 1929, monumental palazzo on the park, he kept his eye on it for his family. And waited. He was never deeply into the stock market, and in the spring of 1929 he divested himself of most of his small portfolio. So the crash didn't hurt him badly, and anyone who had money in those days could name his price. When he moved in to the Beresford, they gave him the first three months rent-free.

Michael imagines: every morning, Jacob leaves the Beresford for his meat packing plant on West 23ʳᵈ Street near the river. He walks to the subway at the corner; his hand in his jacket pocket, his chest out, he strolls into the kiosk and down the stairs. Always he carries coins for the poor—by the subway entrance at 23ʳᵈ Street they gather every morning. He makes it a practice never to judge worthiness. He's asked, he gives. When his pocket is empty, he turns it out and those who know him don't ask. Then there are his greater obligations: the families he helps come over, establish themselves. His own brother back in Kishinev. When his mother dies, then his father, he hears by telegram, but what good would it do to go over? Frankly, he is afraid to go back, with all he hears about Russia, the war—Jews killed by Polish troops, by Russian troops—the terrible pogroms; the Bolsheviks. God forbid, to be trapped there! He worries all the time about his brother and his brother's family. And then he doesn't hear. He stops hearing. He writes letter after letter. Finally, he gets a letter, they have been able to get out, they are living in Vilna.

They are so blessed. Sarah is healthy, he is healthy. All over America, the children are settled, and Belle, his sweet Belle, his youngest, she blooms into a beautiful young woman, a pious young woman. Then this *grubyom* Ira Cooper comes along!

And so, the voice. *What do you need that schnorrer for?*

Michael stops and listens. Was it someone on the street? Of course not. It bothers him, this toughness. In fact, at once he feels like defending his father from attack. *My father the artist.* A father I never knew.

Jacob's Legacy

Where the hell is that photographic supplies store? It's three blocks further down Broadway. Little store with new and used cameras locked away behind glass. The young woman thinks she remembers. Michael wishes he'd brought a snapshot. He leaves his card. He tells her: an old man in a Yankees cap, someone who really knows his photography. And doesn't add . . . someone who makes sure you know he knows.

He finds an off-track betting parlor. His father likes to play the horses sometimes. It's a new interest, the past ten years. No one knows anything about Ira Cooper. So Michael walks up and down along Riverside Drive, sees old men, old women, goes back to the apartment and from his mother's desk makes a call to a distributor in Dallas, then the call to Jonathan—but Jonathan's not in the office. Michael is relieved.

He thumbs the folders of families in the green steel file holder in front of him on the desk, looks at the list attached to his mother's letter. What has the list to do with him? Is he supposed to do something for the children of children of the families Jacob helped? Do what? And why them?

Abelsky/Baumann/Gertsberg/Kerenbaum/Kroilshuk/Liebsmann/ Yotovsky. The list, divided like the file box by families, includes over a hundred fifty names. Some are followed by "Deceased" and sometimes a date. Others—a dash and a question mark. Sometimes Belle typed, "Reported to have several surviving children," or "Reported to have died in Argentina." "Emigrated to Paris; family sent to the camps." "Brother's children and grandchildren murdered 1940-41, Kishinev." Many have the note, "Sister's children sent to a death camp from Holland," "Brother's family killed in Vienna." He's always known about his mother's interest in genealogy. But this. . . . Only for a tenth of the list are there addresses; some with telephone numbers.

The letter—he realizes he's not finished reading it.

> *. . . For many years we met regularly, sometimes many families. My father loved the "Kishinev reunions," as he called them. Your father would say that it "fed Jacob's vanity." I'd say it gave him a sense of wholeness. By the time you were a child, there were no reunions. Your uncle, Uncle David, may his soul rest in peace, was too much the businessman, and anyway he was too shy. Your father has never been interested, but he, too, has connections with certain people on the list.*
>
> *You may wonder what kind of legacy this is—a list of people your grandfather helped. Frankly, I'm not sure how you'll use it. I think you should maybe call, learn about some of the families from Kishinev just so you can see . . .*
>
> *With all my love,*

and she's signed it, *Mother*.

He folds the letter away. It's like her brisket, this letter. Well made, full of the style of the maker, the style of a people. Self-consciously so—still, it's no con. He can smell her perfume on the heavy notepaper. Her handwriting is old-fashioned, schoolroom-taught; not the scribble of people brought up on typewriters and word processors. The letters are even and rounded; only the flourish of the capitals gives away her love of the dramatic. What she's passing on, he thinks, is her kindness and her mystery.

That's *her* legacy. But the legacy of Jacob is another thing. It's impossible for Michael to think the words *Jacob's legacy* and not think of the very strange, befuddled/prophetic legacy of the Jacob of Genesis passed on to children and grandchildren gathered at his deathbed in Egypt. *Jacob-in-exile*: no wonder he's always been fascinated at the story of Jacob, Jacob and Joseph. But he prefers the legacy of his grandfather Jacob Goldstein. Belle used to say, "My father was a peculiar kind of socialist—he gave to each according to *his* ability and according to *their* need."

Michael pokes through the house half looking for clues, half thinking about his mother and her legacy. On his father's desk, a photograph, not one of Ira's, turn-of-the-century—a young man and woman. The man, short, tough, a little stocky, wears a mustache and a derby. He's trying to be American. The woman wears a babushka. These are, he knows, his *other* grandparents. So interesting that Ira left it—took so many photos but left this one.

A different legacy. He can barely remember this grandfather, but he remembers the stories.

A Cigar Roller in Chicago

Ira Cooper's father Nathan sits at a long, pine-plank table on a stained pine floor, with twenty other men—a long, dark loft lit only by small light bulbs, dangling, one at each end of the table. Daylight from the narrow street fades before it reaches the table. Winter is coming, bills for coal. The table has a sweet-sour smell, rank, somehow satisfying, from years of tobacco. Tobacco stains have turned the pine mahogany. He can hardly listen to the Yiddish reader at the far end of the table, the story by I. L. Peretz. They've paid, the workers themselves, for the young man to read to them, and Nathan enjoys the barbed Peretz. But all he can think of is the cost of coal. Chicago! Past the table, he sees a jagged strip of daylight where the window casement has separated from the brick wall into which it's set. No heat. Already, the men wear their overcoats. And it's just the beginning. No wonder he thinks of the coal.

Slowly, at night at Workman's Circle, his English improves. He pays for the lessons by walking every day the three miles to work and back along the broad, straight avenue, downtown to poor town. *Tzu macht mir ein American.* He sees the contempt for them all in the boss's eye—*what!*—as if Ehrenstein were American-born—instead of what he is, just ten years off the boat himself. *Treyf! Proske*, ignorant *grubyom!* Who needs street mobs in Odessa for enemies when the Jews have a pig like Ehrenstein to suck their life blood?

They meet after work to organize. Nathan is angry—but terrified. He can't tell Frieda. He tells her, "more lessons in English," and she is satisfied. English will get them out of these streets. Nathan is a skilled worker—a machinist. In Odessa, until the fight with the boss, until he got totally fed up with family and the enemies of his family, he made a decent living. It wasn't the life his parents wanted for him. Their son should be a student of Talmud. Too bad! In the spring pogrom of 1905 in Odessa, the Jews in their caftans ran and were stomped to death or clubbed to death, or butchered with kitchen knives; their eyes were gouged out, they were thrown from windows in the midst of their prayers. Eight hundred dead Jews in Odessa that spring. Nathan, along with Jewish carters and stone workers, stormed through the streets of Odessa swinging a club, breaking up gentile mobs coming into the Jewish streets. He fought as a Jewish worker. Clubs, not prayers.

Ira was last night sick with a fever. At times like this, Frieda reverts to backward Jew, praying, cursing, rocking the baby and praying in a sing-song, mixed-up Hebrew. Nathan despises her superstitions. And he is afraid: suppose she goes crazy like poor Rachel down the block. If Ira dies, she'll simply *stop*, Frieda, like a horse that falls over in the street. Nathan despises the prayers that still go through his own head, he can't help it, synagogue melodies. But when he catches himself, he chants, *Strike . . . strike . . . strike . . .* as if the word had the power to kill, and half listens to the Peretz story, and his fingers cut and stuff the cigar wrapper-leafs, and the sweet smell comes to him, and he thinks of the fat pigs who will smoke this. He would like to spit in each cigar. He would like to *poison* each cigar. Wait till Ehrenstein—Ehrenstein and all the other cigar makers in Chicago—see what they have in store for them next month. . . .

What can it be like for Nathan Kuperman? What *can* it be like? Twice cut off—first from his family and his religion (his uncle chief cantor in the largest synagogue in Odessa, his grandfather a rabbi, his father all his life a student of Talmud), then from his comrades in Odessa. And worst: he has lost the self-respect of being a *skilled* member of the proletariat—a Jew with muscles and know-how who is part of an international people. Not just Jewish people. All who work for others in the sweat of their brow. But now! To roll cigars, as any fool could learn to do. To come to this flat, bleak city on another great sea, a new, ugly, sprawling city, to live mixed up with Poles and Jews and Swedes and Irish and have no congregation to join. There were workingmen's associations, but he couldn't yet understand the language, and anyway, he despised their ignorance. What had they read? They yelled and swaggered and knew nothing. So who did he have to talk to? Frieda? And what did she know?

Ira the Revolutionary Artist

Ira grows up on these streets and thinks his father is crazy, so bitter, angry all the time. Always, doors slam. Always, curses in Yiddish. He watches out the window when his father goes downstairs in the morning, past the boarder's room, and before the day begins already walks with his shoulders thick. Even when they move to New York in 1925, to Brooklyn, and his father is finally able to work in a machine shop, still, he's crazy. By seven, eight, Ira knows; he's always on the watch for his father's big hand to swoop in a *flusk* to the face. But by then his father has begun to speak good enough English, he's part of Workman's Circle, goes to lectures, is part of a socialist group, is never at home. And that's fine by Ira. Ira can't leave soon enough. He has contempt for his father's so-called socialism. At Brooklyn College, he joins YCL—the youth wing of the Party. It doesn't matter what "career" he's going to have. His real career will be making a new world.

One day in Washington Square Park he meets Belle Goldstein, and he hates her father in advance, because the Goldsteins, having moved from Rochester, live on Central Park West, the Beresford, a palace but bigger. He won't take any crap from those people. He goes up in the elevator in dungarees and a work shirt. When they go off for the day to their country club in Westchester, a day he's supposed to spend with Belle, he sits cross-legged on the sidewalk in dungarees sewed at the knees, camera in the pack on his lap. "I'm waiting for Belle Goldstein," he tells the doorman. "Waiting for the Goldsteins," he tells the building superintendent. "I'm Belle Goldstein's friend." The camera is a used Leica he saved over a year to buy. With this he snaps pictures of the *haut-bourgeois* arriving and departing the Beresford—camera like a gun—until the brand new Packard pulls up and the chauffeur helps Belle's father from the car, and Belle soothes her parents, gets rid of the "disgrace" by going out for a soda with Ira. He takes pictures of her—camera like a kiss. "The revolution needs artists, too," he says. "To show what's real. The truth."

She's seventeen years old, a year younger. It's 1938. To her, Ira is the embodiment of the men fighting in Spain against the fascists, she sees him fighting to save the Jews in Europe. His photography impresses her. His passion impresses her. She has grown up in an Orthodox household; he's altogether different from the boys at shul. He represents no-nonsense truth; even if she can't altogether buy what he believes, she respects its toughness. She doesn't know that he is part of a tradition, ongoing since the eighteenth century, of Jews rejecting tradition. Ira, imitating Nathan his father down to the tightness of his jaw, savoring the same way the sweetness of bitter irony about divine and human justice, also sees himself as new: a rebel against religion and power, with the power of contempt to lift him out of his shame. *What* shame, he can't say.

He is a communist artist.

They make out on the floor of his darkroom that stinks of chemicals in the basement of his apartment building in Brooklyn. He makes her read *The New Masses*. When Stalin and Hitler sign their non-aggression treaty in 1939, he yells at her, "You—you swallow what the bourgeois press tells you to swallow, you don't understand how the world works—Stalin's strategy is always for the revolution. What do the capitalist leaders want? They want the Soviet Union to be bled dry by a war with Hitler—so they can come in and undo the revolution." But even then, yelling just like his father, yelling so that Belle had to cover her ears and weep, weep because it was all over, everything between them was hopeless and over, even then he feels his own bluster. The Party is never the same for him again. And so, after three years in the Army, back from being a photographer in Europe, from seeing and photographing the death camps in 1945, when he's back from the war and much quieter, and Jacob Goldstein can bear to be in the same room with him, Ira subscribes to *PM,* the left-wing daily, but no longer to the *Daily Worker,* and he lets his Party dues slide, and then—it was 1947—Ira writes a letter to a man he admires, his district leader, explaining his reasons for leaving the Party. He knows he will never hear from the man again. Seeing old friends at a rally for Vito Marcantonio, he knows not to bother waving; they don't even meet his eye. He makes sure not to aim his camera their way—they'd think he was a police spy.

So that was that.

It isn't a big step (after he's looked for work as a photographer, as a manufacturer's representative for photographic supplies, after he's worked six months for sixty dollars a week as an assistant for a lawyer who works with the poor in East Harlem) to accepting the idea of a Jewish wedding, the whole megillah, a wedding at an Orthodox synagogue and a reception after at the St. Moritz—so long as Belle knows goddamned well it's just a ritual. It's for her, not God. He has nothing against rituals. He calms his anxiety during the celebration by taking his own photographs. And Jacob pulls him aside while the dancing is going on. "Tell me. I don't want to impose. Tell me, Ira. Would you like to come work for me? I know your views on bosses, but I'll try to be a decent boss, Ira, as God is my judge."

So he works for the old man, works as an administrative assistant, then a supervisor, in the import-export firm that Jacob now runs on Canal Street with his son David. And Ira tells himself that "career" doesn't matter, only now it's not because the Party will be his life, but because he's got his photography. That's what he has, that's his tool, to express his social vision: his camera. He remembers, every day remembers, standing in a courtyard at Bergen-Belsen and finding even his wide-angle lens not able to hold all the corpses piled up, awaiting burial. So. He has his camera.

How much of his father's story does Michael know? The squatting on the sidewalk outside the Beresford; the days he spent taking photographs at Bergen-Belsen; the long walk his grandfather took back and forth to save a nickel? What he surely knows, without being able to say how, is what it was like for his father to take the subway to work every morning, to work for this rich old man who humiliated him with kindness.

Every day, Michael thinks, wandering the apartment, must have been a humiliation, whatever he told himself. *My poor father.* He has always known but now he understands—that his father's real work has been with his camera. From time to time there'd be a showing of his father's pictures in some basement space with whitewashed-brick walls; he remembers there'd be an award, or *not* be an award, and photos crammed the walls of their apartment, replaced by other photographs in the same frames.

Finding Ira Cooper

Michael holds his cheek and rocks, elbow on his mother's desk as fulcrum. Metronome of grief: time and time and time and time. His father's life. And his father's father. Then he thinks, what about his family's earlier exiles? From . . . some town on the Rhine? He rocks; a clock that ticks off centuries.

Abelsky/Baumann/Gertsberg/Kerenbaum/Kroilshuk/Liebsmann/ Yotovsky/

He remembers some of these names. Wasn't there an Abelsky at his Bar Mitzvah? Definitely a Gertsberg. Connections with his father, she said. Who knows? Returning to his mother's desk, scanning the list, he finds several people in Manhattan. Start there.

An Abelsky on Central Park West. Harold and Edith, the children of the *landsmann* from Kishinev Jacob helped at the turn of the century are themselves dead. But Miriam Koplow, Harold's daughter, fifty years old, is at Central Park West and 82nd Street. There's a telephone number for the Koplows, and Michael calls.

Miriam's home. Music in the background. "Just a minute, I'll turn down the music," she says. "Stan? Turn down the music." When he tells her who he is and asks, "You know about my mother, my mother's death?" she moans, "Oh . . . oh . . . your mother! She was so good to me when I was a little girl. I'm so sorry. I haven't seen her for years and years. Once, the families were close. But your father—well, a Communist in those days. . . ."

"I know. He had his troubles."

"According to my parents, it was Jacob Goldstein—your poor grandfather—who had the troubles. Your dear grandfather—he's always been a legend in my family. I'm not saying anything against your father, but to be a Communist after the war wasn't . . . smart. Was it? Never mind McCarthy—you know about Stalin and the Jews?"

"He wasn't a Party member after 1947. Way before Khrushchev's speech."

"It's none of my business. Oh, but your mother, I loved your mother. I'm so sorry, Michael. I remember you a little. . . ."

"We're looking for my father. I just wondered. . . ."

"No. Your *father*?"

"I'm sure he's fine. He hasn't called. I thought you might know something."

"I'm afraid I haven't got the faintest idea. Oh, Michael, you know what your grandfather did for my family?"

"I know he helped get your grandfather out of Kishinev."

"That, too. Of course. But I'm thinking much later, after the war. He found my cousins in England—they had come from Vienna on one of the *kinde transports*—you know about them? A boy and a girl, he found them in a group home, their families were all dead, it was just after the war. And he vouched for them, he paid for them. And it isn't just money. Your grandfather could *hondle*. I could tell you a story. . . ."

He calls a name, another. People are out, he leaves messages; people are home but the wrong people. Then in Brooklyn, a Sarah Bolofsky, daughter of the Liebsmann family, her voice quivering with age, won't let Michael off the phone. First, how sorry she is to hear about his mother. And then—

"I have to tell you, your grandfather . . ."

He hears how hard it is for her to draw breath to speak and in sympathy, not impatience, tries to finish her sentence, ". . . was a wonderful man. Oh, I know."

But she ignores his interruption. "You know the expression, it's from Talmud. . . . 'If someone saves a single life. . . .'"

"—It's as if they save an entire world."

"It's as if they have saved . . . the whole world. *Yes.* Your grandfather . . ."

Now he understands her need and holds back, gives her time to draw breath, though each breath sounds as if she's sucking pain inside. It hurts him to listen.

". . . those he saved. Their children, do you understand? Mr. Kuperman—you know what happened in Kishinev, the destruction of the Jews?"

"Of course. That's how we came to this country."

"I don't mean pogroms, I mean 1940, the Russians . . . as they left, they killed as many Jews as they could . . . And then the Nazis came in and first they killed . . . all the Jewish intelligentsia. Then— they finished the job. Whoever was left, they sent to the camps. Thirty-one thousand Jews. *Then nobody* was left. Maybe some fighters in the woods. When the Germans retreated, they bombed the town. Nothing left. So your grandfather. . . ."

"I do see. Thank you."

"My father never forgot to say Kaddish on the anniversary . . . of his death, your grandfather. If ever there's anything we can do for you and yours, if ever Godforbid you need any kind of help, my husband and me, my son and his wife, please. . . ."

Now he sees the folder for *Kerenbaum* and gets a glint of memory. According to his mother's list, some Kerenbaums are still in New York. Yes!—he remembers learning cello from somebody Kerenbaum—Mark Kerenbaum—in a cheap studio near Columbia. The young man was finishing up at Juilliard in music theory; *it must have been torture to him, having to pay his way by giving me lessons I didn't want. How bored we both were. . . .* He remembers parties with people named Kerenbaum. Their compartment in the folder is thick with photos, letters. Next to one name, Eleanor Kerenbaum, Belle has written, "See photo of Eleanor with her father in Ira's study. Special friend." This notation is underlined twice. There's no address or phone.

He looks—no photo. But he remembers the photo.

He calls information; there's an E. Kerenbaum on East 72nd. He's about to hang up when she answers. Again he explains, but sees at once that he doesn't *need* to explain. Does she know where

his father might be? A long silence. Then: "If I see your father, I'll
have him call you. I really regret that he hasn't called."

"So you expect to see him?"

Again, silence. "It's possible. I might see him. Later on."

The doorman announces him. "It's down the hall to your left
when you get off the elevator. 14E."

Eleanor Kerenbaum lives in a large, unpretentious apartment
house put up in the thirties. During the boom years of the late
twenties, builders were erecting castles, bourgeois palaces—the
Beresford, the San Remo. On the East Side, they were replacing
town houses with narrow, elegant graystone buildings with eight-
room apartments, ten-foot ceilings, two apartments to a floor. This
building, with its flat, modern facade and large, steel-framed, plate-
glass windows, came out of the Depression. No ornate Renaissance
cornices or heavy stone detail on the facade. Art deco designs in
low relief. Ten small apartments to a floor. Recently, the man-
agers of these co-ops have upgraded everything they could: thick
carpeting, fancy tile in the lobby, puffy chandeliers, a brass-edged
elevator in dark, oiled walnut. Everything has been painted in soft
peach and taupe.

"Mr. Kuperman?" A woman in her late sixties, early seventies,
straight and light like an old dancer, peers out from a doorway.
"I'm Eleanor Kerenbaum. Please come in."

She steps back. He enters a tiny foyer, a large living room full
of light filtered through hanging plants, trees in tubs. Books, art
books, many oversized, are in piles by chairs, in a bookcase that
covers one wall. "Please, come in, come in. Give me your coat." But
he holds his coat and stares: the photographs on the foyer wall are
certainly his father's—some he's never seen. He spies against a chair
the black leather art portfolio he bought his father for his birthday.

"I wish you'd said you were in the city—he'd have waited." She
sits on a heavy carved-wood armchair with tapestried back and
seat: faded roses. He lets her direct him to the sofa that backs on
the picture window, an overstuffed sofa that doesn't go with the
table or the art.

Her apartment isn't delicate. He expects it to be delicate, old
fashioned, prim, but there's a rough, bronze ten-pound figure of a

goddess on the low living room table; he can't tell if it's a modern imagining or a reproduction of a ritual piece from some traditional society. And the table—it's a slab of rough-cut marble over a cylindrical base of polished dark wood. The wall behind Eleanor Kerenbaum glows in the late afternoon sun, and on this wall his father's larger pictures hang. As soon as he sees it, he knows it: the missing picture of Eleanor and her father; the same woman, but in her thirties or forties: a very attractive woman. Now, in a pale-cream satin blouse, a strand of pearls, reading glasses on a silver chain, *still* attractive. With a long neck, and a long-boned face sculpted like the bronze goddess—with eyes so deep it's as if someone put thumbs into the clay and pressed; eyes that make her seem both deathlike and lovely; her gray hair pinned back in a swirl; he imagines it would still be long and thick if she let it fall.

On a side wall, under spots, there's a giant abstract expressionist canvas. What would my mother have said? He *knows*. In her husky voice meant to indicate wisdom or tough realism: *Smart— too smart for her own good. Maybe she thinks this is "fashionable." Forty years ago, maybe* then *it was fashionable.* But he argues with his mother: No, this woman takes the style for granted; she has no interest in impressing.

He looks past Eleanor Kerenbaum at her younger self, arms folded, hair in a long, single braid, leaning against a tree; on the other side of the tree, an old man. Her father?

Anything he says would feel false. He sits.

"Would you like some tea?"

"No tea. Thank you."

"You must be a little confused."

He takes his time with this; turns it around in his heart as he looks around this pleasant room. He notices books in French, in German. He is in the presence of a complicated life. "How long have you and my father been friends?"

"Many, many years. We met at one of your grandfather's Kishinev reunions. You know about the reunions? Our friendship is almost as old as you are."

"And he came to you instead of to me or Susan?"

She shakes her head. "No. He didn't *come* to me."

"Oh."

"I mean he didn't *have* to."

"Yes. I do see what you mean. It's that I don't know how to respond."

"Of course. It's better anyway your father talk to you."

She leaves him alone. He hears her on the telephone in the other room. Then the click of a keyboard.

A key turns in the lock. His heart is pounding.

"Ellie? Ellie, you home? Let me tell you what that son of a bitch at the gallery—"

Michael stands up. "Dad."

"*Cle*-ver." His father puts down bags, a newspaper. "Pretty goddamn smart. How did you do that so fast?"

Michael is amazed by his father's cool. Amazed also by his energy—the force with which he moves around. He hasn't been like this—Michael can't remember. Sneakers and a baseball cap, a windbreaker. *The vulgar bastard.* Michael turns away.

"What? Did you hire a detective?"

What really gets to Michael is his father's curiosity about being found!—as if that were the interesting point, as if this were a game of hide-and-seek. "I see I don't have to worry about taking care of you. I was worried—an old man alone in New York."

"Yeah. As if you ever gave one shit! As if you ever took care of me!"

Michael, man of many speeches, is speechless. Or what he has to say is unsayable: (1) When did you take care of *me*? There's that. There are the fatherless years of his childhood. And then (2) Who the hell bought you your apartment? Who bought you your fucking burial plot!

"Your problem is, you think the wrong parent died. I'm sorry to disappoint you by staying in this goddamn world."

Michael doesn't even deny it. "You want to tell me about all this, I'll listen."

"It's been going on a long time. This woman? This woman is my heart." He holds his hand there. "You wouldn't believe how long."

"How long?"

"Thirty years. No. More. More than thirty years. Ellie? Baby? How long? Don't worry. Your mother never knew."

"Oh, she knew."

"What d'you mean, knew? Let me assure you, she didn't know a goddamned thing."

"That's how I found you. My mother."

"Hey—ELLIE?"

And Eleanor in the doorway nods her head. "I've always said she knew."

"Baby, how many years? Thirty-five? Come on—I'd've *known* if she knew. You think she would have missed the chance to put me down?"

"Dad, it's not worth discussing. Anytime you want to visit, I'm not going to turn you away. You can come to Boston, you can stay with us when you want. There's an apartment for you."

"Isn't that very sweet of you. If I wanted to go to Boston, I'd have gone to Boston. I've got nothing against you, Michael, but it's *my* goddamn life, what's left of it." With rage he unzips his windbreaker. "Ellie—what gave him the right to judge me? What is he— a saint?"

"I'm sure you feel ashamed and that's why you sound like such a fool." and Michael gets up and slips into his coat.

"That's it, is it? *That's it?*"

Eleanor stands close to Ira Cooper and takes his hand. "Ira, Ira, it's all right. It will *be* all right."

"Who the hell needs this guy? *My son! He doesn't even keep my name, the prick.*"

And Michael, seeing with his own eyes but also, he imagines, with those of Jacob Goldstein, thinks, *You poor fool, you don't even know your own name. Cooper? You think your name is* Cooper? *How lamentable! Look at all the Jews who died so that an Ira "Cooper" could survive in this world!* It's a comfort to see with Jacob's eyes. But Michael says nothing. Brushing past his father, he walks out, as if from an unsuccessful business meeting, and on the shuttle to Boston sips a scotch. He's only Michael—calm, alone. *There must be a great deal of anger*, he thinks, as if speaking about someone else.

CHAPTER FIVE

"I Just Want You to Be a Success"

"Do I *look* upset?" Deborah asks Martha Corey.

"A bit, yes." Martha laughs sharply. "Oh, yes, I might say you look upset." They're power-walking the footbridge by the Harvard Business School. Or *calorie*-walking; they'd be too embarrassed to walk like maniac athletes with arms pumping. It's so hard to squeeze-in time for a friend. Even a dear friend. Even a friend like Martha, a best friend, whom she's known longer than she's known Michael—ever since they were suite mates at boarding school. Deborah happened to be doing research today at the Business School library—same day Martha was working with a writer at the Kennedy School. They arranged to meet on the bridge and walk instead of having lunch.

"Upset," Martha adds, "but *beautiful.*—I mean it, dear. You *are.* Well. I don't even bother envying. Well. This is so civilized—" Martha drawls, opening her hands as if to offer Harvard to Deborah. "—or it would be if we didn't have to take it at this clip."

"I suppose I am. Upset." But Deborah begrudges the acknowledgement, tenses against the accuser, despises her own dissatisfaction. It's so banal, so banal, the expectation that a marriage will be the center of your life. All right. So this marriage, like nearly all the marriages she knows, has become a tag-team wrestling match. He takes care of Karen and Ari; then she. He goes out to handle the world alone, returns; then she goes out to do battle. *The other night my overnight bag sat open on the bed while I put things away; right beside it was Michael's overnight bag, half-packed for his flight in the morning.*

"He used to be so pleasant! Wasn't he funny, Martie? Now, when is he funny?" In mind's eye she sees him in tuxedo, her big, handsome groom, curly black hair, laughing, yucking it up with her favorite uncle—someone took the picture—Uncle Monroe is handing him an envelope with a check. The ballroom at the Mark Hopkins. Michael pretends surprise, fingers to his cheeks—for us? My big, smart funnyman, my worldly groom. "And now? A Jewish depressive. With a scruffy beard. As if he'd been through the Holocaust."

One day, she doesn't tell Martha, Ari and Misha hid behind a complex structure of cardboard boxes, the detritus of recent purchases. Cardboard cut and flattened into walls of a secret base. This she saw; the rest she got secondhand from Misha's mother. "The Nazis are hunting us," Ari had told Misha. "The Jews used to hide behind the walls. They were scared the neighbors would tell the Nazis. You know what the Nazis did?" Ari asked. "There was this one old rabbi, they made him watch while they murdered all his people in the town. Then they buried him alive."

Misha's mother was very disturbed at the game. *I don't want Misha to be exposed. . . . Is that what a child should be thinking about?*

Oh! Deborah was furious. She stood, arms folded, at the door to Michael's study. "What's got into you? I was humiliated by that shallow woman."

"It was a mistake. He saw me with a book. I told him what I was reading . . ."

Martha Corey, an editor at Houghton Mifflin, savors the complexities of her friends' lives! What would life be without them? Deborah could tell her—*will* tell her one day when Martha's amused snooping gets to her: she'd have to live her *own* life. Martha's already panting a little from the pace and talk, as they walk east against the wind along the Cambridge side of the Charles to the next bridge. Martha's softer, fuller than Deb. She has wit, and God knows she has style. But power walking is definitely not her thing. In sudden sympathy, Deborah slackens pace.

"Why am I so angry?"

Martha laughs. She stops—supposedly to feed the birds, actually to breathe. She's brought a bag of stale bread and tosses handfuls out for the gulls and pigeons. The gulls have caught on; they swoop and pluck it on the fly. "Well, the fact is you're *usually* angry."

"*Am* I?" Deborah pulls away and speeds up crossing the bridge, and Martha has to work to keep pace.

"Oh, now don't get thin-lipped with me, sweetie. You know I love you."

"No matter *how* angry I am."

"Yes, exactly."

Deborah broods. "My husband's mother—and Martie, he adored her—has just died, and I'm annoyed that he's grubby and wandering in a daze?—well, of *course* he's wandering in a daze, what do I expect?"

"So? Does he *want* you again? Sexually?"

"Oh, I swear to God, don't you ever think about anything else?" Then: "No."

"No. Not at all?"

By now, they're almost back where they started. The Business School on one side of the footbridge, Harvard College on the other. Deborah is tired keeping up with Martha's patter and is pleased now to see her have a hard time keeping up with the pace. A gull swoops under the bridge. She stops, has to answer:

"Not yet. Well. One night. But it was during the proscribed period, and I suppose God was watching. Or his mother. And not since. He's got his own rules. I wouldn't be found dead in a mikvah, so he doesn't press. The sad thing is, I don't care. Look: enough, Martie. I don't want to discuss it."

Martha empties the bag of bread to have done with it. "A mikvah—a ritual bath?" She giggles. "I can just see you in a mikvah!" Deborah watches Martha quiet down and spank the crumbs from her fingers. "Then . . . you're not just *angry*."

"No."

Martha says simply, "I think things will turn out. Really."

From the center of the little arced bridge, Deborah soothes herself by watching a two-man scull, noiseless, simple, gliding underneath, leaving a perfect wake. "I'm not so sure."

Martha waits. Deborah finds herself irritated that Martha knows she'll go on. She goes on. "That's not the issue, it's not what happens in bed."

"Or doesn't."

"Shut up, please. Partly, it's that I can't be Belle Cooper. If he wants someone who stays home and bakes a challah on Fridays, someone who makes costumes for the kids at Purim, what the hell are we doing living together? You know, that's really it. I married a brilliant young man doing an MBA at Yale—not an observant Jew."

"Does he impose it on you?"

"You can't live in a house with someone who says a blessing when he urinates or washes his hands or eats a piece of fruit and *not* feel invaded. You know?"

"I think it's lovely. *No*, I do."

"No, you *don't*. Look—the other day, I was in the lobby of the Charles with Ari—we were cutting through to the parking garage— and Ari begins to sing a blessing or a prayer or something."

"Suppose it had been a Bach cantata?"

"Oh, Martie, that's the very point I'm making. Don't make it *for* me." She imagines her son becoming foreign to her. It makes her queasy, and looking down into the river, the small drop from the bridge, gives her a moment of vertigo. For she sees him grown up, with slumped shoulders and an otherworldly gaze, her own son wearing long twisted sideburns and a black hat. "Ari is just imi-tating his father. It's Michael who infuriates me, Martie. It's like a breach of contract. He prays constantly and won't touch pork. Or *lobster*, for godsakes. He says he can't shave for a month—but I think he's growing a beard. He takes a little bag with his tallis and yarmulke when he flies off on business. I'm getting worried."

"Think of it as a sport. Rock climbing. Fishing. Men get obsessive."

Deborah is silent. Martha knows her well enough not to inter-rupt the silence. "I've been having coffee—that's *all*, Martie—with a very interesting man."

"*Tell* me!"

A gray, chilly day. Deborah shakes her head. "No. Not yet."

"Do I know him? What's his name?"

"He's a client of mine. A broker for very expensive boats. It's not the time to talk about him yet, Martie. It's just having coffee." She pulls up the collar of her tweed overcoat and buttons the top button. "God!" She's dressed simply, dressed "down," knowing she's going to pick up Ari at school. There's a scent of murky sea, as if the Charles were a salt marsh. It's probably bad chemicals. The eighteenth-century look of the Harvard buildings always makes her happy. She's often been at the Business School this fall, often stood here alone on this little bridge over the Charles and wrapped herself in the architecture and the curving quiet river. Not today.

The wind whips up and she squints against the dust.

At three, she picks up Ari at the Brattle School in Cambridge. Michelle needed the afternoon off, and Deborah happened to be in town today anyway. Driving over, she looks forward to it, hungry to hold Ari.

Parking is impossible at pick-up time, the tiny lot on the narrow street always stuffed at three, so Deborah arrives a few minutes early. She loves the big Victorian house with its green-copper mansard roof and the incongruous glass-walled classroom wings. Poking towards Ari's room, she reads the notices, sees the art projects hung on all the walls, and it's as if she's shamed by the colorful walls, the shouts of children coming in from afternoon recess. She hasn't been here for a month. Longer. *Ari.* Even for a single afternoon she doesn't know what she's to do with him. He has no music lesson today.

From behind the closed second-grade classroom door she catches something in the sing-song high lilt of Ari's teacher that tells her class is about to be excused.

Ari closes his eyes as he hugs her; it's a real hug. His head buries itself between her breasts, and Deborah looks around to see if it's been noticed. Miss Shaughnessy, bent over a chart, isn't looking; and though it embarrasses her—Ari's too old for that kind of hug—Deborah wishes she'd been looking. *Oh, God, I'm as bad as Michael thinks.*

She'll take him to the Museum of Science; they scarcely use their membership.

So they stand in the Electricity demonstration theater, watching bolts of brilliant lightning snap from giant phallic pole to pole. Ari's always loved this room. Deborah wants to say to him, *I don't want you to lose what we won. I just want you to be a success. An American.* It bothers her: she can't escape seeing Ari, with his curly hair and strong nose, as that small scared child in peaked cap and wool coat, staring into space, his hands up in surrender: photo from Warsaw, 1943.

"You want to do a planetarium show, honey? Or there's a demo of ferrets at four."

Between cuts of a hip-hop album somebody at school just screamed about, Karen hears from downstairs the second movement of the *Hammerklavier Sonata*, and figuring the Beethoven is a hostile statement by her mother, a not-so-subtle criticism of trashy music, is about to turn up the hip-hop to override the downstairs stereo when the piano stumbles, a passage repeats: Oh. It's not the stereo, it's her mother. So Karen turns off her own stereo and opens her door a crack to listen. It's a passage from the movement she herself has struggled over—the sheet music is hers. Now she thinks that her mother is trying to make her feel inadequate. Because that's how she does feel. Mom's so *good*. But standing at the head of the stairs, she recognizes how quietly Deborah is playing, and how often, after running through a passage without a mistake, she repeats the passage. So it's not for my benefit. Running hair through fingers, she sits on the carpeted stairs to listen, listen and envy, but she's drawn, a magnet, a siren song, so drawn to Deborah, so furiously in love with her, in awe of her, feels never, never could she herself be so beautiful, so intelligent. Sometimes Deborah wears a towel turban-like around her hair after a shower, and when she walks through the house like that it seems to Karen as if she has no age; she looks goddess-like, immortal; and Karen feels a glow of love and at the same time diminished.

Karen slips downstairs, tiptoes into the living room, to stand behind her mother, turn the pages for her. Ari's doing his twenty-minutes-of-reading in the reclining chair. Deborah ends a passage, hits a dissonant chord to laugh off the tender depths of the music.

Karen says matter-of-factly, "You're so good. You ought to play all the time."

"Thank you my darling. Once I was all right."

"Once! Then what am I?"

"Good. You're good. Not quite taking it as neurotically seriously as I did. It was for your grandfather, you know. I tortured myself, believe me. Then college—you know—and it became one thing or the other."

"So are you ever sorry?"

"Oh, yes. Yes. Please—listen to this." Deborah takes Karen's hand and leads her to the sofa, goes to the stereo and puts on a CD. "It's Rudolf Serkin, an old recording; re-mastered, but who cares. It's Serkin." She starts up the second movement and sits by Karen. "I suppose I play when I'm a little blue."

"Blue? About what, Mom?"

"I'm not sure." Deborah takes her hand; together they listen to the *Hammerklavier*.

And Karen is wondering, *How can I get so mad at her sometimes?*

He'd said he was coming for dinner; it's seven before he's home. The kids have been fed; she herself has no appetite. She sits in the kitchen with a glass of wine, brooding; she thinks about calling Larry Ackerman. She regrets having mentioned the man—the possibility of another man—to Martie. And now Michael rushes in and tosses his coat over a kitchen chair.

"Deborah? Listen. Listen, Deborah."

She nods, half-listens while she puts the glasses and dishes in the dishwasher. She can't stand looking at his grubby, half-grown beard.

"For all these years, Deb," he half-sings, "—my father—*listen*—thirty years—my father has had a lover, a woman some years younger, actually a very nice woman. I met her today. I saw them both."

"What? Your father? Oh, please."

"No. Really. Maybe my whole life."

Looking into his eyes, she knows it's true. "How did you find out? Someone told you?" Now he's her gossip-friend; she's forgotten she was irritated. "Michael! It's a scream. And he's with her this soon?"

"There's so much to tell you. We've hardly had a chance to talk, you and I. That's not a complaint. No, honestly. My father. I never really got it. He's an artist. Not a casual photographer. I never knew it. And this woman. I couldn't not like her. Well, she must be a saint to put up with him. And my mother knew."

"You're sure? Belle knew?"

"My mother *knew*." He tells her how he came to know the story. Oh! She loves it! It affirms what she's always felt: her father-in-law's flashy vulgarity.

"How cheap," she says. "Oh! The moral socialist. Really, Michael, that's incredible. Oh—" She finds a padded manila envelope that's come for him. "From today's mail—apparently, it's from that father of yours."

Photographs. "Political Photographs," his father has scribbled on a cover sheet. No note, no return address. Just the pictures. Young men lined up, waiting for a draft board to open. But also women shopping on Ninth Avenue near Port Authority. A subway platform (Times Square?) at rush hour. What makes these *political*?

"Oh, God. The 'artist' seems to be sending you some of his oeuvre."

"The thing is, Deb, I really don't know much about him. My own father."

"Maybe that's just as well. Is he coming up here? How am I supposed to act?"

Michael and Deborah lie in bed on their backs, staring at the ceiling the way married people do, each churning, thickly not-saying, and neither is under the illusion that the other is asleep—and it feels more and more terrible, as if it's a bargaining session and no one's bargaining. Each is brooding over wrongs and their own essential goodness. Each is practicing sentences in the dark.

Until finally Michael turns onto his side, away from Deborah, and now she says, "I've thought a lot today. You constantly put me into a terrible position. I truly believe you need me to play the cold-hearted businesswoman. Your mother had the heart. All the heart."

"I don't believe that."

"The more you see me this way, my dear, the harder-edged I'll be. And that's what you want."

"No. I certainly don't want that."

"You know, I think you do. We want such different lives now. Do you remember an evening maybe two years ago—the finance minister from Taiwan was over? We had a little party. We argued hotly about capital intensification, I can't remember what our positions were, but it was good-natured. And, for some reason, that Padraic something, you remember?—the Irish consul to Boston?—was with us, and Jonathan and Jessica, and then that wonderful pianist from the New England Conservatory, you remember she was talking to me about Brahms, and to explain a point—I don't know what we were discussing—she went to the piano and played impromptu a movement of a ballade. Remember?"

"I remember very well. You glowed. I felt proud of you."

"Thank you, Michael. Did I glow? No wonder. Because that night, I saw what our life could be."

"We can do that anytime you like. You're not saying you want more parties?"

"No. I'm offering you an iconic moment. That's my real life. And you know—more or less it always has been. When I was growing up, I mean. Not going to services with a bunch of shabby professors and lawyers with no style. I know I sound awful to you. But that's the point."

"What point?"

"That I'm so different. That perhaps we don't belong together. You judge me, I judge you. Why do you want to be with a dreadful, shallow woman like me?" She turns onto her side away from him. So he picks himself up and takes his pillow into his study.

Mergers

On his way to sleep, Michael dreams down into the complex shape of the merger. As for Chemicorp, well, he's put that aside. He's thought about calling Rosenthal again. But come *on*—sell chemicals for poison gas? Monsanto, Dupont, Chemicorp: too big to take such a risk.

Michael prepares for the meeting a week from Tuesday—having found the antidote for nerve gas, for mustard gas, in the sanctuary of his own mind. He takes notes on the merger. A whole new constellation of forces, of people, will come out of it. It will be less a family, of course, and the stakes will be higher. The possibilities, including possibilities for disaster, enormous. What began in 1983 with three clever people spotting a niche in the corporate software market and seeing a way to fill it quickly, inexpensively, has become an established company with new products coming out every year. At first Michael went to Japan for venture capital; they knew Fusion was making it when venture capital investment groups started coming to *them*. On paper, Fusion isn't making a profit yet; and doesn't want to. Money is ploughed under, back into R&D for Tony and Steve to use, into marketing for Jonathan to use. And Fusion is doing very well by its people—stock options, bonuses. Now Fusion is threatened by Microsoft as it becomes visible to Microsoft—it would take so little for Microsoft to alter their NT platform so that Fusion software wouldn't run. Fusion needs this merger. With it, Fusion triples its strength—and multiplies tenfold the complexity of organizational politics.

All this he cares intensely about. And doesn't care at all. It's gotten to be like a game of Scrabble: in the midst of play, rainy day at the Cape, his pulse rises, he's hungry to stop Karen's gloating over her double word score, to block Deborah's chance at a triple word space. Total joy if he gets to use all seven of his letters in a word. But a phone call, say, and . . . he's out of the game—returning, he doesn't care at all. It's boring. A game.

The most real time for him is the time he spends in prayer.

But what about the people he's responsible for? Over and over it loops: *a game . . . but there are real lives at stake (at least real livelihoods) . . . but . . . a game.*

In the morning, he checks Martine's arrangements for next Tuesday, admiring again her clarity, her precision. And he's grateful: how much he can count on her to handle all the details. Waiting for Jonathan, he calls McNair's point man, makes notes for his speech to the Board of Directors:

> *In a nutshell, what are the advantages this merger gives us? What are the strengths only* one *of us had before?*
>
> -
> -

These he knows, he leaves to fill in later. Then:

> *SYNERGY. The strengths we lacked singly that, now, together, we can develop:*
> - *Financial*
> - *technological*
> - *strategic*
> - *human resources*

He starts on a new line:

DANGERS: how a corporate marriage can potentially **block** *creative development. . . .*

When Jonathan knocks, they talk about the presentation. Dinner is sandwiches and sodas. They don't talk about Chemicorp until they're about to wrap it up.

Jonathan says, "Legally, it seems they're okay. Legally, there seems to be no problem. I called the Commerce Department in D. C., I got someone on then phone, I read him the list. Yes, it's true, they're 'precursor chemicals.' But here's what I was told: there are no trade restrictions when they're going to Britain, Sweden, Austria, countries like that. Chemicorp just has to file papers. It can't exceed a certain total quantity. They have to have an end-user certificate for certain chemicals. But the chemicals are used in pesticides, a bunch of things."

"Well, good. So that's it."

"Michael—that doesn't mean they're *using* them for pesticides. I talked to Rosenthal."

Michael's face is hot. "You talked to Rosenthal?—"

"It's okay, Mike. I told him one of our people found the names of chemicals—nothing about letters, nothing about encrypted files—and I was passing on the concern—this guy wondered weren't these chemicals components for chemical munitions. Rosenthal laughed. He said—I'm quoting—'I suppose they are. So is water.'"

"That's what he said to *me*." Michael caresses his beard and suddenly sees his mother in a housedress cutting up vegetables, a cigarette burning in the ash tray.

"Then, he got serious," Jonathan says. "'You don't honestly think we'd be knowingly involved in such things?' I assured him, *no*, Christ, not at all, of *course* not. I said, Funny how the same chemicals can make life and death. Etcetera. Anyway, he ends by inviting us out to his place in Ipswich, a party, mostly family. I'll be in Japan. My sense is that he wants to show us the kind of person he is."

"Did you believe him?"

"In my role as the CEO of Fusion, I believed him."

A Crowded City Square

Every day he prays, even says Kaddish alone, sitting at the window of his study facing east over housetops and stands of the great deciduous trees of Brookline, leaves turning brown . . . falling . . . fallen, until, in early November, he can see through the web of branches all the way to a patch of Jamaica Pond, a mile away.

He prays so he doesn't have to cope with what's happening outside this room. Deborah has begun to change their marriage: when she's not traveling, people drop by after Ari is asleep, in twos, threes, for a drink and conversation. What is this? Is she reinventing the salon? Does she think she's Mme. de Staël? He says hello, goes back to his study.

Friday night, after candles were lit for Shabbos, she asks, "Shall I come with you to services?" Ari's practicing piano; Karen's on the phone.

"You really want to come with me? Why?"

She doesn't answer. "Karen?" she calls up the stairs.

When Karen comes to the head of the stairs, Deborah asks, "If I go to synagogue with your father, can you stay with Ari and put him to bed?"

His synagogue is a fifteen minute walk. Ordinarily he'd drive, even on Shabbos, but tonight she wants to walk. A mild night. She slows her walk to his Sabbath pace, though it seems to her—God knows—so put-on, like the hat he's taken to wearing, this man who rarely wears a hat, a dove-gray expensive black fedora. A tedious affectation. And this messy, blossoming crop of beard. Now let's be honest, she says to herself. If I saw him for the first time, at a party, say, my head would turn his way. I'd be fascinated. Who is that man? If we were seeing each other, I'd be trying to get that beard shaved—but I'd be interested. "So," she asks, not particularly interested, "tell me how you're doing, Michael . . . I mean about your mother. It's really peculiar. You know, we never get a chance to talk."

"We *decide* not to talk."

"That's entirely possible," she grants. She falls into the dry irony he expects from her. Her eyes narrow, her lips make a smile like a knife.

"I think about her every day. I say the Kaddish for her when I'm driving alone in the car. I've stopped asking Dennis to pick me up. It gives me a little time."

"I thought one needed a minyan."

"That's right. It's one of the prayers, like the *Barekhu*, that has to be said in minyan."

"So does it—count?"

"For her soul? Stop, Deborah. Please. I can hear you're making fun of me."

"Am I? Oh, I suppose I am. Nothing serious, Michael."

He feels choked with hatred for her "*one needed a minyan.*" Her clever amusement, elegant, elevated head. You're my wife, it's enjoined upon me to love you, it's my obligation as a Jew, feelings aren't the point. But I can't offer love. They're walking at the same slow pace past old clumsy houses, once single-family, now condos for young people, a talking pace, man and wife, but at this moment he doesn't know her well enough to speak.

"Frankly, you know, I have no interest in sitting through services at a synagogue. It was just to take this walk with you. I've told you—I can't stand the way you see me—a hard-edged, materialistic woman. Well. I've been considering changes, Michael."

At this moment, waiting for her to come out with it, he stops seeing her at all. He's seeing his own life from a small place inside himself: he is like a homunculus, operating, from within, the strings of this large man walking up Beacon Street; there are hands and feet and breath and gaze to coordinate—too much! Arms and legs will loosen and, strings cut, sag and crumple. He believes, seriously believes, if he could let his attempt at control dissolve, let God take over, it would be all right. *God is with me now; there's no need to pretend, to defend.* Then why is his neck so tight? He wouldn't be surprised if she told him she'd taken a lover. *The children*, he prepares to say, *the children*, but knows she'll wince at the cliché. *As if* she'd already winced, he grows furious.

The street leading to the square is cluttered, mostly with people in their twenties setting out on a Friday night. Outside one bar they have to walk single file. There are lines of cars and trucks in every direction, stopped for the red light, creeping through the green. The heady stink of their exhausts fuses with salty odors from two

Chinese restaurants and a happy-hour place for burgers and beer. Then there's Deborah's delicate perfume. This jumble and his personal jumble also fuse; but it's not a harmony. This city belongs to the young—couples, guys bopping to a single rhythm of the spirit, shoulders hunched over their private laughter, laughter about something sexual.

"What are you saying. . . ? That you want us to separate? Deborah. . . ."

"For a start, I want my own bedroom. We have a guest room we never use."

He sighs. A fraudulent Jacob Goldstein enters this sigh. The *historical* Jacob, faced with such a demand, would have not believed it and so would have not let the words have meaning. If his wife had said them again and again (but of course, Sara Goldstein would never have dreamed of making such a demand), he would have raised his brows, lit a cigar, and said, *So, you mean you want us to speak to the rabbi?*

"You're wondering what to tell the children?"

"No. No, not at all. I was thinking, this isn't a Jewish marriage."

Of course she laughs. "I love it! Isn't that expectation of yours part of the problem? Oh, Michael. We can still pull apart your challah on Friday nights."

Deborah's hair is in a chignon, she's wearing a cashmere coat, nothing showy but it cost almost two thousand dollars. That she put this on tonight, to take this walk, black, close-cut coat and faint blue, translucent silk scarf, seems to define her position. This is who she intends to be. He feels this but doesn't know the details— that the coat is cashmere or that the long elegant boots cost more than many people make in a week.

"When is this move taking place?" he asks.

"Oh, you know me. It already has. I shifted things around this afternoon." she stops, touches his sleeve. "Don't worry. We can still talk—or still not-talk. We've exchanged hardly anything but complaints for months. You hide upstairs under your tallis and talk to yourself. In various voices." She takes a deep suck of air to gain energy for the fight. "Pity there's no monastic tradition in Judaism. You could take vows." And adds: "It's not blatant, the changes—I've put some of my things there, pillows, books and so on."

"Well," he says grimly, "you're not a blatant woman, are you."

At this, she closes her eyes. "Are you going to services?"

"It's still Shabbos, Deborah."

She stops. Brakes shriek from somewhere close. From somewhere else, the rhythmic howl of an ambulance. "I think I'll turn back now."

"Deborah? Tell me. Are you with somebody?"

A beat. "I'll tell you when I'm 'with somebody.'"

A Family Affair

Jessica spends the afternoon marinating a leg of lamb and preparing sushi. It's the Saturday after the presentation in Chicago, and Jessica and Jonathan are throwing a small celebration for Fusion's success, a "family" party. Michael and Deborah, Steve, and Fiona, the young woman Steve's been seeing. Fiona's bringing her ten-year-old daughter. Marcus will be here; Karen and Ari are coming.

Jonathan's house in Cambridge, gray-blue with white trim, is tall and narrow on its small lot. It's a comfortably crooked Victorian (lay a marble down on its polished broad-board yellow pine flooring, watch it roll into the corner of any room) stuffed with books—books with their musty sweet-sour odor: books in sagging cases, books in corner towers. You step past Marcus's hockey gear into a living room of books, CD's, old furniture, antique or just comfortable, furniture he'd grown up with, brought here when his father died.

Deborah drives over early afternoon to help Jessica. She brings a soup of the season—a spicy pumpkin soup in a chicken broth base, served in a scooped-out baked pumpkin as tureen. It may not soothe like brisket, but it's family food, love food, and while she'd never say this to Michael, never even tell herself, her soup is meant as a counter-metaphor to his way of seeing her. She wants to disturb his categories: *Oh, yes? Is that who you think I am? Smell this soup I prepared.*

Jessica entered Radcliffe when Michael and Jonathan were sophomores at Harvard. They were often a trio; still a trio after Jonathan and Jessica married, they went to the Cape or the Green Mountains or into the city together. Deborah met Jonathan when they were both at the Business School, and Michael when he came up for weekends from Yale. She's never made the trio a quartet, but she and Jessica like each other, plan dinners like this together, once went off by themselves for a weekend in New York.

More than *like*: Deborah respects Jessica, even envies. Because Jessica makes it seem effortless: to work a full caseload of patients and to do research, write essays and shape them into books—first a book on pre-Civil War black families in the North, now a book on race and psychotherapy. Yet she seems to enjoy time with her family. It's really annoying. Jessica isn't beautiful; she's small, a little overweight, wears glasses. But her face shines; her skin is soft as a child's, and her tenderness warms you; she's often amused, and her amusement is catching. When they first met, Deborah wondered what a star like Jonathan saw in her. Now she understands.

Michael comes with the kids; drinks and appetizers are on the table. Now Steve comes banging in, pulling a jug of raw red wine from his backpack, and in his usual klutzy way introduces them to Fiona and her daughter Miranda. Steve—God, how he makes Deborah laugh—comes dressed for biking, metal clips still on his ankles. The three of them are wearing sneakers.

"We locked our bikes to your gate."

"They'll be just fine," Jessica says. "You want to take off your bike clips, Steve, honey?" She takes parkas and scarves. "Marcus is down in the rec room," Jessica tells Miranda. "You play ping-pong?"

Fiona is in her mid-thirties, her face soft, mild, dreamy, framed by very long brown-blonde hair. She wears a blue-jeans shirt and bangles everywhere—long Native American earrings, on each finger one or two rings with twisted serpents and semi-precious stones. A bone bracelet. Deborah and Jessica exchange A Look. They know one another so well that in the two-second look they concur on complex awareness and complex attitudes.

All of them—Michael, Jonathan, Deborah, Jessica—are in a conspiracy to marry Steve off. He's so brilliant—and so helpless. They laugh at his bare apartment, high up in a building near the Charles. His kitchen table is an unpainted door on saw horses. His sofa is a ragged Victorian left out on the street; his bookcases, found in an alley, are weathered wooden crates from Table Talk

Pies. But his single scull is worth thousands; and in his apartment, his hi-tech equipment is worth well over fifty thousand dollars. He keeps a telescope at a window so he can snoop into windows across the river, a bank of computers, a great stereo system on which to play Bach and country music. They look at his kitchen and want to save him. All he needs—each of them has said this—is a good woman who won't mind a . . . few peculiarities.

And so the look between Jessica and Deborah says, This one may be just as peculiar! Look at those clothes, that hair. She wants to remain a youth, a graduate student. She's not just sweet; she *believes in* sweetness. Finally!—this may be the right woman for our Steve. The look assumes a shared affection for him and for the innocence he represents for them. It brings Deborah and Jessica closer, sharing this affection. It's a comfort—for if he still has it, this innocence, they own a piece of it by their caring.

Fiona has a degree from RISD (Rhode Island School of Design), works in a bookstore in Cambridge—that's where Steve met her—but her real work is painting and sculpting assemblages. "What do you paint?" Jess asks. Fiona wants, she replies, to capture in paint her "vision of Gaia"—in paint, in beads, in rusty metal, in soft wools.

Jessica fills her in about this strange family.

"The three of them have been extraordinarily successful. Michael is the money man. Jonathan is fabulous with people. But without Steve—nothing."

"He's been wonderful to Miranda. There's a lot of *child* in him that hasn't gotten lost," Fiona says, and saying *child*, her voice grows breathy. Then, embarrassed to have said this to someone she's just met, she breathes a long "Whoooh. . . . You've got so many *books* in this house."

Jonathan waves a bottle of champagne by the neck and starts pouring. He catches Michael going by and wraps an arm around him. "I'll tell you, folks: this guy and I, we flew to Chicago, I laid out the new products, talk about R&D and marketing strategies; then Mike here gave them the financials. Stockholders ate it up. Everybody please drink to Fusion."

Jessica throws invisible tomatoes at Jonathan. Michael grins. He loves it when Jonathan's full of himself. He gets drunk on

Jonathan's high. Michael's okay tonight; he isn't grieving. The seven-letter Scrabble word matters far beyond its fifty-point bonus. "At Purim," Michael says, "we're told to drink until we can't tell Mordecai—the hero—from Haman—the Hitler. Tonight we drink till we can't tell Fusion from Con-Fusion."

"What am I supposed to do about your friend?" Deborah asks Jonathan across the room. They're holding little plates and drinks. "Look at his beard. Jonathan, as a businessman. aren't you concerned?"

He smiles.

"*Jonathan?*"

It's his con of a smile: eyes half closed in pleasure, he looks at you straight on, makes you a gift of the pleasure. After, you realize he's avoided whatever issue you had in mind . . .

. . . While at the same time, Jessica, leaning against the counter in the kitchen, complains to Michael. Jonathan's never home. He keeps taking on more and more.

Michael nods sadly.

"I respect what he does. Of course! A program training minority kids for hi-tech careers? How could I not respect *that*? But I don't want him to have a heart attack. I'd like a living husband, thank you. My dad died at fifty. I work, we all work too hard. Why not? But please, Michael—see what you can do. Two nights a week working with those kids, teaching those kids. It's one thing helping develop the grant. But two nights a week! And that's in addition to all the travel he does. Look at him. You see?"

Michael worries with her. He doesn't have to look over—Jonathan looks haggard.

At dinner Marcus sits next to Karen, and as always, they sing a duet together, the comic "Everything I've Got Belongs to You." Michael's smiling along with everyone else. But halfway through the song, he catches a look between Marcus and Karen, and his breath stops—as if his plane has hit an air pocket and dropped a quick fifty feet. Because the look tells him they've got secrets. They've known each other since they were little kids— but suddenly . . . secrets? That look is a shorthand for late-night phone calls, maybe meetings, maybe more. They're thinking of one another in a new way; they have something going on.

After dinner Jonathan pulls Michael aside. "Take a walk with me down to Mass Ave? Got to get ice cream for the kids."

It's cold, but it's a bright, clear night. Two big men in parkas, fists crammed in pockets. Half a block they walk in silence past Cambridge houses and town houses.

"You're worrying Deb."

"I know."

"You're worrying me a little."

"The beard?"

"I'll let Deb do the worrying about the beard. You're in mourning and you look it. No—it's Chemicorp. I don't get you, Michael. You really willing to keep working for these guys?"

"Not if something's really going on."

"Oh, it's going on." Jonathan stops under a street lamp and looks into Michael's eyes. "See, I've been doing a little detective work." He holds Michael by the elbow and they walk onto Mass Ave. "It took me less than an hour to learn about this Pell Trading Company in England. Ordinary research—basic references about European companies. A couple of calls to London, a few minutes on the Internet—no trouble. Okay. Pell doesn't exist except on paper. It's a holding company. It's never borrowed any money. It has no business associations. A dummy corporation, Mike. You know as well as I do."

"Now Steve's got you snooping?"

"Hey—I'm trying to keep Steve from going to his friend at the Globe. He handed me another letter tonight."

"Does he want to wipe us out?"

"You take a look."

From: M. Rosenthal
        Chemicorp, Boston
To: Frederick Lansing
        Pell Trading Company
        London, England
Re: Response to Query

Fred, explain to General Djouti we're held up on this end waiting for the containers to come through from Marseilles.

Product should be in London by the end of the month. Make sure Djouti understands the need for extreme precaution when containers are being re-shipped from London.

"You don't think this is ambiguous?" Michael says, handing back the letter.

"Precursor chemicals require end-user certification. Here Rosenthal's speaking about *re-shipment*. And extreme caution."

"But maybe the legitimate end-user is in another country."

"This General Djouti? Maybe."

"All right. Maybe not. Maybe not."

"Tell me something, Mike. Don't take this the wrong way. But what is it about this Rosenthal that you trust the guy? Is it because he's a *landsmann*?"

Michael laughs—"Where'd you get '*landsmann*'?"

"From you—where the hell d'you think?"

"Because he's a fellow Jew? That is utter horseshit. You believe that of me?"

"Why not? You think we're beyond such categories, you and me?"

"That's right. We're beyond such categories."

Jonathan's been setting this up: "Well, you tell me—I believe what I saw tonight, at dinner. I saw you—you noticed what I noticed—Karen and Marcus. Am I right?"

Michael breaks into a laugh. "God, Jonathan, you do know me."

"I know you. And what I saw—here's what I saw: It *scared* you. To see them in some kind of boy-girl relation. You scared of her being with Marcus?"

"They've grown up together. You know I love Marcus."

"Well? I love Karen. And?"

"And . . . he's not Jewish."

"He's also not white."

"Oh, Jonathan. Please! That's not it. Aren't we past that? Dear God. Don't you know that's not the point?"

"No? You sure?"

Michael hunkers down his head and opens his hands. *What can I say?*

Jonathan wraps a hand around Michael's shoulder to get him ready for this: "Okay, I'll tell you—for me, it *is* the point. *A* point.

Frankly, I'd worry about it. I wouldn't much like it. I'd like it and I wouldn't like it. It would be tough on both of them and on their kids. But, listen, buddy. I like to think you and me, we're part of the same congregation. I mean *finally*, you understand? Or the same family. You see what I mean, Michael?"

"We are. You know, we do okay."

"We do. I'm not saying—"

"And about Rosenthal—"

"Your landsmann—"

"Okay—my '*landsmann*.' It's not that I trust Rosenthal. I still find it hard to believe—a corporation this big? And all right—I don't want to believe. Our McNair is their friend—Rosenthal's, Braithwaite's. He'd never have broached the deal if we hadn't had this contract. We drop the contract, we lose the merger."

"Maybe. You don't think it scares me?"

"But you want to get out of the contract?"

"As soon as we can. As quietly as we can, as soon as we can. When the first stage is completed, and that's pretty soon."

Michael nods. "Will that hold Steve?"

"I'm not sure."

"I'll be seeing Rosenthal at his party. I'll feel it out."

Visiting Myron Rosenthal

On a Friday in early December Michael and Deborah drive north of Boston to the outskirts of a town near the ocean, a clear, cold night. They are polite to one another. They talk business. He says nothing about chemical munitions; she says nothing about the last two evenings, when she stayed very late in the office . . . or not in the office.

Myron Rosenthal's house, a restored nineteenth-century grand house, federal-style, maybe 1850, sits on a slight rise above a marsh. He's floodlit a finger of the marsh; they can see the reeds. There is already a handful of parked cars. Faintly, on their way from car to house, they can smell the tang of the marsh.

A young black man answers the door and takes their coats. Behind the servant, Rosenthal is standing, smiling. He's overweight, but the blazer that has been cut for him half disguises it.

His hair is in tight, angelic graying curls surrounding a bald spot. He smiles intensely, as if they shared a joke. As Deborah examines the filigree ceilings and the original late nineteenth-century American landscapes and is (Michael can tell) impressed, he smiles back. "Happy Hanukkah," Rosenthal calls and lifts a hand to hold Hanukkah up like a jewel. It won't be Hanukkah for another two weeks, but Michael says, automatically, "*Gut yontef,*" and takes his hand.

"A *landsmann,*" Rosenthal laughs. "That's why I wanted you to come. . . . And this is your beautiful wife. We hardly had time to say hello at your house."

"Deborah Schiff," she says. She extends a hand and a caustic smile.

"I like this new custom," Rosenthal says, "a woman keeping her own name."

Behind Rosenthal, a broad, graceful staircase, grand, polished oak, with a Turkish kilim runner and beautifully turned mahogany banisters; this was never an ordinary house, but now it's surely more lavish than it was a hundred and fifty years ago. On the stairs, a beautiful girl, hair long and black, sails downstairs in blue velvet. Rosenthal introduces them across the big hall. "This is my youngest, Julie. Isn't she beautiful? Like your own daughter. This is Mr. and Mrs. Kuperman, Julie."

Julie waves him off and smiles at Deborah and Michael—and is gone.

"To see her on that staircase . . . Now, isn't she something?"

Michael says, "I can see her walking down that staircase on her wedding day." He knows that Deborah is giving him a hostile look. Deborah has a terrific nose for phoniness.

"You know, it's funny you should say that. When I first saw this house, that was my first impression, that staircase—I saw a wedding! Well, can I get you both something?"

"A glass of white wine," Michael says.

"I'll have a double bourbon on the rocks," Deborah says, and he knows she's being perverse. Michael gives her a look.

"Come. Let me introduce you to my mother." He leads them into the living room to the right of the staircase—a soft room, not in period—and calls, "Mama? This is Mr. and Mrs. Kuperman.

My mother, Esther Rosenthal. I'll be right back with the wine, Michael."

"I'm Deborah Schiff."

"How nice to meet you."

There are fifteen, twenty people here for the party. Heads turn, as they always do when Michael and Deborah come into a room full of strangers. They've grown to expect it. Both have large heads on big, lean frames; they walk tall. Deborah is striking—like a goddess—and knows it. Michael is not conventionally handsome, but he has a complex face.

It's a family affair, with young children chasing each other around the drapes, teenagers standing to one side, laughing at something. But without knowing she was Rosenthal's mother, Michael would have gravitated to Esther Rosenthal. Right away she reminds him of Belle Cooper. She's softer, she wears too many rings on her soft fingers, too many links of pearl at her throat—Belle would never have decorated herself like that—but there's something in the eyes. So he says, "What a wonderful house."

"What I particularly love," Esther Rosenthal says, "is the fireplaces. A fireplace in practically every room."

In the way of the long married, Michael knows approximately what Deborah isn't saying. Look at the pearls, she isn't saying, how they're practically embedded in the clefts of fat at her neck. And listen to that pseudo-elegant voice, listen to her count fireplaces. Where were her great grandparents when these fireplaces were built? He's determined to be especially nice to her. "Do you live here with your son?"

"Not far away, Mr. Kuperman. He bought me a lovely condo near the ocean. Tell me, Mr. Kuperman—"

"—Michael—"

"Michael. Where does your family come from?"

"My father, Odessa. My mother's family, Kishinev."

"We come from Minsk. You know, it's funny, I would have sworn. . . ."

"Well, it's all one stock, isn't it?"

"*One stock*," she repeats as if it's a gem of wisdom. "You're friends of Myron and Carol?"

"No, no. I know your son through business. Deborah has met him only once—he was kind enough to come to our house when I was sitting Shiva for my mother."

"I know. I'm very sorry. Well, I predict you're all going to be friends."

Myron comes with the wine and bourbon. "You'll excuse us, Mother?" Leaving Deborah with his mother, he takes Michael by the arm and shows him through the house. The billiard room. The paneled library with leather-bound books. The new kitchen. "This terrace I had put in last spring. . . ." Floodlights shine onto a path leading to the marsh.

When they come to his office, Rosenthal waves Michael to a leather wingback chair. He pulls his desk chair out from the desk so they can talk. Framed awards, personal letters on government letterheads, letters of gratitude from Jewish charities, photographs of Myron Rosenthal shaking hands with this man, that man, decorate one wall. The rest is oiled wood and leather. "I'm sorry your partner couldn't be with us."

"Jonathan's in Japan this week."

"But it's just as well, Michael. You're a landsmann, you understand? I watched my mother talking to you. I'm slightly acquainted with her little gestures, smiles, and she was quite taken with you. Your wife, too, of course. But especially you."

"And I with her."

"I knew it. But Michael, we have something to discuss. I've been waiting for this opportunity. I wanted to talk to you in these surroundings, fershtaste? In family."

"Is this about what Jonathan discussed with you last week? I really don't think there's a need. It was a misunderstanding. I'd say all that is behind us, Myron."

"I knew I could talk to you. Your partner . . . wanted assurances."

"He told me. Not exactly 'assurances.' He was concerned. Naturally. But you gave him assurances. . . . Isn't that right? He doesn't see a problem. I don't see a problem."

Myron Rosenthal waves him silent, raises a finger. "Exactly. I'm so glad we see eye to eye. But I'll tell you, it disturbed me." He plays with a pair of reading glasses. "He tells me you might decide to renegotiate, perhaps leave us after the first phase of the contract is completed?"

"We talked about that, yes. With the merger, Myron, we have to scale back. But we won't leave you in the cold. You'll have the system up and running."

"Now Michael, look. . . . Chemicals. That's what we sell. We sell chemicals."

Michael understands. "I know, Myron. And they have so many uses. For pharmaceuticals, for agriculture. . . ."

"Exactly. And so, if our subsidiary gives us a list of chemicals being sold to a trading group, that's all we know. Fershtaste? That's all we know."

"And I'm sure your subsidiary respects the agreements on chemical weapons."

"Or how could we stay in business? But let's say we ship through the subsidiary to the trading group, and the trading group sells to a foreign government. Now, you tell me. Am I required to give our customers an exam? We fulfill the order."

"But of course if you had suspicions—"

"Listen, Michael. If a trading group wants to buy chemicals, we sell them chemicals. Nu? Am I responsible for what this trading group may do?"

His speech has altered. Usually, Rosenthal speaks with unusual clarity, precision, a touch of pomp, but now Michael hears a lilt. Lilt of a remembered Yiddish one generation, two generations, gone. I'm being wooed with the music of Yiddish.

And Michael, who came here to assure Rosenthal that Fusion won't ask questions, asks a question: "Myron: you're saying you don't know?"—asks knowing Rosenthal knows, and knowing how hard he, Michael, has been pushing knowledge away.

Rosenthal stiffens. He says, "I'm not here to discuss what I know. Look—I'm going to assume you and Mr. Greene are asking about our customers because in the course of your computer work you noticed that certain products were being sold and perhaps you noticed destinations, and you put two and two together. Okay? I'm going to assume you didn't rifle through private files."

"In the course of our work. . . ."

"Yes, exactly, 'in the course of your work,' that's what I'm saying. Otherwise, I would be speaking to our lawyers. Now. This bothers you, what you stumble upon. All right. I can understand. I can! Michael. Let's be honest. All right?"

"Please."

"Let's say we're told that this purchase is for a government pesticide plant."

"And is that what you think?"

"I'll tell you what I think. I didn't say this to Mr. Greene the other day. You're *my people*. I can talk to you more freely. Frankly, all right, it's quite conceivable that these customers—not the trading company but the customers abroad—are going to use these chemicals to make weapons, to quell disturbances, whatever. What am I supposed to do—undertake political research?"

"If the chemicals are precursors for mustard gas? For nerve gases like sarin? I'm speaking hypothetically, like you, Myron."

"Michael, Let's take a worst-case scenario. Chemicorp ships to our subsidiary in England, and from there a trading company ships to . . . Africa—let's just say West Africa—and ships let's say to a person not likely to be so interested in killing mosquitoes. Maybe he's thinking about putting chemicals together to deal with a rebellious part of his population, maybe against some other dictator. Most likely, only a threat. Now, I do know about such weapons. They have particular value where the bush is thick. It's that or napalm. Neither one is very gentle or selective. So. All right. Maybe these are good leaders and maybe not. Maybe they're in the middle of tribal quarrels that go back to pre-colonial days. None of my business. None of my business. And the question is—now listen to me—*Do I care*? Now, Michael, in fact, it makes no difference if I do care. It's just personally interesting. But between the two of us, I'll tell you—the answer is, *Not a lot.* Do you suppose for one minute I'd approve a sale of chemicals to terrorists?—say, Hamas? Or for Iraq or Syria or Iran?—enemies of our people."

"You mean the Jewish people?"

"Yes, of course, the Jewish people. Or, for that matter, any enemy of the United States? God forbid! Or, say, a terrorist group in a European country? As God is my judge, no way would Chemicorp sell to such people. But if some recognized government in

Africa wants to eliminate population by chemicals instead of by disease. . . ."

He smiles slyly, he pauses—for effect. Michael wonders about the effect, the drama Myron Rosenthal is enacting. Now he raises a forefinger: a judge, pronouncing sentence.

"I'm not in favor of it, it's not something to be desired, you understand me?—but . . . it's not the worst thing in the world. AIDS is worse. If I made machine guns, would I sell them to these people? I'm a businessman. So what's different here? And these aren't even weapons.—Is this hard to swallow, Michael?"

So hard to swallow that Michael can't speak. He wonders for a moment if the wine was drugged. Can he drive home? He's glad Deborah is here to drive.

"We're talking about established governments. Finally, that's who pays for our chemicals. Now, sometimes they ask peculiar technical questions. For producing pesticides? But we don't ask questions back."

Michael is silent.

"So. You consider this. What have these Africans and their conflicts got to do with your company. With Fusion?"

Michael doesn't answer.

"Michael. What's the matter? Michael. You're doing an excellent job for us. Let's be frank. You're a service organization. Like electricians; if we need wiring done, we call electricians. They don't ask who we sell chemicals to."

Michael sits and he sits. He takes a long breath. Now he nods. "Myron, I'm sitting here trying to feel what this does for you. I'll tell you something. I don't think it's a question of money."

"I don't understand."

"You like shocking me. I see that. Otherwise, you'd stonewall me. No, it's something else. I think you think this is—*sexy* is the word that comes to mind. You're not 'just a businessman.'"

"I'm a businessman."

"You're flirting with strange gods. That's what I think. It must be very exciting. Tell me. Doesn't it make you think, 'I'm holding death in my hand'?"

"Are you trying to insult me?"

"I'm trying to understand what this is really about for you."

"For me? That's cocktail party talk. I have an obligation to our parent company, I have an obligation to our stockholders. Personally, I'd prefer to ship medicines to people. But I don't have that option. I'm a businessman."

"There's business and business."

"So let's discuss your business. Please. We have a contract. We expect you to fulfill it. That's all. Absolutely. Finish your work. We don't want trouble, our parent company doesn't want trouble. I want you to tell your Mr. Greene to mind his business."

"You can be sure I'll talk to him on Monday, Mr. Rosenthal."

"Myron. What is this 'Mr. Rosenthal'? Now, please, no quarrels, Michael, let's go back to the living room. My daughter is going to play Schumann for us."

Deborah drives home. They don't speak. On the way here they barely spoke, but this is different. It's curious to her, this total silence. When she's silent it throws him off balance; at times she stays silent as a statement. He's rarely this quiet. He sits and strokes his beard. Did he have too much to drink? When they said goodbye, Michael was polite enough to Rosenthal's mother, and to his wife Carol. But he wasn't *there*. She, Deborah, had to pour out charm to that prune of a wife, Carol Rosenthal, so they wouldn't notice. Now, driving the Lexus along Route 1 back to Boston, she's curious—look at him, he stares out the window. At what? Strip-ugliness. Discount outlets, cheap restaurants, motels, malls. Respecting his privacy—it must be something about his dealings with Rosenthal—she plans her week's work. It doesn't hold her. She rehearses a discussion with Karen: Your father and I. . . . It's a discussion she doesn't look forward to.

She glances over: elbow on the armrest, chin cradled in palm, he's staring out the window at the girders of the Tobin Bridge.

A Discussion in Hell

In his bed alone, Michael dreams: a family travels a muddy road that in his waking life he's never traveled—a merchant from Bratslav is fleeing with his family from Poland into Moldava, with nothing more than what his two horses and one large peasant cart can carry. Note how the flesh of his soul is raw under his caftan from the operation of being ripped from his community. The sun is low in the sky. It will be time to light the candles soon. He has a servant couple, but he doesn't trust them. Ukranians. Who knows what they'll do? The Destroyer, like a demonic plague, is moving toward Lubin.

Waking, Michael knows who this Destroyer must be: Bogdan Chmielnicki, hero to Ukrainians, monster to all Jews. Michael has been reading a lot about him. In 1649 he wiped out whole communities of Jews, more than ten percent—some say three times that—of all Jews in Poland and the Ukraine. Asserting the power of the Ukrainian peasantry, Chmiel led the Cossacks against the Polish nobility who controlled them and against the Jews who served that nobility. From the Polish nobles (except for those who were a threat, or those he wanted to punish), Chmiel took wealth; but the Jews—the Jews were something else again. Jews in Chmiel's path ran, leaving everything. When they stayed, the Polish nobles handed them over. Taking a town by siege, the Cossacks slaughtered all the Jews they found. And worse: Nathan of Hanover, in the *Abyss of Despair*, describes the lust for torture, how they burned hundreds in their synagogues, cut women open and sewed up their bellies with live cats inside, then chopped off the hands of the victims so they couldn't rip themselves open. Did this really happen? Happen often? Nathan was an eyewitness; but what matters is that the stories are part of us. Our children were the ones roasted, eaten by dogs.

Michael imagines it's an ancestor fleeing. Isaac, he calls him. An ancestor of his Grandfather, Jacob. An ancestor of Michael. Isaac, Isaac's wife, two grown sons, the servants, the horses and a farm cart carrying whatever they could carry. In a copse behind a church, with no fire to betray their whereabouts, they stop, drag branches to hide the cart, and, protecting them from the wind with boxes, light the candles and say the blessings for the Sabbath. They sleep.

Rousing his sons, Isaac wakes them in half-light. "We have to move on, we have an obligation to move on. We have an obligation to your children and to their children and to their children, that *they* may have a Sabbath. We will pray as we move on toward Kishinev."

The child of the child of the child, and on and on, is Michael. Is Ari. Is the first-born child Ari himself will have one day.

In Hell's last full moon Chmiel sat down with Adolph Hitler to compare notes. *There is* no comparison, the Führer told him through their pain of being Hitler and Chmiel. *What we brought to the job was organization. You meant well—but you were*, enshuldegen zie bitte . . . *butchers.*

But think, Chmiel argued, as he burned in the eternal fires that suit him so well, *what* advantages *you had. We didn't have a telephone, we didn't have a railroad car, and as for poison gas . . . yet we slaughtered whole cities of Jews. You required concentration camps— they cost you money. We used the* towns *in Poland as concentration camps, and when the nobility made their deals with us, we executed our final solution. And we took their jewels, their gold to pay for our next siege.*

So, the Führer said, *you think we needed the technology? I look with admiration on what was accomplished in Rwanda. A million dead, most simply by machete. Everyone was forced to become an accomplice. So elegant. And the killing rate was eight times faster than our own. Yes. Sometimes I do have regrets about the camps. They cost us far more than we took from the dead; as for secrecy, the smell and the ash of the dead descended on the towns. I ask myself, Wouldn't it have been more sensible to eradicate them village by village? The campaign in the East was simple and effective. Why all that effort, to freight the Jews by rail when there was no secrecy? When trains were vital for carrying soldiers and equipment, we kept Jews as our priority. For death, you see, wasn't sufficient. We required vengeance for their existence. It was a spiritual purgation. We needed to force them to crawl through their own defecation. . . . But why be petty?* the Fuhrer said, grinning through the pain of the fire that always issues from his being. *Let us agree you had a share in shaping our vision; you even were a source for us in our methods—to kill a child in front of his mother, a father in front of his child, and so on and so on. Let us burn together forever.*

Michael can't get back to sleep. He prays but is outside the words. *Help us to lie down in peace. . . .* Now he begins to dream awake. A family sits over its morning meal. A difficult time; still, they have food. The family has nothing to do with the soldiers training on the outskirts of town, but they feel safer, having them there. Now they hear a plane and the usual shelling from the ground batteries; the mother carries her baby, and they run, run towards shelter, but it is no shelter, because the cloud pools in the low spots, and soon convulsions begin and two final minutes of pain.

Michael Kuperman looks at the clock radio. It's 1:30 in the morning. Putting on his robe, he goes into the bathroom and knocks on Deborah's door, goes in, touches her shoulder. "Deborah? Can we talk? Deb? Not about us. It's about Myron Rosenthal. Can we talk?"

CHAPTER SIX

It's past sunset, almost 4:30, when Michael rushes in to "make Shabbos." God! Doesn't he know she's throwing a party tonight? He said he'd be here by four to light candles—sunset so early in December—and that would give her time to get ready, time for the caterer to arrive and set up. Deborah has invited her new friend Larry Ackerman, folding Larry into a mix of fifteen or twenty guests—friends, clients of Thayer, Fletcher and Gringold.

They've been meeting every few days for a drink after work, she and Larry.

But this past week she's been uneasy—since Michael came to her bedroom to tell her about Rosenthal and Chemicorp. Uneasy because she'd felt moved that night by his depth of pain. She thinks: *Larry Ackerman wouldn't be capable.* Not that he's especially shallow, Larry; but he couldn't grieve this hard. To see this big man weep—of course she was seduced into temporary tenderness, but it's not that; it's the respect she felt for his seriousness. It reminded her: *this serious man I married.* Larry talks aesthetic trends, talks swings in the market, knows a lot about world trade, especially with Pacific Rim countries; and of course talks sailing—owns a marina, a sailboat-manufacturing company, a brokerage firm for expensive boats. Talks sailing with great joy.

Maybe that's what's led her to invite Larry tonight. To see what she feels for him when she's in her ordinary life. And because she's been sympathetic for Michael, she's especially annoyed with him tonight. Turning her back on him, she pours herself a glass of white wine; embarrassed at the gesture, she asks, "*You* want wine?"

"I know it's late, but I want to make Shabbos—wine, sure. Candles."

Without saying a word, she calls, "Ari? Karen?" Her neck strains, as if to pull them into the kitchen faster; she hardly breathes, waiting. She hears signs, and at last they come and Deborah breathes again and lights the candles, Michael chants the blessings; Ari harmonizes "Shalom Aleichem," pleased by his own boy-soprano voice; Karen isn't listening: the song is background for her observations. Oh, she can smell hostility. She's the world expert, she sometimes feels, in nosing out unspoken anger.

They go upstairs—Karen to dress for a party, Ari to watch a video.

"All *right*?" she asks. As in: *Well? Is your hunger for Jewish ritual appeased?*

And *this*—this is the moment Steve Planck chooses to show up, unannounced. He's dressed in jeans. How long is he going to stay?—the caterer will be coming any minute. Deborah is of course furious. She says, *Hello, Steve, hello, how nice*—and leaves the kitchen to the men. But a minute later, simply not able to *stand* it, she calls their house line from her business line in her study. "Michael. I've got to get ready. What the *hell* does he think he is—a graduate student? To walk in like that?"

"Right, Fred," Michael says into the phone. "Thanks. I appreciate your sympathy. And maybe what you say is correct. Maybe it's true of me, too. Yes."

"You know the trouble with you?" she whispers into the phone. "You found your success too young. You never had to grow up. I'll be in my study if you need me."

"Well, thanks. I appreciate your analysis and your concern."

"Oh, *just balls!*"

Michael hangs up.

"So? What are we going to do?" Steve asks. He sits on the counter, dangles his legs. "You saw the letter about Djouti."

"Oh, Steve, listen. I saw worse. I *heard* worse. Steve? I spent time with Rosenthal. We went to his Hanukkah party. He's got a fancy house on the North Shore. I couldn't sleep after."

"What are you saying? He actually acknowledged—?"

"He might as well have. Okay, Steve. You were right. We're getting out of the contract."

"That's not the goddamn point, Mike. 'Getting out.'"

Michael closes his eyes. "Let's *start* there, okay? Isn't that plenty to wreck Fusion?"

"You're putting the blame on *me*! I can hear it."

"You're right. I'm sorry."

"The bastard! Listen, Mike—I'm preparing a little surprise for these guys."

"What are you talking about?"

"I'm slipping them some software. Let's call a spade a spade—a *virus*, okay?"

"Are you crazy?"

"It's not ready. But I'll tell ya, it's gonna cook them. Not the kind of virus that shuts a system down. Oh, much better."

Michael's face is hot. "Oh, grow up, will you? Will you, Steve?" He pours himself more wine, drinks it down.

Steve picks at a cuticle, bites another. Shrugs, slips off the counter, waves himself out the door. Michael calls after, "Come on—take it easy, come back here, will you?"

"Oh, balls!" Steve yells on the way down the back steps, just as the caterer pulls into the driveway.

A Catered Affair

As always, Deborah's hired a caterer and someone to serve drinks and appetizers; tonight, and whenever possible, it's Panaigiotis Miropoulos, a beautiful young man, son of a colleague, who does this kind of work to help pay his way through Harvard. He's there in his usual bow tie, black pants, white shirt, swathe of black hair.

This morning, an acquaintance from the World Bank, Georg Severain, called, and she asked him, and said, yes, of course he could bring his friend along. "Who is he?"

"His name is Geoffrey Slade. He does research for Interpol."

"Interpol? How interesting. Yes, of course bring him."

The two stubby white Shabbat candles are burning in the breakfast room; eight, ten, unsanctified tall blue candles are lit here in the big living room. Panaigiotis is taking coats. Michael is shaking hands. And here's Larry. She can't hear what they're saying.

Larry is explaining: Ackerman Boats is a client of Thayer, Fletcher, and Gringold; Deborah did a wonderful job for them as consultant. "Do you sail?" he asks Michael.

"I once did. I get seasick. You must compete—what?—big boats, little boats?" *Are you the one having an affair with my wife?*

"I hardly have the time anymore."

"The young man over there will get you a drink," Michael says. He wanders, smiling, listening in, says hello to Martha Corey and gets away as fast as possible. When he slips inside Jacob Goldstein, he's perplexed. All these *strangers* in your house, Jacob says. Jacob, even as a successful man of business in New York, had no one to his apartment at the Beresford except relatives or members of his own synagogue. But to Michael as Michael, this is old hat. He talks for a few minutes to Georg Severain of the World Bank and meets Severain's friend, Geoffrey Slade.

Slade doesn't look like a banker. He's oddly tall for a man not in basketball shorts, taller than Michael, who's almost 6'2". Slade is ectomorphic but looks strong, with wide bony shoulders and long fingers, even a long head, Michael notices, accentuated by a severely close haircut. What makes for an *intelligent* face? What is it about the eyes? The man has smart, amused eyes. Michael talks to Slade—Georg has told him that Slade crewed a shell for England in the '88 Olympics and still coaches. So Michael talks about Steve Planck, his *wunderkind*, rowing on the Charles—Steve's nine percent body fat, his fanatic love for sculling—but Martha Corey takes him aside, kisses him, congratulates him on the merger. And she's off. He wanders the party, Wild Turkey in hand.

And he learns so *much* about the world: *learns that at Henri Bendel there are these glorious shoes that are so "fifties." That the pool of skilled labor in Indonesia is growing fast, and that the Loach woman paid—no, it's true—over $3000 for the gown and wore it exactly once. Once. And. And that outsourcing will find its own level. But Charles Rosen's article on Mozart didn't take the late influence of Bach into account. And Nietzsche's breakdown from syphillis shouldn't be treated as metaphor for ideological failures. Well, no wonder—it was a hideous chartreuse, and a terrible color for her. As a matter of fact, next spring I'm coming out with a final refutation of that jackass.*

It's like standing at a listening bay at a music store with headphones on, flipping channels, Mozart to Stravinsky to the Beatles. Or floating, yes, say floating in a bay of words, pleasant, but which can, after all, buoy you up only so long. The trick is to ride from swell to swell and know when to come out on shore. Shore in this case is the kitchen, where he can appear to be expediting the party in some way, then smile at Panagiotis and pop a couple of tiny mushroom tarts, and it's up the back stairs to his study, where he sits down to read an essay by Abraham Heschel. *Shabbat shalom.* Through the closed door he can hear occasional laughter, baritone, contralto, and from the stereo a tenor sax that strains towards alto to be more than a part of the blur of sound.

Mom! Suddenly she fills him and like a wave, recedes down the beach.

A knock on the study door. Geoffrey Slade, friend of Georg Severain, has been looking for Michael. Oh, he knows he'll find him. No hurry. In the meantime, Geoffrey's the kind of guest who examines the weaving of the kilim hanging over your stairs, pills in your medicine cabinet. Door at the end of the hall.

"Yes? Come in?" Geoffrey Slade is already in. "Mr. Kuperman. I *am* sorry."

"That's all right. Really. I don't like these parties either," Michael says, happy to see him. "You're a friend of that young man from the World Bank?—you rowed for England."

"Yes, doesn't that sound comical—'rowed for England'? Yes. Georg Severain's friend. Geoffrey Slade. Rowed, yes. More recently, coached the Oxbridge entry. I'm a bit old to keep up with the twenty-year-olds." He holds out a giant hand.

"Geoffrey. Right. I'm Michael Kuperman."

"Yes, yes, of course."

They're both flustered. They both smile at their evident embarrassment, smile at their shared truancy. Michael says, "You're at the Bank?"

"No. With Interpol, actually." And adds, grinning, "No, no, I'm *not* a detective. I know that's what people think when I say I'm with Interpol. I simply advise in international law. I work for the Secretary General in Paris, but for the past several months, in New York and Boston. Lately, I've been doing research."

"But *Interpol.* Please, sit down. I have a question for you." Michael has a giddy sense of pattern—to find someone from Interpol. But lately, Michael has begun to sense often that he is dancer, actor, or rhythmic line and moment of color in a pattern he can't fathom. He is swimming in time, one pixel of temporary light at the decree of fingers on a keyboard.

It makes sense to Michael: he accepts this feeling that he's in a web of souls beyond his knowing, and why *not* talk to this stranger about precursor chemicals, about an intermediary trading company, about a General Djouti. It's unlikely, of course, that Slade will know anything, but what has he got to lose? He's actually considered calling Interpol, but he knows Interpol is not an international police; just an organization that coordinates the work of national police forces.

"Interpol. Interesting. Have you been with the Secretary General long?"

"No. A little over a year. Before that, I taught international law at Sussex. Is there something about Interpol that interests you?"

"Oh. Well. It's not likely to be your department, Mr. Slade—but has the name François Djouti ever come up that you can remember? A *General* François Djouti?"

We Shall Not Be Moved

He's back to work after the weekend. Jonathan's in from Japan, and Jonathan's in contact with McNair. They'll meet, the three of them, tomorrow. It's a tough day for Michael, having to keep planning for the merger when he knows it's likely to go bust. Michael attends the strategy session with Doug Shaughnessy and Doug's marketing team—how to integrate people from InterCom with their own marketing staff.

On his way home, Dennis driving, he checks his messages from the car.

❏ *Message from Steve*:
"I need you and Jonathan ASAP. I know you'll be meeting Jonathan at O'Hare tomorrow. I want you both to come down to Bloomington. I'm blocking out tomorrow afternoon, Mike. We need to talk. Things to show you. Christ. You just wait. I'm calling in whatever favors, Mike. *Please.* I want both of you here tomorrow. . . ."

Michael closes his eyes and sinks back into the vinyl seat.

❑ *Ira Cooper has called.* The message brief, a grunted, "Hello. Just thought I'd call, Mikey. I've got a little problem. Fact is, I'm calling from Precinct 24, NYPD. . . ."
From jail? Dad?
Ira Cooper's in lockup.
Last night, he came on like a little tyrant to Eleanor, and she got hard as a wall. Her eyes floated to the ceiling: *Let the vulgarian rant.*

Your tiny apartment, it's like a cell, and on the hoity-toity East side, Ira yelled. *Who needs this? You know what I am? A kept man, a kept man—how can I work here?* Finally, after all these years, he doesn't have to make up excuses to sneak over to her place, and all of a sudden, it's "cramped," she's trying to turn him into an old man, so he blusters like this, it'd make you laugh it's so transparent, because he wants so badly to give it up and rest against her, to stop blustering, stop *needing* to bluster, who the hell cares? She's so calm it pisses him off. Belle had a barbed tongue, but Eleanor is a *lady*— he draws the word out: laaaay-dyyyy—and who needs a goddamn lady? He thumps his chest like a monkey, knuckles on breastbone, me, me, me, yatada yatada yatada. So the upshot is, he packs a bag and heads across town to West End Avenue, sets up shop in the old bedroom, though the place is so musty and full of Belle's perfume, it works on his asthma. But he spends three hours in the darkroom with Coltrane keeping him company, and he listens for the phone, but nobody calls.

Morning, the day begins in anger, so Ira doesn't shave, to hell with shaving, takes his old heavy Hasselblad, gets breakfast on Broadway, sits in the booth under his own 8 x 10 of fighting cab drivers and listens to the heavy wheezing of the deli owner.
It's after this he gets into trouble. He's in jeans, grubby old man is how he looks, to hell with Eleanor, let her eat alone for a day, he grumbles. He's an artist. With camera. Out in the streets is where he belongs.
You know where he belongs?—where he belongs is at the strike at the hospital, down a few blocks, one block over. He read about it in the *Post*—it embarrasses him to pick up his political news from that rag—hospital workers squeezed, productivity jacked up,

people laid off a third round, and they're out on the street picketing, cops on the scene. He finishes breakfast and goes down
there, and he's catching shots with his big Hasselblad, excited like
a kid, it's like his early days. He shoots a cop blocking a picketer
trying to swing the picketing circle closer to the entrance, and Ira's
right in the cop's face—hostile, no doubt about that—and they
come after him, and (as he tells Michael over the phone) "I thought
they were after my camera, and it's precious, it's irreplaceable, I've
had it forever, you know that. Nobody's going to get my Hasselblad
without a fight."

"So you fought the cops?" Michael says on cell, as his cab
breaks free of traffic and heads west on Storrow Drive.

"They call it 'resisting,'" he guffaws. "Ahh, but Christ, I'm an
old man!"

His voice is quavering with self-pity like a cello now, and
Michael closes his eyes, not wanting to get sucked in. Michael says,
"So did you call Eleanor?"

"You keep Eleanor out of this. This is just the kind of goddamn
thing'll give her fifteen, twenty points of power, and that I don't
need. She's still trying to tame me."

"Look. I'll get my guy in New York on it. I'll have you out, Dad,
in an hour."

"You tell 'em I get my Hasselblad back. *With pictures.* Tell 'em
I'll sue their ass."

"Dad, did you hit a cop, Dad?"

"What, 'hit'? Me? I'm a weak *alte kocker*. 'Hit!'"

"Okay, let me get on it. You coming up here if you're allowed
out of the city?"

"My work's down here, Michael. What am I going to do
hanging around? And I don't like to remind you, but your wife isn't
exactly fond of me."

Fonder of you than of me. Home, he calls Fusion's law firm in
New York, talks to Jerry Williams, who did Yale Law when Michael
did his MBA, and Williams talks to a paralegal who goes down
with bail money. "Charges will be dropped," Williams says. "They
were just trying to get this old guy out of their hair. They were
afraid he'd have a heart attack."

"I can't tell him that."

"He gave our paralegal a message for you—he says *thanks*. Says he'll be in touch. Oh—they gave him back his . . . Hasselblad— what's that, a camera?"

"In between a camera and a lover. Maybe I shouldn't tell him that charges will be dropped. So—can he leave the city?"

"He just has to be back for a hearing. That'll be dropped, too."

"Thanks, Joe."

"Sure. I hear the cops liked him. They spent most of the time talking baseball with him, 1930's, 1940's. Did you know he was at Yankee Stadium when Lou Gehrig gave his 'Lucky-to-Be-a-Yankee' speech?"

"He means he was at the movies when Gary Cooper played Gehrig."

"I guess your dad isn't easy."

"I've got no problems with my dad," Michael says. "I just know the guy."

"But he *is* a real photographer?"

"Oh, yes. A real photographer," Michael says, getting off the phone and finding papers he needs. Oh, yes. And sees, as he has *been* seeing every day at odd times, some basement (?) room somewhere in New York, a cheap exhibit space, some show in Soho or the Village—when was this? Keeps seeing plastered walls, rough like white-on-white relief, and must be his father's pictures hanging, he was a kid. *Political pictures*, his father called them. He goes into his study and looks through the pictures his father sent. That subway at rush hour: *foreground*: commuters packed four deep, bunching as a train (slightly blurred against the staring faces) pulls in. If I'd taken these, Michael thinks, they'd have been expressing the emptiness of urban life, mechanical life. That's not it. Nor is it a shot of interesting, turbulent, ethnic, urban life.

In the middle of the subway platform, very still, a mother and little boy. Iranian. . . ? Something like that. All of a sudden, he gets it. It's as if his father, pretentious, vain, foolish old man, has somehow taken a photograph that gets at complex life and does so without putting his ego in the way. Subway billboards behind the woman's head. He stares. And loses it. It's just a subway picture again. Then it happens again, though he can't put it into words. For a moment he thinks, That's going to change the way I see things.

An Assignation

Monday morning. It's raining a cold rain in New York; he's glad he zipped in the lining of his London Fog. By 11:30 he's in a cab from La Guardia to a quiet lounge on East 54th. Geoffrey Slade is sitting at a small table past the bar. This feels like an assignation. In dim light Michael sits across from Slade, dwarfing the little table.

The room's painted in muted pastels, and past the bar are tables small and separate enough for secrets to be comfortably shared. Slade is six-four, six-five. He's wearing a beige suede jacket that sets him apart from the New Yorkers in the bar. Its softness doesn't go with the look of the man. Slade's hands are long and muscular; they look like exaggerated, sculptured hands; his face is crossed by heavy, suntanned creases. Put him in different clothes and, with his big body and big hands, he'd look like an oil rig worker, a cowboy. But spy to spymaster, that's how it feels to Michael. That's his agenda, and he imagines a wire taped under his shirt, amateur turns spy, film ends in a commando raid on a warehouse on the London docks. "I suppose you checked up on me?"

"I checked, dear boy, before I spoke to you in the first place."

"Of course."

"Of course. Enough to know I have good reason to talk to you. Reason to trust you. And then, well, you were so disturbed on Friday night. Well, let me say this: you have good reason to be disturbed."

"You mean you were right about this Djouti?"

"Oh, yes. I was right, but it was much worse than I remembered. I knew the name from my research, but I'd never learned all the details. General Djouti?—he's someone you don't want to have dealings with, Michael. No, you'd best steer clear of that one."

"Because of his government?"

"No. Not his government. He *has* no government. Because of his *trading partners*."

"His 'trading partners'? But isn't he buying for his government?"

"This is one very nasty man, Michael. The reason we have him in our files—his trading partners are Libyans, Syrians, Iraqis, Germans, Japanese. He's not particular. He sometimes does represent his own government in a transaction, but . . . you see, he's not a 'general', not a representative of his government at all. Of *any* government. He's an independent agent. And his customers—we know some of his customers are terrorist organizations. Not in West Africa—organizations in the Middle East. It's weapons he sells—conventional weapons, explosives. But not exclusively. I can't say more. You understand. Actually, there's not enough evidence to convict him in any country. My colleague tells me we're working on this with the French and British."

"But you're pretty sure.—In the Middle East?"

"Oh, yes. Another thing: at your house, I noticed the Jewish books, lovely collection, I noticed the Jewish art on the walls of your study. Even from that point of view—no, I doubt you want to have anything to do with this man."

Michael bristles. He sees a village. Jews, Arabs, Kurds. . . . "That's not the issue. Victims are victims."

"Of course, yes, of course. Still. . . ."

"Yes. All right. I grant you."

"I can't show you files, I can't discuss this much further. Actually, I don't know a great deal. But this Djouti is a very dangerous man, absolutely without scruples. And maybe the most dangerous thing—I'm told he's not a fanatic, Michael. Not a terrorist himself. As for his religion?—he believes in Swiss bank accounts. That's Djouti. But he's the tip of a nasty iceberg. There are organizations upon organizations. Chiefly, there's a French-Russian syndicate—a man named Reynard in Marseilles—my colleagues tell me that's the organization behind Djouti."

"Thank you. Oh—I brought you the letter."

"Good. Fine." Slade holds it, doesn't read.

"Obviously, you didn't get it from me."

"Right. Right."

They sit in silence over a glass of wine; Michael sees white stucco walls, the planes, sees corpses in a square. "Look. Have you thought about my helping you? You say you're not a policeman. You do research. I don't believe you. Not for a minute. But I'm willing to help. Nothing heroic. But maybe if I go along with our original contract . . . I can learn more about the sale."

Slade smiles. "I spoke about precisely that possibility to my colleagues in Lyon first thing this morning. And this is what I'm told:

Interpol is *interested*, we thank you Michael, this goes into our files on Djouti, our files on Reynard, information goes to various authorities here and in England. But this particular transaction isn't strictly illegal, you see—not the actual export of chemicals. Not if they have end-user certification, as of course they will. And it's hard to trace the shipment after it arrives in England. Easier with conventional weapons. Now, if the shipment of chemicals went to an interdicted country, then yes, Export Enforcement would be all over them. But it won't, you see. Not directly."

"I told you Friday about our system designer, Steve Planck."

"This Planck fellow—yes, the one who's developing some computer virus or other."

Michael asks, "Aren't you going to read the letter?"

"The letter? Oh. Yes. Yes, of course." Slade glances through it, folds it away.

Michael notices that Geoffrey Slade is busy sketching on a paper napkin. It's a long boat on stylized water, oared—a single scull, he supposes, remembering that Slade is a champion oarsman. A wake radiates behind. On the shore behind the boat are cartoon people with arms raised in triumph. Michael watches him add smiles to the spectators. Now Slade turns the paper Michael's way. "I think there's something you need to understand about me, Mike." With the napkin upside down he adds in the prow of another boat to the left edge of the picture. "I am a ferocious competitor. I don't just like to win—everybody *likes* to win. I'm afraid I'm rather preternaturally disposed to win. In this case—"

"All right, Geoffrey. So you're not even pretending to be a 'researcher.'"

"Of course I do research."

"Right. So do we all, we all do research. Geoffrey, look—what if I can do something to stop these shipments?"

"You feel guilty, don't you, *not* doing something."

"Shouldn't I?"

"Oh, you should. Indeed. Suppose one day you turn on the TV and see Tel Aviv being gassed."

"Suppose I can dry up this particular source? I won't step on your toes."

"I'd like to hear more details about this Mr. Rosenthal. You say he already knows your feelings. And what are *his* feelings, assuming he has such things?"

"It's Rosenthal I'm thinking of. I want to talk to him. Look. People have to justify the things they do. Rapists, murderers were '*driven to it*' by their victims. Or child abusers, or men who beat their wives. Even the SS. I remember Himmler's speech to the men who were going to be in charge of killing Jews in the East. 'You will feel revulsion because of your advanced humanity at some of the things you have to do. But if we are going to get rid of the cancer that's destroying our own people, you will steel yourself to do your duty.' And Rosenthal—Myron Rosenthal thinks of himself as a good man, a good Jew, who has to be part of 'unpleasant business arrangements.' It's those who *use* the chemicals who are responsible. But he's lying to himself—actually it excites him, the tough world view he's got."

"And you don't think he knows where it's really going."

"You mean whom Djouti is buying it for? No. No, I doubt it. I'd like him to know. I'd very much like him to know."

"Really, Michael. I'm serious. We want you to drop it—but keep us informed if anything happens. Oh—" He hands Michael a card with his name, telephone numbers in Paris and two in New York. "If you want to get in touch, the second number's best. But let my colleagues do their job."

"All right. I hope I won't get anywhere near Djouti."

"I enjoyed meeting you," Geoffrey says, crumpling up the napkin. I'm so glad I wandered upstairs Friday night. I rarely meet such a serious person. No, really. It's startling. I'm glad I could settle your doubts."

Michael smiles. "You didn't 'wander' anywhere Friday night. Tell me—you have a British accent, Geoffrey, but it's faint. Were you brought up in England?"

It's a transatlantic accent, Slade explains; he went to school in London and New York, spent summers on the Cape. "My aunt's in Boston. . . ."

Breaking With Chemicorp

Flying is as ordinary to Michael as driving to work; not today. The takeoff from La Guardia howls in the cave of his stomach. Impossible chutzpah—to invade the sky this way. What gives him the right to thrust himself through clouds? He's dizzy with the thought of his insufficient body controverting gravity.

McNair and Jonathan are meeting him in Chicago; McNair is on his way to Los Angeles, so they're to meet in the US Airways Club at O'Hare. For a moment, in the accordion tube that connects plane to terminal, Michael feels the cold of Chicago's actual weather through his suit; then he's rescued by the manufactured climate.

The US Airways lounge is divided into comfortable inner "rooms," with soft carpets, upholstered armchairs, end tables with telephones. They could have taken a conference room, but, Jonathan told him, that would be too formal for what he wanted. So they're waiting for him at a corner table. Ken McNair is squat, neck thick, head broad, hair cropped close, giving him a military look. Jonathan grins; he's not looking into Michael's eyes, but the grin is secret communication: *Hey. Looks like it's going to be all right.* Michael wants Jonathan to lead, trusts Jonathan more than he trusts himself, and finds Hebrew words he doesn't understand— words of a prayer, he can't remember which—going through his head, and it's Jonathan who "fills him in."

That's in quotes because what Jonathan is *really* doing is shaping his previous conversation in such a way that Ken McNair will concur—*and not quite realize that Jonathan has defined the problem in a new way*, moving them closer together than they really were. But that's all right with McNair, who smiles as Jonathan calls him "far-sighted"—("No, I really mean that, Ken—") and seems eager to be moved.

Partly, it's because of the beauty of the man who's moving him. This handsome man in the beautiful gray wool suit hand-tailored for him in London. Jonathan's tie from Louis' in Boston. But it isn't the elegance of the suit, the tie. There are people who have such physical grace that you want them to smile at you. You want them to nod and pick up your words and carry them further in the same direction. Jonathan does that to other men. They want his approval. He's not stingy with approval either. But he's never off-balance, worried what you think of him, of his ideas. You pick up, unconsciously, his talk-rhythms. Michael has seen men who could buy and sell Jonathan slip into his language, say "sweet deal," "sweet strategy," because of the music of "sweet" as Jonathan says it. As now Ken McNair, who woke up this morning with "objections," "concerns," "issues," picks up Jonathan's "symbiotic"—"The real symbiotic aspect of our relationship," McNair says, "is a sweet interplay of capital and research." McNair's speech has this pseudo-intelligent sound of corporate bullshit; it makes Michael wince. But "sweet interplay" tells him Jonathan's being successful.

"Thing is, Michael, Ken isn't overly upset about our making a clean break with Chemicorp—of course within the terms of our original contract. There are confidential elements here. We know Chemicorp is selling precursor chemicals, probably in good faith—let's agree to that, hey, no one's pointing fingers—but we don't want to get too close. We realize it could blow up in our faces, one or two years down the line, isn't that so?"

"It's *possible*. Mind you, Jonathan, not likely."

"Absolutely. *Not* likely, Ken. But *possible*. A few weeks, we'll be out of this phase of the contract, and we'll call it a day. We've done one sweet job for Chemicorp. They'll pass the next phase on to another vendor. But InterCom and Fusion—we have a lot more at stake. We have long term value, each for the other. Am I right, Ken?"

And Ken says, "Of course I think that. Certainly."

"Right, or you wouldn't have come near us. We're too small—but *not* our R&D. Now, that's not small at all. And that's what InterCom needs. Just as we need your capital strength—let's be honest, we need you, no question. It's symbiotic, as you said."

"No question," Michael repeats. "Ken—you're not . . . tied in financially, are you, to Chemicorp? I don't remember seeing anything like that in the financials."

"No," McNair kind of drawls, Midwest version of a drawl, "but your contract with Chemicorp was a selling point for us. And I happen to know Myron Rosenthal. He's an upright guy, Mike. And his direct boss, Max Ferguson—a very strong manager."

"No question."

"Then there's Al Braithwaite—now, that's something else. Al's been my close friend for years. Whatever's happening at Chemicorp, Braithwaite is clean."

Jonathan skews the talk toward their merger. New logos, coordination of technical support. And in twenty minutes, they stand up to shake hands, and Kenneth McNair is off to catch his plane.

"We're out of the woods," Jonathan says, and sighs a contented sigh. Laughs aloud. "Out of the woods. Lord! I could hardly sleep last night, Mike."

"You were amazing. Well, you know that."

"Nothing magic I do, Mike. I'm just his golden African-American, his one special friend, that's all it is. Same as at school. *You* remember. Lot of American men want to be on a first-name basis with me. I don't mind it, Mike. I feel a little phony, but I use it. Don't you bet, when McNair gets home he tells his family how *smart* I am?"

"Well. And aren't you? You are."

"Not the point."

"Okay, it's true, sure it's true, but you don't know how much stuff you've got."

But Jonathan disregards this. "My brains, that's not the point. I'm saying, why—*if* I'm right—is he gonna go home and *talk* about it?—*that's* my question. The answer? It's to show how gracious he is to have this opinion. And Mike—there's something smells even worse: '. . . *for a black man*' is what isn't being said. *So smart . . . for a black man.*" He smiles. "I don't mind. Need all the help we can get. I was afraid," he says, "we'd never be able to extract ourselves from the contract, not without losing the merger. So. That wraps it up. We go on to Bloomington, we hear what Steve has to say, we calm him down."

Leaning back, Jonathan clasps his hands together over his chest. Keep watching those hands. They're going to come apart in a few more lines.

"Jonathan," Michael says, hardly wanting to look at him, "the thing is, maybe you were right, what you said weeks ago. I mean. I mean there *is* no way to extract ourselves."

"We just *did*, Mike. Weren't you here?"

"Don't get pissy. Think about it. You said it yourself—the problem is, *we know*. I haven't slept much since Friday night."

"Friday? You mean Rosenthal? Oh, oh. Mike, don't do this. Mike, I know you."

"You've been saying it all this time—I didn't want to listen. No—not Rosenthal. This past Friday. I've been talking to people at Interpol. What do we do? Let Chemicorp, Orion whatever it is, sell poison gas, nerve gas. We just forget about it?"

A woman's voice in an echo chamber—a flight postponed, a flight ready for take-off. Mr. Bradley, please call the Delta ticket counter. The click of laptops from the cubicles at the club. But here go Jonathan's hands—one to a cup of water, one to his cheek, he's back in Cambridge, it's spring over twenty years ago, they've been working in Widener Library on term papers; Cokes in hand, they're walking the footbridge over the Charles (the bridge where Deborah met Martha Corey). And at this late hour, one, one-thirty in the morning, Michael begins worrying about absolute and relative morality. *Mike, enough.* Jesus, Mike. It's too late for this shit. Drink your Coke. Until finally Jonathan gets seduced into taking a position—he can't remember what anymore—and they don't stop chewing it over till nearly three.

Well, there's something nostalgic for Jonathan, something takes him out of his understated, hand-tailored suit and back into jeans—gone, funny, high-carbohydrate life of college. After all this time, he doesn't need Michael's explanation to know what he means. He lets out a big laugh, totally inappropriate for a frequent flyer lounge. "All right—we've passed the word to Commerce. And we're extracting ourselves. What else are we supposed to do? Mike, there's terrible evil in this world. I *like* it that you can't get used to the fact. I always *have* liked it. It bugged me when I saw you sloughing this off. But don't turn around and go crazy on me. First you didn't want to give up the contract. Now you want—what?—what *do* you want? First Steve. Now you."

"I feel a little crazy."

"What else *can* we do? Michael! American companies in Central America, they spray pesticides over their fields while the pickers are working—same pesticides we don't let them use here in America. Right? Well, last year, we organized the computer systems for one of their subsidiaries. Remember? Just the other day we were talking about subcontractors in Malaysia and Korea using production methods that wouldn't be allowed here. Resins in closed spaces—cementing bottoms onto shoes—well, we know about that too, don't we? We put in an integrated network system for True Step Shoes—we were blown away to find out what their Chinese workers are paid. What've we done about that?

"I know."

"You *do* know. Michael: there are engineering concerns in Switzerland happy to make stainless-steel factories for chemical munitions, biological munitions, for both Iraq and Iran. I'll bet our investment portfolios include stock in one of those companies. Or one of the companies we hold stock in, *that* company holds stock. So what about Chemicorp? We blow the whistle on them? And *what* whistle? *What whistle?* Far as we know, they're *legal*, Michael."

"I know."

"Legal. So let's say we go to the newspapers. We'll get our ass sued. Nothing else will change. We'll just wipe out everything we've built. What about our responsibility to the people who work for us? Hey! Not to mention Jessica!—she'd kill me. Not to mention Deborah, who wouldn't look so classy in the poorhouse."

Michael doesn't argue. Michael doesn't say, Look at the time you put in, working with the kids in Roxbury. Don't make out like I'm the idealist. He doesn't say this, doesn't argue, because come *on*—Jonathan's making the speech Michael wants to hear, and here's the clincher—it's the speech Jonathan *knows* Michael wants to hear. *If he didn't make it, I might have.* A ritual is what this is, to give Michael the moral advantage of groaning in guilt *without doing the company any damage.* You think Michael wants to make waves? Especially now! If Deborah leaves, what then? He'll need money. He'll need Fusion to ground him. In pretense of argument with Jonathan, he can bow his head and nod, reflect on universal grief and injustice, feel moral and comfortably helpless in this lounge of glass and aluminum, vinyl and other polymers, then fly home to Boston reading prayers for the dead, maybe the future dead in some other country.

Now Michael blurts a laugh and keeps chuckling. He doesn't know what's so funny, but he laughs broadly, in waves, not a bitter, sardonic laugh but a big laugh that turns the heads of other men in suits, a huge, if temporary, release of self-righteousness.

"*What*, Mike?"

"I don't know what." But he knows. "Sometimes I'm a terrible fool." He gets up, he puts his arm around his friend, feels closer to him than he has for a long while. "Okay, man. Okay. Okay." And he's grinning as they walk out of the lounge toward the flight to Indianapolis. But once they get to the gate, the smile dims, fades. They check in. Michael waits for the boarding call. He's tired as hell. He takes up his book on medieval Jewish history. But at 21,000 feet he falls asleep hard, and he dreams.

His dream is a residue of his reading. He's back at the time of the Plague, fourteenth century—1349. He had dreamt about an ancestor, Isaac, fleeing Chmielnicki, the Destroyer. Now he's dreaming of an ancestor who lived three hundred years before Isaac. In the dream the ancestor has a name. Shmuel. A strong man of middle age, bearded, in black kaftan, Shmuel walks beside a two-wheeled cart pulled by a sluggish horse; his daughter and wife are in the cart, and his son-in-law holds the reins on the other side of the cart. A servant goes with them. All are silent. The cool of the morning enters their kaftans. Half waking, Michael keeps his eyes shut so that Jonathan, reading a book beside him, doesn't start up the conversation. Michael tries to keep the dream going.

. . . Thanks to the Holy One blessed be He, it is a dry day, and over low spots in the road, the cart is able to move without the women needing to get out and walk. The wood of the cart creaks, creaks. Menachen, the younger man, ancestor of Jacob Goldstein, and so of Belle, prays, *Adonoi, may it be your will that the wheels hold up this long way over such roads.* What they have left (most of their possessions they gave to the community or to the city guards they had to bribe) is piled in the cart, covered with hides and sacks of grain, except for florins, ducats, guelder, and seed pearls, which are sewn into their clothes, clothes of *each* of them, in case one is taken. Passing east through the valley, they see from a hillside the little steeples of villages, spires of the great cathedral behind them across the Rhine, take the morning sun. Now a forest, a merchant road, cool from the night, forest of great trees and very little underbrush; the trail is easy, but there is no protection.

In the voice of an imagined ancestor who sees everything, who knows what's been and knows what's coming, Michael thinks,

Protection. And what protection have we ever had? In Vienna in just a few more centuries, the most distinguished, comfortable professors in the University will be Jews, and after the Anschluss their students will be pleased to throw them out the University's windows onto the pavement. As now, 1349, we give to the barons, we give to the Bishop, and we do our business, we make our trades and our marriages and vie for seats at the East wall in the synagogue. Except for being spit upon, except for that, or occasionally robbed, except for that, or one of us pulled from the street and beaten, kicked in the skull by young men who've drunk too much, except for the yearly humiliations at the steps of the cathedral, and the threats and curses of the fanatics, we go on with our ordinary lives. We treasure the dignity of our position in our community. We may, during the week, have to cringe, to bow down, as we buy and sell, but in shul, when we are called to the reading of the law, and in our homes, we have dignity. We don't forget the armies who came to rob and murder, but that was two hundred years ago, armies on their way to Constantinople and Jerusalem, who needed Jewish gold and Jewish blood. Worse— the rabble sucked into the wake of the armies by Peter the Hermit. Oh, we don't forget. Nor the fanatics—even the ruler of their Church tried to squelch them—who accuse us of killing a child for blood, here in Germany, in France, in England, we who won't even eat meat tainted by animal blood; and we were exiled from our homes again. We don't forget, but that was fifty years ago, and we have been (more or less) safe since. We have, some of us, prospered.

But now everyone is dying, especially the poor, especially the Jews. The Plague spreads till there are too many dead for the authorities to take the bodies off the streets, and it is on account of the Jews—we must have poisoned the wells. But aren't we dying the same as everyone? That must be one more Jewish trick. And we are at the mercy of bands of crazy men whipping themselves from town to town, gathering numbers, praying and slaughtering. Penitente, who "repent" by slaughtering the Jews.

We hear news of the slaughter and tremble—oh, but that was far down the Rhine, and our peasants and our nobles, we live in peace with them. But the rumors of well poisoning have spread. They have

"proof." They have crazy stories, rabbis have sent bags of poison to this one, to that one, and they get Jews to confess by taking strips of their skin off their bodies and salting the human meat underneath. They haven't yet learned how to make the skin into lampshades, the fat into soap, but give them time. There are things that can be done to anyone. In Speyer, they tortured an old man until his mind went from him and he told them, Yes, he had received secret instructions and a little cloth bag of poison from a rabbi in Turkey, and thus had he cloaked himself and come upon the well when there was no moon and poured in the poison according to instructions. And in Nuremberg, the same, and some of the lords tried to stop the rumors and some profited from them, destroying whole districts of Jews and taking their possessions.

We wrap ourselves in prayers and prayer shawl, we accept martyrdom, the Kiddush Hashem, we say, You are holy and your Name is holy and the holy martyrs of Israel have sanctified and will sanctify again your Name. They will suffer all manner of death and torture for the sanctification of your Name and for the deliverance of the nation of Israel.

But there are things that can be done to anyone. And so we are leaving: everything.

We are leaving the Rhine, our adopted city, our home, our congregation—whoever is left alive. We are leaving our contracts and our positions, we are leaving for Poland and the East as once we left the Holy Land for Babylon, as one day we will leave the East for America or the Holy Land, eretz Yisrael. We go, mostly at night, until we come to the next Jewish town. We abide with them for awhile and leave again. Always east.

The wheels of the cart are singing now. One of the wheels has a twisted spoke, another has a brace where the rim cracked, so the cart bobs and the joints are slowly coming loose. In a day or two they'll need a wheelwright. Twelve miles today to a town whose lord is well known for protecting Jews . . . at a price.

Eyes shut, Michael becomes fearful for them and for himself. If these ancestors die, he will never be. No Michael, because no Jacob Goldstein, and what about those families Jacob Goldstein helped almost six centuries later? They will simply be fuel for Hitler's ovens, rot turned to rich soil in a forest pit outside Kishinev. This man, his wife, his son-in-law, his daughter, have to reach Poland, where the king-who-is-good-to-the-Jews, who needs merchants like Shmuel and Menachem, will protect them. Word has reached them along with goods from Hungary, from Turkey.

Towards noon a band of peasants comes along the road on their way home from the fields. They might be friendly—who knows? They look exhausted, not in the mood to kill Jews. Thick, reddened faces. But Michael can't take the chance. He diverts them with words. Here, rest yourselves, this way, come on, good folk. Look, I have wine for you. Oh, wonderful wine. And a story. Let me tell you a story. They troop after him, singing. He provides a feast, feeding them on words, an old Jewish trick, and they eat and sleep. A horse and cart rattle by over the road. No one wakes.

A fragile thread runs taut between this Jewish merchant family in 1349 and Michael Kuperman, 1994; they are precious; the line through the centuries so fragile . . . as the plane touches down to the high singing of wheels skidding and the shrieking whine of the engines revving up in reverse.

Dogs

Michael tries to avoid Bloomington, Indiana. Jonathan, too. That's Steve's province. You take a flight to Indianapolis and rent a car, drive about fifty miles of flat, straight highway until it starts to curve and rise and dip into Bloomington, "All-American City." Tree-lined streets, a big small-town, a little city, still active as a center for limestone quarries and mills but it's the University, that's where the energy is. Their laboratory—Fusion's training facility—is in Bloomington because of Indiana University. Steve had connections with their computer science people, and he found a facility they could buy cheaply. Bloomington is well situated for them— close enough to a lot of places, especially Chicago, to make it easy to bring computer people from corporations for the training in using Fusion systems.

But it depresses Michael every time he has to come, two, three times a year to show support for the troops. It feels so drab, especially in December, light coat of snow on all the buildings, mounds of bulldozed snow along the sidewalks. He drives past the old-fashioned courthouse square—it's like a city in the South, old stone courthouse, patches of snow, pigeons. A Starbucks has made it to Bloomington. And a Gap.

At a refurbished two-story warehouse Fusion's built a lab and training facility. A group of tech support directors from a chain of video stores are at work today in one of the classrooms. Jonathan cruises the cubicles, shaking hands, listening—he's got a listening posture Michael's always admired: head bowed, tilted to one side as if to decrease the distance your words travel, head rocking a little, yes, yes. Not—like most people—waiting for his turn to talk: just listening. At times Michael's tried to imitate his friend; it's made him quieter, more patient. But Michael's own way is to dance and console. A shoulder-toucher, shoulder-patter, he touches and watches the screen as Okike, Dmitri, Tony Kim or one of the interns shows off a new protocol, some link that will lop away a dozen steps, flip between screens and programs in an instant.

Now Steve is ready for them; they follow him into his office cluttered with thick loose-leaf books of documentation, folders, loose paper. Wasn't the computer going to create a "paperless office"?—there's more paper now than ever. He'd know Steve's office from all others by the smell of garlic—lunch, breakfast— just as Michael says morning prayers, Steve does garlic on whole-wheat toast at six AM. Then there's the poster of a crew race on the Charles, and the unpainted counter running three sides of the room, loaded with consoles, printers. Paper.

Jonathan sits on the edge of Steve's desk and sips coffee from a thermos. Michael clears away the papers from a side chair. This is Steve's realm. They know he feels it. He's not the kid among them, they're not the uncles. He's the magician.

Steve takes from his laptop case a CD-ROM diskette between thumb and forefinger. "This is it. It's something you should see. I want us to see it together. It's already been downloaded onto my hard drive. I'm . . . working on it."

Michael sighs. "So that disk you're holding—something you downloaded? It's Chemicorp? I want you to know—we're out of the contract with them."

"Contract! I'm not talking about contracts. Who gives a damn for contracts? The sons of bitches. Wait till you see. Dirty sons of bitches."

"I know. But what's to be done? We've given the information to Commerce, Steve."

"*Not this information.*"

Jonathan silences Michael with a brush of fingers.

Steve boots up. And now they don't say anything. Michael realizes how unusual this is, to sit with Steve in silence. Like a meditation, the three of them, waiting. Or not-quite silence, because even silent, Steve murmurs thoughts, murmurs so that only the peaks of words, an occasional sibilant or voiced consonant rises above Steve's thick breathing. It's being privy to the incomprehensible stream of his consciousness.

Emitting garlic and sweat, he tugs Michael toward the screen. Over Michael's shoulder Steve clicks on **Experiment-Canine.3**, and an icon of an hour glass replaces the arrow. Now a title page—a date, **Experiment-Canine.3** again. Steve scrolls down: a chart of figures, a second chart, **subject #** along the horizontal, **time** on the vertical axis.

"Wait."

Steve clicks on an icon: **Demonstration.** Now we see a film of the experiment: a white room, steel plate halfway up the walls, filmed through a one-way mirror. We see three dogs, one of them large, prowling the room. At the bottom of the screen a digital clock has been superimposed. At 00:30 a word flashes, flashes: **Gas Released**. 00:40. 00:45. Now, the animals go crazy, careening from wall to wall to find a way out. 1: 00: the smallest dog has stopped running and is in spasm, now he's down, legs twitching. 1:20, the next. 1:40 the third, all down now, all twitching. The camera rolls on. 2:30: no movement. The frame freezes. Steve clicks on the chart. This time Michael looks more carefully. Fifteen subjects—so there must have been more "trials." And a graph: in the vertical axis, time; on the horizontal, weight.

"Oh, Steve."

"And then there's this letter." He clicks again: a letter from Pell Trading to His Excellency General François Djouti:

> These trials are samples of an experiment carried out last June 5th on fifteen canine subjects. Mean elapsed time to jnd effect, 1 min., 11 sec. To termination, 2 minutes,

16 seconds. Dosage held at .03 milligrams per cubic meter air. This should answer the questions you had.

> Respectfully,
> Dr. Allan McNeil

"I came upon this *off-system*."

"Off-system?"

"You don't want to know."

"Oh, my God, Steve."

In the silence Michael clicks onto the demonstration and lets it run again. He's not seeing dogs. He's seeing with mind's eye *through* the pixels. He is equipped—not by his own virtue—to see through the one-way mirror and white walls and the trembling flesh of these dogs, to a village in sunlight. Chalk-white stucco over stone and cement block. Planes come from the sun, so are invisible. The drone brings people to the steps of their houses. Now the town square flowers red and black; walls crack and rise, stone and mortar rain down. People run from houses, screaming. And now, with the families away from shelter, a second wave of planes comes in, and this time there is only a puff and hiss, and yellow clouds, thick, descending like fog. Women are weeping, howling, reaching for children's hands; he sees a few villagers stagger above the fog, reaching the hillside, howling. From the village below, silence.

Now, again, he hears the murmur of Steve Planck thinking. Jonathan's resting his forehead on his fingers. Steve hands the disk to Michael, who puts it in his jacket breast pocket like a pistol.

"A little window into hell," Jonathan says and rubs his eyes.

"So what are we going to do, Jonathan? Mike? We've *got* to do something. Don't we? These dogs—you can't run an experiment like this."

"No . . . No, you can't run an experiment like this," Jonathan says, congregant answering prayer leader.

"I brought you down here because you're different here. Both of you. Maybe you can think straighter."

"Stop being so damned condescending," Jonathan says. "Of *course* we'll talk to the FBI. Give them the disk—we'll give them the disk and try to stay out of it. Is that your point? Of *course*. Today."

Steve holds up a hand. "Good. But here's the thing. I don't *want* us to talk to the FBI. Not yet. A few more days. I'm almost there. I'm working on something. *We're* working on something." He picks up the phone, punches numbers. "Tony?" While they wait, he buries his face in a file cabinet, comes up with a folder.

Michael smells his own sweat. "Jonathan? You okay?"

"Yeah, I'm okay. Glad I'm not a dog."

Tony Kim comes in. He's been here in Bloomington while this story has been in Boston, but he's important to Fusion. He's Korean, grew up in Seoul, came to MIT on a scholarship and never went back. Now he's brought his parents. He's thin, long-faced, not like most Koreans Michael has known—more Chinese.

He takes them through the plan:

"The principle, we got that down, basic software strategy we know, but awful lot of code to write. I work with an intern. We make a kind of virus. And some virus, man! State-of-art Black Plague. We slip this into the Chemicorp computer system—actually, Orion sub-system. No good to go after the whole Chemicorp system—we'd be swamped by so much information."

Steve takes over. "See, it's a kind of a Trojan horse. You know—you let it in, it ruins your day? But with a twist, Mike. We slip it in, encrypted the way the rest of the Orion data is. Okay? It does no damage to files, no damage to anyone's hard drive. Its action's invisible, okay?—and—I'm pretty sure, Tony's pretty sure—undetectable by current virus-protection programs. If they hunt, I guess they'd find it. But not right away. What it does—*all* it does—is copy all e-mail addresses from the host hard drive. Invisibly it sends all electronic communications back to us."

"And next," Tony says, "the virus tags along with all messages, enters each *new* computer and sends back *its* list as well."

"Sends *where*?" Jonathan asked.

"Well, that's *it. Where?* The FBI, I guess," Steve said. "*Somewhere.* That's why I want to wait a few days. So we can give it to them *in place.* The information does *us* no good. But the FBI, Treasury, whoever—they'll be getting a direct line into Orion."

"You keep saying 'Orion.' What *is* Orion?" Michael asks. "*Who* is Orion?"

"I don't know, exactly. It's not top management—at least I'm pretty sure. It's a marketing group within the corporation. I'll know pretty soon."

Jonathan grunts a kind of laugh. "You, you're like a teenaged hacker, you know that? You *love* it, this is right up your alley. And how can we say no—after seeing those dogs, how can we say no?"

"How *can* you say no?"

"To a little industrial sabotage?"

"Right."

Jonathan nods and closes his eyes. No one interrupts. "We can't. Problem is—hell, Steve, all right, the *real* problem is I'm scared what this could do to Fusion. But there's this, too: the FBI can't build a case on evidence obtained this way, no warrant."

"Still . . . it could be useful to them," Michael says. He says it for both of them—for himself, for Jonathan. He wonders whether Rosenthal has ever seen those dogs.

Glad I'm not a dog.

CHAPTER SEVEN

Meeting A Very Handsome Man

Martha Corey is delighted with the story.

"You know," Deborah says, placing to one side of her salad the green onions, "it's really nothing Michael's responsible for. He can hardly help it, can he, if his father's something of a lowlife." She stares at those green onions that have somehow become Ira Cooper.

"What I love," Martha says, almost *sings* to capture the theater of it, "is how Michael felt all this guilt, oh, his poor father, poor papa, alone somewhere in the granite canyons, eating his old heart out, pants smelling of pee. And lo and behold—the old guy is living with his *mistress*. Not a 'girlfriend,' Deb. When it's a thirty-year affair, we're talking old-fashioned serious mistress here. *Did* he say thirty or did I make that up?"

"Thirty. He doesn't really know. At least thirty."

"Now. What about you? What about your own 'outside' friendship?"

"It's odd. I don't frankly know what's going on with me," Deborah says. "Larry called, and I put him off. You know what it felt like?—*Oh, yes, Larry Ackerman, I forgot.* Martha!—I haven't given him one moment's thought lately, and this is a man I'd been thinking of very seriously. Very. I'd actually been imagining being married to him."

It's turned fiercely cold, just a few days before Christmas, so they've met for lunch at the Charles Hotel.

There are people who make you feel good just to be in their presence. Martha Corey does that for Deborah. Even the way she dresses—understated, simply, a silk blouse, a tweed skirt. She has a wonderful color sense, a palette of pastels, and she speaks in the subdued classy drawl that's almost a quote from films of the thirties; it's conscious of its own affectation. Deborah doesn't mind at all. She likes the way it lets her, Deborah, feel mischievous, witty, and grand. And—let's admit it, all right?—it's always, since they were fifteen years old, been a little comforting that Martha has a plain, full, good-natured face.

"Look, my dear," she says, holding the stem of her wine glass between thumb and forefinger, using the glass to make her point. "From what you tell me, your life with Michael is full of—oh, you know—*drama*. This business about what's his name—"

"Rosenthal. Myron Rosenthal."

"Rosenthal. And you're married to a man who's got this thing about good and evil, who sits in a prayer shawl groaning prayers. So no wonder. Larry is ordinary life. Untried, I know, but ordinary—with—I understand—a terrific sloop. And ordinary life is bound to appear trivial. But it's not, you know. It's profound. No, I *mean* that, don't laugh. After all, it's a question of how you want to spend your days, day by day, for the next forty years. It's whom you want to speak with over breakfast."

"I don't speak with anyone over breakfast. Hardly even Karen or Ari."

"Oh, *please*."

"Martha, are you saying I'm not going to live a good life staying with Michael?"

"No! Not at all. In fact, you know, having met your Larry, I happen to *prefer* Michael. Even *sans* sloop. Michael's lovely . . . oh, you know, a little bit too solemn for my tastes, but sweet. And Larry?—but what's the difference? *I'm* not marrying either one. I'm saying, *Don't underestimate the ordinary.* . . . Oh," she stops. "Aha. Deborah? Don't look, do *not* look, but there's a man across the room, diagonally over your left shoulder. Not at *all* ordinary. Oh my God, you see how he's looking at you?"

"How can I *see* if I can't *look*?"

"Well, look *casually, accidentally.* The art of the casual glance: *lost!*" She lets out a long musical breath. "The well-tailored gray suit. You see? Now he sees me looking. So of course he's *never* looked at you at all, he's been looking elsewhere all this time. *You are a* very *handsome man, whoever you are.* Well, and *you*, Deb, you *do* look lovely, I think."

"Thank you."

"Drama becomes you. It *does*, I think. You look different. Do you know that?"

"Oh, Martha, it's so late, I had no idea—I've got to met Karen in ten minutes."

They kiss goodbye in the lobby of the Charles. Martha takes the garage elevator down to her car; Deborah is off to Harvard Square. With Martha gone, it's as if the Technicolor balloon they fill and float when they're together sags and sinks, and their friendship, instead of lofting her spirits for hours as it usually does, seems tedious, shabby. Tinsel.

But there's music in the Square. Santas ring hand bells. Reindeer pull a sleigh full of packages dancing from a wire hung above the street. It's crisp, cold, gray but exciting in the Square; a shopping frenzy is on, hooded parkas and woolen hats rushing one way with bags, rushing the other way with bags. *She* should be frantic; she has a million little Christmas presents to buy.

Near the Booksmith she thinks she spots that man again. Isn't it the same man? She can't see the suit under the overcoat. And she didn't get a very good look before—Martha wouldn't let her. But *isn't* it? Is he possibly that guy in polymer science she flirted with at the Guilfords' party? We talked about the Bosnians? Is he following her? No one has done *that* in years. She smiles, stops and looks around. He's disappeared.

As she approaches the Coop, she hears a voice right behind her: "Ms. Schiff? Mrs. Kuperman?" She spins around. At once she's uneasy. Fear must show in her eyes. He smiles and, like an old friend, lays a hand on her arm. "It's all right. Just give me a minute's time. No, really."

"I'm meeting my daughter."

"I *know*. I know you are. Let's step over to the stationery counter?" And, confident she'll follow or wanting to indicate that she's not his prisoner, he walks a little ahead of her. It gives her a chance to look him over. He's about forty, tall, a strong man, with salt-and-pepper wavy hair, a patrician face and a wool overcoat with fur collar that *cost*. Martha's right—he *is* attractive. Maybe she *has* met him at a party. There was someone she spoke to about helping an immigrant Bosnian family—didn't she agree to volunteer some way or other? And maybe he just *happened* to see her at the restaurant, in the square?

Oh, she wants it to be innocent. He's so relaxed, so distinguished.

The man rests an elbow on the counter and says, "First, let me assure you that you're in no danger. I simply want you to understand something and communicate it to your husband. My clients are disturbed about his peculiar interest in corporate details that don't concern him."

"You're speaking about Mr. Rosenthal?"

"No. In fact, I'm not."

"But Chemicorp—you represent Chemicorp."

"Actually not. But we have common interests."

"Why are you talking to me? I have no authority to speak for my husband."

They're in the eddy of mingling streams of Christmas shoppers, but no one has time or interest to listen. Handel—a muddy *Music for the Royal Fireworks*—the high trumpets blur in and out of the shoppers' voices. They could hardly have more privacy.

"Mistakes may have been made. My clients wish to avoid further complications. I could have said these things over the phone, but it makes an important point this way. You understand?"

"No. Do you mean it demonstrates our vulnerability?"

"We are asking Mr. Kuperman that he avoid pursuing the matter. Mr. Greene as well. I'll be in contact with Jonathan Greene."

Deborah hears the music of this correct speech without analyzing—the subjunctive, *avoid*; *wish* rather than *want*. "You haven't told me whom you represent."

"My clients are from abroad. I don't wish to make a mystery of it, but I've been asked to represent them under conditions of anonymity. I apologize."

"And are you suggesting repercussions? This is a warning, I take it?"

"Your son gets out of school early today, isn't that right?" he looks at his watch. "I'm sure you're in a hurry to get on with your shopping. I certainly don't mean to make you late." Now he looks past her, points with his eyes. "Your daughter is just walking into the Coop now—she doesn't see you yet. I suspect you're not interested in introducing me. Here. Take my card. If you think of a way for Mr. Kuperman and Mr. Greene to assure us of their cooperation, I would appreciate that."

He turns away and is swallowed up by shoppers.

"Karen? Karen—over here!"

It's as if she'd been told a moment ago she has a tumor. Is it benign, doctor? The doctor looks past her shoulder at a noncommittal painting. *We'll . . . have to run a biopsy before we can be sure . . .* and everything becomes permeated with the music of terminal illness. All conversations become charged with irony. Posters for travel, love songs, business deals. In a few minutes a new story supplants the stories of Personal Success. It takes time for the new story to pluck out of our lives just the right elements, but the process begins.

Karen looks ruddy and strong in clean jeans, holding large bags with handles and wearing a backpack fat with presents. Her red hair, as she whips off her cashmere hat, flies up with static electricity, expresses the same energy as the swing of her body through the crowded first floor of the Coop: *Let's shop!* They hug and Karen, oblivious to Deborah's mood, is full of news: gossip about classmates, a concert, oh, and Jason Koren.

And Deborah transforms everything. It's the gap: *I* know; *she* doesn't *know*: it makes everything Karen says *ironic*. It's *not* like a terminal illness. Rather it's like knowledge of, say, the Nazis taking over Boston, freezing bank accounts, telling all Jews to appear with small suitcase at Back Bay Station in the morning. And then someone who doesn't know speaks to you about hairstyles or the opera or plans for a Ph.D.

Deborah is suddenly furious. Terrified, but even more, enraged. She's glad she didn't try to appease the bastard.

Michael's somewhere between here and Bloomington. How can she reach him?

Karen takes her mother by the elbow and walks toward the toiletries in the back. "You know, Mom, I wish we could just all-out *do Christmas*. Without guilt. Look. I have to keep presents in the closet, I'm supposed to have presents for you guys but not too much enthusiasm and no lights, no tree. I think it's a great holiday, Christmas, a fun holiday, and Dad gets to be a Kosher pickle about it. We ought to go on strike."

Expecting her mother to groan and sympathize, that's all. But Deborah is grim, and when Deborah sees Karen looking up at her, curious, she says, "Your father's a serious man. Honey, there's things we haven't talked about. It's about a client of your father's. I'll explain. We're a little concerned. It's not about money. Your father discovered something seriously illegal. No. Worse than illegal, Karen. Much worse. So let's not worry about Christmas. All right? Anyway, your father *doesn't* make a big deal about presents. Where did you get that idea? You can do whatever you want, Karen."

"Great. Now I'm really in the mood. Merry Christmas."

Deborah, in her terminal condition, just takes one of the shopping bags, takes Karen's hand, fakes a smile. "Come on, honey. I'm *desperate* for your help shopping, my dear. Please. Let's divide up the names. So—you enjoy Christmas, do you? Well, you just wait till you see my list!"

Two Glasses of Wine

As soon as Deborah spots the headlights of the taxi making a U-turn out front, she pours two glasses of white wine and puts them down on a side table, opens the door. "We have to talk, Michael," she says before he can put down his attaché case and his laptop. "I've been trying to reach you everywhere. My God!"

And she had. At work, on his cell, at the lab in Bloomington. By now she's built up a terrific pressure of interior drama, as if he were *refusing* to be available, *refusing* to call or answer calls. This beautiful foyer—the Artimide lamp that cost $1400, the 4 × 6 gold and blood-red rug from Iran, and past that the cherry and mahogany inlaid flooring whose pattern gives the illusion of a third dimension—boils in dark turbulence as if she's on a bad drug trip. It's terrible for her. Her eyes dart everywhere. "Sit with me. Michael! You don't know what I've been through." She keeps her voice low, though upstairs Karen's playing the stereo too loud to hear them. The thump of a bass vibrates the house like a heartbeat. "At the Coop," she tells him, "at the Coop in Harvard Square, a man was following me. Here—have a glass of wine. Sit down."

"So a man was following you," he prompted, sitting on the couch. "Well, you *are* a beautiful woman—"

"*Don't*. He stopped me. A lawyer. Kevin Murtaugh. I have his card. Here—see? Engraved, letterpress, not just printed. It was a clear threat, but terribly polite and all that. He knew everything. Knew I was waiting for Karen. He knew when Ari gets out of *school*, for godsakes. He asked me to tell you to back off. To keep your nose out. You understand, Michael?" As he starts to answer, she says, "I don't want to hear it. This isn't a moral dilemma, whatever it is you're facing, this is your family, Michael. Just get *finished* with this Rosenthal. Let them know, let them understand you have no further interest."

(She can hear the bravura; though she'd deny it furiously, it's as if she knows she's acting. Earlier, she got in touch with Jessie, who called her back between patients. And with Jessie, why Deborah was calm! They were able to laugh. "These guys," Deborah said.)

But in fact, Michael isn't making trouble. He's replaying what she said. *This is your family.* He says it over to himself. *This is your family.* Sitting in the soft-lit living room on the plush taupe velvet couch, he sips his wine, pours another glass, tells her, "I like it— you think we're 'family,' Deb. That's what we are. Family. Of *course* I'll drop it. It makes me as frightened as you are. We'll let the FBI handle things."

"The FBI?"

He's silent, *not* telling her about the dogs. He rehearses, *I saw something pretty terrible today* . . . but thinks better of it. "Listen— what about taking the kids out of town for a few days?"

"The kids? If it comes to that, they'd be better off staying at friends' houses. I'm leaving for New York day after tomorrow."

"I know. Why not take them with you?" The two glasses of wine let him run his fingers along the sleeve of the taupe cashmere sweater he bought her for Hanukkah.

She looks down at his fingers but doesn't brush them off. "But that's so hard, Michael. I'll think about it. But thank you for being reasonable. So. You'll give those people a sign? Let them know you're not going to get involved?"

"Oh, I'll let them know all right."

He's not exactly lying. As she calls a take-out place for chicken, he goes into his study, picks up messages, including the message from Steve, and calls Myron Rosenthal.

Steve Downloads Evil . . .

. . . *downloads evil,* and when he's finished, Steve links in to a CD burner, puts text, data, videos on a CD-ROM, makes two copies. It's late; with everyone gone home, place feels like the warehouse it used to be. The cubicle walls muffle the old warehouse echoes, but he hears them. He has to stop and rest. He keeps an exercise mat rolled up in the corner of his office; in an open space between cubicles and classrooms, he lies down. He hasn't the words. Jonathan would take shelter in words about Jesus; Michael would mumble a blessing in Hebrew and close his eyes. Fiona would close her eyes, too, and imagine a shimmering, pulsing light that could heal her spirit or defeat the darkness. Illusions? Maybe. But the things Steve has seen would remain. Steve has no container for this evil.

He stretches out on the mat and looks up at the high steel ceiling, bare except for ductwork and electric lines. His eyes get used to the dark. Maybe he should call Fiona and ask her to meet him somewhere for the weekend. Usually, he likes being alone. He doesn't understand people who say they're lonely. But this is loneliness like a weight of loneliness and evil. Machines in their cubicles, he sees their silhouettes; they don't seem user-friendly. Fiona would say they're inhabited by bad spirits—which is foolish. They're *not* inhabited—which is worse.

He can't rest, so he goes back to his office and puts in a call to Michael. To Michael's machine he says, "Listen. I've got an appointment in Indianapolis day after tomorrow with the Feds. Call me if you want to be there with me. We're in *deep*, all sorts of stuff, I've downloaded a video—you won't believe it, man, FedEx-ing it to you tomorrow and then we'll talk. It's fuckin' scary, Mike. Makes what you saw before like a Disney cartoon. Oh—and by the way, our program—you remember—well, I think it's going to do the job." He thinks about Geoffrey Slade, telling Michael about Slade, but promised Slade he wouldn't.

It was bizarre, the way they met. No *chance* meeting—of course not. He's rowing on the Charles River, taking it easy, building up to a sprint—this was yesterday morning, Sunday morning, and he's taking his last hour on the river before coming back to Bloomington for a couple of weeks. For December, it's warm, sun shining, but of course nobody else is crazy enough to be out. So he has the river to himself. Suddenly there's a one-man scull, an elegant wooden beauty, a King, built in Putney, giant of a rower hulking over this javelin of a single scull, six-five, six-six, who could row (okay, if not circles) *ovals* around Steve, pleasure just to watch his swing, watch him glide the river. Guy rows through him in two strokes, flies by, heads up river towards the dog-leg bend near B. U., then down again. Now he stops, waits, balancing, oars raised, as if he were in a rowboat; he comes abreast of Steve's scull and grins. On the gray, flat water, the two sculls float downstream, Steve's scull of hi-tech fiberglass, blue fading into white, Geoffrey Slade's of oiled dark-wood. Steve's black brows lift up in a cartoon of surprise.

To himself, Steve says, *Wow—amazing. What club is this guy with?* To Slade, he just nods. "You're a hell of a strong rower."

"Thanks. It's what I *do,* you see." He clamps the boats together with his hand on the oarlocks, and they rock together—it's a chilly, wet morning but Steve wants to talk with that good a rower. "I'm Geoffrey Slade. Last chance of the season perhaps, a bit difficult to row on ice. You are Steve Planck, aren't you?"

"Yeah. Slade. Sure. I know your name. Who you row with?"

"Well, with *you,* actually. Scull borrowed for the occasion. It seems we share another interest—in a loathsome business enterprise that's been going on. Michael Kuperman mentioned you a couple of nights ago. He told me some marvelous things. Would you like to try a sprint together?"

"You're kidding. You think I could keep up with *you!*"

"I'll keep *down* with you, then. Let's pull in at the Union Boat Club dock. All right? I'd like to talk to you. By the by, you're a really strong rower, but you work at it unduly hard. No offence? You put such demand on those wonderful strong arms and legs of yours. Result is a bit rough at the catch. I wish you'd try for more of a swing, l o n g recovery, swift stroke, you see? L o n g recovery, swift stroke. A fuller, easier glide, all right? Let your boat do more of the work."

No offense at all. He knew Slade's name. To discover Slade was coach of the Oxbridge crew gave him enormous credibility for Steve. And there's no lying about skill like his nor about his ability to spot problems in position or stroke. "Those thumbs, Steven. Your finish starboard will be cleaner if you just move your thumb a little further under the oar. You don't mind, do you?"

Mind? It was like being back at MIT, Slade one dream of a coach. "Elbows, my dear, closer to the body, not like a chicken, you see?—*that's* it. Now let's pick up the pace a bit, shall we? We'll close with a power forty, but remember that swing . . . that's right, here we go." Hiss of the hulls cutting water. Steve's kind of music. Trying too hard at the end, Steve splashed a spray of near-freezing water over himself.

Stepping out onto the wet, sloping boards, Slade wasn't even winded. Steve needed time to recover. Slade took from his bag a couple of pair of sweats, and they put them on. Sitting on the sunny dock, they talked about last year's Head-of-the-Charles races, about new boat designs, new computer programs to form and test those designs. And then computer systems. And Chemicorp. And General Djouti.

Slade was particularly interested in the virus.

Jonathan was right, Steve thinks; I *am* a hacker, a snoop; Slade must have sensed it. He had blankets, a thermos of hot coffee for them to share. They sat on the dock wrapped in blankets, children playing Indians, and Slade told him about Djouti. "This virus—you see, I want it to get to Djouti—and more important, I want it to get to his trading partners in Marseilles."

"That's cool. It can happen. Michael must have told you—I've got access to the Chemicorp systems. Soon as it's ready, I'll plant it."

"Yes, precisely. But beyond that—well, perhaps a little more *direct*—I want you to send a corrupted disk with new data—really, Steve, it doesn't even matter *what* data—to Michael. Then again, the important thing is, the virus should be planted in it. And don't mention me, you see, I'd rather he didn't know. I want him to act naturally. *Not* that I suspect Michael of anything, no, no, not at all—it's this: I believe someone will catch on. He's already spoken to this Myron Rosenthal fellow. Michael's so upset. I'm certain someone will be watching him. And if they intercept a disk, why then, we'll have them. We can listen in on their electronic communications. The other night, when Michael told me about this virus, well, I was delighted, you know."

"It's pretty damn elegant," Steve said, grinning.

"You keep in touch. I'll give you my telephone numbers. And please, Steve—*don't* get heroic on us and call the FBI. I'll be the go-between. My dear man, I don't want anything to happen to you. You understand? I'd like to see you at Henley one day. Now—I know where you store your lovely boat," Geoffrey Slade said, rubbing his fingers along the gunwale. "Come, let's row back to the Cambridge Boat Club. I'll stay just ahead and observe, and—if you like—give you a few suggestions when we dock."

Then, today, Monday, here in Bloomington, he went back to probing the encrypted files at Chemicorp. And this is what he found. This is what he found that makes him sit at his desk shaking his head. It's all on the disk in his fingers. Data from hell.

Steve leaves a message on Fiona's machine. Monday: it's the night Fiona takes Miranda to rock-climbing class at the Y. He walks through the lab turning out lights, checking doors, locking up. He'll spend a couple of hours eating chicken wings and talking basketball at a bar, get this thing off his heart. Heartburn. *But oh, Christ, oh, yes, we are definitely gonna* get *those bastards.*

Jews at the Athenæum

It's possible, isn't it, that Myron Rosenthal, of Chemicorp, is Michael's relative? Ashkenazi Jews are all related somehow—by blood or by marriage. Rosenthal's family is from Lubin, but his grandfather came west from the Pale. A *landsman.*

Rosenthal sees himself as a "loyal" Jew. He doesn't say "good" Jew, maybe he's too tough-minded to be a "good" Jew—though he believes he is not without merit. But certainly a loyal Jew? Didn't his daughter Julie do a magnificent job for her Bat Mitzvah? The new synagogue—could that have been built without his help? Not just his money (oh, that, too)—he was at meetings night after night, whenever he wasn't traveling for Chemicorp. When he is uneasy, when he needs bolstering like this, he sees behind his eyes the new synagogue, Yom Kippur last year, sees half the Jews on the North Shore crammed in, rows of folding chairs in front and on the sides, and he pressing past people to climb to the bima, and touching the fringes of his tallis to the Torah and kissing the fringes, with Carol,

Julie, and his mother there to watch, go take the honor of the first aliyah. In a few years, when he retires, he may have time to be the president of the congregation.

And now this fellow Kuperman insists on seeing him, this Michael Kuperman, self-righteous sonofabitch—as if he thinks it's angels—angels who come down from the heavens and hand Fusion Software checks every month? Does Kuperman—and what about that loudmouth Jonathan Greene—do they scrutinize every company to see how Fusion software is being used? *If we sell chemicals to a government, and with those chemicals, the government puts down a revolution, this is not something I'm going to brag about to my rabbi. But there are things you do.*

What could be so important? But Myron Rosenthal has suggested, if they have to meet, let it be at the Boston Athenæum so they can talk privately. As if he *needed* to take out an hour from his day. Something that can't be said on the phone? But you know, this guy Kuperman—all right, he may be a self-righteous pain in the ass, but . . . there's something Rosenthal likes about him. Last time they met he'd played tough guy to Kuperman's idealist. There are things he could have said—Kuperman doesn't know the half of it. And frankly, Rosenthal is *bothered*—he wouldn't give Kuperman the satisfaction, but all right, it's true. He's spoken to people in New York and St. Louis. That's all he can do.

He's a businessman.

The Boston Athenæum is a private library, with reading rooms, stacks, exhibits—a private club at the foot of Beacon Street. Rosenthal has been a member for years. There's a panache about the Athenæum—its high brocaded ceilings, its Renaissance palazzo facade—Rosenthal just thinks of the style as "fancy," thinks of the place as "classy." Well, why not?—it was established by Boston society in the 1840's. Imagine a Cabot or Lowell a hundred years back learning that someone with a name like Myron Rosenthal would ever be a member!

Rosenthal gets there early, leaving Kuperman's name downstairs so that Kuperman would be coming to *him*, and near the wrought iron spiral library stairs in the corner, in a wingback chair in a bright alcove, he keeps the tall window behind him so that Kuperman will be forced to look into the light; and he waits. It's pleasant to sit in the high wingback leather chair. He thinks, Chemi-corp should have our next function here. A layer of fat presses into the sides of the chair. It may not look so svelte, he thinks, but, you know, it's *comfortable*, his extra flesh. Except when his family nags him into a long walk on the beach and he can feel the extra baggage he has to carry around. It doesn't look so dignified when he wears work pants. But now? Here, sheathed in soft wool and surrounded by leather, he's *portly*.

Or so he thinks, and certainly no one he knows would tell him differently. Rosenthal sits decorously in this decorous space, but his face shows everything. There's a bagginess tugging at the flesh under his eyes that makes him look dog-like and sets his eyes deep. But it was unavoidable. He needed the flesh there to hold and enwrap the thick grief he couldn't swallow, there since childhood. He could tell you stories about his father, who went from dress shop to department store *schlepping* a line of blouses, skirts, he could tell you the story of a night of smashed mirrors and humiliations, but what's the difference? We all have such stories, we all have these bags under eyes or twitches or headaches to keep us balanced, cane for a cripple, and as if the work of carrying these thick bags justified it, Myron Rosenthal clenches his jaws, and the scalenes of his heavy neck are taut in anger: repayment.

Michael knows the Athenæum from private functions held there; he's always admired it. Now, coming across the lovely book-lined room, shaking hands with this fat *grubyom*, this peasant Rosenthal, and taking a seat, he's barely aware of the place. He's barely aware of Myron Rosenthal. No small talk. "Look," Michael starts. "Tell me: are you aware *who* this General Djouti is really buying for?"

Not waiting, he tells Rosenthal the real story and listens to the denial he expects: *That's impossible, as a matter of fact, I've met Djouti, and he's interested in his own country. Do you really think I'd have anything to do with terrorists? I know. You hear rumors.*

And Michael pauses, looks deep into his eyes. He expected a denial—but not this kind of denial. He himself is a poor liar; other people are capable of looking you in the eye and telling you *No* when it's *Yes*, *Black* when it's *White*. Unable to lie, he's not confident of his ability to detect a liar. But this morning he's certain. *The bastard is shaken. He's telling me the truth as he knows it. Now Rosenthal's not so sure it is the truth. Oh, he's shaken.* Michael says, "You just check, Mr. Rosenthal, will you? I can see you make a special case when it comes to terrorists. To Israel. And the United States. Am I right? Well. If you really don't know, maybe we can do something. But Mr. Rosenthal, don't tell me you don't know about the dogs. I've seen things. You'd better check."

"I'm not denying there've been experiments conducted. I've heard that in one case dogs were used. But as for General Djouti—you don't know what you're talking about."

"And of course—you had nothing to do with threatening my wife?"

Rosenthal opens his hands, rubs them over the leather table-top. "Threaten? Why would I threaten your wife?"

"That's it, then." Michael can't bring himself to shake Rosenthal's hand. "Don't worry. You tell your employers *I'll* make no trouble, *Jonathan Greene* will make no trouble. You understand? We know nothing." Walking past the reading tables, he already has a headache, feels nausea, is seeing dogs in a sterile white room. He says a blessing to himself, a blessing for the life those chemicals take away.

Rosenthal sits a moment, then stands by the window until he sees Michael walking up Beacon Street toward his office. Now Rosenthal hurries off to locate a telephone.

So Michael will let Geoffrey Slade know that Myron Rosenthal is definitely *not* aware of everything that's going on. And that's it. He'll fulfill his promise to Deborah, wash his hands of filth. The tricky thing will be to get Steve to back off.

He puts it out of his mind most of the day. There's no time to talk to Jonathan. For a minute—as they're walking in to a conference together, Jonathan says, "Jessie's scared. You know anything more?"

"I spoke to Rosenthal—I'm sure he doesn't know about the threat. We'll talk later—I've a lot to tell you."

But the client is there.

When he's in his office alone, a *dybuk* walks into his body without knocking, twists inside his stomach, a silent howl of anxiety.

Deborah calls; he tells her, "I spoke to Rosenthal."

"Michael—you promised!"

"Don't worry. I let him know I won't give them trouble. But Deborah, listen—Rosenthal doesn't know. That scares me. Now I'm scared."

"Doesn't know about the threat?"

"That, too."

"About who's using the product?"

"Right. Not that this makes him any less loathsome. Maybe it's worse—that he can distinguish among victims. But if he doesn't know—"

"Are you all right, Michael?"

"No. Thanks for asking. I mean it—no irony. Thanks."

"Michael? Here's why I called. You won't *believe* who's paying us a visit tonight."

Ira Pays a Visit

Of all nights for the prodigal father to come to them! Ira expects to be met at Route 128 just after five o'clock. But Michael is tied up in meetings and has to send Dennis. It's nine o'clock by the time Dennis drives Michael home. "How'd it go with my father?"

"Your father? What an interesting old gentleman."

"Yes. Yes, definitely interesting."

Dennis laughs. "Tough old guy, huh? You know what he said to me? He said, 'I hope you're getting double-time for working after five.' Protecting my interests. I told him it all works out. . . . I liked your father."

The interesting old gentleman is waiting up for him in the kitchen listening to jazz over the radio. Ira doesn't get up, keeps his eyes on the newspaper.

Michael doesn't have the strength for a fight. "Dad, I had a business meeting."

"Yeah. I know. Deborah convinced me—or you think I'd still be here? When you couldn't find the time to pick up your own father yourself—"

"—On five-hour notice?"

"—when you sent your chauffeur to pick me up, I'll tell you—I was about to turn around and shlepp my carcass straight back to New York." Ira is wearing denims and a turtleneck. He suddenly reminds Michael of this old Greenwich Village beatnik he once knew, a poet, who used to "chair" a table at Rienzi's, a coffee shop on Macdougal. "Anyway, I'm going back tomorrow. This is just to break the ice. . . . Fuck it—you're my son, am I right?"

"Tomorrow?"

"I figured I owed it to my son after he got me out of jail. Oh—I told Deborah about Eleanor. But you'd told her already."

"So? Wasn't that all right?"

"Sure. *Sure*. It's no secret. This is the love of my life we're talking about. Yeah, I mean one of the *two* loves, Mike. But different. I don't frankly give a shit what you think about it."

"That's why you came up?" Michael pours himself a glass of wine. Doesn't offer.

"I figure I owe you an explanation. Then you can take it or leave it."

Michael sits down at the kitchen table under its soft, recessed lighting, and remembers to breathe, ahhh, breathe into his belly, breathe and let his shoulders drop. Michael gets it: his father wants to come off outrageous as he can—take me with my stink or don't take me at all. And now he notices—there is an actual stink. Of what? Old man? Unwashed shirt? My father the Beatnik. At this moment, for Michael, it's balanced, like rainwater at the very top of the Continental Divide; it could go either way: he's so close to saying, *No, no thanks, I know you feel ashamed or embarrassed, so you want to moon me, and frankly, I just don't give a damn. Especially right now. I've got bigger troubles. You, you're a lousy father; you've always been a lousy father. I'll see you next at your funeral.*

So easy to just get rid of it, write him off, a total loss. And yet he's feeling *just* as close to saying okay, okay, not giving a damn what kind of love life the guy has had. Drop it all. No explanations required. "Okay, Dad," he says. "So you love this woman. Eleanor seems like a fine person. I liked her."

"You did? Good. At least you got taste. This is the way it is. Your mother and I, we kind of stopped being husband and wife. You remember what it was like, the arguments? But I always cared about her. She always cared about me. You probably don't believe that."

"I do. Yes."

"Your mother was one terrific woman. Actually," Ira says, as if he's considering his stock portfolio, "I've been very lucky in my choice of women."

Michael laughs. "You think I want to hear that? You're something, Dad. Look—I don't need explanations. Let's just be decent with each other. Okay? Well. It's late. Deborah gave you towels? You need help?"

"*H e l p!*"

This one word, the syllable protracted through descending notes of sarcasm, really gets to Michael. He can hear the italics. *What help have you ever given me?* "Look!" Michael says. "You go somewhere else with your nonsense." Then, quieter, afraid the kids will hear: "I've got a big day tomorrow, Dad. But midday I'll take off, okay? We'll go see Ari at his school if that's all right with you. We'll have a chance to talk. Day after tomorrow, Deb's going down to New York. I'm going to have Dennis drive her and the kids—you can go along, okay?"

"So you're kicking me out?"

"Didn't you just tell me you were leaving *tomorrow*?"

"So you're granting me an extra day?'

"Stop this already. Look. There's things happening—I've gotten mixed up with some rotten people. Bad timing. I need to handle things here." He's about to turn and walk away. But he finds himself stuck at the door to the kitchen. Stuck. He can't leave. He stares at his father, breathing hard. Maybe because it's late at night, maybe because Ira's sitting under the glow of the overhead light while everything else is dark, Michael sees him in a fine precision of vision: the crooked nose, the subtle pockmarks of his cheeks beneath the old-man lines and a shave maybe sixteen hours old. The collar of the turtleneck is ragged, its elasticity gone.

Under the chin there's a wattle he's never noticed.

"Dad? Hey. Come on, let me help you get settled. It's late. You get into bed. If you don't feel like sleeping, there's a TV, you can bring the paper. Get comfortable."

"Yeah, it's pretty late. I've been up since six."

"You been sleeping okay?"

The guest room is on the main floor. It's painted in a warm taupe, there's a wall of bookcases with all sorts of books. Dürer engravings of animals. Tapestried drapes Deborah's mother sent them when she moved into the condo. A nice room. Michael pulls down the covers, puffs up the pillows. Ira thumbs through a book of photographs by Robert Capa.

"Dad? You know, I wanted to talk about your pictures. Your photos. They're really something. I don't think I ever got it—how big a deal they've been to you."

Ira looks up. "That's right, kid—you never got it."

"I like that one of the two cabdrivers arguing after an accident. I saw it down at your corner—in the lunch place? Two guys going at it. Really good, I liked that."

"It's not the two guys. Everybody misses the point. It's the crowd. You remember the crowd in the back, like a frame around the fight? That's the main thing. It's like street theater—very New York. They know it, too, the cabbies. They're pissed, but not oblivious, get me? They're playing the scene for the benefit of that crowd—you can tell, you look close. I like that picture. You want a print? I can make one up for you. Ari'd like it."

"*I'd* like it, Dad. So goodnight, then. You got everything?"

"All set," Ira says. "All set."

So it's ending well. Michael's backing towards the door; he dims the overhead lights and is halfway out when Ira says after him, "When you were a young guy, you were something. Remember the institute in Rochester, Saul Alinsky? You learned community organizing. An idealist. You never had an analysis, but I was proud of you, you were a fighter."

"When I got arrested?"

"That, too. Yeah. But I was thinking, you wanted to help out the people who get pissed on in this country."

"In every country."

"But here is where you happened to be, my friend. You remember the time you organized to save that hospital in Bridgeport? I got a good memory. And then, all that goes out the window."

"Out the window. Goodnight, Dad." Shaking his head, *Enough, enough,* he goes upstairs, tiptoes past Ari's room, whispers "Good night, honey" as he passes Karen's door. He finds the bedroom already dark, Deborah back in their marriage bed, her eyes closed. He slips in beside her.

The Burning Bush

He has no time, but middle of the next day he drives home to get Ira, and they stop by Ari's school in time to see him during recess. "Watch this, Dad," and "Watch this, Grandpa." They watch, Ira tells Ari how impressed he is with his tree climbing, his ability to shoot a basket. "This is a kid needs a hoop," Ira says, and Michael agrees. "You bet—tell that to Deborah, Dad." He decides to try again to talk Deb into letting him put a hoop up over the garage door. Loving the limbs, the grace, of his own child, he feels in the middle of a family line: grandfather, Michael, Ari. Nice. All at once he half-sees a thick cloud of yellow gas descend on the play area, and these children he's known since they were four—Alex, Misha, Zoe, Ben—he sees them caught by the cloud, and Ari stumbling, and Ms. Koenig falling. There's a digital read-out of the seconds elapsing until the yard is still. Meantime the actual yard is anything but still. There's so much shrieking, so much laughter, and he hugs Ari to break the haunt, kisses him and leaves his father with Ari— later Margaret can bring them home.

It's a late night for Michael. The fewer people who remain at Fusion tonight, the more depressed he feels. He spends the late afternoon looking over new contracts, as if nothing else is going on. Jonathan's playing catch-up; they talk for a minute, not about Slade, not about Rosenthal. Steve is out in Bloomington for a couple of days working with technical liaison people from an enter- tainment group. Calling home to pick up messages, Michael hears Steve's voice:

"The package I mentioned should be coming your way tomorrow, Mike. Fed-Exed to your house. A CD-ROM and some print documents. It's worse stuff than what I showed you already. But the good news is this: it's definitely *not Chemicorp.* I mean not the corporation as a whole. It's one part of a *division* of Chemicorp. 'Orion.' So not company policy, okay? Chemicorp itself is going to want to know this. You'll see. It names people who are to be kept out of the loop—Braithwaite, as we expected, also Max Ferguson. . . ."

It's seven-thirty when Michael takes the elevator to the garage.

No matter how late he works, there are people coming and going, but he is alone on the descent from the lobby down to the garage, and he has a daydream: in the dream he sees himself packing a bag. No one else knows. He tells Deborah tonight. In the morning, they drive to the airport. Just a vacation, he tells them. But he's been secreting money in off-shore accounts, and in the plane he tells them, We're never coming back, except for visits. We've bought a fifty-foot sloop, we'll home-school the two of you. And Deborah takes his hand. *I've been waiting for you to do something like this. . . .*

—Except what she'd really do, of course, is laugh. Get on a plane without an itinerary so she'd know what clothes to pack? She'd say he was running away from the world. She'd be telling the truth. What's bad about that?

"Mr. Kuperman, someone left an envelope on your car," Hank says. Michael's called down, the car's running as usual outside the garage office.

The letter's scotch-taped to the windshield of the Lexus.

> There's something you need to know, Mr. Kuperman. Please drive down to Atlantic Avenue in the North End. Stop at the fish market on the waterfront. Across the street, there's a telephone booth at the corner. Park and cross the street and wait for a call. We need to talk. **No need to be afraid**. You know the street; you know it's not deserted. Get to that phone booth as soon as you can.

He thinks, *Geoffrey Slade.* He's the one person who might not want to call him at work or at home. Then: *Or Rosenthal?* But the letter doesn't sound like Rosenthal.

Neither does it sound like Geoffrey Slade.

It's a five-minute drive at this hour. He parks, goes across the street to the phone booth, not a booth really, a plastic shelter for the phone. He's there only a few seconds when the phone rings.

"Yes?"

"Mr. Kuperman?"

"Yes, this is Mr. Kuperman. Who am I talking to?"

"Tell me—there's no one in the car, is there?"

"No one."

"No, there *is* no one in the car. But you see, there *could* be. That's one of the things you need to know. Your son or daughter, your wife. Anyone could be in that car. You could be driving home right now."

"Who is this? Are you trying to threaten me?"

"You can see the car very well, can't you? Keep your eye on it."

"Yes, yes, what about it?" Michael peers, as if there's something he's not noticing. But in a moment, it becomes obvious. There's no explosion: silently, black smoke curls up from the hood; he cringes against the booth. A flash of light now, flame snakes from under the hood, flames from everywhere—doors, undercarriage.

"What are you doing? My car—"

"An electrical fire. It's just an electrical fire."

"You bastards!"

"You haven't listened. This is a demonstration. We're demonstrating how dangerous it would be to continue to concern yourself with the sale of chemicals. Look, Mr. Kuperman: you *are* permitted to get out of your contract. In fact, now we *insist* on that. Then you drop the matter. Next time, it won't be just an electrical fire. You understand?"

There's a click, dead air. He calls 911, but before anyone answers, he hears sirens, fire engines—and hangs up. Fire has spread to something in the interior—the seat fabric? Michael's blood is thumping fast in his temples, but he feels calm. *Understand?*—oh, sure he understands. Who wouldn't? We've been taught by the movies. He stares at the car, burning. He wonders: did they set it to go off after a certain number of minutes? Is someone nearby with a remote?

There's something final, definitive about this. He's been taught by the movies how to experience this moment.

I'm no hero.

The paint is scorched.

He whispers in Hebrew the prayer for being in a place where God has performed a miracle. *She'asa li nays bamakom hazeh.* He stares at that car, as if it were not a warning but a mystery. But what's so mysterious? What's the miracle?

He has been permitted to continue living his life.

Kuperman's Fire. The burning bush? The way God is present in a village being destroyed by soldiers. The way God was present in Rwanda when the taste for chopping into bodies grew hot in men's mouths, when ordinary men in ecstasy hacked and beat, with what joy, all humiliations and human limits gone and terror in their hands, a whole village herded into a church to be butchered or burned. "Insects," they called the Tutsi, but that was just to make the joy acceptable. And God is there, in the ultimateness, mach two, defining God by knowing what is not-God, and *still*, God is present—human power showing us the holy by its absence. Or somehow there even in the burning. *This is what is.*

God demanded Moses speak. He stood tongue-tied in the face of the fire, "the bush all aflame, yet the bush was not consumed." Who, me? You got the wrong person—I can't speak in public.

I'm no hero.

He'll call Rosenthal, say it again, *All right you bastard, you win, I'm out of this. You'll have no problems from Fusion.* It could have been Ari in that car; there could have been a bomb. As the engines pull up, as a police car, light spinning, blocks the street, the fire dies, there's just smoke, whitening, thinning, and a stink of melted plastics. Just an electrical fire. He'll say nothing to the police. A couple of thousand. Maybe much more. He's insured. This kind of situation he's equipped to handle. He walks over to handle it.

It's not especially late when the taxi drops him off. He often works later than this. Deborah calls hello from her study. "Have you eaten? Margaret's made a nice stew for us. Your father ate two helpings."

"Margaret's not still here?"

"She came in at noon today. She's just leaving."

He says a polite goodbye to Margaret Corcoran. Her first grandchild is having his first birthday Saturday. Ari made him a picture. Karen's doing homework, Ari's taking a bath, and his grandpa is reading to him. Michael hears Ari's boy soprano—he always sings in the tub—made-up melodies in a minor key. "Hi, honey." And to his father—Hi, Dad."

"He can really belt out a song, this guy," Michael's father says.

"Hi, Dad," Ari says. "You're too late. We ate already." Ari takes a deep breath and holds his breath and nose while he submerges himself and becomes a fish. When he rises, he asks, "How long was that?" Michael kisses his wet head and pats his father's shoulder and quietly goes into his study. He hears his father call, "Hey, Mikey?" but pretends he doesn't. He's breathing heavily, he can't take in enough air. The thump of his heart throbs behind his eyes.

No need to disguise this call to Rosenthal.

A muffled, blurred voice that must be Carol Rosenthal.

He has no politeness for her. "Mrs. Rosenthal? It's Michael Kuperman. I need to speak to your husband right away. Is your husband there?"

For a moment, she doesn't speak. He hears breathing. "Mr. Kuperman? Myron's dead. He's *dead*. Just like that. My husband's dead. Some filthy animals, some scum, tried to carjack him, that's what the police say, he was coming home tonight, he must have fought back, who knows, they shot him in the head, they took the car. Then they left it in Charlestown, they must have gotten scared. Just like that. He's dead. He called just before he left the office." Now she's weeping, as if they were old friends.

"Oh. Oh, God. He's dead? Mrs. Rosenthal. Carol. I'm so sorry for you."

"That a thing like this could happen. He was such a good man."

"I'm really sorry for you. You'll be sitting Shiva?"

"You'll come?"

Cheap Poisons

Frightened? He's frightened. *So*—you want to be Grandfather Jacob? You want to feel the connection between your life and the lives of your Fathers and Mothers, generation to generation? You want to know what it's like? So go, cower in a cellar. The boots are stomping on the cobblestones, soon the screaming will begin.

Putting Ari to bed, he feels like two people—one talks about rollerblading, Ari's piano lesson, the Bruins; one moans over and over, *Oh, my God, oh, my God.*

Rosenthal wouldn't be dead if Michael hadn't informed him.

Why should I give a damn?

"Deb? Dad? I'm stepping out for a few minutes," he calls out casually; he's humming a nigun, knowing without saying to himself that his father will avoid him when he hears "rabbi music," as he calls it. From a phone booth at the corner he telephones Geoffrey Slade, afraid to call from home—suppose the line is tapped—but knowing he won't find him in. "Geoffrey? I'll try you again. Try to stay by the phone." He talks to Dennis, he leaves a message for Jonathan.

At a local video store Michael looks at video cover art, buys a Laurel and Hardy for Ari, returns to the phone booth to call Slade. Still not there.

Home, he stops at the foot of the stairs, prepares himself like an actor going on stage. The actor has just learned he has cancer. But the part calls for him to be a wise, calm doctor. Deep breath. His chest hurts as he takes in air.

Upstairs, he touches Deborah's arm and sits on the daybed in her study. She finishes typing a paragraph, looks up.

"Myron Rosenthal is dead, Deborah. It's because of me he's dead." Methodically, calmly, he goes through the meeting with Rosenthal, the burned car, Rosenthal's murder—a "carjacking"—*oh, sure.*

Now, she looks into his face. Answering what she hasn't asked, he says, "I don't *know*, Deb. *How* dangerous it is. I don't know. Look. If they'd wanted me dead, they wouldn't have bothered with a warning. They could as easily have killed me, too."

"Maybe not the same day they were killing Rosenthal. What are we going to do, Michael?"

"I don't know."

"Have you called the FBI? We'll need protection. Can we get protection? Look, Michael. Can't you just let them know you've taken their warning?"

"I think so."

"*Please.*" She keeps looking at him. "Make sure they know. Please, Michael?"

He feels her panic. He strokes her hand. "You think I want anything to happen to us? These are . . . the kind of people you read stories about. We'll get out of this, drop the contract. Tomorrow. I promise. Commerce Department knows about the sales. And Interpol. Enough."

"Should we take a vacation, Michael? That might let them know you're out of it."

"They'll know. I promise. But Deborah?—I'd feel a lot better with you and the kids out of here for a few days. In the morning you take them to New York. Dennis will drive, my Dad will go with you. Ari will love it. Christmas in New York? They'll both love playing hooky with you."

"When is Dennis coming?"

"First thing in the morning."

She stoops past dresses and shoes to the luggage at the back of their walk-in closet. He helps her lug the small suitcase out, lifts it onto the bed, then turns, puts his hands on her shoulders, kisses her cheek.

"Michael!" She doesn't pull away. "Michael?" There's something in her face that makes him touch her cheek. She moans a little; it's as if they're going to make love, he thinks, and for the first time in weeks, he's suffused with sex.

Ira calls from downstairs, "Hey, Mikey?—what the hell's going on around here?"

"Sorry," Michael calls back. "Sorry, Dad. I've got a real emergency. I'm coming down, I'll tell you all about it."

"I've been on my feet since six this morning," Ira calls up the stairs. "You gonna talk to me or what?"

"I know. I'm coming." He exchanges a look with Deborah, the kindest look they've shared in months, and goes down to his father's room. "You sit down. Can I get you a shot of bourbon?"

Ira waves off the suggestion; he's sitting on the bed, shirt unbuttoned, pants unbuttoned, no undershirt, his chest hairy, gray but still with peninsulas of black, the chest sagging down to his little belly. "I hope to hell it *is* an emergency and you ain't just been blowing me off all day."

Michael walks back to Beacon, back to the phone booth, and this time Geoffrey's waiting for the call. "I need to let you know . . . Myron Rosenthal is dead."

"Dead—I see. How?"

"It was made to look like a carjacking that went bad. Geoffrey? This call is just to let you know. Okay? I'm out of this. Rosenthal's dead, murdered, my car was burned—a warning, and, Geoffrey?— I've taken it. You understand? I'm no longer involved. But Interpol ought to know."

"Start again. Slower," Slade says. "I hear the panic. Breathe."

Breathe! Michael laughs!—as if Slade were a yoga teacher. He breathes. He takes him through the meeting, the warning, the telephone call. "All I can imagine is Rosenthal really *didn't* know. I know from Steve Planck—remember I mentioned him?—that Orion is *not* company policy. It's a group inside Chemicorp. Maybe a small group. And I guess even within that group there are different levels of knowledge. Anyway, Rosenthal didn't know where the chemicals were going. He must have called to complain—and called the wrong people."

"Indeed he must have. Well. I'll pass this on. When I say 'pass it on,' Michael, I mean to Interpol people in liaison with Export Enforcement in the Commerce Department. Yes, we'll let them handle it. And we'll get in touch with the Cambridge police—"

"—Charlestown—"

"All right—Charlestown. They need to know it was no carjacking. And the FBI. Sorry about that car of yours. Sorry about your scare. That must have been quite something—to see your car on fire." He laughs. "Now. You see what I meant the other day?"

"So you think it's this General Djouti who's behind this? Is that what you're saying?"

"No, no, I don't mean that exactly. What can I know at that level? It may have to do with Orion itself. I'm saying, please be very careful. We'd prefer that you stay alive. I believe this is an agenda item on which there's total agreement."

"'Careful.' Of *course*, careful. I've got a family. Oh, yes. My God. . . ." Michael is suddenly embarrassed, aware that he's called Geoffrey not just to inform him, but to get some kind of assurance, and what assurance can he get? They're silent. Michael's standing in a lit phone booth watching for guns at the windows of the cars that pass. "Geoffrey? You *are* a cop of some kind, aren't you? It's not an accident you came to the party that night?"

"An accident? No. *Not* an accident. I *have* taught international law at Sussex, I really do research for Interpol. Well—in a *sense* 'research.' Your name came up—I made a point of meeting you."

"How did my name come up?"

"We've been following Chemicorp's dealings here and in Great Britain. When Fusion contacted the Commerce Department, they let us know about it. We found out that you were the one negotiating with Myron Rosenthal."

"Why didn't you tell me?"

"Couldn't take a chance. Suppose you knew very well what was going on? You see? Suppose you were working with Rosenthal?"

"What *is* going on?"

"Well. There are organizations sending heroin from Europe to the States. Heroin goes one way, money comes back. But they're also involved in arms trafficking. And of course the money needs to be laundered and invested. So it gets complicated. At some point they realized, you see, that they could send drugs one way and get back chemicals, then sell the chemicals. Both poisons are quite cheap, actually. It's the overhead that costs—the security, the payoffs. So the containers for chemicals—or containers of the same sort—began to go back with a different kind of poison. Orion is the supplier. It's part of a complex, lucrative business."

"So the warning—they're afraid I'll pass the information on to the police, the FBI. But I think they're also afraid Orion's cover will be blown *within* the corporation. Afraid certain people will find out."

"If they knew you'd been passing information along to us, you'd be dead right now. No question. But they don't know."

"I'd be dead right now," Michael echoes.

Stories

Deborah is packing; she packs for herself, tiptoes into Ari's room to pack for him. She lets Karen know, and Karen is delighted. "I'm bribing you, my dear. You look after Ari hours I have to work, take him to FAO Schwartz, the Sony museum, you know—I'll buy you some fabulous clothes. *Your* definition of fabulous, not mine. . . ."

Michael sees the suitcases when he comes in. "Good. Thank you."

"Oh, we'll have a good time in New York."

Her playful, elegant voice is back. The moment of eros and innocence is past. She's guarded—but friendly. Michael says. "Listen—we'll all be all right. But the people we're facing. Can you imagine the corruption of soul?"

"Please, you're *not* going to talk *religion*," she says. "I couldn't stand it. I'm going to take an Adavan and go to sleep."

He laughs and squeezes her shoulder, the soft taupe sweater, and now he touches his fingertips to her cheeks, lifting away the worry lines. She lets him.

"Do you remember a man named Geoffrey Slade—at our party?"

"A friend of Georg Severain's? A tall, peculiar-looking man?"

"He was here that night to meet me. He's with Interpol. He's working on the case. That's who I was meeting in New York yesterday."

"You promised you'd drop this. Michael?"

"I am dropping it. I want you to know someone else is picking it up."

Deborah is disturbed. It's something in his voice, something she's not used to hearing, and as she finishes packing, laying out the right clothes for her luncheon meeting with the Chief Operating Officer of Danmart and for walking around the city with Karen and Ari, she knows she's been hearing it lately. It's a new firm timbre. He sounds like—well, himself. His voice doesn't grate. Even his beard doesn't particularly bother her.

Her story is breaking down.

Deborah's story is disintegrating, and she has nothing to put in its place.

Patches of Deborah's old story, stuck together with tape, did well enough until now. It was sad—but *comfortable*; it had a known shape and a more or less happy ending. It wasn't fully enacted yet, but she knew where it was headed. The story she told herself went something like this:

We were a couple of clever young people, definitely first-rate—Michael working at Yale for his MBA while I was at Harvard working for mine. He was this sexy guy, with thick, curly hair, not an MBA type, thank God, and our politics were different and fun to fight about. He was a benighted liberal, but that was perfectly acceptable since I was sure this man was going to be a Big Personal Success whatever he felt about poverty in America.

Michael soon enough got into the private sector, then built this amazing start-up firm with Jonathan, and while I was on a healthy salary plus stock options, he was building wealth.

And the sex was good from the first, and how often can you say that?—and we traveled well together, loved, both of us, art and serious music, and while we were both Jewish, it was merely a cultural patina. A flavor, a scent in the house—nice, really.

But, oh, well, you know, we grew apart. It was already shaky before Karen was born. And then Karen, and then Ari came, and of course we loved them but, like everyone else, had no time for each other—a tag team, negotiating work and child care, bickering over business trips; then he lost interest in sailing and in collecting paintings and became seriously Jewish, and to put it mildly, we began to want very different things. It's as if we began by dancing the tango and right in the middle he started to waltz. And the waltz, let me tell you frankly, bores me to death. No hard feelings, but the dance was a flop. Nothing against Michael. He might be happy with a good Jewish wife, but believe me, I am not that wife. And I—I would be delighted to work hard, buy a little place on one of the less spoiled Greek islands, have fabulous friends and a husband who likes to tango.

And that's what will *happen. I expect to share Karen and Ari with him, even to stay friends—better friends once we're not tugging at one another. But it has to run its course, like a virus, this poor sickness of ours. Soon, very soon, it'll be finished, and we'll both be able to say, "That wasn't a bad first marriage."*

So that was the story. At the same time, to get on day by day this had to be covered over—again for *herself*—with *another* story: *There are differences between us but we're both working on it, we'll probably get through this.* She couldn't let herself know that she was waiting for a *Final Straw*, the sign of a gap between them that was unbridgeable. This almost-lover of hers, Larry Ackerman; *that* might have done it; that, in fact, was his role in the story she was going to tell, but then came Chemicorp and Rosenthal, then came the threat of death.

Now she doesn't know what story she's living. She finds herself turning to him, wanting him there in the house. Her story of class, of style and shrewdness triumphing, of personal victory, has been shaken. She's soothed by Michael's voice. The old story—everything she'd wanted—is beginning to seem meretricious.

To be without a story.

CHAPTER EIGHT

In the morning, awakened much earlier than usual, Ari hears his mom tells him they're going to take a vacation in New York, they're going to see amazing things. It's gonna feel weird, missing the all-school Hanukkah-Christmas-Kwanza sing, but . . . New York! The store windows!—you won't believe how fabulous! she told him, packing his teddy in his bag.

He keeps glancing up at his father at breakfast. His father keeps his eyes lowered. But the hug he gives Ari—it squeezes all the air out of him. "I *love* you," he tells Ari. Now he leans down to Karen and presses his check to hers. "I *love* you. Have a great time in New York."

She looks up, curious, shrinks away a little at this effusiveness. "Sure. Thanks."

"Dad?" Michael calls out. "You ready?"

"Yeah, yeah," Ira calls back.

Deborah feels the gnaw in the pit of her stomach that comes with walking into the unknown world not dressed in a story.

Willing to Be a Coward

From the kitchen table, Jessica, cramming manila folders into a briefcase, scribbling onto a leather-bound pad, keeps glancing up at Michael. "Coffee's made, Mikey. Jonathan'll be down in a minute." What's he doing here at seven-thirty in the morning?

Mikey—his father's name for him—Jessica's the only friend who could call him that. Anything she does is okay by him; she goes right to his heart. Always has. Always there's been this gallant, decorous *generosity* between them. Sometimes, meeting, they each hold hand over heart and bow slightly.

"So? Is this about the lawyer, this . . . Murtaugh?"

"Worse. Much worse."

"I wish you'd told me last night. I've got a patient—I can't cancel now."

"We'll talk."

"It's that bad? You can't just *say*?"

He takes both her hands. "Rosenthal was murdered yesterday."

Her arms go slack. "*Michael.*"

He holds her, kisses the top of her head. "It'll work out, Jess. Go ahead—I know you have to go. Call Jonathan from the car. Okay, Jessie?" When she's gone, he pours coffee and puts a slice of bread in the toaster. And Jonathan's there.

"Hey."

"Hey."

"You look terrible."

For a moment, Michael feels the giddy power of knowing something Jonathan doesn't know, the knowledge that it's going to shock him.

Jonathan is self-consciously pouring coffee. Michael feels the stiffness, as if Jonathan feels a camera watching him. Michael waits for him to pull up a chair. In this kitchen with its new equipment but comfortable old look, old maple table, oiled-wood floor, bulletin boards with schedules and photographs, these two men in business suits seem oversized, out of place.

"Jonathan, my car . . . was burned last night." He holds up a hand to stop questions, then realizes Jonathan isn't asking. "As a *warning*. I was lucky. Myron Rosenthal didn't get a warning. He's dead—he was murdered on his way home."

Murdered? Jonathan says. *Have you called the police? Won't we need protection?* Michael holds up a hand. He tells him: Geoffrey Slade; this "General" Djouti; Rosenthal's shock when he found out where the chemicals were going; the way the car began to smoke and burn, the warning over the phone while the car burned. And Rosenthal.

Michael hands him the "B" section of the morning *Globe*. The story's on the first page—carjacking, philanthropist murdered. A photograph of Rosenthal. Jonathan reads the details—the body dumped in an alley near the docks in Charlestown; the car, bloody, found on a residential street nearby. *Mr. Rosenthal, an executive. . . .* Jonathan looks up. "Mike? What the hell? You took your damned time telling me about this. And this—what's his name—Slade? You've never hidden things from me. Now how come? Why couldn't I call back last night?"

"Suppose our phones are tapped."

Jonathan's about to call him paranoid, thinks better of it. "I got a call last night from Steve. He's sending another disk. He's going to the FBI."

"He called me, too," Michael says. "We've got to talk him out of it. These guys *murder*. Slade says they'd kill us in a minute. I want us to get out, get all the way out. I'm willing to be a coward."

Jonathan hunches forward; their elbows are almost touching. "Jesus."

"I'm worried for you guys just as much. You're in the same hot water."

Jonathan turns a spoon over and over.

"I'm hoping," Michael says, "we show them we're not getting involved, we'll be okay. We get a letter off to Chemicorp dropping the rest of the contract 'for internal corporate reasons during a time of restructuring,' suggesting alternative 'vendors.' A friendly letter. Of course, except for the guys in Orion, Chemicorps won't understand. Ferguson, Braithwaite won't understand. Orion represents a small group inside Chemicorp. Steve says we'll have evidence of that today."

"Mike? We'll have to do better than a 'friendly letter.'"

"A statement of intent. We can fax it this morning."

"It's a start. But not near good enough. Let me think a minute." Jonathan stares out the kitchen window, using the sky over Cambridge as his scratch pad.

Not for the first time Michael realizes that Jonathan's almost military-short black hair has gray sprinkled in. Oh, we're *getting there*, he thinks. Meaning *old*. He wonders which of them will die first, which one will have to speak at the other's funeral. And how soon. Nice morning thoughts. "I come from a long line of people who hid in cellars, got out any way they could. Not a warrior tradition, not for two thousand years. At least until 1945. But we've survived. I'm here." "Well—" he laughs at himself—"of course, you, too, man."

"You recall that story about my great-grandfather?"

They grin, they nod, breath comes. Sure. (Jonathan told Michael the story long ago. How his great-grandfather William came up from Charleston with his family by ship. This was in the 1870's. A skilled worker, a shipbuilder, he'd saved some money and knew of a job in New Bedford; hearing terrible stories of folks traveling by road, he figured it was safer to go by ship. But at night the sailors put a bag over his head, tied him up and stole his small purse, and afterwards, of course, no one knew a *thing* about it, not the captain, not the crew—and he was warned he'd better not complain to the owners. He would have come to New Bedford a pauper if he had not had the foresight to sew up almost all his savings in a leather bag inside his baby's pants. The foresight was his; the location his wife thought of—that was one place no one was going to want to stick his hand.)

"What's your grandfather got to do with it?"

"My grandfather didn't do battle with those sailors. Nor your grandfather. But they didn't think of themselves as 'cowards.' They saved their families. My plan, Mike, we're gonna talk face to face with the people from Orion. And smile a *lot*. Start with Rosenthal's office in Boston, maybe fly out to St. Louis, see Ferguson and Braithwaite."

"They're probably not involved."

"I'll put in a call right now to the Boston office. I intend to let them know how friendly we are."

"It makes me sick."

"And I'll call Steve. No. *You* call. Tell him to cool it. Let Interpol take over. Michael! Damn! Sometimes you piss me off—like you're the only one who feels these things."

Michael nods.

"So Rosenthal's wife thinks it was a mugging?"

"Seems to. Yes, I'm sure. I felt for her. I don't think she knows a thing."

"I got no sympathy for Rosenthal. But it makes me want to stay real cordial with those sons of bitches."

They're stuck at the table. In silence—twenty-five years support that silence. Jonathan reaches out a hand, grips Michael's shoulder; Michael meets his eyes. There's no other friend with whom he can dare do something so intimate. Even with Jonathan, this shared look is not so much intimacy as a *sign* of intimacy, a testimony to intimacy.

Jonathan heads for the phone to call Chemicorp. But before he can get there, it rings. "Jessie?" Slipping out, Michael drives his rental car to Mass Avenue and pulls over, calls Steve in Bloomington, reaches his voice mail. "That appointment we spoke about, Steve, the appointment's *absolutely not necessary*. We need to talk. Myron Rosenthal is dead, Steve. Please listen to me. I'll try you again later. We need to talk. Call me on my cell phone. You have the number."

Mr. Death

The Chemicorp International Sales offices aren't far from Fusion, downtown Boston. Promptly at two o'clock Michael and Jonathan are escorted into Rosenthal's office. His name still on the door. Pictures of Rosenthal's family, framed awards, on the paneled walls.

A short young man steps out from behind the desk to shake their hands. He's suntanned, powerfully built, his smile is warm. "I'm Anthony Carulli," he says. Michael sees Mr. Death. . . . Michael is dizzy from lack of oxygen. His chest is like plate armor; no room to take in air.

Maybe Carulli is not Mr. Death. Maybe he's a young executive with a family, knowing nothing, handling the contracts for Chemicorp, filling in, not part of Orion at all. Michael doesn't believe this.

"I'll be taking over for Myron. At least temporarily. I got pulled in from the New York office. So much to handle down there, but we've got international contracts to fulfill, and the Boston office is crucial. So I'm here. Well, gentlemen. Terrible thing, just a terrible, rotten thing. Myron was such a central player for us. You saw the nice article in the *Globe*? We got your fax. I do appreciate it, Mr. Greene. That cleared things up for us. I'm pleased you came in to talk. Myron wasn't sure how the two of you felt. He told us you had concerns about certain chemical experiments Chemicorp had subcontracted. Is that right?"

Jonathan says, "We've dismissed those concerns, Mr. Carulli. Absolutely."

"We want you to know—we consider those experiments trade secrets under the terms of your original contract with us."

"We do, too," Jonathan says. "Oh, we're very, very clear about that. They're not our concern. Our concern is to make your systems talk to each other." And Jonathan smiles his biggest damn smile. You'd have to know the man for years to sense the parodic quality of that smile. "And we're doing that. This has all been a misunderstanding. Mr. Planck needed to go into your encrypted files to make sure the systems were compatible. He wasn't trying to spy, he assures me of that. He was made a little uneasy." A magician, Jonathan spreads out his hands: "But that is *finished*. That's *over*. You can be assured Mr. Planck will keep hands off. Chemicorp is a very important contract for us, Mr. Carulli. I don't know if you know that. We're going to do everything we can to finish this stage of the contract and get your systems connected perfectly."

"Fine. That's what we're hoping to hear." He leans forward, shakes his head. "Poor Myron." Carulli shakes his head. "There are people in this world who'd kill you for a car." He pauses. "You can imagine when the stakes get higher . . . I happen to know he liked working with you, Mr. Kuperman. He was a bit disappointed, losing your help after this phase of the contract. But as you said in your fax, Mr. Greene, it's a transitional time for your firm. And Mr. Kuperman—Myron said you were having personal problems—with your father, is that right? I understand your father was in custody— some sort of political protest? Now what was that all about?"

Michael has to suck in breath to be able to answer coolly. "Yes. Hospital workers. He's a funny guy, my father. It turned out to be nothing."

Carulli pats them on the shoulders, shakes their hands, escorts them out. Michael and Jonathan say nothing until they're out on the street.

"I think it went well. Oh, those sons of bitches. He's part of Orion."

"Jonathan, now I'm *sure* my phone *is* being tapped. It's not just fantasy. I never spoke to Rosenthal about my father. Never. I spoke to Susan in Seattle about it. I spoke to Deborah. Maybe I mentioned it to you on the phone, but not to Rosenthal. Look—I told you I'm expecting a package. When it comes, if I call you, you've got to assume I'm talking for an audience. And your phone? We don't know. When I call for real, I'll call your cell from my cell."

Steve Closes Up Shop

Most nights it's Steve who closes up the lab. When the new training group from BRT Cosmetics finishes up for the day, he shmoozes over coffee with a couple of the tech support people but can't wait to get them out so he can pull together his documents for the morning. His appointment with the FBI is at 9:30 in the morning, so he has to finish tonight. Printouts of letters, instructions, sales; and the videos—especially those. Michael wants him to hold off, Slade wants him to hold off. But can he be sure about Slade? He can't hold off. He's worked hard on the virus, it's in place. Information is already coming in.

Steve could hear how guarded Michael's message was. And Rosenthal dead? Mike must think the phone's bugged—his phone, this phone. But all he has to do is walk in to FBI offices in the morning and he's safe.

He decides not to sleep at home tonight. He decides to drive up to Indianapolis and stay at a motel, anywhere.

He walks through the lab, shutting off lights. He's told his mother how it makes him feel: like a captain standing watch over his ship. Now, as he does every night, he goes back to his office to shut down his electronics. . . .

Orders for Zyklon-B

It's 6:30, middle of December, a cold night.

Usually, Michael likes the Christmas lights on Boston Common. There's a Childe Hassam painting at the Museum of Fine Arts, Tremont Street in winter, snow, trolley lights, a slim, pretty woman holding a muff. Or that's how he remembers it. Christmas season, though it's not his holiday, has always made downtown Boston seem for him like that painting. Not tonight. Tonight it's grubby, snowless, cold; Christmas lights an irritant. A cover-up of ugliness.

When Michael gets home from work he finds inside the door the FedEx package sent from Bloomington. Margaret's taken it in.

Nobody's home—everyone in New York. The answering machine's flashing; ignoring it, he stares at the package, imagining a bomb. But it's Steve's friendly scribble on the label. It's no Christmas present, he's sure of that. Disposing of the packing material he takes the package to his study: computer disks, a CD-ROM, hard copy—thirty-odd pages of letters and data. He feels like a criminal. I suppose he *is* a criminal—a receiver of stolen goods. But imagine this is 1941. These are orders for Zyklon-B.

Hasn't he decided he's a coward?

Steve has wrapped the disks and documents in yesterday morning's *Indianapolis Star*. He smells—or imagines he smells—garlic; newsprint and garlic from Steve's morning garlic and butter mash. While his computer starts up, he skims the hard copy—the internal memoranda. In a few minutes, he knows this: it's not a question of a chemical manufacturer looking for additional sales. It's not a subdivision. *Orion*. Clearly, Steve's right: within the company, only a few people know about Orion. Others, who know much less, are, it seems, looking the other way. The documents speak about a concern for "intra-corporate security." This is a relief to Michael. So it's first of all the company itself that should handle this. But who knows, and whom is it safe to tell?

His only clue: There are two memos warning someone to keep data out of Max Ferguson's hands. It doesn't mention Al Braithwaite—maybe because he's part of Orion, or maybe because he'd have no call to learn about Orion. He works at too high a level. But the two memos definitely mention Ferguson. So he knows someone, at least, he can trust.

He sits at his desk skimming correspondence (Steve's penciled note—"from company electronic garbage"). There are no names, but he's sure Steve can tell who's writing by looking at the headers.

Orion. The hunter.

Now he puts the disk into his CD-ROM port. He clicks on a few files. Data on effectiveness, on schedules for deliveries, notes within the company about the cost effectiveness of Orion, about the need for secrecy. The need for laundering profits. Methods of laundering profits. Rosenthal, he imagines, was told only what he needed to be told with regard to shipments.

He clicks on the icon: *Canine.2*.

The same white room, steel plate halfway up the walls, filmed through a one-way mirror. Again, three dogs, one of them large, prowl the room. At the bottom of the screen the digital clock starts. At 00:30 two words flash: **Delivery commences**. This time, the chemical agent is not released through a vent. Off-camera, a panel in the ceiling must open. A foot-long canister, olive green, with an aluminum-gray mechanism at the top, drops into the frame. At 00:40 the canister erupts, a white cloud of gas explodes from the canister and quickly permeates the picture, then dissipates. At 00:44 a spastic dance begins.

Michael wonders what he's watching. A nerve toxin? Sarin, he remembers, was used by the Iraqis against the Iranians; it was made in chemical plants built by the Germans, the French, the Dutch. Nerve gasses cause a very different death; faster, more spasmodic. These dogs dance to their deaths.

Michael thinks of the bank of television monitors on the second floor of the Holocaust Museum in Washington, fenced off and lowered so that young children can't see the images, but the effect is to make visitors squeeze in and lean over. You can't look casually. You look over someone's shoulder, it's a committed looking; you feel implicated; an accomplice. The images: SS film archives, medical experiments on prisoners. Film of a prisoner subjected to extreme cold. A series of still photographs:

a body clothed,

the body naked,

the body dead and flayed;

the body as skeleton;

body parts.

In those films, in the film on this CD-ROM, the same unspoken trope: objective, detached rational investigation.

Michael doesn't pray. He closes his eyes and sits in silence.

The silence leaves room for a gathering of his ancestors. The silence fills with voices he can't make out, and if he could, he'd imagine they were inner voices. So much they've gone through for their children and their children's children that they can't put down their end of the delicate thread that joins them to Michael Kuperman. If he doesn't survive, of course there's Ari, there's Karen, but they need a father. Yet if he only *survives*, what good is he?

And so he almost hears whispers inside the silence and sits up, feels the kind of calm that might save your life in an auto accident, those three seconds that expand and slow down while you negotiate the wheel.

Getting Out

He sits there, afraid to move, knowing that when he does move, he will do something that might change or even end his life. He can't bring himself to click on **Demo.1**. No time—but that's not it. He wants it out of his hands, let the FBI—someone—handle it. So much data. He wants to think of it as *data*. He sees in mind's eye the olive green steel file case, his mother's "legacy" of names.

He remembers one telephone call, to Mrs Bolofsky wasn't it? From the Liebsmann file . . . *If there's ever anything we can do for you and yours.* . . . "You and yours"—he remembers that locution.

He gets up, takes the file case from the closet in his study, finds the Liebsmann-Bolofsky family, makes notes.

He takes up his tallis bag—his prayer shawl and yarmulke.

He packs a few things—prescription medicines for himself, for Karen. A hunting knife. A change of shirt, jeans, a pair of underpants, a razor. His address book and a prayer book. Credit cards he's accepted but never used. From his personal files, important papers. Their passports. From Deborah's office, her current files, her Rolodex, her file of "IMPORTANT DOCUMENTS." The big hiking pack is very heavy—the Chemicorp files, some of his mother's files and Deborah's files making up most of the weight—maybe sixty pounds. One bag for the belly of the plane, one to carry on.

The simplest thing, of course, would be simply to drop the car at the body shop, take a cab to the airport, and make the calls he needs to make from the Four Seasons when he's had a chance to talk to Deborah. But his mind quiets, as it often does when he's working on a problem; he grows calm, clear, and feels himself physically in relation to a hologram of a plan superimposed over the house.

All right.

He's counting on the phone being monitored. He calls Jonathan, breathes deeply: *An Actor Prepares.* The machine picks up but as he starts to leave his message, Jessica takes the call. "Sure, Michael. I'll get him. He's just talking to Marcus."

When he's on the line, Michael says, as if holding anger in check, "Look, Jonathan, I *know* you want to drop this whole thing, I know *you* don't give a *damn.* But it *makes me sick.* Do you understand?"

"Go on," Jonathan says. "I hear you."

"I'm calling Ferguson and Braithwaite at company headquarters. I'm going to get things straight. I'll be flying out to St. Louis in the morning. I'll call and let you know what they say."

"You really think that's necessary?" Jonathan says.

"Now, you keep telling me to drop this. But you know me, Jonathan—I've never been a coward."

"No. No, you haven't; *never been a coward.* Like . . . oh, you mean like the time you swam in the Charles in spring?"

"That's right," Michael says. "*Exactly.*" Remembering the morning Jonathan refers to. It was Jonathan, not Michael, who jumped off the boat dock near the foot bridge. Jonathan's got it.

"I don't see the point. Listen. *Really.* We've decided we won't get involved in this. Haven't we, Michael? Haven't we said it's none of our business?"

"None of *your* business. I want to get to the bottom of this."

"Michael? *Michael?* No, I mean for real."

"I'll call you from St. Louis."

How much of that was really real? He knows. He could hear the urgency. That's not Jonathan trying to save himself. He's trying to protect me. Now, to stay alive, Michael has to run. *Suppose Carulli knew this morning that the package was coming*? Suppose they're outside this house now, right now.

I could call Carulli, tell him it's here. Tell him I want to get rid of it.

I can't do that. Even if they were to believe me. I can't.

Now Michael calls United and books a first-class reservation on the 9 AM flight for St. Louis. It's a flight he's taken often. He leaves a message on the answering machine at the auto body shop: "Jimmy, I'm dropping off the loaner tonight, key in the drop-slot.

I'll be getting home by cab. Please put a message on my machine—
tell me when I can get my Lexus back." Another red herring; in
point of fact, he wonders if he'll ever see that car again. Finally, he
calls for a cab to pick him up at seven-thirty in the morning.

At seven-thirty in the morning, the cab will come to an empty
house.

He hopes that he really has a legacy in the list. *You and yours.*

He picks up the big knapsack . . . and puts it down again. Wait
a minute.

Steve.

He replays in his head the call Steve left on the machine
yesterday. *Oh my God.* Now he remembers the flashing of the
answering machine downstairs and half-leaps down the stairs.

They're the usual messages left on answering machines of
families in which both spouses work. From Margaret, a memo
saying she'd not be coming in tomorrow; a sitter telling them next
Tuesday night would be fine (Karen at a rehearsal, Deborah away,
Michael at a class at the synagogue, Ari needing a sitter). But the
third message is from Steve:

*By now, Mike, I guess you've got the disk and the printouts.
There's a lot of stuff. There's account numbers—bank accounts off-
shore and in Switzerland. These guys can be nailed. Jesus. You'd
better take a shot of whiskey before you watch **Canine.2**. But Mike
—the file labeled **Demo.1** is much worse. Mike, that really did it for
me. I didn't want to take the lead in this, but you'll see, I couldn't let
it go. I've got an appointment at the FBI field office in Indianapolis
tomorrow morning. You want to talk about it, give me a call—I'll be
at the lab.*

Oh, my God. He should get the hell out of the house, call Steve
from the airport—but now he can't wait that long. He calls the lab.
Tell him to get police protection. The machine picks up; he presses
1, 3, 2. Steve's greeting comes on. Knowing he's being overheard
on this end, Michael doesn't know what he can possibly say and is
about to hang up when someone picks up. "Yes?"

"Is Steve there?"

"Mr. Kuperman?"

"Yes."

"It's Dmitri. Something terrible happened. I just got back here. I got a call. There's police and firemen all over. Listen—Steve Planck is dead."

"Oh, my God."

"Steve's dead—blown up. I mean, he's *dead*."

"Oh, God, no."

"There was an explosion. About an hour ago. The police think it was a bomb. It's a real wreck around here, Mr. Kuperman. His office is like a meltdown. Computers all fried. Steve, he must have been dead before he knew anything."

"Dmitri—did you call his mom?"

"First thing. . . . I called her. She's coming out in the morning."

"Oh, his poor mother. You take care of her."

"Sure. The rest of the place is pretty bad. It's still smoking. It stinks of burning polymers. But we can rebuild, Mike. We've got backups of training materials, everything. . . ." Dmitri's silent. Then: "No backup for Steve."

Michael says, calmly, "Better call Jonathan. He's home. Dmitri, you get things sorted out."

"What kind of crazy guy would do a thing like that?"

"I don't know. I don't know."

"You think it's the Unabomber? He goes after high-tech people."

"Maybe."

"Police have got yellow tape around everything. Tony's out of town. We've got a training group coming in tomorrow—Mr. Kuperman, I've got to start canceling everything for the rest of December."

"You do it, Dmitri. You're in charge. I'll get out as soon as I can."

He sees the fire and the smoke. It will have to lead him into exile. He is thinking of the pillar of cloud that accompanied the Israelites by day, the pillar of fire by night.) He takes deep breaths. *Can I do this?* He has no choice. *If I want to stay alive.* He feels the presence of abomination outside all his windows. He thinks, *Jacob*—and at first he means his grandfather. He says aloud, "Jacob." This time he means the patriarch. The shrewd Jacob, our

Odysseus, who runs off to save his life—first from Esau, then from Laban. Now, he has no choice but to be Jacob.

They may be outside this minute, waiting to come in. But it's hard to leave. He wanders the house. What does he need to take with him? How long will he be away? A few days? Forever? What will he curse himself for forgetting? He notices the samovar; the silverware means nothing to him, but this brass samovar, maybe two hundred years old, lugged from Kishinev, he takes down to the cellar where it will look like a cast-off pot.

There must be a blessing to say upon embarking on exile. The prayer for travelers doesn't seem strong enough. But he says in his head what he can remember, the prayer he says every time he flies. *May it be Your will . . . that you lead us to peace. . . . Rescue us from the grasp of every foe . . . and from all forms of punishment that rage upon the world.*

Michael is alone in his lit-up house. He calls for a taxi to meet him at the body shop and bring him home again. (Please God they've been listening.) He puts a CD on the stereo, picks up his pack and, leaving the lights on, walks out the front door to the loaner Dodge parked in the driveway. He's wearing a good suit and his London Fog overcoat with the liner zipped in. He drives slowly toward the body shop on Huntington. In Brookline Village he stops at a convenience store where there's a phone; he calls Deborah at the Four Seasons in New York. He doesn't tell her much. He calls Margaret Corcoran: Take care of things. Then he leaves a message for Geoffrey Slade.

A minute later, he's eating a bar of candy—just in case anyone's been watching him walk into the store.

No one's been watching.

The taxi meets him at the body shop. "We're not going back to Brookline. We're going to Park Street Station. And I'll tell you how to go," he says. "I don't think anyone's following, but I need to make sure. Okay?" At Park Street he takes the T to Logan in time for the eight o'clock shuttle.

CHAPTER NINE

Christmas on Fifth Avenue

Ira offered her the apartment on West End Avenue—she'd have it to herself; she was dropping him off at Eleanor's—but Deborah decided they'd be more comfortable in a hotel. She chose Four Seasons partly because it's near MOMA and near the windows of the department stores on Fifth, intricately made up for Christmas. But partly because it's so grown-up a hotel. *She* feels like a grownup here. Though it turns out that Ari, too, is delighted with the hotel—an Egyptian temple, he says. They've just studied Egypt, and he's thinking of the high, cool, marble and limestone lobby, the huge pillars: he's exactly right. He thinks it's got secret passages for priests. But what he loves most is the whirlpool bathtub in the marble bathroom that fills completely, with a great gush and a waft of steam filling the lungs, in less than sixty seconds. He sits on the window seat pressing cheek to glass and looking twenty-seven stories down into Madison Avenue and out over the park. Karen walked in here last night and immediately entered a role: Deborah could see her body metamorphose into young lady; *she hasn't spoken one acerbic syllable since we walked in.* Today, while Deborah worked at an office in the Seagram's Building, Karen took Ari down Fifth to look at the windows.

Waiting for Michael, Deborah feels the peculiar mix of this safety and luxury with uncertainty, danger, chaos in the heart.

When he called tonight she was looking at the presents she bought after work today: the robin's egg blue and terra-cotta bowl made by Hopi in New Mexico: this, for Jessica and Jonathan. Hundreds of dollars, but lovely placed by itself on a glass cube under a halogen spot, so museum-alien from its origins. And for Martha, a pendant from Tiffany's, an Elsa Peretti gold heart. This out of friendship—*and* in calculated revenge for the tourist-quality Florentine diary-journal Martha had given her for her birthday. There were the lovely bears from FAO Schwartz for Susan's little girl; Ari, though too old, could hardly keep his fingers off the soft fur. She'd placed the presents on the bed and Karen and Ari were admiring; then came the call from Michael:

". . . *need to slip away. Go into temporary seclusion . . . Deborah— look—I mean we have to go into hiding.*"

When Deborah was a child her mother would take her to New York at Christmas to stay with Deborah's aunt and uncle, who lived in a town house on East 63rd. She would wear fur gloves and a fur muff, her mother would wear the mink she rarely got to wear in San Francisco, and they would walk glove in glove down Fifth. It was the only time she could count on being close with her mother. She remembers that, and the dollhouses at Schwartz's Toy Store. And the Christmas windows: when she thinks *Christmas windows* what she's remembering is one series at the old Best & Company one year, a family of bears that moved, window after window, through the story of Goldilocks—while surrounded with bourgeois luxuries. The bears enter a bedroom and throw up their paws as Goldilocks sits up and rubs her eyes.

The day before Christmas, her father would join them.

The Christmases blur together. But once, when she was Karen's age, he came with one gigantic box for her. It didn't fit under the tree. Last present opened, it held five smaller boxes: a tent, a sleeping bag, a mountain pack, cross-country skis in a canvas bag, a Coleman heater. "We'll get boots tomorrow," he said. "You and I, we're going into the White Mountains—we'll be camping for three nights on Nick's land." Nick was Dad's friend from college, his lifelong friend, who died just last year.

"And Mother? Are *you* coming, too?"

Everyone laughed at the thought. No, she'd stay on East 63rd, thank you very much. Deborah pretended to try to tease her into coming, but was overjoyed. And the snow that year! They camped five miles from where they left the car.

Waiting for Michael, she remembers that camping adventure. Porcupines after salt ate the gas line, so on the morning they were ready to return to New York (he had an operation to perform in San Francisco in two days), they had to pack everything away in the car and ski six extra miles to a phone to get help. She considers this memory, why it came just now; three years in therapy have taught her something: this is how she feels right *now*, waiting. Skiing out of that forest, tired and sore from three days skiing, with a bad shoulder bruise (and a torn ligament, she discovered later), she didn't panic, because her father, so extraordinarily competent, was with her, but she skied at the edge of panic: what if they were lost? What if there were no phones? What if they skied till dark (which came on just after four, and it was noon by the time they left the car) and all their supplies were back there?

By the end of the following summer, he was dead from cancer.

The children are watching television. Not panic but the edge of panic. This is a hotel suite whose every chair and strip of polished wood trim says *safety*. Michael, like her father, is a competent man. Lately, she's been thinking of him as a fool—an ersatz (Jewish!) saint. Her father would be *furious* at him if he were alive. But yes, competent.

Where *is* Michael?

She begins to worry before he could conceivably get to the hotel—even without traffic. Karen and Ari are watching a sitcom before Ari goes to sleep. A laugh track. But the *under*-hum of the TV, with its hollow voices, carries with it echoes of dark movies; she feels threat as a churning hollow, in the bottom of her chest.

She loved her father's spontaneity and despised her mother's rehearsal of everything. A party. An outing. A visit to France. Mother drained everything of its excitement by knowing every trip in advance, *restaurant by restaurant*, so it could stay under her control. When Deborah was a child she promised herself to "delight in the serendipitous." As soon as she learned the word *serendipity*, she used it to death. *But look at me—I've become just like my mother.*

This is, she knows, a cultural sickness. You see ads on television—Americans on a spree, out in the wilds—desert, mesa, forest trail—bouncing in an off-the-road vehicle. Their hearts are free? But all the skills, all the qualities of mind, that have permitted us to own that luxury sports vehicle have made us unfit to live in the wildness, without itinerary, with a free heart. The same hunger to express self, the unbounded American self, produces the assertion of will that makes us want to control everything. But if it's a false, foolish, vulgar attempt—like hunting lions in New Jersey—it's also heroic, an attempt to lift the self into the realm of the lost-sacred.

Deborah sees her mother wearing a mauve loden jacket, sitting in a narrow-gauge train in Switzerland, her head bowed over schedules while the Alps went by unseen. Deborah promised herself then, never would she become like *that*.

Now her own life—it's even more scheduled.

Here's what all this is leading to: if these qualities of organization have been useful for getting her through her weeks, they've unfitted her for this new thing, for going into hiding. She's being thrown into a life she can't schedule, can't control. *Hiding*. What does he mean, *hiding*? They'll leave records everywhere. Their credit cards, bank cards. Records of telephone calls. And for how long? She has her work; the children have school.

She shuts down her laptop and goes to sit between Ari and Karen. When the program ends, she shuts off the television and puts an arm around each of them. Rosewood soffits hiding soft lighting catch her eye and soothe her spirit.

"What's wrong, Mom?"

"We're going to have to keep you both out of school for a couple of days. It's got to do with your dad and his business. It's better for him to stay out of sight right now."

"*What?*"

"It's nothing illegal. He'll explain."

"'Stay out of sight?'"

"Think of it as a family vacation, honey. We'll have a spectacular time. Come on—help me finish packing."

The Other Side of the Moon

When Michael comes in, he's lugging the heavy knapsack and the kind of cash only a drug dealer carries around. He's made telephone calls before leaving Boston; he's left a straight message for Jonathan on the answering machine in Jessica's office. They sit around the small table in the living room of the hotel suite. A family meeting. When was the last time? Ari, oversized, sits on Karen's lap. "Okay," Michael says, apparently to Ari and Karen, secretly in terms Deborah can't refuse, "so these people are selling chemicals to make poison gas—and we've got to help stop them. We have no choice."

"Why? Why don't we have any choice?" Karen asks.

"Don't you hear me? They're selling chemicals for poison gas, nerve gas. I've seen a film of an experiment with dogs—"

"Michael!"

He drops it. "And we've got the evidence. What else can we do?"

"So we're going to the FBI," Deborah says to Karen and Ari.

"*Tomorrow*," Michael says. "I don't want to scare you kids. We'd probably be safe even if we stayed at home. Or here at the hotel. But why take the risk? They want to shut me up. So we're visiting some people. I've called. They're expecting us. Tonight. So go get ready. No discussion. Karen—help Ari, okay?"

Alone with Deborah, he whispers, "Tomorrow I'll be in touch with Geoffrey Slade and with Max Ferguson, and I'll try to get police protection for us. If that doesn't happen, I'll hire somebody. A security person."

"A bodyguard?"

"I have some names."

This amuses her. "I've always wanted a bodyguard. Preferably the young Sean Connery if you have a choice, Michael."

He smiles, "Sure, sure." More than in all their time together, the four of them feel to him tonight like a real family. Ever since he came to her bed that night after Rosenthal's party, things have been a little better. He thinks, *Maybe this is God's design for us.* It embarrasses him to think of something as small as the intimacy of their single family or even the *safety* of their single family in terms of a divine plan. *There's providence in the fall of a sparrow.* He can't imagine such a God—but then, he can't *imagine* God at all. It's beyond him. It's *supposed* to be beyond him. Any God he *can* imagine or explain is an icon. And if so, why *not* pray for his own life, for their lives?

Why not? Because of all the families who prayed for protection as the Romans or Chmielnicki or the SS were sharpening their knives. He doesn't know any of his cousins whose parents and grandparents stayed in the Pale. But he imagines a family in Kishinev before the SS liquidated the remaining Jews in that city, imagines them asking for Divine refuge. *He is my refuge and my rock.* Deborah is outlining possibilities and asking questions, and even while answering, he's thinking, . . . *and though He slay me, yet will I believe in Him.* But to imagine God's intervention? Still, Michael closes off nothing from possibility, and as she speaks, his consciousness feels like a balloon seen from the inside, expanding and expanding until its skin is out of sight.

"Tomorrow you're calling Chemicorp? But suppose this Ferguson is part of it."

"It's not likely. The memos say that he's not to be informed. We know that only a small part of Chemicorp is involved in Orion. But of course I'll be careful—I'll call Ferguson on my cell phone. Nobody will know where we're staying."

"You haven't even told *me.*"

"You remember my 'legacy'? The list of families my grandfather helped? It suddenly came to me—no one else knows those names or could connect them with me. They're not friends, they're not relatives. But they have a debt to our family. I've called one family on the list. They live near here. In Brooklyn."

"In *Brooklyn,*" Deborah groans, as if he's said, *On the other side of the moon.* "I'm going to hate this. It's all right if it's a day or two, I suppose."

"You see why it's a good idea. Any hotel, any plane tickets—everything can be traced. But with a Jewish family who never met us—"

"Yes," she says simply. And she reaches across the table and takes his hand. "Well."

"Well. Their name is Bolofsky. An old couple and their son and his family. The younger Bolofsky owns a small computer store. The woman I spoke to, Sarah Bolofsky, is in her late seventies. I talked to Lazar Bolofsky, her son. He didn't hesitate."

"What did you tell him?"

"A little. He's going to speak to his rabbi about us, in case we need to stay a week or two. But for a couple of nights, they'll put us up. After that—well, I have a long list, a rich legacy."

"So you expect to stay more than a day or two?"

"Please, Deborah."

"You know, it's possible Debbie Harrison is out of town, and I could get the key from her brother. She's on East 73rd Street."

"It's possible. But she's one of your best friends, Deborah. If they're able to trace recent telephone calls—"

She laughs. "Oh—you just want to rub my nose in Jewish life. Michael—please. Let me call Debbie's brother. How much of a risk can there be?"

"Deborah. . . ." He takes her hand. No. That's not enough; he pulls his chair next to hers and puts an arm around her shoulder. He whispers. "Deborah, listen. The lab in Bloomington was blown up tonight. Steve Planck . . . was blown up. Steve Planck is dead, the lab is a wreck. Shh, shh, Come on, no, *no*, don't panic on me, *shh, shh*, no need for them to hear. *Don't panic.* Please, Deb, please?" She pulls away, he pulls her back, holds her until she slumps against his chest. She turns to look at him. He says, "They knew where my information was coming from. They've been tapping our phone."

"What!"

"I think that's why he's dead—they must have known he was going to the FBI. And now I'm counting on it, on the phone being tapped. I think *they* think I'm still there. That I'm leaving in the morning for St. Louis. Oh—I brought you some of your papers. I probably forgot things."

"Steve? Oh, my God. Oh, my God—who *are* these people?"

"Come on."

"What kind of animals? Now, I'm terrified."

"I'll get the elevator."

A bellhop takes their bags down. At the desk, Deborah pays with a credit card. "It turns out," she tells the desk clerk, "we have to fly to St. Louis tonight." The Kupermans step outside. *A well-dressed family from out of town.* She doesn't look terrified. She wears a beige cashmere dress, long and flowing, and over that her black velvet coat with fur trim at the hem and collar. It's after ten. Late for a little boy to be out, but no one seems to notice. Under the cantilevered steel and glass canopy, a doorman flashes the light for a cab and goes out to the curb to blow his whistle. Above their heads is a giant stone oculus lit by huge lamps, a post-modern vision out of a German expressionist film. In a minute the suitcases are wheeled out of a side door and loaded in a cab, while Michael holds on to the hiking pack. From outside the cab he says to the driver, "Kennedy Airport, please, we've got a plane to catch," and hands the bellhop his tip, but as he slams the door, Michael says, "Forget that, driver. No plane. We're going to Grand Central."

Ari's excited being out this late, excited to be escaping from the bad guys. All through his childhood he's been practicing for this moment. When he was four, he and his dad and Karen made a home video together. The bad guy (Michael, wearing a disguise) tries to break in, but Ari takes him down with a squirt to the eyes (spray bottle, label to the camera: *AMMONIA*) and ties him up with duct tape until the police (Karen) arrive.

Their disappearance would be easiest to pull off if they took a subway instead of a taxi to Brooklyn, but Michael didn't even bother suggesting it. Besides, dressed as they are, this late at night the subway might not be a good idea. So dropping the cab at Grand Central, they take another. Michael asks the driver to cross by Manhattan Bridge. "Look, Ari—that's Brooklyn Bridge over there—isn't it just beautiful? Look at the pattern of cables; see, it's changing as we drive? And look there—the Statue of Liberty—way off in the harbor. See?"

There! It's tiny as the nail of your little finger held up to the black window of the subway car, but the dark outlines of low-lying buildings put it into scale, and he says, "Wow! It's *huge*, Dad! It's all lit up! Can we go there tomorrow?"

"Not tomorrow." He's watching Deborah out of the corner of his eye.

She catches the look. "Don't worry, Michael." For the first time in months, they stay with each other's eyes.

The statue holds a torch, but from the Manhattan Bridge you can't really make it out. He sees it, that light, only in his mind.

Displaced Persons

Flatbush. It's Thursday afternoon. Karen is in a foreign country. On Coney Island Avenue three young men in black Hasidic hats hurry by, arguing, fingers writing fast on imaginary blackboards. Women push baby carriages, pull shopping carts. It's late afternoon, and Karen's helping the younger Mrs. Bolofsky with her shopping. Last spring they spent a week in Tuscany; Coney Island Avenue looks more foreign. They pass another *Glat Kosher* market ("Under Supervision by the VAD") another kosher pizza parlor. Signs in Hebrew, signs in a Cyrillic alphabet—"The Russian-Jews," Rebecca Bolofsky explains. Crossing the street, two more men together, these in yarmulkes—again young, mid-twenties. Then a couple of middle-aged men in the same broad-brimmed black hats. "Mrs. Bolofsky? What are all these men doing—middle of the day I mean? Don't they work?"

Some, Mrs. Bolofsky explains, are students at a yeshiva or in personal study with one of the rabbis; some are able to arrange their schedules. Maybe they're on their way to study Talmud, or to pray Mincha in one of the shuls. "But lots of the Orthodox have jobs in the city. Like anybody else. They own stores, like Lazar, or sell hi-tech or something, but it's not like the Hasidism. The Hasidim, they work on 47th Street in diamonds, or they sell hi-tech. Around here, the men do everything. Our congregation—the big synagogue, I mean, not the little shul—has a mathematics professor, a professor of chemistry, a radiologist. You'd be surprised. You've noticed how simple the houses are? Well—most of them. Nothing fancy. But big. We have big families—five, six, seven children. And inside, often the families are doing very well financially, *Baruch Hashem.*"

Karen has never seen so many shuls! Ten, fifteen, in just this neighborhood. A regular grand synagogue here; across the street a little sanctuary and study room in the basement of a rabbi's house. A *stiebl*, she's told. "Then why only men?" Karen asks.

"By us, we believe a woman has a different place. Not worse, just different. *Different.* Tell me." She stops, stands up the wire shopping cart and, arms akimbo, faces Karen. "*Tell* me. Do I look so oppressed to you?"

"No, of course not. God, no. I'm sorry, Mrs. Bolofsky."

"Not at all. It's a common confusion, this mishegos about women should do everything the same as a man. By us, the women are very proud to be what they are." She adds with a little smile, "We pray, too."

Mrs. Bolofsky wears a heavy cloth coat, and a simple brown wig, a "sheytl"—if Karen saw her on the street she'd never know it wasn't her own hair, but why anyone would *choose* such a thing is beyond her. She looks lumpy and dowdy, no style at all, God!—she could be thirty, she could be fifty. Her youngest, a boy, Shmuel, is just a year younger than Ari, so she can't be that old. Then she laughs, and everything comes alive in her face.

She must find me as weird as I find her.

Karen's trying to brush it off by being a tourist. Oh, she thinks, it's *exactly* like some *really* foreign country. But in her chest her breathing is almost spasmodic, as if she were holding back tears. It's not fear of being killed, or her father being killed. She thinks it's just a question of waiting until the lawyers settle everything, the way lawyers do. She doesn't mind missing school for a couple of days, it's not that. But this place—Brooklyn spooks her. It's as if she's tainted by it. Or trapped inside a dream. She's fifteen, and whatever is happening right now this second, it's always *been* that way, will always *be* that way. And she can't wear her own clothes, so this really feels, even in a single day, as if she's a permanent displaced person.

Everything's *so* weird. Her father last night reached out to shake hands with Rebecca Bolofsky, who pulled back and held up her hands to keep him off. "Please don't mind. It's our way." "I'm sorry. I should know better." He told Karen later, he didn't *mind*— he just felt foolish.

Karen is freaked every time she sees her reflection in a plate glass window. Warm today, so her borrowed overcoat is open. Whew. What bothers her aren't the beliefs of Jewish Orthodoxy— their beliefs are as remote and kind of funny as if this were an Amish community. A boy can't touch you? There's no such thing as a *date*? Dumb. But what weirds her out is this pretending to be like them. It's especially *style*—like this borrowed, straight-cut, long-sleeved dress. "As an unmarried girl," she was told, "you don't have to wear a covering on your head."

Well thank God for small favors, as Grandma loved to say! The women's hats—polyester mushrooms with a brim—look absolutely ridiculous to her. As freaky as the men's black broad-brimmed . . . "fedoras," she was told. The *biggest* shock was to see her own mother in one of Rebecca Bolofsky's stiff polyester dresses, sleeves down below her elbows. Oh, my God!—my own mother, Deborah Schiff, in one of those hats!

And when she laughed, or, rather, mimed laughter, in their bedroom this morning after Dad was gone, hand to her chest, eyes googily, her mother turned on her. "Get over it, Karen. Right now. They're being very kind."

"I didn't say—"

"They're protecting us, the least we can do—"

"Oh, Mother. Do we really need that much protecting? Isn't this a little extreme? You really think somebody's going to spot us here? We're not on America's Most Wanted."

Deborah kissed her.

When was the last time she'd done *that*—I mean, just out of the blue? "It'll just be a couple of days, Karen. Just imagine you're playing dress-up. No one's going to know we're here. We just want to fit in."

Karen doesn't want to fit in. Weird—when she's with prep school kids from Andover or Choate, she feels they're not like her at all. These people are even more not-her. They're nice enough: *old* Mrs. Bolofsky almost cries when she talks to Dad, because he makes her remember her own parents and Karen's great-grandfather Jacob. The young Mrs. Bolofsky, Rebecca, she's been terrific. Karen hasn't yet met Rebecca's husband. He was at shul, then at work, by the time she got up, and the kids were off at school. It's like discovering cousins. Weird cousins. She can imagine what dinner's going to be like. Kosher. And like Seders. Lots of prayers.

And Dad. What if he *likes* it here and when we go back home he makes us live with the Hasidic Jews in Brookline?

I'd have to really learn Hebrew. Oh my God!

No I wouldn't. I'd get Dad to send me to prep school.

It hits her now: a lot of these people, they have an accent. They're Americans but they have an accent. It must be Yiddish! Of course. It's like Hispanic kids—second, third generation in America, they still talk with a Spanish accent.

Loaded down with bags, she and Mrs. Bolofsky come to Eichler's. It's a huge store for Jewish stuff. Mrs. Bolofsky stops in for a book her husband wants, and Karen pokes. Unbe*lievable*.

Whole tables of yarmulkes, glass-fronted case after case of meno-
rahs. Karen's research paper last spring on the Spanish expulsion
of Jews in 1492—this would have been the place to come! Jewish
history, Jewish religious texts in gorgeous leather bindings. She
finds herself across the table from a big man in black clothes
and a fur hat. She knows it's not nice but she kind of flirts, tries
to get him to *look* at her. Well, he looks—past her, back down at
his book. Now she can examine him freely, head to toe. He looks
doughy, not in great shape. His black suit is cheap and shiny. His
beard is raggedy. He's pasty, his skin so pale it makes her feel sick
in the stomach. Really. This gets her. *Uch.* What is it? That this
man is in a sense *related* to her? I mean, *as a Jew.*

Get over it.

Okay. Okay. Smiling, she takes the bags of bread so Mrs.
Bolofsky has her hands free. She even thinks of buying herself
one of those cool Israeli pendants on a chain, but Mrs. Bolofsky
pays and they go on to the butcher's. *A foreign country*, she thinks
again, trying to be upbeat. "I like the way you shop like in the old
days or in Europe. Lots of little stores."

On the wall of a building, between two stores, a poster. She's
seen them all over the neighborhood, but this is the first time it
really registered:

KOACH
—Jewish Defense Network
—lessons in street fighting
—course in the legal use of firearms
—Learn to talk back to Christian Missionaries and Anti-Semites

It must be she's stopped to gawk. Mrs. Bolofsky says, "Oh, *that*
we don't believe in. People need an excuse to be tough or violent,
because they're so angry. It's a sickness."

"What's 'Koach'?"

"'Koach' is *power*."

"*What* Christian missionaries?" She can feel her own whiny
irritation, as if that poster were this nice woman's fault.

"Well, there are some. They come around."

"Oh sure—but Mrs. Bolofsky—you mean a bunch of crackpots
who go door to door? No big deal. Nobody takes them seriously."

"Karen. You're a Jew. Don't you think we have good reason to be wary of crackpots?"

Karen is quiet on the way back. *I can spend my time reading and playing piano.* She's got a room to retreat to, the room she shares with Ari, and Ari's always downstairs. But unease is big inside her. She'll be here forever, wearing long dresses, avoiding Jewish weirdos, and saying *bruchas* from morning to night. And not touching boys' hands.

So this is exile. For all of them, but especially Karen. Deborah minds much less. For Deborah it's like visiting a Hindu village in India, *that* disconnected from her; not threatening—quaint. She's just afraid. For Michael, it's a strange exile-in-reverse, exile *from* America. He's back in the shtetl. But he wasn't thinking about this when he went out this morning. "I'll call and tell you what's going on." He takes her hand. "Deborah? Look. Nothing's going to happen, but in my pack, there's a long letter explaining things. The evidence, I'm mailing. But the letter, make sure it gets to the F.B.I."

"Nothing's going to happen to you."

"No. Of course. I'll be fine."

Deborah refuses to worry, but when he finally calls, she's relieved.

"We're set for tomorrow."

"Why tomorrow? Why not today"

"I'll tell you later."

They've been billed as visiting cousins. There's no real need to disguise herself, but it's better they don't stand out. The Bolokskys have these cousins who aren't Orthodox, that's all. Still, she tries on a wig, a "sheytl," and she and Rebecca laugh like girls at the new Deborah in the mirror. It amazed her to look at this make-over. What she might have been if, God forbid, she'd been born two hundred years ago. For a day or two . . . why not? In wig and borrowed clothes Deborah took Ari for a little walk this morning around the neighborhood, and it was like being on stage with other actors but without an audience. The clothes feel scratchy and stiff, but she's not complaining.

Ari has been complaining all day. Breakfast, there was the wrong cereal, he's bored, he has nothing to read, this is a lousy place. He pretends they're on the run from bad guys. Well, they *are*. But it's all play to Ari, it's the bad guys of his fantasies. When they went out, he kept pretending that people in the neighborhood were spies or allies. In the house, he watches with a pair of binoculars from the upstairs windows. He's worried about his bird. Suppose Mrs. Corcoran forgets to feed Pedro and give him water. He's never thought about that bird so much.

But Deborah—when she's not feeling pangs of fear in her stomach, she's a tourist, it's like a visit to a spa like Canyon Ranch but with strict rules: she can't use the phone or fax; she has her laptop but can't plug into the phone line to use e-mail. She has to take a chance using her cell for one call, to call her company, and tells her assistant, "You'll have to cancel the Seattle trip. Tell everyone I'm taking care of my husband—it's a medical emergency. I'll reschedule. . . . No, he's going to be fine. . . . Yes, it certainly is. But I have plenty of work at home to catch up on."

But she doesn't work; she disconnects her *internal* systems. Since she can't do much else, she talks to Ari or Karen or Rebecca Bolofsky; and she observes. It's pleasant to see three generations more or less getting along in one house. She was up early enough to see old Mrs. Bolofsky fixing the children's breakfast while Lazar—what a squat giant of a man!—and Rebecca worked out living arrangements for their guests. Then the old woman, Sarah, and her husband actually talked about a passage of Torah—talked very loud because he's nearly deaf. Deborah could see that their voices irritated Rebecca, but she herself was fascinated: never in her whole life, except at a synagogue, has she met anyone who talked about the Torah. There's a sweetness in their relationship, the old people, she rather envies. For a moment she has a fantasy: she and Michael, old, sitting by the fireplace in their own living room and talking about the Torah. Only for a moment.

There's a great deal, God knows, she does *not* envy. White shirts for Lazar and the boys hang on a rod in the hall beside an ironing board. To think that anyone still does their own ironing! And the house is so middle-class and drab. She couldn't possibly live here. Plastic slip covers over the living room furniture! But this Rebecca Bolofsky is a strangely attractive creature. She'd be extremely pretty if Deborah were to do a makeover. *No.* Even as

she is. Unlike a lot of the women Deborah sees around the neighborhood, Rebecca actually has an original sense of style—within
limits set by what she calls "modesty." Instead of the usual boring
hat worn by the Orthodox women they saw today, she wears a
swatch of bright color, a warm red, half-turban, half hat. They have
to make do—seven people crammed into one small house (and
now, with them, eleven). But the kitchen is spotless and bright, the
house is full of books—Hebrew, Yiddish, English—and the books
make all the difference.

"I really like being here," she told Rebecca this noon. It wasn't
a polite lie. But condescending? Oh, yes, condescending, and
Rebecca, who's quite a powerhouse, shrewd and unafraid, turns
from her preparations for dinner: "Mmm. And that surprises
you?"

"Let me cut up the apples," Deborah says.

A Shtetl in Brooklyn

Michael has been wearing his black velvet yarmulke all day—in the
house, in the neighborhood. He'd stand out if he didn't. But let's be
honest—it's not just a question of fitting in. It feels good; by the
end of the day it feels natural. Lazar wears a yarmulke at home, a
black fedora to work in the city, and going to services, also a black
fedora, but broader-brimmed and very expensive. They're walking
to Ma'Ariv service at a little shul around the corner. "Many nights,"
Lazar says, "I can't get home for Ma'Ariv. It's good you're here. I
made sure to come home early." It's early enough for them to have
dinner after they return from services.

Lazar Bolofsky is a couple of years older than Michael—
forty-four, forty-five. A big man, not as tall as Michael but much
broader, he looks like a wrestler gone to seed. You might look at
him and expect a big tough voice. But his speech is dignified, his
eyes are gentle. He speaks with a subtle Brooklyn-Yiddish lilt, as if
English were his second language, though a language he's perfectly
fluent in. The Yiddish quality is in the music of the phrasing, the
rise toward the ends of sentences. But there's a nasality that's like
chalk on a blackboard for Michael. Michael is a snob about speech.
He respects Lazar; but when he hears him, he winces.

Lazar owns a small store off Canal Street, downtown Manhattan, that sells computer systems. He has computer hardware and frames built for the store, is able to offer customers a lot of capacity at a good price.

What's important for Michael is that Lazar has a CD burner at the store—he was able to dupe the CD-ROM Michael got from Steve.

"I made two copies for you. One, like you asked, I mailed off to the FBI at 26 Federal. The other's a backup."

"I'm grateful. I'll take that copy with me to the FBI."

"So tell me. About the sales of these chemicals."

Michael's unwilling to get started. But once he begins, he explains everything—the initial discovery, the dogs, the sales to customers in the Middle East. Lazar offers to help. He could make a few calls and there'd be a bodyguard of strong Jews. Lazar himself is a hell of a strong Jew. He'd like Lazar by his side in a fight.

"I don't think it's necessary. But thanks. Lazar, if you want, when we get home tonight—*if* you have the stomach for it—we could look at the CD-ROM together. I don't want Deborah to see it. But I could use the company. And I need to see it before I talk to the FBI tomorrow."

This morning Michael sat in a deli on Coney Island Avenue and over his cell phone, which couldn't be traced to Brooklyn the way a call from a pay phone could, called the police in Bloomington, had a long talk with the detective in charge of the bombing. He refused to give his whereabouts. Then a scheduled call to Geoffrey Slade at Interpol, a call to the FBI confirming the appointment Geoffrey had made for today.

Finally, a call to Max Ferguson in St. Louis.

He remembered Ferguson from the meeting in St. Louis when they won the Chemicorp account. He's a big man—maybe two twenty-five, two fifty. But when lunch arrived, he ate almost nothing; Michael wondered: did Ferguson feel that being seen eating gave him less authority? Vice-President for International Sales, Ferguson sat beside Al Braithwaite.

"This is going to be a long and tough conversation, Mr. Ferguson. Chemicorp is in very deep trouble. I'm calling you because I happen to know you were specifically kept in the dark. . . ." Of course Ferguson assured him, "Orion is a legitimate project, Mr. Kuperman. We know about Orion." "No, I don't think so. I certainly hope not. I'll start from the beginning. . . ."

A long conversation ending in the account of Steve's death. "Within Chemicorp, Orion is a tiny operations group," Ferguson said after a long silence. "But if any of this is true, well, it's terrible. And it's liable to damage Chemicorp badly. We're a publicly traded corporation. Can you imagine what will happen if this comes out? Mr. Kuperman, we have to survive."

"That can't be our chief concern, can it?" Michael said. But he agreed—he'd wait a day, change the appointment for tomorrow.

"I'll call Al Braithwaite," Ferguson said. "One of us or both of us will get to New York tonight. We'll be coming in with lawyers. Where can I reach you?"

"You can't reach me."

"Well, then, call me back with details. Please, Mr. Kuperman."

And he did. He made calls, put off his appointment till tomorrow morning, let Geoffrey know, let Ferguson know. Then he found a copy center and duped the print material from Steve, put it in the mail to Interpol and the FBI, both at 26 Federal Plaza, downtown Manhattan.

Suppose Ferguson starts checking files, documents, asks questions of the wrong people, and they learn about his ten AM appointment. What then? Maybe he *should* take Lazar up on his offer of a bodyguard. But he's embarrassed to ask.

Lazar sighs, "How terrible, that your colleague was killed by these people."

"My *friend*. My good friend. More. It's like a younger brother dying."

"I'm so sorry. You and your family will be safe here. It feels like a gift to have you with us, to be able to complete the circle."

"What my grandfather Jacob did for your grandfather?"

Lazar doesn't answer. He asks, "Tell me, do you wear tefillin? No? If you'd like, Michael, while you're here, I'd be happy to teach you."

Tonight they walk slowly. *And I'd be happy to learn.* A quartet of young men—The brims of their broad hats like a black horizontal from building to street. But they move to let Lazar and

Michael pass by. There are Jews and non-Jews. They pass a number of young black people, black and Hispanic men and women. Angry music blares from windows, from car windows. A young man's carrying a boom box down the street. There's lots of street action. One black woman seems to aim at Michael and Lazar a look of contempt, even hatred. Michael can't put that look down. It stays with him.

Terror and sorrow. Grief for Steve keeps welling up. All day, all day. Grief for his mother, grief for Steve, a cloud of grief that sits in his chest. On the street today Michael wept, turned to look in the window of a shop to hide his face. This afternoon he stopped in at an early Mincha service so he could say Kaddish for Steve as well as for his mother. He's never in his life been directly at the mercy of evil. This is his Chmielnicki. He's Tutsi, he's Bosnian; his neighbors are coming.

Halfway down the block they pass the men's *mikva*, the ritual bath, closed for the night. A couple of black teenagers passing by pay them no mind. Michael imagines they're all here, all the ancestors. A black man in jeans and windbreaker too light even for a mild winter night is coming home from work, too tired to pay attention to them. Up ahead is a brownstone, like a storefront church except Jewish, painted sign in Hebrew and English *B'nai ha Bereit. Sons of the Covenant.*

Climbing the steps of the brownstone, they step inside. Twenty, twenty-five men attend this Thursday evening service, but they take up more than half the chairs in the room for men. Women, if they came, would sit behind a screen in an adjoining room, but middle of the week there are no women. "I can't help thinking of the politics of space," Michael whispers as he thumbs the Siddur. Lazar Bolofsky is murmuring to himself. But he's heard, and later, on their way home, he'll answer, "What 'politics'? We have *our* place, the women have *theirs*."

The service is brief. The rabbi, a thick man in an untidy beard that adds ten, fifteen years to his age, says no more than the page number. Michael can't help using mental scissors to trim the ragged ends. He offers the rabbi a program in exercise and weight loss. Meanwhile, the chazzan, a man about Lazar's age, hunches over the reading stand and chants, building to little explosions of intensity, tuneless, no voice and hardly the pretense of melody, sometimes lifting his head to shout a phrase and slam his hand down on the wood. Each man davens at his own pace, and what a pace! Faster even than at the Orthodox synagogue in Brookline. But whispered. Here, Lazar is like a fish in water; glancing at him out of the corner of his eye, Michael finds respect, admiration, even envy. Michael can't get his mouth around even the prayers he knows by heart before they're onto the next. The men rock each to his own drum, head back and forth, back and forth, weight from backward to forward foot, as if each were alone, as Michael is alone, too worried about tomorrow to focus properly. He thinks, *If some gentile were to walk in, he'd think we were all crazy, that this was a crazy house.* Well. Too bad. Closing his eyes, touching his fingers to his own beard, Michael lets himself rock, too, through the Amidah, until it takes, and he's caught up by the murmured praying followed by the chazzan's repetition, and finds that the men are *not* praying each alone.

It frightens him, this crazy praying; he's half-observing, half-observant. Frightens him—as if he might belong here, has come to stay. He sees his own synagogue in Brookline, with a woman rabbi, the congregation chanting prayers in unison, *contemplating* the words of the prayers. The rabbi may say some words to unlock the passion within one of the prayers, the *kavannah* (intentions), then they chant only a part of the prayer together—not chant, sing—a traditional melody, men and women intermingled, and the chazzan (a convert, a woman, a gay woman!) chants some of the rest in her pure soprano. He can imagine what the men in here would think!

All of a sudden, he's Jacob Goldstein again. *As* Jacob, he's home. He feels his breathing deepen. The stale air in the little sanctuary seems to have become a denser medium, half liquid, in which chairs, bima, ark, vibrate in fuller being. The accent's a little funny, the intonation more nasal, but it's the same service Jacob took part in, morning and night, his whole life, in Kishinev, in Rochester, even in Manhattan. And Michael-as-Michael says to himself, I want it both ways: to be Jacob and to be a modern Jew. To live each day bound by mitzvot to the Covenant, by the Covenant to

God; *and* to live as I feel like, adventurer in the world of spirit. The service ends and the rabbi makes a couple of announcements.

Not thinking, he stares at the lamp above the ark, always kept lit in every shul, a splinter of fire from the light over the ark in the mishkan, in the tent of meeting in the desert, "to burn from evening to morning before the Lord." And that light over the ark is a metaphor for the cloud of fire of God's presence at Sinai—"The appearance of the glory of God was like a consuming fire on the mountaintop before the children of Israel." The same fire in which Moses first encounters God—the "bush all aflame, yet the bush was not consumed." Kuperman's fire.

On their way back from services tonight, he's seized by what his mother would have called a *shreck*—but not exactly: a *shreck* is like a momentary internal shriek in the guts, while this . . . it's a pain . . . it goes on and on, the way he imagines a cancer being born—it twists, it tugs, a siren in the belly. He has trouble breathing. But Lazar needs to talk to him about the store. Lazar asks for advice about venture capital.

Should Lazar take up the offer of venture capital in return for a share of the business? Michael pulls himself together. He finds it strange to discuss business with someone whose *tzitziot* (fringes) on the little *tallis katan* worn all day under his clothes show at the bottom of his shirt.

"Can't you go to a bank?" He wants to offer Lazar a low-interest loan, no strings; he'd be *happy* to loan him some capital. But it seems a bad idea—Lazar might think Michael felt pressured. Perhaps later on. Meanwhile the siren screams on. That they might be waiting for him. Are Deborah and the kids safe? For how long?

"It's tricky, accepting venture capital," he tells Lazar. "That's how they get their hooks into you. Let's talk about it tomorrow night. I'll give it some thought."

A Different Shtetl

Lazar slips the disk into the CD-ROM port and brings up the directory. They're sitting side by side in Lazar's study; the walls are bookcases with leather-bound volumes and computer manuals. Lazar insists Michael take the desk chair; on the side chair he looks outsized, gross. His thick arms are folded.

"*Canine.2*—it's an experiment: killing dogs in a laboratory with nerve gas. We see the dogs die. Steve said over the phone to take a drink before I watched. But I want to turn to *Demo.1.* He says that's worse. Can you handle it. . . ? You know, he died because of the call."

"You said."

"Steve . . . he was the sweetest guy. A real maverick. He used to row on the Charles River in the morning—worked out technical solutions while he rowed. He was smarter than I'll ever be."

"I'm so sorry." Lazar closes his eyes. "*Baruch ataw Hashem, Eloheynu melech ha'olam, dayan Ha'emet.* Blessed art thou . . . the true judge."

"I know what it means," Michael snaps. He takes a big breath. "Look. Lazar. It just sounds too pat. You know? It puts it away. In the sense of *gets rid of it.*"

"Not at all. It leaves us with the obligation—"

"Here, watch this. This one I haven't seen." Michael clicks on *Demo.1.* It comes up with a freeze-frame rocky landscape. He clicks on the icon, **BEGIN**. Black and white. Silent. A helicopter shot, maybe a thousand feet up, rocky hills, sheep or goats grazing, a bit of cultivated land, another patch, then the copter seems to rise, rise above a ridge and swoop toward a village spreading irregularly down a hillside along a road, each stone and stucco house seeming to find a niche among rocky places. Where is this? Michael wants to say Afghanistan, but it could as well be Turkey or Albania or Iraq. At the bottom of the screen, time is overlaid in digital figures: −6.0, −5.0, −4.0 . . . Not many people in the village. But a little farther on, in a flat cleared spot, maybe fifty, sixty, seventy men are gathered. It looks like only men, or mostly men, but you can't be sure. −1.0, 0. The words flash: **Delivery commences.**

The men hear the copter or spot the copter. They're running in every direction up the hillsides. The camera captures a tiny parachute opening below, a flash and white smoke that dissipates almost at once. +2.0, +3.0 . . . +5.0, +6.0.

There's no need to keep watching this. There's no need— Michael knows what he'll see, but he can't click it off. It's masochistic to suffer this, and cruel toward Lazar. Maybe he wants to be cruel. As if to tell Lazar, *Go ahead, say* . . . da'yan emet *now.* But it's also that he needs to feel this terror that Steve died to send him. It's Iraqi planes gassing Kurdish or Shiite villages, but gas isn't the point, it's Dresden or Cologne or Serb soldiers in Bosnia or Kosovo, it's Hutus with machetes, SS units forcing Russian Jews to dig a killing pit. Except—isn't there's a different level of evil in this film?—to demonstrate the capabilities of your product in a promotional video. To be able to distance yourself as much as that.

At +.9 seconds the camera captures the first signs: as the brain functions are destroyed, the bodies dance; arms flail, he can imagine what the faces show, but the camera is too distant to read faces. Fewer and fewer men are on their feet. It's as if they were swimming, swimming on the dirt, swimming into the rocks.

+26.0, +27.0. . . .

The copter drops lower, the camera pans a dance of death, and now it zooms in.

+45.0 . . . +1.35.0. . . .

Now you can make out the faces, they seem fractured by trails of—it must be blood—seeping from eyes and ears. The camera sweeps over the area and rises, rises, pulls away, a few people running from the village, now rocky hillside, beautiful empty landscape. At 3.0.0 minutes: freeze frame.

Michael clicks onto the directory. To blur his feelings, he says, "The rest is just data. I haven't had time to read it. Clients, bank account numbers, encrypted until Steve got a hold of it. This isn't a company CD-ROM—Orion didn't put this together. Steve culled it from various encrypted files."

He looks up, sees Lazar's eyes are closed, Lazar whispering words; now he looks back at Michael and nods and nods and cradles his own cheeks with his own hands.

"Sorry. I shouldn't have done that to you."

"Michael . . . Michael."

From the kitchen: "Din-ner!"

Chapter Ten

Fences

Ari has already eaten, but he sits with the two families at the long dining room table with a good white tablecloth and takes the blessings very solemnly, the blessing over the washing of hands, then the silence until the bread is blessed. Ari has been given a yarmulke decorated for a child. Needing comfort after watching men drowning on bare rock, Michael stares at Ari: the boy's face glows. Ari seems to be broadcasting something that doesn't originate in himself. It's just an ordinary Thursday night. So this must be simply the way it is every night Lazar can get home. Candlelight refracted through a decanter of juice: violet shadows on the white cotton cloth. There's a comfortable, required, silence. Lazar looks at Michael, looks and nods.

Now—quick—Lazar says the blessing over the bread, over the meal. Rebecca laughs at something Deborah says to her, and they plan for tomorrow, Friday. Deborah will help Rebecca get ready for Shabbos. Extraordinary! Deborah's face is mild, her laugh girlish. Maybe it's just that here's a place where she doesn't have to compete.

Even knowing that tomorrow will be frightening, may be dangerous, knowing that after he sees the FBI and Export Enforcement he's still not going to be safe, Michael feels, if not peace, at least a promise of peace tonight. To bring home to Brookline this way of eating together, eating a sanctified meal together! His pulse jumps at the possibility. It's so much the way he wants their life to be. Will Deborah accept that—or is this make-believe for her, like putting on a costume for a funny portrait at a mall? That it can be like this, so simple!—it feels like a treasure he's had at hand all the time and never picked up. He pats Ari's knee under the table.

Oh, he feels a slight strain—he so much wants this to be perfect. He wants to shed complications, the need to re-imagine what it means to be a Jew, what it is to love God. And this is a treasure. The families they know back home eat on the run, catch-as-catch-can. Imagine: every meal might be a blessing. Now, Michael feels overwhelmed by images: the helicopter in grainy black and white; and though he hasn't seen it, the lab in Bloomington, everything charred, mangled, Steve spattered throughout the lab.

Lazar's father and mother have already eaten; they go to bed early. The Bolofskys have a grown son in Chicago with a family of his own. At the table tonight there's a twelve-year-old daughter, Leah, and a handsome son, Samuel, a little older than Karen. He's sixteen, maybe seventeen, but seems so much more placable and innocent. Samuel's quiet until asked—about his school, his plans— and then he answers in full, eager sentences with tongue clicking staccato on teeth and palate in yeshiva style, citing authorities. A teenager citing authorities! (". . . as Rabbi Hillel tells us . . ." and ". . . as Rashi tells us . . ."). It makes Michael a little uncomfortable to hear a teenager use secondhand formulations. "As Judah Halevi says in the *Kuzari*. . . ." Of course Karen's friends are loaded with received ideas, too, ideas just as hand-me-down, about "finding themselves" or "being who they are." Is this so different? Samuel won't look at Karen. Just shyness—or is he obeying a rule? To find out, Michael gives Samuel a reason to look at Karen, asks her, "Honey—can you imagine yourself going to a school that's essentially religious? A Jewish high school?"

She says, "I never thought about it. I guess I'd find it pretty weird. I don't know."

As she speaks, Samuel doesn't even glance her way. Rebecca, maybe sensing that her son is being watched, speaks about their belief that men and women need to stay apart unless they are married. "We would never permit them to go to school together, boys and girls together."

And Samuel, looking very serious, says, "We've found that it's not good." *We*—it would be inconceivable for any teenager Michael knew—Jew or gentile—to say "we" comfortably, whether the "we" meant "we Jews" or "we young people" or "we Americans."

Karen pushes away from the table, stares at Samuel. "So how come you're so afraid of a man and a woman being alone?" Deborah arches her eyebrows; it's a complicated gesture, ironic, amused, supportive; at the same time it reminds Karen: be polite. It doesn't stop Karen, her face hot with righteousness. "I mean, don't you trust yourselves?"

Samuel bows his head and still won't look her way. Lazar says, "You can answer, Samuel. Go ahead. It's a discussion. It's not immodest to answer."

Not looking at Karen, he says, "I have friends who go to secular high school. I know what goes on. We have a better life. We have Torah, the life given us by Torah. We live as Jews. It's no good living like gentiles. Look at what happened in Germany."

Michael doesn't understand.

Lazar explains. "Samuel means—my family has heard me speaking about this—assimilation in Germany gave the Nazis a big target. It's not a complete explanation. Samuel, this we shouldn't get into tonight. Germany isn't the point. But look at the culture we're staying apart from. Here in America. Michael, don't think I'm proselytizing. It's because I respect you that I feel obligated to explain about us. Look at it—your American culture. Every day I think about this. Look what magazines and television and movies are selling us, teaching us what's important. The images. Every day I need to get on the Internet for my business. I wouldn't want to say at this table everything I see. Money is success, and expensive cars are success, and fancy restaurants and fancy clothes. Speed is success. And unnatural titillation. You know what I'm saying, Michael. We've seen images, Michael, you and I, tonight. For money, they debase human life. They make this place polluted, evil. For money. You're in business, like me. I mean ordinary business, not this terrible evil I saw tonight. Debased images become idols. It's truly idolatry. Is that a life? But we can fence the unclean out, *Baruch Ha-Shem*. All right"—he hammers a forefinger on the white cloth—"not completely, but enough. We're protected by the fences we put up. We live by Torah. They say we're unwilling to adapt to American society? Nu? Frankly, we are. Of course we are. We have a plan given to us at Sinai. '*Emet v'yatziv v'nachon v'kayom*. True and firm, certain and enduring. For all eternity.' We have been given a way to live. God forbid we should forget it."

"God forbid," Michael says.

"Why is it that it's so marvelous for Native Americans or Hispanics to be proud of their separate culture, but not Jews? How is it we're not allowed? Look what the world is like! Look at what we've witnessed tonight."

Rebecca says to her husband, "*What*? What did we witness? This has been a good discussion. Are we so afraid—?"

"That's not what I meant. I'll explain later. *Fershtaste*?"

"I go along with your revulsion," Michael says. "But Lazar— can't we disagree about the details of God's plan? I don't think it was written down at Sinai that I can use an electric razor but not a razor blade. Or take Shabbos. In our world, what does it mean to 'keep the Sabbath'? I agree, sure, it's hard to live as Americans and still keep a sacred space and a sacred time. It's just as hard for Christians, for that matter. But if we spend time concentrating on all the things we mustn't do, for instance, on Shabbos—like turn on a light switch or carry keys outside the house—we do injury to the spirit of Shabbos—its peace and joy, and that's what it's about."

"Absolutely. The laws of the Sabbath insist on our being joyful. I always say that. But excuse me, Michael, that's not what Shabbos is *about*. It's not like a weekend. America has the weekend. 'Party, be happy.' Jews have the holy Sabbath. It's to remember God resting on the seventh day. It's to remember the gift of freedom from slavery in Egypt. But you're right, it is a mitzvah to be happy. The Sabbath is a 'foretaste of Paradise.' Of Messianic times. Our family keeps the small obligations of Shabbos, and I think tomorrow night you'll see we haven't forgotten the spirit."

Lazar sits higher in his chair at the head of the table. He's remembering the Talmudic passage that clarifies the passage from Leviticus on why it's forbidden to use a razor. But he's silent.

Michael wonders: Does Lazar really believe in Messianic times? Are we really moving toward a time when people will be close to God that Mosiach will arrive, the dead will rise, and we'll live in the world according to God? Michael can't believe. He sees that rocky video-landscape, the digitized numbers spinning at the bottom of the screen. Are we moving toward Messianic times—or toward a society like the one in *Blade Runner*, that vision of Los Angeles split into a small, powerful, rich, and highly technological sector . . . and the rest of us, shabby, grubbing to survive?

Rebecca takes the soup bowls to the kitchen and Deborah follows to help her bring in the main course—a beef stew and a big serving bowl of kasha varnishkes. "We don't always eat like this," Rebecca says. "More and more we eat vegetarian. But this is the food I was brought up on, and you're a good excuse. Do you cook varnishkes?"

"I don't cook," Deborah says.

"Not true, not true," Michael and Karen both say.

"My dears," Deborah says, "just imagine Rebecca were a great diva, a professional, and you'd want me to say I'm a 'singer.'"

Everyone laughs or pretends to laugh. But now comes a mistake. Karen sings. She's done musical comedy at camp and at school, and she's got a rough-and-tumble voice people enjoy. She sings, "You say t-*may*-toes and I say t-*mah*-toes. . . ." Michael grins, grateful for the change, but quickly Samuel turns to his father, "May I be excused?"

"Samuel, just sit. It's all right." But Lazar puts up a finger. "Karen, dear?"

She stops.

"There's nothing you've done. In fact, it's fine for you to sing. Samuel doesn't quite get the subtlety. A man, by us, mustn't listen to a woman's voice, her singing voice. A woman's voice can be very beautiful and very arousing. But in this situation, it would have been much better to listen. You're like family." He casts a side-glance at Michael and smiles at him, and Michael nods and smiles back.

"I didn't know."

"Of course, Karen. How could you know?"

"Please, everybody, eat," Rebecca says.

Coded Communication

After dinner, Deborah disappears to get Ari ready for bed. Karen goes up to his room to kiss him goodnight. And maybe to complain. She rolls her eyes, hoping her mother will laugh. But Deborah shakes her head.

Michael comes in to say prayers. Sitting up, Ari asks, "Dad? Are we going to go home tomorrow?"

"Oh . . . I think we'll stay for Shabbat, Ari. Shabbat with a family like the Bolofskys, a family that really keeps the Sabbath; it'll be fun."

"They pray a lot. Even after dinner."

"They do. You mind?"

Ari shakes his head. "You know what?

"What?"

"I'm in a James Bond movie."

"You think?"

Ari rolls off the bed, falls to the floor, arms spread, head askew, eyes freeze-frame. He comments like a voiceover: "And there he lay, sprawled on the floor."

"God forbid."

Back in bed, Ari reaches up and pulls his father down to him for a kiss.

Deborah takes Karen by the hand and leads her into the hall.

"You're no fun. Admit it, Mom—this is a weird scene. What's going on?"

"I wasn't going to scare you, but you need to be oriented, Karen."

"Oriented?"

"Uncle Steve—Steve Planck. He's been murdered. The lab in Bloomington's been blown up. We're here because we could be killed too, and there's no way to trace us at the Bolofskys."

It's as if Karen isn't even shocked. She lets Deborah hold her, like a doll, being held. And slowly, she lets go. When Michael comes out of Ari's room, she calls to him. "Dad!"

"You told her."

"I think it's better. Of course don't say anything to Ari."

"Uncle Steve? Uncle Steve?"

In their own room, Michael watches Deborah organize her things. Now that they're alone, she's changed into the only comfort clothes she brought to New York, a Gortex navy-blue running suit. He watches her straightening the bed. It's where the Bolofskys' son slept before he married and moved away. Not really a bed— it's a box spring on the floor. He's ashamed—as if it mattered. "Want help?"

"No. No, thanks."

Now, something's cooking in his brain. He takes a snapshot of Deborah making things nice and scans it through his inner software, where it transforms itself into . . . a different marriage—he the Jewish husband, she the Jewish wife. There's an erotic charge for him in the scene. Is it the patriarchal authority that excites him? Much more it's like looking through a gap in a high hedge, a view into a secret garden. At the same time, there's something else, something he can't admit: wouldn't it make him tremendously uneasy to enter that garden?

Admit it's no accident he married Deborah. She didn't pretend she was someone else.

"Deb?—"

"Are you all right about tomorrow?"

"Sure. Well. No. Are you kidding? A little scared, matter of fact."

"I should hope so. I am, too."

"Lazar offered to come with me. To get some strong young men to come along. But that's not necessary."

"You're going by subway?"

"Sure. . . . So, did you call work, let them know you'd be out?"

"On cell phone." Suddenly Deborah laughs. "You know, Michael—I'm going to enjoy helping Rebecca get ready for Shabbat. You see? Finally, I'll be what you always wanted me to be. A maker of chicken soup and Shabbos, like your mother. Oh—I didn't show you what I look like in a wig."

"The dress was enough," he laughs. "But you know, you don't look bad. Well. You never look bad. You're an exceptionally beautiful woman. You know that."

Listen to the conversation under the conversation:

"Deb?—"

"Are you all right about your meeting tomorrow?"

"Sure. Well. No. Are you kidding? A little scared, matter of fact."

"I should hope so. I am, too"

"Lazar offered to come with me. To get some strong young men to come along. But that's not necessary."

"You're going by subway?"

"Sure. . . . So, did you call work, let them know you'd be out?"

"On cell phone." Suddenly Deborah laughs. "You know— I'm going to enjoy helping Rebecca get ready for Shabbat. You see, Michael? Finally, I'll be what you always wanted me to be. A maker of chicken soup and Shabbos, like your mother. Oh. I didn't show you what I look like in a wig."

"The dress was enough," he laughs. "But you know, you don't look bad. Well. You never look bad. You're an exceptionally beautiful woman. But you know that."

Deb he calls her, not Deborah: Can we be friends? The music of her name, "D e b"—one syllable rising, gently, into uncertainty—tells her—is *meant* to tell her—he's ceding power to her.

Now he hears in her questions a concern for him he hasn't heard for years—or hadn't heard until the night he wept in her bed after hearing Myron Rosenthal talk about lives that matter . . . and lives that don't matter. Now their own lives are taking place on a different plane. Imagine—perhaps pettiness can be shed! He can tell her he's afraid. Suddenly, they can simply converse. Just the exchange of words seems a wonder.

He knows-and-doesn't-know that her own generosity to him— she hasn't blamed, hasn't complained—is making her generous, generosity breeding generosity. She makes fun of herself in the role of *frum* wife. That means it doesn't threaten her; still, it lets him know that she's aware there's a price to pay. He acknowledges his debt by reminding her of her beauty. "Exceptionally" makes it easier to say, as if he's stating an objective evaluation.

And something else. Her distance from the role; this doesn't upset him. It relieves him!

Relieves him. Suppose she said to him tonight, "Michael? I'd like to live this way. Aren't there congregations in Brookline? I'm up for it"—If she said that, if she left her role as secular rationalist, he'd feel dizzy, in mid-air. But she's letting him know her limits.

It's so subtle, what's going on in this strange bedroom. It's in millimeters of the fleshing out of lips, the softening of focus in the eyes, the way Michael scratches the back of his neck, a Jimmy Stewart gesture of uncertainty that opens her breathing. It's the scent of her perfume. Something in the tilt of her head, a gesture he knows from a long time ago, when she loved him—a gesture he still sees, from time to time, at a party, say, when she gets interested in a man, usually a powerful man but sometimes just someone nice looking. Oh yes. That little tilt, chin pointing at him. As now.

Actually, not talking about it, they're dancing towards the bed. This is a courting dance composed by tongues, by eyes, the tilt of a head. He wants to know, can they go to bed tonight, make love, first time in weeks.

They've been given the third-floor bathroom for themselves. They wash up, get into bed, he with his Siddur, she with a folder. He reads his prayers in a whisper, she makes notes for a report. This lasts all of ten minutes. She raises her eyebrows, he nods, she turns off the light. Now they lie there looking up at the cracked-plaster ceiling. He finds a map there—coastline, rivers. There are hills where years ago a drip puffed out the plaster. The map is absorbing because it keeps him from the landscape of the bed, the map between them, negative space formed by elbow and curve of hip.

But that land between them is fluid, its edges shifting slightly, and the fluid is charged, dangerous, an electrical field, positive/negative—or a mine field. Half-glancing, he sees the lovely bones of her face against the near dark, and—maybe to imagine her less dangerous, or love between them easier—he sees her as terribly young, no older than Samuel and Karen, younger than when they first met.

He turns toward her onto his side. She turns onto hers. They're opponents across no-man's land; it's still a kind of battle; after all, this is Deborah—general, judge, prophetess. This is part of a long, tough war, and she's a force to be reckoned with. But the rules of engagement are changing. Because she's suddenly—not suddenly at all, but that's how he wants to imagine it, because "suddenly" costs less, seems more the play of impulse, something coming from outside—precious. Maybe it's the real danger, too; that he feels responsible for their lives. The negative space between them diminishes.

Sometimes, across it, they touch, accidentally. And then, talking about tomorrow, touch to emphasize a point, fingertip to shoulder. That her skin should be so charged for him!

And his for her.

He touches Deborah's hip. Now he can't bear to stop; it's as if he's already making love, there's such pleasure in it. "Deborah? Deborah?"

She closes her eyes and laughs. Opening them, she leans over him, breasts against his chest, and kisses him. She plays with his beard. "Funny man."

"Oh, thank God, Deborah. Thank God. *Baruch Ha-Shem.*"

Deborah gives him a look.

Mourners' Kaddish

On the floor below, Lazar brushes his teeth with fury, annoyed at himself for arguing. And brushes, too, to purge what he's seen. His stomach is giving him trouble; clicking off the light, he says the prayer of wonderment at, gratitude for, our bodies. Blessed art thou . . . who has formed the human being in wisdom. . . .

Rebecca is already in bed. He can tell by the set of a shoulder that she's upset. Lazar finishes his prayers, makes sure the two-handled jug of water and the basin are ready for morning oblations. He touches her shoulder, and she turns and looks into his face. "What did you witness?"

"A CD-ROM. A video. The death of a village."

She waits.

"Rebecca? Please? It's not a time to speak of it. I keep no secrets from you. I'll tell you, but not before we sleep, or I promise you, we won't sleep."

He slips under the covers and puts his arms around her to comfort them both.

But the death he doesn't describe permeates his sleep. He doesn't see the dead or the village, but the landscape is the same. The dreamer is sitting wrapped in tallis on barren, rocky soil. But now he sees that the mourner is not wrapped in tallis; it is a kittel, the white robe worn for High Holy Day services and as a shroud. There is no minyan; alone, he is murmuring the Kaddish.

Getting Ready for Shabbos

Deborah wakes in time to say goodbye. Michael leans down to kiss her. She's grateful: it's not a special kiss meant to remind her of last night. Then from the window she watches Lazar and Michael walking to morning services. Michael carries an attaché case and a paper bag. What could he have in the bag? A black yarmulke covers his bald spot.

She thinks of herself as a clearheaded person, but this morning it's as if no story holds her life together. She doesn't want to fool herself, to get swept up in movie emotion. Like an affirmation of religious faith, she says aloud, as she straightens the bed, "Listen, Michael, you listen—there's too much in my life, too many things I care about—I won't stick with one way to live": an inverted Shema. Before the turn of the century, her grandfather escaped from the tyranny of Judaism as much as he escaped the Germans. She isn't going back!

She's almost angry at him for last night. She feels herself in a country that's strange but not wholly undesirable. The strange country isn't Orthodox Judaism. That, it's clear, is simply not for her. The strange country is rather some alternative version of marriage.

Karen will be sleeping for a couple more hours. But Ari's up and calls for her from next door. "Mom?" She goes in to kiss him, reassure him. "You get dressed. I'll be downstairs with Rebecca, and we can have some breakfast."

"Mom? What about my bird? What about Señor Pedro?"

"Oh, he'll be fine. Señor Pedro will be just fine."

"Will Margaret feed him?"

"Of course."

"Will she pet him?"

"That I don't know."

"Is Daddy here?"

"No. Daddy's got some business to finish so we can get back home."

But in a sense Michael is there. There's a filament of feeling, sewn last night, connecting them. Or it's more like a radio frequency, and last night they tuned to the same single frequency, so that when she stops for a second at the top of the landing to listen for sounds of Ari getting dressed (noticing the bare spots in the decrepit runner), she feels as if she's with Michael at services in the dark little synagogue around the corner, with a bunch of pallid strangers in black hats or yarmulkes and prayer shawls.

Michael feels it, too. His body is humming, a body tune, he'd forgotten you could feel like this. He's praying, but she's there in his skin, Deborah. At the same time, there's the same gnawing pain high in his belly; it goes on and on, through the Shema, through the Amidah. It's a Friday. This morning the prayers of supplication are short.

> O Lord, punish me not in thy anger; chastise me not
> in thy wrath. Have pity on me, O Lord. . . .

He's glad Lazar is there with him. But all around him, the men in skullcap or fedora, they don't feel like home to him. He breathes in the stuffy, sour smell of the little shul, smell of oxidizing books and prayer shawls in need of cleaning. He doesn't want to be tainted by it. Then, a moment later—as he sways through the standing prayer, the air seems suffused with the Shekhina itself, the Presence of the One, and all he needs to do is breathe her in. But he is physically sickened: the doughy skin, so many bad complexions, most of the men out of shape; and the spastic rocking from the shoulders by some, especially the younger men. Young men look like middle-aged children; middle-aged men look old. Many seem out of sync with their bodies, as if they didn't belong in them.

But does it matter? What matters is that he is with men who permit him to mourn. Their prayers, all different, make one strong prayer. When Michael stands for the Mourner's Kaddish, he is thinking of his mother, he is thinking of Steve, but he is also remembering that rocky village, the gas, those dead. "*Yitgadal v'yitkadash, shmey raba. . . .*"

His body suddenly becomes clammy: Dad! Suppose they go after Dad?

We Should Say a Prayer

"Have you ever had cholent?" Rebecca asks as she gets the kitchen ready for Shabbat cooking. She's wearing surgical gloves. Deborah has never in her life seen a kitchen this immaculate. "It's for tomorrow, cholent, the dish we eat for after Saturday morning services. Stewing beef and tongue—well, there's lots of recipes. It's like a stew. We use kasha, stuffed derma. I put in chicken fat. It's 'heart-attack food,' but once won't hurt you."

"I'm looking forward to it. Now, put me to work, Rebecca."

Rebecca hands her surgical gloves and a bag of apples and pears. "Good. We'll make a dessert kugel for tonight. You want a cup of coffee? It's made."

Deborah feels like a child playing hooky. She's wearing the same plain dress. Not to disguise herself, but because none of the clothes she brought with her to New York make any sense for housework. "Thanks. Have you ever worked outside the house, Rebecca?"

"Oh, for years and years. First, as a teacher, then when the children came, I stopped. But then Lazar opened his business and I learned to do the books, I took care of the billing, I *hondled* with dealers. Now, thank God, the business is on its feet. Once Samuel is in college, I'll find something. But I'll tell you—this is plenty."

"Please. Rebecca. Of course it's plenty. I'm not saying that keeping a life together the way you do, I'm not saying it isn't work. But it's work I wouldn't be good at."

"And it would bore you to death. Be frank. You weren't brought up the way I was. So? What do you enjoy about your work? Travel? I hear you travel a good deal."

"It's exhausting, travel. No. What I like is the analysis of structural problems in business. I like solving problems. I like being respected for my competence. I'm a lot like Michael that way. And frankly, I like making money. But this is extraordinary for me—of course I'm frightened, but there's something good—this time with your family."

"I have a good feeling about it. Michael will do fine today. He's going to the police this morning?"

"The FBI. But Rebecca, there may be people looking for him right now."

"We should say a prayer. Will you say a prayer with me?"

A Meeting With Max Ferguson

Michael walks to the subway with Lazar. The disagreement of the
night before has disappeared. Lazar wears fringes under his shirt,
but under the trench coat, no one can see. It seems like half of
Brooklyn is walking with them. Hispanic, black, Jewish, it's like a
scene out of a forties' propaganda film about America as a melting
pot. The subway is elevated here; they climb the iron steps. The rest
of Brooklyn is on the subway already or crams in as the subway
heads northwest.

Michael's anxiety seems a thing outside as well as inside his
body; it's expressed in the tapping of the young black man in the
next seat—the man drums his fingers on his book, drums to some
inner beat, but the tapping seems uncontrollable, frantic; he's
barely in the same car. The man grabs his own hand to stop the fingers, but they explode—yet it's an articulated explosion, producing
a complicated, accurate rhythm that rules him. It's turned against
him; it could wreck him.

The subway climbs Manhattan Bridge. Lazar taps the glass.
"Just look at the Brooklyn Bridge in morning sun. Isn't that something? Those huge towers that hold the cables, when the bridge was
built—what, a hundred thirty years ago?—those towers were the
highest point in Manhattan. Can you believe it! And now look."

Michael nods. "Thank you for enduring that with me last night."

"Aach—you have such a burden. Please—whatever you need,
please call; you have my number at the store."

"I have it." The train descends beneath Manhattan. Lazar
gets off at Grand Street, a couple of blocks from his store.
Michael knows he could walk from there, through Chinatown,
but can't remember how—it's been too long; so he goes on to
Broadway-Lafayette.

Alone, Michael grows a little dizzy. He looks up; the young
black man has gotten off. The disturbing energy is only in his own
body. He doesn't know what to do with himself. Subway ads above
the windows tell him—learn English; find out about AIDS; here are
sexy jeans. A subway poem, Williams' "Red Wheelbarrow." Suddenly he realizes how smothered he feels in the packed car. He's
choked by stale breath, patchouli oil, after-shave. Someone's talking

in Spanish. Someone's talking in—Russian? He's only got a minute, but from his attaché case he takes out a pad and looks at a list of points to go over with the FBI As always, lists soothe him. He adds:

> Call Dad.

At Broadway-Lafayette he changes for the Lexington Avenue line. As soon as he gets to the Brooklyn Bridge-City Hall stop he finds a phone.

"As a matter of fact," Ira says to him, "I stopped by West End Avenue yesterday to water the plants, and you know what?—ten minutes later, somebody rings from downstairs, he says he's a private investigator, and have I heard from my son. You think it's one of the bastards?"

Michael has reached him at Eleanor's. "I think. Did he bother you, Dad?"

"Bother? No. No. Not at all. He said he's with the D. A., he needs to check some facts with you. It could be about my case, but I don't think so."

"Listen. Do me a favor—you stay away from West End Avenue for a few days?"

"I intend to anyway. Eleanor and I are getting away for the weekend. You know, I got a big show coming up in New York. A retrospective."

"Really! Good. That's good."

"My agent is hoping to sell to a couple of museums. So, anyway, we're going up to a place Eleanor knows in the Berkshires."

"That's close enough, Dad."

"Oh—I get it. Those sonsabitches. Ahh, there's no way they'd tap this phone."

He wonders if he'll ever see his father again. He wants to say something loving, something kind for his father to remember him by. But he can't get the words out. "So, Dad. Take care of yourself."

"Yeah, yeah. But Mikey, what about you? Are you all right?"

Now, for the first time since he left, again from cell phone, Michael calls home to pick up messages. The tape is pretty full— eight, nine messages. The fifth is the one he was expecting:

We want back the material that was mistakenly mailed to you. Our clients say that you have no legal right to any of it. Mr. Kuperman, you can stay away only so long. You have a family. You should remember Mr. Planck. You must understand how insistent we are. All we want is the material. Is that clear? The material and your assurances. We get those, we'll have no further issues. Leave a message on this machine, and we'll make arrangements to meet you and take the material. Our client asks that you consider this offer very seriously.

Surrounding this are messages from friends, the house painter setting up a date to do the estimate, information left by Margaret Corcoran.

Scaffolding surrounds City Hall. He skirts the park and goes up Lafayette past court houses, city buildings. Where in the world are there this many cop cars?—County Sheriff cars, NYPD, detectives' cars, State Police. Mostly witnesses for court cases, he guesses, but the presence of the cars cheers him. Already, before he reaches Foley Square (he's starting to get his orientation now), he's watching for people who might be watching for him.

Scaffolding up over the street-level floors of most of the buildings, wooden canopies shield the sidewalks. A bright wind, dust in the air, so he has to squint constantly. Scaffolding and chain-link or wooden fences, and against the fences or the walls of buildings, street vendors—immigrants, most of them—sit behind with big trays set up on boxes. Asians, Hispanics, a few blacks. They sell whatever—watches, scarves, African statuettes, tee shirts, souvenirs—a hodge-podge. Who'd buy? He feels the weight, the grubby sadness: they don't even call out an invitation, don't smile a welcome. Maybe they're not permitted to hawk their wares? They just sit. He supposes they put whatever money they have into whatever they can buy cheap, then sell what they have and go back for more. How do they make a living? Even if they stole what they sell, he can't imagine anyone buying. He fantasizes going up to one of the younger ones and giving him a free business consultation.

Walking past him or alongside, so many worried-looking people. Families, brooding or talking fast, the husband or the wife maybe trying to get a green card, trying to extend a visa, trying to find a job.

More than half the people on the streets seem to be immigrants. Then there are the crazy ones. On this short walk he passes two men, one woman, talking to themselves.

"So am I crazy? I talk to myself," he says to himself.

The FBI is located, along with Immigration and Naturalization and other Federal agencies, in the Jacob Javits Federal Building, about thirty stories, architectural glass and aluminum, heavy vertical shafts of concrete. A cold wind blows around this tall shaft like crazy; he has to squint even more. The main entrance is only for Federal employees with badges. To one side, there's a visitors' entrance—a temporary structure, one-story box of attached panels. It looks like a place that sells hot dogs at a football stadium. I'll bet the architect grinds his jaws every time he passes, because it louses up the elegant, severe hi-tech look of the building.

The FBI is here at 26. So is the NYPD Intelligence Division and, in the same set of offices, a liaison group from Interpol.

Attaché case in one hand, paper bag in the other, Michael walks around the building. There's another entrance for visitors, closed today. So he'll have to go into that little pre-fab to explain his business. He's promised to wait for Max Ferguson; together, they'll meet Blair on the 28th floor and talk. Geoffrey Slade will meet them there and they'll head over to the other side of Duane Street, where they'll meet with the anti-terrorism squad and an agent from Export Enforcement.

But not yet. It's an hour before his appointment. Michael crosses and buys a newspaper at a tiny newsstand. Then he stands at a pay phone at the corner pretending to make calls. At the next phone stall a wired-up man with a Southern accent is talking loud to some agency. "So I can't get her off my back, ma'am, she keeps following me. Follows me up to New York. What I come to New York for? How would you like it, ma'am? Well, then, who'm I supposed to talk to, t'get that bitch off my back. . . ? Well, excuse my language, no, I apologize, I'm so damned overwrought. Now you tell me. I send her money. I got to send her money. Nothing she'd like better than drag my ass into court. . . . Well, you tell me. Well then, who? You got a number. . . ?"

Michael wishes he and Geoffrey had decided to meet up at the Interpol Liaison offices. Everywhere, he sees hit men after him. He goes to sit on a bench in the little park next to the building. The benches are in long, curving ribbons that form a pattern, each surrounding a hillock where in the summer they must plant annuals. Now the hillocks are bare and no one's on the benches.

To look busy, ordinary, he takes from his attaché case the manila folder with the memos Steve mailed. He holds the folder on his lap. He takes out his prayer book. He pokes through it, keeping one eye open. He reads the Hebrew aloud, a psalm of joy, praise for God in a world from which God seems absent. That's why the psalms still work, he thinks. God still seems absent.

He remembers last night: Ari's eyes. Deborah's breath.

With twenty minutes to go, he closes the Siddur; he's too anxious. He decides not to wait for Ferguson after all; let him find his own way up to Blair's office. He gets up from the bench begins to make his way toward the building. Now a black Lincoln pulls to the curb and a man—isn't that Max Ferguson?—steps out. And another man. So Ferguson brought his lawyer. Makes sense, Michael thinks. I would have done the same. The car stands there, but a policeman walks over, and Ferguson waves the driver on. He's met Ferguson only twice—once when they pitched the contract, once at a technology conference in Chicago. But the man's easy to remember—very broad, nearly bald, with eyes close together and a natty little mustache. So we'll go in together after all. He puts the Siddur into the paper bag, the folder into the attaché case.

But as Michael gets up to walk toward Ferguson, another car stops at the curb; two men, both big men, get out. One has long black hair; the other a blond brush cut. Both are wearing suits, but these aren't lawyers. Ferguson gestures, points one forefinger right, one left. Right away, he *knows*. Right away, he's sweating. The men separate, one toward Michael, one away. Toward Michael, yes—but Ferguson still hasn't spotted him; so Michael keeps his eyes averted, and walking slowly past one man, changes course for the street corner and waits to cross, his heart beating like mad.

Where's that damned policeman now?

Now, as he quick-steps across Broadway, he glances back over his shoulder and sees the men running. Ferguson must have recognized him; they're running. No time to figure out what's going on. Is Ferguson part of Orion after all? Or is he ignorant but trying to eliminate any report that makes Chemicorp look bad? Michael breaks into a run, down Broadway, back toward the only subway kiosk he knows. He runs, broken-field through crowds, into the open, out on the street and back onto the sidewalk. No chance.

These guys are younger, stronger. No chance. If he can find a few seconds to get out his cell phone! 9 - 1 - 1. But no time. And how could the cops get to him on the street? Cops! A thousand cops within a few blocks of him! Where are they?

His only chance, he thinks, dodging down Chambers, crossing, trying to get lost in a crowd, is to find a cop down by City Hall, cops in a patrol car. No cops in sight, and the distance between him and the men is shrinking. What about one of the courts! Courthouses all over the place—get into a courthouse, he'll be safe.

The little lead he started with has been cut in half. Sometimes, when he glances over his shoulder, the view is blocked. Then— they're there again: closer each time. Should he start yelling? All they have to do is grab him and say they're cops. So he runs. He's losing breath. Where's a courthouse entrance?

He retraces his route past the immigrant peddlers. As he runs, some shrink back against the building; some just sit. Brooklyn Bridge is just across the open plaza, but he'll never make it.

Near City Hall, Michael-the-legacy, beneficiary, distillate, of centuries of suffering, of running and surviving, makes a break across Lafayette Street, barely squeezing between the back of a truck and the hood of a taxi—and here's the kiosk.

These several blocks, he's envisioned a train, but why should a train be coming just now? There are two of them. They'll trap him on a platform, nobody will dare to stop them, people will look the other way. They'll throw him onto a third rail! And the long trek of Shmuel and Menachen and Isaac and Mordecai will end with him. No—there are the children! Tails of his trench coat flying, for an instant he sees Ari's face. If he's killed, they'll go on.

Now, thank God, he gets a crazy idea. It's not that he hasn't thought of it earlier. In fact, here's what the paper bag was for! But not like this—so fast! Taking the steps three at a time, ripping off his coat, he's maybe ten, fifteen seconds ahead of the faster of the two men.

At the first landing he swings to a stop, takes out of the bag the black Hasidic hat he brought for just this, for a disguise, just in case, and jams it on his head, and holding onto the Siddur, he drops the bag, pops the clasp of the attaché case, and tosses the case, open, with a tennis backhand, down the subway stairs, so that papers float and scatter. The manila envelope with the CD-ROM's is among them. Now, forcing his breath to quiet, he pulls off his trench coat, shrinks himself and bows his head, pulls the hat lower, and, eyes half-closed, praying both as disguise and comfort, he walks up the stairs—quiet, solemn Hassid, *alte Jude*, the fringes of his talit katan showing at his waist, past the rushing men.

They leap down the stairs past him, the long-haired man ahead, and follow the trail of paper. One stops to collect papers and the leather case, then takes off after the other. One of them is shouting instructions. But Michael is on the sidewalk, and he hurries through a crowd toward the great columned archway over the New York municipal buildings.

Just inside the courtyard, he presses against a column, calls Blair's office at the FBI. He can't get through the telephone menu. Again. This time he pretends to be on a rotary phone. Somehow he's taken seriously. *Wait*, they tell him. *Wait right there.* He waits until he sees an unmarked black sedan. An FBI uniformed policeman gets out. "Mr. Kuperman?"

A sagging, middle-aged Hasidic Jew in broad-brimmed black hat comes out of the shadow of a column and walks toward the car. Looking around, he straightens up into a tall, athletic, "modern" Jewish-American businessman, and gets in.

It's only when, as he steps into the car, the crown of the broad-brimmed hat bumps the ceiling, that he remembers—and removes the hat. But then he takes his black velvet yarmulke from his shirt pocket, puts it on, and keeps it in place with a bobby pin Rebecca gave him.

Why? So he can remember who he is, where he came from, when he talks to the FBI? At work, though he's forgotten once or twice and left it on, he wouldn't purposely wear a yarmulke. It would feel ostentatious. It would be disconcerting to clients. And there's no need. Only the Orthodox feel it necessary to wear a head covering outside synagogue or Torah study.

Nevertheless, he leaves it on as he follows the large—large like a professional football player—FBI policeman through the lobby at 26 Federal, past the glass doors to the elevator bank for the FBI. At the 28th floor, he leaves identification—his Massachusetts license—with another officer at a receptionist window, and he's given a visitor's pass to wear. "Agent Blair is expecting you in conference room B."

A young woman leads the way and knocks.

Intermittent humming of printers, fax machines. The conference room is practically bare. The walls are decorated with plaques, framed awards looking like baccalaureates, photographs of FBI directors and recent U.S. presidents, some in handshake with FBI big shots. The lighting, fluorescent, sends out an irritating high-pitched hum. Through slats of the blinds he can see down to the street, out between buildings, over roofs toward the Hudson. New York is almost silent from up here, insulated out. It smells of a new building. It smells of his own suspicion. Suspicion makes sense: these are the people who bullied employers into firing leftists in the fifties and in the sixties, spied on Martin Luther King, on Vietnam protestors—maybe on Michael.

He needs these people, as they need him.

The agent in charge, Curtis Blair, gets up to shake hands, introduces himself and his partner, Frank Beaudoin, and they get down to business. Business—when what Michael wants to talk about is his narrow escape, his fear for his family. There's no opening for that. And where's Geoffrey Slade? He asks at one point; the question is ignored.

If only he had the CD-ROM's with him. Copies will be coming in the mail, but today he's walking in with just a story.

The odd thing about the next hour is how little he finds out, how ordinary, businesslike, the meeting seems. Even boring. It's like discussions with his marketing team. Do they believe him? He can't tell. Curtis Blair, a heavy-set man in his late thirties who speaks slowly—slowly and in monotone—is not Michael's idea of an FBI agent. A corporate manager, not a cop. Beaudoin looks like the pop image of a detective—at least he's solid. The muscles in his neck are delineated the way they are on the covers of body-building magazines. But he's silent. The senior agent, Blair, he's not stupid— Michael can tell by his questions. But he has no interest in being liked, no real interest in Michael. Is it my beard, my yarmulke? They sit around a long, imitation-wood grain table: Michael, Blair and Beaudoin, then, after a few minutes, a young man, Anthony Paglia, an agent from Export Enforcement. Paglia takes notes on the chemicals, on the British subsidiary, on General Djouti. But what the FBI asks about is Steve's murder and the bombing of his lab—not the sale of precursor chemicals for munitions. That they seem to ignore. And where's Geoffrey?

They take names, dates, and content of telephone conversations; they listen to Michael's description of the CD-ROM without comment. Then more questions about the lab and Steve's work. Then the same questions, phrased differently, by Beaudoin.

Still no Slade. Now Blair and Beaudoin take him across the street to a different office building, where Michael answers the same questions for two men from the Anti-Terrorist task force. These people don't even perk up when he mentions Djouti. They nod. Do they already know?

Michael's statement is recorded. Now, he tells his story from the beginning, but no one in the room seems to be listening. Blair is organizing the folder and taking notes.

By the time they stroll back to Blair's conference room across the street, Michael is silent with anger. No one wants his inferences. And he's a successful man; part of what it means to be a success is getting to play with your own set of conceptual tools. *You* can write the story—of sales strategy, of problems, of how software is changing. Blair and the others—they're not interested in his narrative. As for his feelings—they're simply irrelevant. In his whole life he's only been chased once before—in New York, as a sixteen-year-old, by a teen-aged gang as he was coming home at one in the morning. But that was nothing; they just wanted to hassle him. This time, it was life and death. He's irritated at his childish hunger for concern. Nobody seems impressed. Waiting for the elevator at the Javits Building, he asks about protection. No one replies. They go up in the elevator in silence; when they're alone again, on the 26th floor, Blair asks, "So—you think they know where you've been hiding?"

"Certainly not. They'd have come after me."

"Think you can stay there till Monday? We'll send a car for you this time," Blair adds. "I'd like to talk again after we've gone through the memos—and we'll want to see that CD-ROM."

"And after Monday? How do we go back to having a regular life? I can't stay hidden. I've got to protect my family, Mr. Blair. What do we do?"

Blair shrugs. It's an expression of superiority, the little bastard. "Oh, I wouldn't worry too much. If it does become a problem, we'll have someone assigned to you."

"'If it does become a problem'—and how will I know that? If they come after me again?"

Blair ignores this. Not even a shrug.

"Who were those men who chased me? A private security service?"

"Possibly."

"They picked up printouts on the subway steps. And the disks. But they won't know what else I've got. And they'll think—they'll think I can identify them." *They'd be wrong*, he thinks. *Long black hair, short buzz cut. Suits.*

"You can identify a couple of guys who chased you, Mr. Kuperman. What is that? That's nothing. Can you connect them with anything? What does it mean, that you were chased?"

"Exactly. Why *was* I chased? You've got a murder in Bloomington, a murder in Boston. I want you to look at the larger picture."

"You don't have to worry, Mr. Kuperman. We'll look at the larger picture. If it turns out that the bombing and murder are connected to chemical munitions, don't you think we'll go after that connection?" Blair asks. Deadpan.

Michael feels Blair's condescension; it rankles. "And the sale of chemical munitions," Michael goes on. "The sale to Djouti?"

"I'm sure the anti-terrorist people will look into that. We're not sure at this point you're talking criminal activity."

Meanwhile, Michael says, "You'll drive me to the subway?"

"We'll drive you to Brooklyn, Mr. Kuperman. We'll make sure the police keep an eye on the street tonight. All right?" Blair says. *Will that do you?*

Michael is no pushover in negotiations. Like Jonathan, he impresses people with his power. Not as sparkling as Jonathan, but a tough negotiator. Fusion didn't succeed these past ten years just because of smart software. The chase today got him rattled; the loss of Steve, the threat to his family—he came in here shaky. Now, he's not shaky, he's calm. And angry. Standing, gathering his notes, Blair tells Michael the car is ready to drive him "home" now.

But Michael sits; finally Blair has to look at him. Michael says, "You sit down, Mr. Blair. We're not finished."

Blair sighs. He sits. "Yes, Mr. Kuperman?"

"You don't listen very well. You're looking for an indictable offense. You seem to have defined the problem as a series of crimes. And they're terrible crimes; I'm very glad you're going to help solve them. I've lost one of my dearest friends. But what I'm not hearing you talk about is the meaning of it. The meaning is money. The sale of chemicals for chemical munitions. Wait till you get the disks. Then you'll understand. Those sales have to stop. I'm going to expose what's happening in Chemicorp. You listen. I've got contacts in Congress, I've got contacts in the media; this will get to be a very public case. I promise—I'll make a public and political stink. You'll be surprised—I can be a real sonofabitch, Agent Blair, so let me suggest to you that the FBI take the connections seriously. I want you to *get* it. People were hired to stop information getting out. We're talking murder and arson. But what are they about? They're about money . . ."

"They're almost always about money, Mr. Kuperman."

". . . and about death, they're about death—the villagers in the video, and people who are still alive. Villages of people somewhere—maybe Iranians, maybe Kurds, maybe North Africans—and if you don't put these crimes in perspective, the sales will go on, more villages will be gassed. I'm not going to let that happen."

Blair shrugs; he steps out, comes back, leans over Beaudoin and whispers.

Now there's a knock at the door; three men walk in; first, Geoffrey Slade, then Max Ferguson—and someone with him—a lawyer?

Slade nods to Michael and sits down; he begins writing on a yellow legal pad. Ferguson smiles solicitously at Michael. "Heard you had some trouble down there."

"You dare show your face here?" Michael, unbelieving, stands. Blair points a pen at him. He sits.

"Mr. Kuperman, please, you seem to be under some misconception." Ferguson is unperturbed. "I hope we can clear this up." Concerned, dignified, he smiles at Michael. He eases himself down into a conference chair, half-spills out the sides. He's powerful, not just fat. People describe Ferguson as a "sumo wrestler." He's the kind of guy so big he needs to travel first class. His neck is thick and muscular, he has big eyes in a big head, reminding Michael of those massive portrait busts of late Roman emperors. It's cool in the room, but Ferguson's skin gives off a sheen of heat, of sweat. Is it fear? Every time he looks over at Ferguson, Michael is filled with nausea. He remembers a passage in the Book of Job. Somebody describes a wicked man, a "man who drinks wrongdoing like water. . . . His face is covered with fat/ And his loins with blubber." It's not the weight—but in this man the weight seems like a metaphor. Ferguson is gross and unclean, stuffed with corruption.

Blair, reading from the papers in front of him, says, "Apparently, Mr. Ferguson, Mr. Kuperman believes you had men try to kidnap him."

"'Believes'? Please! I *saw* Max Ferguson directing those men. It's hard to mistake Max Ferguson."

Ferguson shakes his head. "Please. You're upset, I understand. Mr. Kuperman—you saw me with a couple of men from our legal staff. That's all. This is James Seltzer, this is one of them. My legal people. We were supposed to meet, isn't that so?—suddenly I saw you running, Mr. Kuperman."

"Why, you murderous, lying son of a bitch," Michael savors the words (how often do you get a chance to say *murderous, lying son of a bitch* in a conference room?).

Ferguson closes his eyes. "I understand you're upset. You've been through an ordeal. I'll let that pass. There were allegations made against Chemicorp—that's why I'm here. Mr. Kuperman, you called me. Isn't that right? I'm here because you said you trusted me. Isn't that true?"

Michael picks up a folder. "The company reports—Orion's memos—said not to inform you. I was conned—I see now that must have been your way of staying safe."

"—Not to inform me. Exactly. That's what you told me. So I'm afraid I'm in the dark." Ferguson leans forward, says this in his thick, heavy voice. "I'm not informed. If it's true that some people at Chemicorp had illegal dealings, of course we need to know that. We're looking into the allegations. Orion does exist—it's a small marketing group within Chemicorp. It reports to me. So we're concerned. We'll be examining company computer garbage. We're not sure—perhaps the disks you have are doctored. Believe me, this means as much to us as it does to you. Think how badly this could damage Chemicorp. It's doubtful. But it's possible. But I do know this, Mr. Kuperman: we're contemplating a civil suit against Fusion for industrial espionage." And to Blair: "His people invaded our files—encrypted files—apparently downloaded some."

"Agent Blair! You wait till you see what's in those CD-ROM's I mailed you. Has Mr. Slade explained?"

So far, Geoffrey Slade has said nothing. He's sat quietly, in suit and tie; he looks diminished. He seems embarrassed for Michael, embarrassed for being connected to him. He murmurs, "Of course, well, of course it's all conjecture."

"What," Michael says, "what's conjecture?"

"Well, the source for those videos," Geoffrey says. "And how Chemicorp is connected to the material. Conjecture. We simply have certain surmises, not much more than that, you see. Apparently—is this correct?—Mr. Kuperman has additional material. I under-stand there may be potential international connections. That's why Interpol is somewhat interested. Someone named . . . Djouti. Someone named . . . Reynard. I believe that's the name. Reynard."

Michael stares. Geoffrey seems so uncomfortable. As he speaks, speaks haltingly, he looks down at a piece of paper in front of him. He seems to be writing.

No. *Drawing.* He's drawing.

"That's not our concern right now," Blair says. "We're more con-cerned with the bombing of the lab. Mr. Planck's death."

"What are you talking about, Geoffrey? What about Djouti?"

Slade clears his throat. "Yes. Exactly. Someone named Djouti. And others. I understand that there's a good deal more data in Mr. Kuperman's possession. Something about a M. Reynard—is that the name you gave me, Michael?"

"Reynard in Marseilles?"

"*Exactly.*"

Michael can breathe again, for now he's *got* it; he's noticed what Slade is drawing: a cartoon of a race, two sculls, figures on the bank, cheering. He remembers Slade sketching that cartoon in the little place on 52ⁿᵈ Street. *I'm a ferocious competitor. . . . I'm rather fanatical about winning.* "Well," Michael says, "Yes. I've been under some stress. It was terrifying, those men after me."

"I can imagine," Geoffrey said blandly.

"Yes—Reynard," Michael says.

Taking up coat and black hat, Michael lets himself be ushered from the room. "You've got to let us do things in our own way," Blair says, as he escorts Michael to the elevator. "Don't worry." His tone has softened. "We'll do what has to be done."

Shabbos

Mid-December; candle-lighting (eighteen minutes before sunset) is just past four today. All the Jews in the world seem to have left work early and are rushing home through the streets of Flatbush. No Christmas decorations on Coney Island Avenue. The siren goes off—*Jews, just fifteen minutes before you light your candles.* By the time Michael gets dropped off, he has only a few minutes to rest, no time to talk to Lazar or even Deborah. He's trying to put it together. What was Slade doing? But he doesn't want to lose the Sabbath.

They welcome the Sabbath—Old Mr. and Mrs. Bolofsky, Rebecca and Lazar, Samuel, Karen, Ari, Michael and Deborah. Rebecca lights the candles, one for each member of the family, one for each of the visitors. No one speaks as she says the blessing, shading her eyes from the light, drawing the holiness of the Sabbath toward her with open hands as if she were welcoming a sweet aroma, or a guest. Then the blessing over the wine, over the bread, and so the Sabbath has begun. He wants to call Slade—what was Slade trying to do?—but can't now that the Sabbath has begun. Lazar takes Michael off to Kabbalat Shabbat service.

Michael is afraid he'll lose concentration—the glass of wine knocked him out, and he can't stop thinking about Geoffrey Slade the competitor, the guy in the winning scull. And what does winning mean in this case? But the service moves him. He's especially grateful to be able to welcome this Sabbath.

Home from synagogue, they ritually wash their hands and, silent, sit at the table, laid out with linen and silver, lit by many candles. The barucha over bread, now they can speak. It's clear to Michael, even clearer to Deborah, that the Bolofskys want to give them a gift—the taste of a perfect Shabbat. Deborah has been part of the preparation, has seen the care with which Rebecca got things cooked, ready. Samuel set the timers for necessary lights; the oven's off now, but the cholent, inside its earthenware insulation, is steaming for tomorrow.

But Michael, who wants to be at peace, is not. ("Michael? Are you alright?" Lazar asks.) There's herring, there's soup, there's roast chicken, roasted vegetables, and kugel. But Michael is in Warsaw, it's 1939, no, it's 1940, the Gestapo might be just outside the door. It's like that morning at the Orthodox shul in Brookline: he can't get rid of this vision: of Rebecca, of old Mrs. Bolofsky, Lazar, Karen, Ari, Deborah, too—each of them, their heads shaved, herded into a cattle car. He looks around the table and sees numbers tattooed on forearms.

He goes to the window to look out. Sees nothing. What could he see?

It's Shabbat. He doesn't want to ruin it for the others. But he hears a sharp rapping on the door, hears boots thudding on the floors, on the carpets, hears breaking glass, crying, praying, while at this beautiful candle-lit table, this Shabbat in 1994, Samuel begins "Sholem Aleichem," and everyone joins in but Karen. (Rebecca asks Karen with her eyes, but Karen tightens her lips.) "Bless me with peace, messengers of peace, angels of the Most High. . . ."

And they do, the angels do, but you can't take away the works of time. Those jackboots are never going to stop pounding. Will a Rwandan Tutsi ever be able to see a machete in the same way again? Or see a Hutu neighbor in the same way? Still, there are songs to sing for the Sabbath.

Deborah gets Ari ready for bed. Michael comes in and they say prayers together. Ari's well-kissed, he's comfortable, but he's been thinking about his bird. I suppose it's his home he's been thinking about, really, and Señor Pedro is merely its symbol. But he sees Pedro with no water, no food, in a dark house. What can he do?

No one sees him tiptoe into the hall to the Bolofskys' phone. It's Shabbat: no one is supposed to use a phone. He knows this. He knows, too, that no one is to know where they are. So he won't say. But when Margaret comes in tomorrow, she'll get his message; he dials.

"Hi, Margaret, it's Ari. Margaret, I can't tell you where we are, Mommy says. I want to make sure about Señor Pedro. Please take him out of his cage, okay, and let him sit on your shoulder sometimes, and please put out bird food for him. And don't forget his water. I'll see you soon. And please don't tell Mommy I called. . . ."

CHAPTER ELEVEN

"They Make Their Own Laws and Rules"
—Book of Habakkuk

His father's career at Lever Brothers forced the family to move from state to state. So Max Ferguson was like a military child, but without the continuity of officer clubs and PX's and base culture. Three elementary schools, two junior highs, two high schools. He was always the new boy, always the fat boy. Since his academic record was blurred from all the moves, his parents put him in a prep school for a thirteenth year, and there he was "Max the Elephant"; by the time he graduated, five-foot-eight, he weighed almost two hundred pounds. He spoke slowly, guardedly; in spite of good grades, he was thought stupid.

But he wasn't stupid. By the time he was eighteen, he had invented a secret, aloof self that despised the others. He separated a part of himself from slow, lumbering Max; this created inner self would bide its time, hiding inside Max the Elephant. He managed to make the teasing stop. He was, first of all, a strong boy. And he turned his quiet, heavy look on the boys until they shrugged and, uneasy, let him alone. And he let them alone.

Except once. He was good enough in chemistry to put, in two tubes inside a beaker, two chemicals, harmless separated; noxious, acrid, sickening when combined. A film of tissue paper at the mouth of each tube separated them. He placed them at the foot of the teacher's desk, stationed himself at a stool and sink near the door, and when the papers dissolved and the reaction began, he walked out before he could be affected. There was wild confusion, screams, banging and breaking from the lab; he stood outside and listened. Then, calmly, victoriously, he pulled the fire alarm. An absent troublemaker was suspected but couldn't be held accountable. No one was badly hurt. And Max?—why, he was in the lab himself until he ran for the fire alarm. Besides, no one could suspect Max the Elephant.

He doesn't consider himself *evil* or *not evil*; he considers himself *smart*. He made sure that Orion memos indicated he had been kept in the dark about Orion's activities. Were there revenues that came through Rosenthal to Ferguson, not to Chemicorp? Internal documents won't say so.

It's his French associates (Reynard and the others) who take care of problems and launder money. Ferguson would have no compunction to eliminate someone who got in his way. But in the normal course of things, he doesn't need to dirty his hands. He's generous to subordinates while they're useful, has made himself learn how to tell a joke, has learned to follow football and basketball like an ordinary person. But he knows he's not an ordinary person. At times he's wondered how he came to be so fortunate—to see things so rationally. He's wondered about his brain chemistry. If a colleague—this happened last month—loses a child to a tumor, he knows what the man is going through and knows the facial expressions and gestures that are appropriate. But his secret childhood self, still alive, is busy estimating the cost in productivity of the man's grief.

He is no longer an object of contempt. And working every evening with free weights, he has grown physically very strong. He likes to hurt—only slightly—the man he's shaking hands with, smiling all the while, stopping just before he can be called on it.

He is still, quiet. He looks at you like a Buddha. Women are intrigued. He has stayed single, but he has no trouble finding attractive women who don't mind his extra weight.

It is with women that something odd happens. He is a surprise to women. They take an initial interest in him because of his success. But when he is naked, he is seen to have great strength. He uses that strength, edging on sadism, never making unusual demands but forcing a woman to submit, to lie helpless—it's no act; she becomes helpless under his force. Not his weight—his force. As if he's holding a cat or a small dog down, he holds her down. He opens her body to his with enough pressure to make her want to stop him; but he won't let her. She might think that lost in all his bulk he'd have a small penis, but no, he's surprisingly large, and he forces himself into her until he presses against her cervix, *painfully*, smiling into her eyes; then, when he knows she has given in to him, knows she recognizes her own helplessness and is afraid, he holds back—is suddenly subtle, gentle, arousing. Two or three women these twenty years have gotten furious, have scratched or bitten or yelled out. He hasn't hurt them. He makes sure they know that he is refraining from hurting them, that he is not humiliated nor even angry. He smiles, and very, very gradually eases up, holding their hands away from him. The two or three women became afraid. But most become aroused and come back to him, keeping him like a wicked secret.

Last year, on a trip to Marseilles, he met Reynard's chief assistant and made final arrangements for protocols; then he was taken in a limousine through back streets near the old port and led down cement stairs to a cellar, then along a corridor to a room with a one-way, heavy glass wall. The floor and other walls were white, made of some plastic material. From the observation room nothing inside could be heard until a switch was thrown.

They were meaning to frighten him. He took the situation in, in all its threat, but he knew that they needed him, knew that like him, they didn't act irrationally. A man, naked, hands taped behind his back, was brought in. For half an hour, two men went to work on him methodically, with garrote, cigarette lighter and knife. At first the screaming was audible, then switched off. It was explained what the man had done. It was explained what it was they needed from him before he would be permitted to die. And when the torturers were satisfied, they stopped, looked toward the mirror to make sure, then at the tap on the glass, slipped a knife between his ribs and twisted slightly. Max nodded, as if it were a demonstration for his edification. He knew he'd impressed them: no ordinary businessman. Since then, they've worked together as equals.

Reynard himself, Ferguson has never met. He's a legend, Reynard—soft spoken, reasonable, terrifying. His own employees would sooner oppose any of the Russian Mafia bosses, sooner betray God or Satan. Max is wary, but calm: he has what Reynard needs.

Rosenthal needed to be disposed of. One call to France took care of that. As it will take care of Kuperman.

"Hear O Israel, the Lord our God,
the Lord is One."

Lazar is willing to wait for him Shabbos morning, but Michael says, *No, you go*—because Deborah woke up and said, "Michael? I'll come with you to synagogue if you like." It's not that he expects her to turn passionately religious; it's a gift, and he wants her to know he appreciates. So Lazar goes off, taking Samuel and Ari. Michael waits for Deborah. There's an upper-class drawl to her voice; Michael is aware that it's there as a cover. It's when she's being most yielding, most open to him that she needs that voice. It's a cold, sunny day. He looks down from the window at men bound for shul. A wire has been strung up around the entire neighborhood to create the legal fiction that this is a single "domain," within which one can carry things. But the thoroughfare!—according to the Code of Jewish Law, if 600,000 people pass through it in a single day, it makes establishment of an *eruv* illegitimate. So there's dis-agreement in Flatbush among the Orthodox: should Jews be per-mitted to carry their tallis? One rabbi has declared that an *eruv* has been established; a second, whose word, according to Lazar, is given great weight, says *no*—since there is a major road. So some wear their tallis under their coats, while others carry them in a bag. Lazar, whom Michael watches walking down the street with his father-in-law, *wears* his.

Not to carry even a key! Not to carry—of *course*—money, a wallet. All the articles that define identity and everyday activity must be left behind. No cell phones, pens, appointment books. No driver's license.

It's wondrous and funny to think of how seriously people can argue about things so arcane. But, the argument goes, if the Torah has been given to Moses by God at Sinai, if the Torah includes the *oral* Torah and thus implicitly the Mishna, the Gemara and the commentaries and debates that make up Talmud and provide the basis for the Code of Jewish Law, then nothing, *nothing*, is small. For everything, implicitly commanded by God, must be immensely important!

He decides not to speak of this to Deborah. But he has to warn her—"I want you to understand—the women sit by themselves.

Not behind a full screen—we're going to a 'Modern Orthodox' syn-agogue—but to a separate section raised up above the main floor. Is that all right with you? You know—you don't have to go."

"*Ce n'est rien.*"

He's about to turn from the window and say, lightly, *All right, I won't make too much of it. But it's a kindness, an act of loving-kindness.* His hands on the windowsill, he looks down at the dark suits and overcoats, the black hats, everyone going to shul. *Stops breathing*: for he notices a car parked near the corner, an American sedan, blue. A Buick. It could be anything, but he knows it wasn't there last night when, just before going to bed, he looked the street over. It's too early for visitors. Of course, it could be somebody's son getting home in the middle of the night.

On the Sabbath?

And what about that van parked on the Bolofskys' side of the street? Is anyone inside? The glass is tinted.

"Deborah?"

"Oh, Michael, if I were in India, I'd visit a Hindu temple."

He says nothing, knows before he picks up the phone in the hall that the line will be dead.

It's dead.

There's a break in the back fence, boards hanging diagonally by one nail, he remembers. That neighbor's house fronts on the next street over, and from there to Coney Island Avenue is only a couple of blocks. The shul is even closer, and Lazar's at shul. Michael says nothing, gets dressed, waits for her. She says, "I'll tell Karen we're leaving. Do I look all right for synagogue? He says, only in his head, *I think we've got trouble. A couple of cars. Across the street, a blue Buick and on this side a gray van.*

He comes away from the window and finishes dressing, Sab-bath or no puts his wallet in his pocket, goes down to the kitchen to say Good Shabbos to Rebecca and her mother and kiss Karen, who's telling Rebecca about the soup kitchen she volunteers at, and Rebecca, nodding, half listening, organizes the midday meal. He drinks coffee and looks out the back to see if he remembered that gap in the fence correctly. Yes, just big enough for him to squeeze through. Now he tells Deborah—fast—"So I'm going out the back way. They'll be after me. You watch those cars. If you see them leave, you leave, take Karen, get to a taxi or subway, leave everything, get to Evelyn's place—my Dad's place—on East 63rd." Breaking one more Sabbath restriction, he jots down the address and telephone number, Geoffrey's numbers, the FBI. And wait there. If I make it, I'll catch a cab."

He hands her the slip of paper with the numbers, and gives her no time to suggest alternatives—he's out the kitchen and squeezing through the fence.

The kitchen door opens behind him. "Michael! Michael, you're right!—both cars are moving—I'll call the police."

"And the number I gave you. Call that! The house line's dead. Use your cell."

And he's down the neighbors' driveway and up the street, pumping hard, Jew in fine black fedora, tails of his overcoat flapping as he runs down the street, passing one, two, three men on their way to shul, and one, a father holding his son around the shoulder, both of them in black hats, calls out, "What is this? On the Sabbath? What are you doing, running on the Sabbath!" He's running on the Sabbath all right, he's at the corner before he spots the van coming down the street. A woman's voice from an upstairs window calls, "Don't you know it's the Sabbath? What? Is there a fire?"

Michael sideswipes a baby carriage, gets more grief. "Police!" he shouts—and in his army-sergeant voice, his great-grandfather the cantor gave him, loud enough for anyone in the nearby houses to hear: "Call the police! Life and death! Police!"

Up ahead at Coney Island Avenue he sees the Buick and knows he can't make it, but he gets to the doors of the shul, rushes past a couple of men into the lobby, and now through the inner door to the sanctuary.

This shul is large, room for hundreds, women seated on the sides, raised up five or six feet, a low, decorative lattice screen you can see through or see over between the women and the men; men on the main level of the sanctuary, the floor dense with them standing, seated, a sea of full-length tallises, over shoulders, over heads, and all striped black and white; waves of black and white covering everything so you can see only random flecks of polished floor; it's like a single strange black and white creature, undulating.

The bima, raised, is not at the end of the sanctuary but in the middle, and it's there Michael runs, shouting in his biggest voice over the chanting of the morning service, "Fellow Jews! Fellow Jews! I need protection. Hide me, for God's sake! They're going to kill me!"

He's running through this sea of black and white, yet it's in slow motion. For while he's in the middle of a cloud of fear, rushing toward the bima, there's an observer within Michael taking in the sunken eyes of one bewildered man wrapped in full tallis, a black and white striped tent over his head, peering out as Michael passes, gaze locked on this . . . maniac, terrorist! Women along the sides are standing; he notices that one is unusually beautiful, dark, Karen's age. He notices the carved wood of the columns that support the canopy over the bima. He's even able to do complicated math (in the sense that an outfielder running for the ball at the crack of the bat has done extraordinary feats of mathematics): running this many yards he'll easily make it to the bima so many seconds before whoever's after him can park, get out of the van and into the shul.

Lazar Bolofsky climbs the steps of the bima and whispers to the rabbi, hands churning the air, and the rabbi nods, gestures to Michael, *Come, Come quick!* and the chanting stops, starts up, questions go through the sanctuary, and Michael climbs to the bima and takes refuge standing under the rabbi's own tallis; for a moment they share the tallis while the rabbi unfolds another for himself. Lazar slips away to find a phone.

"This is the Sabbath, but it's my life or death!" Michael calls out. His voice rings again like the voice of his great-grandfather, the cantor, and the young rabbi puts a hand at the back of Michael's head, cradles his head, and the terror washes out of Michael; now the rabbi puts a finger to his own lips and Michael closes his eyes and, standing on the bima, tallis over his head, a tent of peace, quiets himself. He looks around for Ari—where's Ari? Michael, not knowing where they are in the service, begins murmuring the prayer for a safe journey, and when he stumbles, the rabbi puts his hand on Michael's hand and continues the prayer beyond the few words Michael knows. Now the service goes on again, and while the chazzan chants, Michael takes up a Siddur and finds his place.

"Nishmat kol chai," "The breath (soul) of every living thing shall bless your Name." He rocks under his tallis, feeling foolish for having made such a fuss; the congregants must think he's crazy. Surely Ferguson's men—if that's who they are—won't come in here! And the police have been called.

But now the door to the sanctuary opens, and two men—the same two who chased him yesterday?—stand at the back, long hair, short hair, and one calls out, "We're police. Sorry to interrupt. We're looking for a Michael Kuperman." Their voices echo in the great hall.

The Jews turn back to their prayer books. Already, magically, crowded as it is, a space clears in the back.

"You're *here*, Mr. Kuperman. We know you're here. Mr. Kuperman—you'd better come with us."

The voices echo like prayers. No one looks at Michael. They look at their prayer books but the davening has stopped, their bodies are still. Now the other man, the one with long, shaggy hair tied back, takes from a steel box—the kind of box used for musical equipment, camera equipment—takes a long, green aluminum canister and holds it over his head. Michael recognizes it. He's seen a canister just like it in the video in which the dogs twisted and died. The men fit gas masks over their faces, giving up all pretense of being police. One holds the canister, the other a machine pistol. Their faces look like skulls in olive green. "Mr. Kuperman," the long-haired man says, his voice muffled by the mask, "*you* know what the choices are."

Michael Kuperman keeps his eyes on that canister. He knows what the choices are.

"You come with us now, right now—or there's going to be a lot of dead Jews in this room. Including you. *You* know what I'm saying. You don't want that."

Six million Jews are in the sanctuary this morning—there are those who are praying, and there are the children of the children of the unborn children of those in this shul. A multitude of nations, as plentiful as the stars. There are Ari's unborn children, children of his own child, who's here somewhere in this sanctuary. And Lazar's Samuel. Then there are Michael's own ancestors, from generation to generation. He is almost one of them at this moment. He has, as Belle Cooper told him, become the legacy. It's not that he sees, under invisible tallises, his ancestors Shmuel or Menachen, or Isaac; his mother is not hiding behind a pillar in the women's gallery. Michael sees only two men in olive-green masks, one with a gun, one with hand upraised holding a canister.

This is only Michael Kuperman, a good businessman, no holy man. And he's not being killed as a Jew; he's being killed because of what he knows or might know, what he might do. Yet standing on the bima, wrapped in tallis, he feels himself one of a long line of murdered Jews.

Michael sees the canister held high in the man's hand, and he lifts his own hand, removes the tallis and folds it, hands it to the rabbi and walks up the aisle. "All right. Here I am." Someone's moaning; a few whisper; most are silent. "People stay back. *Please.*" *This is the end of my life.* He whispers the *Shema.* The congregants shrink back from him as he walks. He's very much in his own space. He feels like an actor in a tragedy. Even *now,* can't he get away from watching himself? Can't he even *die* in one piece, in peace? *Dear God, help me be simple and whole as I come before you.* Hineini.

His legs are trembling. *Help me be strong.*

The man holds the canister high. "You hurry the hell up, Kuperman."

He hurries. His legs move. No one touches him. At the back, he's grabbed by the arms, one on each side. It's deep belly-terror, but something comforts him in this being beyond choice. One of the men, the one in long hair who almost caught him at the subway yesterday, has put the canister back into its steel container. Their gas masks are off. They say nothing, they lead him down the steps of the synagogue, past the two men and a group of teenagers who seem to be outside every synagogue; he's held so firmly, and though he's a big man, he's lifted between the men so that his feet only scrape the ground. The door of the van is open; they shove him into the back, the long-haired man follows, and the van starts up, the short-haired guy driving; it turns the corner, stops; they drag him out, shove him into the Buick, and Michael sees he's sitting between the long-haired man and someone he doesn't know. The little fat man with sunglasses is dressed for a boardroom in dove-gray wool.

"You were right. He thought it was a live canister, Mr. Kadar."

"So you see—already we have information. So he's *seen* one of these. Isn't that right? Well, that's the sort of thing we need to find out, Mr. Kuperman. How much *have* you seen, how much did you give the FBI? And so on, and so on. I apologize. I have nothing against you. It's just a question of damage control, containment of a problem. If you were to be a witness, just what do you know? What other material—do you see? What do you know about M. Reynard? We need to know what has to be changed. The less the better. You'll come with us and we'll be asking you some questions."

"It was an empty canister?"

"Please! Of *course*, empty. Think about the repercussions if we actually gassed a synagogue full of Jews!" Kadar laughs, cheerful. Then the joke gets to him, he emits high-pitched explosions of laughter, now settles down. "You think we want that?" It's a good-natured laugh—as if he expects Michael to see the humor. "No, we'll leave that for people on the other side of the ocean. And you know, it's got nothing to do with *Jews*. Please! Don't be stupid, Mr. Kuperman. Jew, non-Jew, not the point. Who knows? The chemicals might end up being used against Palestinians. Not the point at all. Now, we require your help for damage control. We need to debrief you. You can understand."

"And then you'll kill me."

"There's killing and killing, Mr. Kuperman. You understand what I'm saying? And then, you have a family. No, I don't think we'll have a problem with you. Will we?"

"No problem. And you'll leave them alone?"

"No reason not to. I just expect cooperation. If we get the truth, believe me, things will be better for you and for your family."

Quietly, as if this *were* a business meeting, the man in sunglasses says, "The first lie or imprecision and I promise you, we won't fuck around, we'll go into your spine, straight into the root nerves, we'll use a knife. You have any idea what that will be like?"

"You'll get the truth," Michael says. "Of *course* you'll get the truth." But at once he's sweating. His own smell sickens him. *What about Jonathan, what if they ask about Jonathan, what he knows? Or Lazar? Or Deborah?* "Please. One thing. It's important to me, my family gets my body. You understand? For Jewish burial?"

Kadar doesn't answer. The little bastard! "You work for Ferguson? Or General Djouti?"

Kadar is making notes on a little pad. Where are they taking him? Bastard with pig eyes deep and close together. The car has turned up a side street, turned again, they're not bothering to blindfold him—he'll not be able to tell anybody. Out of the corner of his eye he sees they're followed by the van. Morning sun's in their eyes, so they're heading east or southeast. He imagines making a grab for the door handle, diving over Kadar onto the street. But the door's locked. No chance. And before he could get up, grab the wheel, and twist into an accident, he knows they'd pull him down again. No chance at all. What about the police? Someone might have seen the van, but not the Buick. Lazar will make a huge outcry, but what good? Again, he whispers the *Shema*, then. the first words of a psalm that a few weeks ago he'd read each day during the Ten Days of Penitence, the days between Rosh Hashanah and Yom Kippur, go through his head. *The Lord is my light and my help; whom should I fear?* Well, here are great candidates. *Ana Adonoi hoshiana.* (We implore you, Adonoi, deliver us). Delivery, this he doesn't expect, not this morning in the material world. He can barely control his hands. His breath is on its own. Time is a spastic series of still pictures instead of a flow. Yet he feels he is in the hands of God. It's not that he will live. But he *is* in God's hands. The thought flits by—I'm soothing myself, fooling myself. This is the God Who comforted those being led to the showers. The God in Rwanda. Still. *Still.*

"Let's begin the questions right now," Kadar says. "What *other* material did you get from Mr. Planck?"

Perfect English but something foreign about the whining voice. *Kadar.* Isn't that Hungarian? "Nothing. What I had, the FBI soon *will* have. It's in the mail."

"Oh, my. Well, you see?—that makes a big difference. That's what we were afraid of. Bank accounts have already been changed, but we have other juggling to do." At once, he punches numbers into his cell phone. "What we spoke about earlier?" he says to someone, "Yes. Yes, the changes *will* have to be made. No. . . . That I don't know yet." Then, to Michael: "You and Mr. Planck have caused us a devil of a lot of trouble. And millions of dollars in expenses to make this problem disappear. Now, please—we know there's *more* material—about a M. Reynard? What *is* this material? And where is it?"

Michael rehearses a speech of moral outrage, but what's the point? Better quiet himself, better pray. *Think of yourself as dead.* He wonders who will say Kaddish for him. Ben from his shul? Lazar? Ari is too young.

I won't be there for his Bar Mitzvah.

"No. Please—I know Mr. Slade mentioned more material—but there *is* none."

At the corner up ahead a small bus used for taking the old and disabled around Brooklyn blocks the intersection, and the Buick slows down to wait till it gets rolling again. Mr. Kadar is irritated at the delay. He taps manicured fingers on the window. He has a plane to catch. Well—but the questioning won't take any time at all. He takes a small bag of peanuts from his pocket and dips into it again and again, crushing the shells and skin inside the bag, extracting the nuts and popping them into his little mouth.

The bus hasn't moved. Kadar touches his driver's shoulder, and the driver honks, creeps forward. Kadar says, "What's wrong with that idiot?"

The next thing Michael feels is a tremendous jarring—he swivels around; the van's been smashed from behind into the back of the Buick. There's a Jeep backing up—it smashes again. Michael makes a play for the door, but he's slammed hard in the face, and blood drips down his shirt front. Now an explosion makes the car shudder. He shakes his head clear to see, and there's dense smoke, and young men with machine pistols emerge low out of the smoke, running—dressed in jeans, in bulky sweaters or leather jackets. The driver's window explodes and with it the driver's head, which, shattered, coats everything. Coats Michael, and he smashes out, smashes out, flinging arms and fists, more to get free of the blood and fragments of bone and brains than to escape. Now the doors open, Kadar is dragged out, and from the other door, the man with long hair, and Michael hears screaming and thump, thump, thump. "Mr. Kuperman, stay down, you stay *down,* Mr. Kuperman," and next thing, someone's on top of him, keeping him down, pinning his arms, saying in heavily accented English, "Okay, you're okay,

Mr. Kuperman. We'll get you out of here in two seconds. You're okay, just don't move now, please, Mr. Kuperman."

Move? The guy's so big, no way to move.

The attack is over. He sits up, is lifted bodily out of the car, and someone's checking him over. By the time he looks around he can't see Kadar or the SWAT team or whatever the hell it was and now the Jeep is gone, the bus is gone, and Geoffrey Slade is holding his arm and leading him to a car half a block back. "All over now. You did remarkably well."

"Why the hell didn't you tell me?"

"Better this way."

"Better this way! For who?"

"For *whom*," Slade says, laughing.

"You set me up. You set this whole thing up, you sonofabitch, and you didn't say a thing. What right do you have—?"

"You mean I was willing to take a chance on your life?"

"Weren't you?"

"You have every right to be annoyed."

"Annoyed? And what about the gas canister? At the synagogue. How could you take such a chance? Not just *my* life! You bastard!"

"Oh no, *please*, we had directional microphones listening in. We *knew*. Got all *sorts* of information. No worry about gas. We knew for certain. I might add, we were terribly impressed with your courage."

"Who the hell is *we*, Geoffrey? Who's we?"

"Can't say."

"Heavy accents."

"Sorry, can't say."

"A couple of voices. Thick accents. Was it Interpol?"

Geoffrey grins. "Definitely not. Not Interpol. God, I wish we *did* have commando teams like that. Remarkable, how clean, wasn't it?"

"Clean!" At once he feels drenched in slime. "SON OF A BITCH!" he screams. "I'm filthy with blood and brains. Uch!" A shudder passes through him.

"Don't complain. You're alive and in one piece. Except for your poor nose. I'm afraid that's broken."

"I've got to wash this off. Geoffrey, you had no right!"

"We've got to get you under wraps right away. See those people across the street? Someone's going to call the police. Someone already has, I'm sure."

"You lied to me. You said you didn't know about Djouti!"

"That's right. Had to lie." Slade steers him toward a Chrysler sedan, borrowed, Michael knows, from some pool of cars. He pops the trunk, pulls out a blanket, and spreads it over the seat. "Come on now. Want to get you to a doctor."

"And who's this Reynard?"

"Good doctor waiting for us. Nothing to worry about. . . ."

Sitting on a stoop, Isaac of Bratslav holds a hand to his cheek. *If only we'd had such men, trained men with automatic weapons, when Chmielnicki came through Poland like the Angel of Death through Egypt.*

Michael takes a sheet of today's newspaper wet with window-washer fluid, and wipes his face. A prayer he says every morning comes into his head. Ignoring Slade, he mumbles, in the Hebrew, "*Blessed are You . . . who has made the human being with wisdom and created within him openings and hollows. . . . If one of them were ruptured or if one of them were blocked, it would be impossible to exist and stand in Your Presence. Blessed are You, Adonoy, who heals all flesh and performs wonders.*" Michael, intact, runs his hand over his body in amazement at its ordinary miracle. And weeps, quietly weeps, and can't stop.

"We'll go to my place. You can shower. I'll put you in clean clothes for the Sabbath."

"Deborah. Give Deborah a call."

"It's already been taken care of. Do sit down and let's be off."

Rescuer

So he sinks back against the wool blanket and, closing his eyes, lets Geoffrey Slade drive him to an apartment in Sutton Place to have his nose set, doctor and a nurse expecting them, "our special medical friend," Geoffrey explains. Michael's not talking to him. He's shot up with painkillers. He closes his eyes. They work on him, he's a rag doll, an object in their hands. It's a kind of passive resistance—even passive aggression.

Now down to the car, over to Geoffrey's small apartment not far from the U.N. Building. Slade leads the way, telling the doorman, "Slight accident, Chang. My friend's quite all right."

It feels so good to shower. But his own death is something that he can't wash off. He feels a little giddy at walking around wearing his own death. Wearing it for the first time. A new suit of clothes for a second Bar Mitzvah. An invisible kittel for burial. And he's got a buzz on, as if he'd swallowed a mix—narcotic, amphetamine. Maybe it's the courage. Or maybe just the shot. He thinks of himself as not physically brave. But when he slipped into his death, terror singing shrill in his belly, he didn't disintegrate. He stayed calm. And now he's taken inside the knowledge of both his fear and his courage, and it's that, and the death he wears, that have produced this giddiness. He knows he'll forget, after awhile, that he's wearing his death. But right now it's palpable.

"When you didn't take me back to the Bolofskys right away, it wasn't 'just to clean me up.'"

"No. That's right."

They're driving back over the Manhattan Bridge. Under their tires the bridge hums.

"*Nor* to set my nose. You were stalling for time."

"That's quite right. Give them a little head start."

"For what"

"Our fellows. But your wife *was* informed. She'll vouch. How do you feel now?"

Michael just laughs. Now something comes to him. "Geoffrey—was it *you* who lifted me out of that car?"

"Afraid so. Did I hurt you?"

"I weigh almost 190. How the hell did you do that?"

"Research," Geoffrey says. He smiles and lays a hand on Michael's shoulder. They wait for the light at the Brooklyn end of the bridge. "You know, the traffic we're trying to stop, it's very much like the slave ships that returned by way of the West Indies, where they took on rum to fill their holds. Slaves one way, rum the other. Now it's cocaine or heroin one way, weapons the other. Weapons, money laundering—it can get complicated. But in this particular case, it's fairly simple. Chemicals one way, chemicals the other. Michael, it was unfair to you. But you helped us—you helped us do something important. We're not finished, but we're well on the way. Now, isn't that precisely what you wanted?"

Wearing His Death

You can go home to Boston, Geoffrey tells Michael and Deborah, Karen and Ari, at the Bolofskys'. "There'll be someone watching your back for awhile," he tells them mysteriously, "but you shouldn't have any problems. Your phone lines will be checked on a daily basis for intruders. We'll be in touch next week."

The Bolofskys stare at this ectomorph, this odd, long-boned gentile with secrets, with an educated voice, and with spatters of blood on his overcoat. Old Sarah Bolofsky shakes her head at all this confusion on a Shabbos. "Cars on a Shabbos," she says. "In this house, people who drive on Shabbos."

Smiling—no, *grinning*—Geoffrey Slade shakes Michael's hand and Lazar's hand, and he's gone. Sarah Bolofsky won't give him another look.

Slade is gone, but half the neighborhood seems to be dropping by. The news has traveled fast. Now, at the end of Shabbat, at the Havdallah ceremony that separates Shabbos from the everyday, Lazar hands Michael a Siddur and they say blessings of gratitude: ". . . Who has preserved us with a miracle . . ." The room is already packed. "*Oi, your face, look at his face . . .*" Michael's swollen nose has been set and taped; there's already black and blue under his eyes. Ari stares. "I saw you. I wanted to go kick those guys. I was too far away. Why didn't all those men stop them?"

"They couldn't. Remember the green thing one guy held up? There was nothing in it, but they pretended it was poison gas. And the other guy had a gun, right?"

"Still. . . ."

They open a bottle of schnapps, and soon Lazar is a *bissel* drunk, and Michael is groggy with the mix of schnapps and painkillers. The women are laughing at them. Now, an hour after sundown, the telephone starts ringing and doesn't stop. The chazzan. More neighborhood friends stop by. You would have given up your life, they say to Michael, fingers tapping chests. You were willing to hide me, Michael says. Everyone except Michael feels joyous.

Michael is, God knows, grateful. But joyous? He's weeping inside his chest. Why?

The Sabbath over, they light the many lamps, and this family room, that had seemed so drab when they first arrived, glows in the warm lamplight. Dark wood and books: you don't notice the plastic covers on sofa and easy chairs.

One of the men with him on the bima stops by with his wife, another man brings his son to meet Michael. Then another family. Now the rabbi comes, says little, smiles, and Michael feels almost embarrassing love for this bearded man he doesn't know, who hid him under his great tallis. *Destroyer of Amalek*, he whispers. "This is our rescuer and the grandson of our rescuer," old Mrs. Bolofsky says, and tells them about Jacob. *Nonsense*, Michael laughs. *My grandfather brought your family to America. I just brought you trouble.* He tells them again, the canister was empty. "But . . ." Lazar lifts a forefinger, ". . . he didn't *know* it was empty!"

Everybody wants to hear about the canister of gas. Three times at least someone mentions *"the showers."* He's promised Geoffrey not to go into details about the rescue, but he tells them about the gas, and Lazar describes the film, telling them what seeing it did to him. More schnapps. Lazar let the answering machine take calls. People come and go. It's all over Flatbush, there was poison gas released in a synagogue. Anti-Semites. Thank God, no one was hurt. Somebody (some say a goy, some say a *baltashuva*, a returning Jew) was a hero. Lazar's thick face is red and wet from tears and schnapps; he hugs Michael, kisses his cheek. Ari, Karen laugh a lot, Samuel laughs. The women, too; this laughter lets Deborah hold Ari tight, as if he had been the one in danger, lets her kiss Karen as she rarely did these days.

Time to take Ari to bed, to get to bed themselves. At the foot of the stairs, Lazar grabs hold of Michael's arm and pulls Michael against his chest. That's all.

Everyone feels high. Michael feels the ache in his head returning. Deborah is quiet. She sits with Ari, who can't stop talking. He puts his father and James Bond in the same sentences. He tells Deborah how he'd set a trap for the bad guys, and when they walked in, a net would drop on them. No one's coming in, she tells him, and rubs his back in the spiral he loves, inward and inward to a single point, the center of the world.

Till then she's okay, but by the time Ari falls asleep, Deborah's unraveled.

"You're crying," Michael says as she gets ready for bed. "Don't cry. Why are you crying?" But he finds himself excited by her tears. That, he can't say. It's the tenderness glowing through him.

In bed, they hold each other, and as if a new drug was taking effect, at once he's groggy, can't keep his eyes open or move his body to make the pillow more comfortable. He's asleep.

And awake! Heart beating like mad, blood thumping at his temples. He gulps huge breaths. *Well what do you expect?* He says to himself, doctor to patient. *What you've been through.*

But it's not doctor to patient. It's his grandfather, it's Jacob, back with him, but inside his head so Deborah won't wake up. *It's no different from 1903 in the cellar, when we expected any minute, God forbid, the Jew-haters to come into our hiding place and do what they do. Nights and nights afterward, I couldn't sleep.*

And Michael can't sleep. *Post-traumatic stress,* he says to himself. Maybe that's right, but he's not afraid. He's not reliving his own near-death. This is the feeling: that he *has* died. This is the feeling he'll live with from now on. So if he's not dead now, soon he will be—in ten years or forty years, does the little bit of time make such a difference? It's that he gave himself up to dying. And this is the thing: it *is* good, as if a lump, an accumulation of unnecessary worries and guilt, like old fragmented computer files loading up a hard drive, has been cut loose.

The words of the Amidah come to him? The eighteen blessings, praise, petition, thanksgiving, are murmured without interruption three times a day. Maybe it's only once a day for Michael, but the Hebrew gets in your bones after months, years, and at the edge of sleep comes, unbidden, the music of the words. He doesn't know if he's awake or in a dream of Hebrew blessings, but it's as if he's breathing the blessings, as if there's nothing else of him but this music. If it's not sleep, it's even better.

But if it's so okay, then why is the blood thumping in his skull?

How Rare Is a Good Wife

The peculiar thing is that home hasn't changed. Senor Pedro trills a greeting and Ari trills back. Margaret's left a long note. There's nothing in the *Times*, there's nothing on television. None of them know what to say. Michael carries the samovar from the cellar, and Ari drums in triumph on its brass belly.

And Michael doesn't let on that he's had this sea-change, that he's as good as dead. He thinks of Dostoyevsky, who was condemned to be executed; on the morning of his execution, he was taken to the parade ground where the sentence was to be carried out, dressed in a fresh white shirt, given the cross to kiss, and a sword was broken over his head. He and two other revolutionaries were tied to posts. They had less than a minute to live. But suddenly they were *untied*, led away from the grounds, and told that by magnanimous order of the Czar, their lives would be spared, their sentences commuted to imprisonment in Siberia. A new life began for him. It's a story that's always moved Michael. Now, he feels he understands better what it was like for Dostoyevsky afterwards. He has been through the worst, all his fear should be burned away. But it is not.

Steve is dead. It's as if Steve has died in his place.

Every few minutes Steve's death hits one of them. Deborah cries, and Ari caresses her hair.

Tonight, it's Jonathan he needs. Deborah doesn't want to see anyone, not even the Greenes, but Michael's the one with the swollen nose.

Jonathan and Jessica bring pizzas and a bottle of wine.

"Your face," Jessica says, stroking his cheek. She sits beside him. "Tell us."

Michael tells them about the commando force. "No one's to know about this, friends. If it weren't for this Slade and those soldiers. . . ."

"Israeli Intelligence," Jessica says. "Mossad."

And Deborah nods. "Of *course*."

"Operating on American soil?" Michael says. "I don't know. I can't see that. I suppose it's possible."

"Sure. No question. Mossad. You think it's over?" Jessica asks.
Michael shrugs.

"It's not over," Jonathan says. "Geoffrey Slade called me this morning. He told me roughly what happened. Whoever this guy is, he's not finished."

Slade called *you*?—Michael isn't asking; he's examining Jonathan's face. He thinks he understands what Jonathan's after. "Look. Yes. You can trust Geoffrey. *If* that's even his name. Trust him to lie to us. Trust him to get us into trouble—he just about got me killed, Jonathan. But you can also trust him to *try* to save our lives."

"Well, that's something," Jessica says.

"I asked Slade about Orion," Jonathan says. "He didn't know or wouldn't say. And those men who kidnapped you—they must be in somebody's custody—or dead?"

Michael's Sermon in the Bedroom

Tonight, Michael takes a pill. Looks in the bathroom mirror. His nose, still swollen, looks *Jewish* for the first time in his life. How damned funny!

Deborah doesn't look at him as she gets ready for bed. She massages lotion into her face, upwards, gently, erasing imaginary lines.

"I've been thinking a lot about evil," he says.

"My God"—an ironic *My God*. She cups her jaw line on the tips of her fingers as she examines the effect of days of anxiety on her skin.

He ignores the irony. "A few minutes ago, I thought I had it. I wrote it down. Here: 'Evil is simply the extreme state of separation, defining yourself as separate from other people and from God. No one else is real.' And yet each of us is a child of God."

"I am not a child of God, if it's all right with you, Michael."

"It's all right you think so, Deb," he says, touching, unaware, his hand to his heart. He goes on. "Extreme separation as the basis of evil. But then I thought about it some more. Agents of evil are often anything but separate. The SS—they were brothers in evil. People become part of Hutu Power or the Third Reich. Or the Mafia. Or the Palestinians. Or the Irish. Or the Jewish people."

"Oh, my poor, poor honey."

"They see other groups as not-human. But one another they see as real."

"This is charming talk for one in the morning. And look how bruised you are. Between your bruises and that beard. . . ."

"God says, 'You will be a holy people.' We are to be separate from others. We are not like 'the nations.' *But* we will be 'a blessing' to everyone. So I keep thinking about separation as holiness and separation as evil. If we're separate from the world, if we live by Torah, children of the Covenant, then we're connected to the holy, to God. But suppose we cut ourselves off from people outside our own group? Take that far enough, we can go into a mosque and shoot people. We can blow up houses and uproot olive trees. We become the nightmare.

"At least," Deborah says, "you're saying all this in your own voice. You've lost the phony Yiddish lilt. If you want to talk, I don't mind listening."

But soon she's asleep. Like Geoffrey Slade doing research on evil, Michael takes up *Tehillim*, the *Book of Psalms*. He knows what he's after. The evil man, says the tenth psalm, "waits in ambush near open cities, in hidden places he murders the innocent, his eyes spy on the helpless. He lurks in hiding like a lion in his lair, he lurks to seize the poor. . . . He says in his heart, 'God has forgotten, He has hidden his face. He will never see.' Arise, O Lord, raise your hand, do not forget the humble. . . ." The psalm doesn't tell us whether God arises. Michael is too exhausted to imagine God's reply.

Deborah is so busy catching up at work that danger, exile in a strange country, Brooklyn, has to be kept at the bottom of her intake bin. Because first at Thayer, Fletcher, and Gringold's home office in Cambridge, then in San Diego on Tuesday and Wednesday, she has to sew the threads of procedures and relationships that have frayed. Just a few days away, yet she feels continually on the defensive, laughing too much, trying to charm, succeeding but critiquing the attempt—vulgar!—apologizing to clients and coworkers. Still, this part of her life is basically intact.

But at night, oh, *exhausted*, lying in the dark in a hotel room in Seattle or Austin, that might as well have been in any city, she takes a long time getting to sleep. She succors herself with a Valium and the chocolate truffle placed on her pillow by the maid who turned the covers down. But behind her eyes Michael keeps running, running through the Bolofskys' yard; he squeezes through the fence. In endless replay, she fumbles through her purse for her cell phone. Rebecca is whispering prayers, not upset that a phone is being used on the Sabbath. . . .

In turbulent sleep, a bomb is waiting to go off. There are too many doors. The dreamer, searching laboriously, knows she'll never find it in time.

Back from Seattle, she has to face him again. There he is, *not* blown up. Well—thank God. But it's hard to be in the same room with him. They should be talking. He's done well by them. But she's raw, and everything rubs her the wrong way. She can't watch him measure out his evening glass of bourbon, can't stand the way he clears his throat before speaking on the phone. Uch—and the way he sucked up the fettuccine from his fork, and it slides through his beard!

Long talks between him and Jonathan; after dinner Michael stays shut up in his study or hangs out in Ari's room. Wednesday night he spends an hour with Karen reworking an essay. And *that* irritates her too!

She feels irritated that she feels irritated.

Friday night after "making Shabbos," as he puts it, the blessing over the candles, a long kiddush before the wine, a blessing over the bread, the song about "angels, messengers of Shalom," he lays his hands on the children's heads, "May God bless you and keep you. . . ." Then again in Hebrew. And then he *praises her, Deborah!* *How rare is a good wife . . . worth beyond rubies . . .* something, something, from somewhere in the Bible. Narrowing her eyes to hunt for irony in his, she finds none. Unable to reply, she feels her face grow hot; she concentrates on the challah and the wine.

CHAPTER TWELVE

Blood thumping painfully through his left temple and behind his eyes, Michael walks past the carpenters, past the electrical contractor and his men, past the mess of construction, to the office Jonathan is using. Bloomington police, FBI field agents are gone. Michael's been shuffling training sessions, finding ways—and there *are* no ways—to fill Steve's place. Jonathan's been talking to the tech support people, listening, reassuring.

When they see each other, Michael and Jonathan, except when they've got another emergency, just look at each other in silence for ten, fifteen seconds. Jonathan's haggard; it's good Jessica can't see him now. His beautiful Italian suit is streaked with sawdust and powder from dried joint compound.

"You tired?"

"Tired!" Jonathan just laughs.

Michael sits down and puts a hand to his mouth. "What could get someone to *do* this?"

"You okay, Michael?"

Michael opens the catch of his attaché case and examines some papers, then stops pretending and closes his eyes to see better. "Isaiah says, '*We have made a covenant with death.*' It's something like that, Jonathan."

"Come on," Jonathan says. "Let's take off, take a walk." Not saying much, they walk down through the Indiana University campus in its thin coat of snow. "We've been taking walks like this for twenty-five years. You're some intense guy. I knew what I was getting into when I asked you to help me start Fusion."

"I've got your number—you figure I need healing. It's a kindness. But I can't stop thinking about those Swiss and French and German corporations that made chemical munitions plants for Saddam in the eighties. What did a CEO say to himself when he looked at the reports? 'Someone else will make the sale if we don't. My responsibility is to the shareholders.' Maybe. But beneath his rationalizations, what was happening in his heart?"

"Nothing. That's the *point*, you clown. Nothing was happening in his heart. Ferguson takes his identity from money and power. He's not in love with evil—he doesn't experience it *as* evil."

"God help us," Michael says.

Demonstration

Michael makes another copy of the CD-ROM, taping his original to the base of the brass samovar. Copies have gone to Interpol, the FBI, the police in Bloomington. At night, in Bloomington and then back in Brookline, he finds himself turning on his computer, returning to the CD-ROM. Not to the video. To invoices, to letters. Letters to Orion—questions about *volatility, requirements for the corrosive-resistant glass and metals, combinatory agents.* The letters are boring, but he feels he has the obligation to keep it real. He notes formulas of dispersion and effectiveness, logarithms of dissipation. He examines bills of lading.

. . . Be advised that exposure to combined elements without prior protection is potentially lethal. Chemicals must be kept separate, in vessels meeting our specifications, until. . . .

All this while, he has a business to run, a merger to hold onto—he's not sure how long he'll be able to hold onto the merger or even Fusion. McNair and Braithwaite are, he remembers, close friends. He tries to charm Ken McNair by sending him notes about new clients, new contracts, and a new product. But McNair doesn't acknowledge his notes, doesn't return his calls. Michael keeps busy developing staff and vendors, as if there were to be no trouble with the merger, no potential suit for illegally breaking into the Chemicorp computer system. He helps Tony Kim cover for Steve and rebuild the training facilities in Bloomington. Dr. Rabin puts Michael on a new pill to cope with anxiety.

He has bouts of weeping. The windows of his car rolled up, he howls like the Hispanic mother at the hospital. He weeps for Belle, unwilling to lose her. When he can't sleep, out of a trick of streetlight through the window and Deborah's blouse on a chair, Michael summons up his mother sitting by his bed in a blue-flowered housedress and Chinese slippers. He thinks: *if I can keep her with me only in grief, if it's that or lose her, I'd rather grieve.*

But the grieving casts its net wide. For Steve. For a village God-knows-where. He is putting no limits on the breaking of his heart.

Finally, McNair calls and wants a meeting. Right away Michael knows and Jonathan knows. "It's over," Michael sighs. "Merger's dead. I suppose we've got to figure on paying a price."

"Hell of a price," Jonathan says. "Could be the beginning of the end for Fusion."

Already, the young woman from Fusion serving as liaison between working groups at Fusion and InterCom is told by McNair to return to Boston. Bad, bad sign. Now, Doug Shaughnessy, who came from InterCom, has stopped functioning as National Sales Manager; back in Chicago, Shaughnessy is not returning Michael's calls.

Then, late in the afternoon the day before they are to meet McNair in Chicago, while Michael's trying to work out a strategy for talking to McNair, Dave Posner collapses, writhes on the floor and loses consciousness. An ambulance takes him to Mass General. Dave's wife calls—"We had no idea how serious, what a serious case, the diabetes. He'll stay overnight for some tests."

Every time he's about to fall asleep, dead tired, Michael sees this fat man rolling on the floor, then sees the gas released over the village and he's sweating, heart pounding. Another pill.

Their in-house legal department consists of one woman on staff and one assistant, and their main function has been protection of intellectual property. So they take along Fred Waller, Fusion's hired gun, to Chicago. Michael sits next to Waller on the flight—first class, because that's how Waller travels. Michael can hear the meter ticking as Waller finishes his *Times* and peruses company documents. As the plane taxis to the gate at O'Hare, he turns a sad smile on Michael. "You do know we haven't got a leg to stand on?"

Jonathan, en route from L. A., meets them in the lounge, and they take a cab into Chicago. Cold wind, wet air. From time to time he gives Michael's arm a pat, smiles at him. Jonathan looks bedraggled but he's offering cheer; can he, Michael, look even worse?

Boardroom's the same—walnut paneling, window wall on the city, but the atmosphere has chilled a lot since those honeymoon days. McNair's not there when the meeting begins. No one even mentions Doug Shaughnessy. It's the InterCom legal team, all business, coffee in giant steel thermoses. Jonathan's charm sits useless on his face. Michael sees how much effort it's taking him. Jonathan's football shoulders slump after the first half hour while the lawyers go through the clauses in the contract that will let InterCom back out of the merger. And Waller picks away at some of these, points to penalty clauses; these are acknowledged.

McNair comes in. It's a divorce, McNair providing the *get*, the document that nullifies the Jewish marriage contract.

Now the lawyers—including Waller—go into working session down the hall, and McNair straightens his Fusion file and looks sadly at Michael, as if *he*, McNair, were the one who bore the weight of this breakup. Jonathan he won't look at, and Michael imagines that somehow McNair is trying to reshape Jonathan for himself, see him as troublemaker, Michael as unfortunate accessory.

But watching McNair's body language, Michael's fantasies change: McNair's not a dissatisfied husband handing out a divorce but captain of a platoon about to court-martial two lieutenants. He looks at the documents and picks at the bristles of his close-cropped hair. "As you can imagine," he begins, drawing out the words as if each had a long echo, giving the words weight and himself confidence, "I've been on the phone with my dear friend Al Braithwaite quite a bit. Quite a bit. Yes. InterCom's relationship with Chemicorp—well, you can imagine how important that is. For us, it's either you go—or we lose Chemicorp. That's InterCom's bottom line. But my own friendship with Al—well, that goes back twenty years. And that's *my* bottom line. Max Ferguson, he's an unknown quantity. I don't know what sort of trouble he gave you. That's in the hands of the government, I understand. But I know Al too well to think he'd go along with anything illegal."

"We're not saying anything about *his* role—" Jonathan begins; but, wincing, face wrinkling like a prune, McNair waves him away.

"I don't want to hear it. All right?" And tapping the file on the desk and leaning forward, McNair prepares to get up from his chair and take his leave.

They can't imagine how heavy McNair's heart is. Because Michael has it backwards; in McNair's own mind *he's* the betrayed lover. To cut ties with Michael—well, that's a sad business decision; to cut ties with Jonathan is something else—to lose this youthful energy, lose grace and power. When McNair has talked with his wife about Jonathan, he's described him *not* as a black man who gives evidence of McNair's tolerance. No. He speaks about him as a prince. He even dreams him.

He can't look him in the face.

But now Jonathan raises himself; Michael turns, heart pounding, at some signal he can't name—the shoulders? The turn of Jonathan's head? The rustle of hand in briefcase? And Jonathan produces from his soft leather briefcase a long, heavy, green-metal canister and rolls it across the conference table, scratching the polished walnut, to land right in front of McNair. Jonathan stands, takes off his suit jacket and folds it lovingly over the armrest of the empty chair beside him. McNair freezes, comically, half-standing.

Jonathan sits back down in his shirtsleeves and fills the boardroom with his voice. "*Pick! That! Up!*"

McNair looks up at him, mouth open, is about to say something, thinks better of it, sighs, sits back, picks up the canister and glowers.

Quietly: "Heavy, isn't it, Ken?"

"What the hell are you doing? What *is* this?"

"You see that release pin? This is a poison gas container. You pull that and in ten seconds the room is filled with cyanide gas—or mustard gas. Or sarin."

"What are you—crazy? Jonathan? Are you threatening me?" McNair looks about him for help, ready to press a button, when suddenly Jonathan stands up—big man, remember, six-three—reaches across the table for the canister and—pulls the pin.

The three of them watch nothing happen.

"It's not loaded, Ken. This is the canister Ferguson's goons carried into a synagogue in Brooklyn. Two men—they put on gas masks and demanded Michael Kuperman come out—or they'd use it on the congregation. And Michael knew what that meant, so he went with them. It turned out to be empty, but Michael couldn't know that. He'd seen what this canister could do. Here—*you come here, Ken—*" and opening his laptop, Jonathan clicks onto a file he'd already loaded. Now he draws McNair to his side of the table, beckons with his fingers, smiles, and McNair comes. **Experiment-Canine..3** "Tell me," Jonathan says as the video begins, "You like dogs, Ken?"

They have lunch brought in. No lawyers—just the three of them. Waller is sent back to Boston. McNair never bothers to say he'll try to patch the merger together. He just shakes his head and groans about how damned upset Al Braithwaite is going to be. The dogs—the dogs stopped McNair cold. But the village—the hillside of men running, stumbling, choking on the gas—made them all fall silent. The issue of the merger isn't so much resolved as bypassed. They eat in silence. McNair begins to ask, Michael to answer. McNair goes off.

Michael asks, "Jonathan? Where did you get it? Did Geoffrey Slade give that canister to you?" Jonathan doesn't say; McNair comes back, nods. "I think we'll be all right."

And that's all it takes. Michael *knows* it's going to be all right when Al Braithwaite himself asks to get together and doesn't ask them to come to St. Louis. No—suppose he comes up to Bloomington and meets them at the lab? One morning, Braithwaite brings along two of his young men—not lawyers but assistants, tokens of his authority. It's not the first time Michael's met him. But the other time was at corporate headquarters in St. Louis, Chemicorp turf, and the man was framed by cherry paneling, outer offices, a huge inner office with a desk the size of a conference table. Here's a man who makes many millions a year. He sits on the boards of some of the largest corporations in the world. He's trim, well-groomed, late-fifties. He puts in his time on exercise machines, Michael is sure. But away from his own office, he isn't all that impressive; even the slowness of his speech—as if he's dictating to someone, as if he cherishes every verb (because it's especially the verbs he caresses, as in "we neeeeeed to ascertaaaain our options. . . .")—doesn't enlarge him to his accustomed semi-divine status. He's . . . oh, a high school principal, a country doctor, a college administrator, except that his clothes are too expensive for that. Michael notices Jonathan checking out the pin stripe as they stroll down the temporary hall. Braithwaite's eyes are narrow; it's as if he's sculpted his face to indicate savvy. The comedy is that savvy isn't needed; hey—they're just looking at temporary cheap construction on their way to a small seminar room, so the role pulls apart from the situation and shows itself clearly as a *role*. His majesty inspecting the servants' quarters.

But majesty is clearly unnerved. Catching Michael's eye, Jonathan grins and adjusts his walk ever-so-slightly—no one except Michael would discern the parody.

Debris has been cleared, training sessions are back on schedule, but you can see where walls used to be, where new wiring is temporarily strung up, taped to new framing and duct work. "You people have done a hell of a job in a short time. Terrible thing. Just a terrible damn thing." The two young men trail them. Braithwaite stops at the door to the seminar room and grasps their arms, Jonathan's, Michael's, and looks into their faces like a football coach inspiring a team—"Now, look—I want you to know, I will swear this to you on a stack of Bibles—I had nothing to do with what you saw on that goddamn video. In fact, I haven't had the opportunity to observe firsthand the material you showed Ken McNair, but I don't need to see it. I've been informed. Now, now, Orion never amounted to very much in the first place. We've done our own internal investigation, and, frankly, it's clear there were mistakes made, excesses, overzealous marketing decisions. We've rectified those mistakes." He looks up for confirmation; Braithwaite's assistants nod.

"It could be called tampering with evidence," Michael says quietly.

They sit around a seminar table. Michael fingers the streaks of burnt shellac.

"Mr. Kuperman. Mr. Greene. Do you really think Chemicorp would get involved in selling chemical munitions? I'd have to have my head examined to try tawdry crap like that! A small operating group took advantage—and that group—Orion—doesn't *exist* anymore. Its members are no longer employed by Chemicorp. If there are criminal charges brought, we'll cooperate in every way with the investigation, deal with the sonsabitches. Now, Michael, I know you were molested, and I know you believe it was by some of our people—"

"I *saw* Max Ferguson on the sidewalk in New York, directing the men who were going to kidnap me. It's hard to mistake Max Ferguson."

"Acknowledged. But you might have misinterpreted. Isn't that so? The case is in the right hands now, I think you'd agree, and so far the FBI hasn't touched Mr. Ferguson. Now why is that if he's been engaged in criminal activities?"

"That's a damned good question," Michael says. "I'm bewildered."

"*But we're willing not to press the issue,*" Jonathan says.

"And in turn," Braithwaite says, "Chemicorp is willing to agree not to sue Fusion for industrial sabotage. You understand? That's what it was. Wouldn't you agree? Braithwaite says this smiling. "You invaded encrypted files. We'll forgive and forgo. I know there were excesses."

"Excesses!" Michael catches a look from Jonathan and backs off.

Margaret Corcoran has left them a roast chicken and pasta for dinner. It's the first night since they got back from Brooklyn that they've had dinner together as a family, and Karen gets giddy about Brooklyn. She sings "*Doe,* a deer, a female deer . . ." in full voice and stops: "Oh! I'm so sorry! Does my voice excite you too much, Ari?"

"Come *on,* weirdo."

"We're *family,*" Deborah says. "Apparently, your feminine voice doesn't wreck the spiritual concentration of one's own family."

"That is one *gorg*eous wig you're wearing, Mom."

"You gooney old cynic. The Bolofskys, weren't they wonderful to us?"

"Well? They can't hear me all the way from Brooklyn, my dear *mamela*. So now I guess you're going to arrange my marriage?"

"Perhaps not for several years," Michael says. "*However,* if you keep that up. . . ." He puts a hand on hers: "Life at the Bolofskys really, really got to you, honey. You think maybe there was something about it—the devotion and the discipline—that *attracted* you?"

Karen rolls her eyes. "Oh, sure."

Ari can't get over it. "Were you scared?" And though Michael tells him, "Sure, really scared," Ari keeps asking, "How come you weren't scared?" One day Chris Canzanutto comes over, and the two of them shadow Michael when he goes for a walk before dinner. Michael knows they're in the bushes, hiding and giggling. He walks on. Ari is his secret agent, also his bodyguard.

After dinner, Ira calls. It's Karen who takes it; hanging up, she tells Michael: "Grandpa says, if you can't be at his opening, he'll 'manage to live.'"

Michael laughs. "His opening. What opening?"

"He says it's a 'retrospective.' It's next Thursday night."

"Eleanor's pulled strings," Deborah says.

Michael says, "*Next* Thursday? He never even sent an invitation. That way, if I don't get there, it's not such a big deal."

"I can't go," Deborah says. "I'll be in Seattle."

"So it's down for the memorial service, back home, back down to the city. Well, he's been a second-rate father, and I've been a pretty lousy son. I'll go. Ari, mind sleeping over at Misha's?"

Ari never minds.

Michael asks Karen—"You feel like coming down to New York with me?"

When Ari is in bed and Karen is installed on the phone, Michael puts the CD-ROM into his computer, and Deborah pulls up a chair.

"You don't have to do this."

"Oh, Michael."

Now the village, the time to tenths of a second at the bottom of the screen.

"Is it Iraq, do you think, Michael?"

Delivery Commences. . . . The little parachute, the running men. After a minute she turns away and waves her hand; he exits from the file and shuts down. Deborah puts her hand over his. He turns his hand and holds hers. They sit.

Steve Stories

Deborah wears a simple black dress, pearls. In the taxi on the way to the church, she takes his hand.

It's not really a religious service, but it's in a large church in a Jersey suburb, and a minister offers a blessing and welcomes mourners. After he steps aside, Steve's friends, who have come from everywhere, take over. Four men sing in *a capella* harmony a Sam Cooke song from the seventies. His friends tell "Steve-Stories." "I don't dare cry for him," Phil Skibiski says. Steve would just say, 'Oh, give me a break, Archibald.' 'Archibald' was for when you were acting like a dope."

Sylvia Planck's a tough lady in her late sixties. Only a couple of years ago did she stop running the Boston Marathon. She's been kicked out of the New Jersey legislature quite a few times for raising issues from the gallery. No tears from this lady. She says, "Steve would have wanted you all here just like this. Music, no frills, jokes, not too much about God and heaven. Here it is: my son had the best heart in the whole world. Being a genius was just a nice addition. Now, he didn't have a political bone in his body, and as some of you know, I'm a fighter for progressive causes, I always have been. He used to heckle me. So it's ironic that he's the one who died to change things for people. He had no politics, but he couldn't stand evil. Listen: I'm too old to get over this. I'm going to miss the grandchildren he would have had when he finally got around to it, I'm going to miss his cantankerous conversations. I've hung up on him for making fun of me. I'm going to miss calling him back. If I told you what he's meant for me, well, like Phil, I'd have to listen to that boy's heckling in my head. I'll just thank you for coming."

Michael doesn't cry. But on the plane ride home, he heaves in waves of grief. Deborah rubs his back in slow circles.

Eliminating the Source of the Problem

"Stanley Fish is here for his appointment."

Max Ferguson tells his secretary to show him in.

Usually, they set up a meeting at an airline club members' lounge at an in-between airport. This time Kevin Murtaugh (the attorney who terrified Deborah)—"Stanley Fish"—called him at home at six this morning; and here it is, only eleven. Boston to St. Louis: it must be urgent.

"Kevin."

"Max. It's good to see you again. We have a problem. Can we take a walk?"

"Of course. I'm ready for you this time. A change of clothes waiting at the gym." Ferguson doesn't blame Murtaugh for suspecting that there might be recording equipment in the office. Two men—one tall and athletic, one broad enough to turn heads—stroll through the halls at Chemicorp headquarters to the lobby. They've done this once before. There's nowhere to walk outside, especially in January; they head for the employees' gym and, in sweats with the corporate logo, walk the running track, empty at eleven. Ferguson doesn't like the man, but he admires his style. Murtaugh lends class and ease to what could feel—frankly—ugly, tawdry. Max himself has never been a graceful person, but he admires grace. Their mutual employer in Marseilles—Reynard—knew what he was doing when he hired Kevin Murtaugh. He lubricates deals.

"We understand you've been subpoenaed."

"No, that's mistaken. No grand jury, no indictments. Simply questioning. I've been brought in for questioning. It's the bombing that concerns them—and really, I must say that was overkill. You should let Marseilles know. Bombs make them nervous. As for the chemicals, as Reynard well knows, my name was on nothing. Everything is deniable."

"We're also a little concerned about the disk that came to me from Fusion. I sent it on to Marseilles."

"What's the difference? There are other copies."

"It's this copy that concerns us. I know very little about such things," Murtaugh says. "It seems there are odd lines of code. Marseilles queried me. Our computer security people see odd lines of computer codes, but they don't see any damage. As I understand their feelings, Max, well, they're a tad uneasy. Mr. Reynard is uneasy."

"But if there's no damage—?"

"No discernible damage, no. But until they were eliminated, the codes duplicated themselves. Like a virus, but there's absolutely no effect. Now, there's nothing—but sectors of the disk are unaccounted for. Perhaps it will remain nothing. I've been asked to sound you out."

"Well—you were the ones who asked Kuperman and Greene for the disk. Are you planning to eliminate the source of the problem?"

"We've erased the material from our hard drives. The security people are still in the process of analyzing it."

Ferguson, breathing hard and not wanting to show it, doesn't like this pace around the track. But he stays abreast of Murtaugh.

"I meant eliminate *Kuperman*. Eliminate *Greene*."

"They're simply businessmen. No. They know nothing about sophisticated computer programming. We've decided to leave them alone. Kuperman's frightened. He knows nothing that can harm us. If something happens to him—or to Greene—it would simply add to the mess. No. Our people are fairly sure it was this fellow Planck who was trying to inflict damage on our system. We think he was taken care of before he had finished his programming. Well—don't worry about it. Marseilles didn't think you could help us on this."

"They don't hold me responsible?"

A pair of runners comes out of the locker room and passes them. Their feet echo off the steel walls.

"Responsible? I really doubt that. You'll have to discuss it with Reynard and the other directors when you meet next week. But this has gotten much too complicated. We brought you on board to make things simple."

"And they will be again. So . . . next week? I wasn't planning on meeting them so soon."

Murtaugh nods. "Marseilles wants to discuss the new sources you've established. They *are* in place?"

Ferguson is panting. It's getting hard for him to lift his feet off the beautiful composition track—the Nikes are lead weights. "In place," he manages. "Oh, yes. Reynard can be assured."

"Then perhaps we'd be better off making direct contact."

"No, Kevin. No—Marseilles makes contact through me."

"As you wish. When we go back to the locker room—I have your ticket on the Concorde to Paris for next Monday. You'll need to discuss protocols for future shipments. Tell me—am I tiring you? We might walk more slowly."

"It's good for me," Ferguson puffs. "Afterwards, let's spend a few minutes with free weights."

"No time today," Kevin Murtaugh says, checking his watch.

Ferguson stops; hands on hips, he takes great draughts of air. "The security people you sent, your people—what happened to them?"

"They were never 'our people.' They were hired for the one job—it seems they fumbled the ball, Max. But they have little to tell anyone."

"Good. Good. But who took them out?"

"We're still investigating."

Afterwards, when Murtaugh leaves, Ferguson—oh!—resents; will repay. Oh, yes. The pace of that walk was meant as a demonstration of dominance. Skipping lunch, he works out with barbells and weighs his position in relation to his associates abroad. They don't brook complications with good humor. But he has them, he feels, by the proverbials. The new sources for chemicals are his. He knows the people, understands the materials, can expedite shipments.

Was he responsible for taking Fusion on in the first place? That decision was corporate—nothing to do with him.

Still, he's uneasy.

He'll get to New York on Sunday. He thumbs his Rolodex for Caroline Balisdell's phone number. Lately he's been making his intention clear to her. She's hoping to get the catering contract for the Chemicorp international celebration—the yearly gift for their industrial customers, their executives and head sales reps. This year the affair's on an estate overlooking the Hudson near West Point. Catering contract alone is worth $150,000. She wouldn't dream of trading sexual favors for the contract. Not directly. But she's intrigued. Caroline is a beautiful woman who in about five years will be called *handsome*. He enjoys the illusion of superiority her beauty gives her; he will enjoy showing her that it's an illusion. So he will ask her point blank, may he stay with her on Sunday night in New York before he flies to Paris? She's not likely to refuse.

Chapter Thirteen

The Jewish Artist

A "retrospective" for Ira Cooper: as if, Michael thinks, he's a famous artist with a long history of shows. By the time Michael and Karen arrive, the reception is well in progress. Thirty, forty people mill around the big, whitewashed space in Soho, walls crammed with photographs, small prints, large prints, color, black and white. How many people are here!—especially how many African-American people. Part of the show concerns the recent strike; a lot of the hospital workers are African-American.

Eleanor, her gray hair loose, long, held by barrettes at the sides, shepherds Ira from group to group. He's like a pugnacious ex-boxer, dapper but tough in clean jeans and a navy hand-knitted wool sweater, his energies jutting out every which way. He's a gruff dog held in check by Eleanor's hand on the leash of his elbow.

"Well, I told you the guy'd make it," Ira calls out, seeing Michael.

"*I* told *you*," she says.

"Deborah is in Seattle. She sends her apologies, Dad."

"Well—glad you could find the time in the middle of your busy schedule of praying. Ellie—this guy stops praying for fifteen minutes, the whole world comes to an end. . . . And my *baby*!" he shouts, "Sweetheart!"—grabbing Karen around the waist and giving her a kiss on the cheek. "Oh, Christ, I've got to go check on the wine. You can't trust people. Those sons of bitches were supposed to deliver 1.5 liter bottles, they deliver fifths. You believe that?" And he's off.

"He's just pleased," Eleanor says quietly. "So many people are here. You should have seen him an hour ago. He kept revising his estimate downwards. Fifty would satisfy him. Twenty would be sufficient. And look. There's more than that many just from the various unions. You know, Michael, Ira has quite a reputation as a labor photographer."

"There's a lot I don't know about my father."

Eleanor doesn't answer.

A young man in a ponytail is pouring drinks. They stand across the room hearing Ira complain, hearing just the "sonofabitch!" and "What the hell kind of. . . ."—the rest blurred out, Ira's hands wild—mad conductor. Karen snags three plastic glasses, wine for Eleanor and Michael, ginger ale for herself. It's like watching a comedy: *Ira Has a Fit*. But it's not a fit—no! It's meant for Michael to observe. Ira swings around to shake hands, left hand, right hand together, with a young couple; he's grinning, opening his hands wide, a gesture of plentitude. They go off, he pats a young, hip-looking woman on the rear.

"With my Dad," Michael tells Eleanor, "you're expected to give a lot of leeway. 'That's Ira, that's the way he is'—the way you give slack to an exasperated child. The guy's seventy-four years old. I don't care if he *is* an artist. He bullies people. He thinks about no one but himself—"

"—Now, that's not true. Look at these pictures, Michael."

Michael laughs. "He's one lucky man to have you, Eleanor."

Ira's back, arm around the shoulder of a big man, black, with a moustache and bad complexion. "Anthony, you know Eleanor. And this is my granddaughter, Karen. And I want you to meet my son Michael. He's an ex-lefty. Ahh, it's an old story. *Red diaper baby puts on black-and-white tallis*. But I got hopes for the guy. He's got credentials. Studied organizing with Saul Alinsky, went to jail a couple of times like any decent American. Michael, this is Anthony Porter, he's head of the local, and I predict you're looking at the next President of the whole damned union. Recently, Michael got into a fight with a big chemical corporation. They tried, Anthony—no shit—to assassinate him. You ask him. I was worried sick—worried sick."

And he's off again.

"You've got some gutsy father, Mr. Cooper."

"The name's Kuperman—I changed it back. Yeah, some father. I think I'll go look at his pictures." Michael reaches for Karen's arm, but she's off, talking to the bartender, flirting with him. And Eleanor's busy with someone, so Michael does the gallery shuffle.

A whole lot he doesn't understand. What makes these photos art, not journalism? That they capture more than the moment? Here's victory; here's hatred of cops, any cops anywhere. A photo of scabs, protected by police, walking past a line of jeering workers: Ira's caught the laughter that's mixed up with the rage. Both groups playing roles. Here's a single nurse or nurse's aid, exhausted, sitting on the sidewalk in hospital greens, smoking: a photo of battle fatigue.

Jews and Blacks face off through a cordon of police in Brooklyn. Another: outside a shul, Hasidic men stare at a silent march of blacks, the police watchful between them.

A homeless, misshapen woman wheeling a shopping cart of plastic bags past Bendel's on 57th. Next photo: same woman passing the Russian tearoom by Carnegie Hall. Next photo: a patrol car, reflected in a window. Finally: the cart turned over, the woman being pressed into the patrol car. The cop's hand is covering the crown of her head, protecting. Shoppers have stopped to gawk.

Now Michael comes to a picture of a four-year-old kid with a picket sign in hand:

WE SUPPORT THE FREEDOM RIDERS

An old photo. The kid's in the middle of a march; his head is at the level of belts, and he's hardly able to hold up the big cardboard sign on its wooden frame; its top is steadied by a grownup. Michael doesn't know the grownup, but the little boy—he knows from family snapshots—is Michael himself.

"Karen!" He calls. "Karen, honey! Look here." When she comes, he says, "That's me. There. I don't remember a thing, but that's actually me."

"That's right," Ira says, coming up to them. "I was wondering if you'd recognize yourself as a kid. Ha! You *see*?"

As always, this pisses him off. "What am I supposed to see, Dad?"

But Ira's off again, shmoozing. They hear his strident cackle. "Well, I ain't wasting my charisma on every sonofabitch," Ira says to somebody halfway across the room.

This is a one-artist show, but there are in fact a number of shows on the wall. There's the Look-What-Michael-Never-Realized-About-His-Father show. Another show goes by just beyond Michael's vision—the Jew wearing tefillin seen from the midst of a march by blacks is, for an instant, Michael Kuperman. Those two cab drivers battling on Broadway are Michael Kuperman and Ira Cooper. The homeless woman is Belle Cooper.

Eleanor is talking and laughing in another language to a young man wearing thick glasses. Michael picks up the intonations— it's Yiddish! He goes over. "Eleanor—I didn't know you spoke Yiddish."

"I grew up in a Yiddish-speaking household. Oh, it's a child's Yiddish, but it's fun to practice. Michael, I want you to meet Sam Gladstone. Sam is with the *Forward*. He's doing a piece on the show."

"The *Jewish Forward*? So . . . you consider my father a *Jewish* artist?"

Gladstone doesn't seem to get the question. "Don't you?"

Before Michael can answer, Gladstone is pulled away. By now, Eleanor is speaking to someone else, this time in French. She's wearing an off-white embroidered blouse and matching long skirt. She looks so much in her element. Michael thinks about his mother, how strange this world of Ira's must have been for her.

Gladstone is back. "You know of course about the show next year at MOMA?"

"No. My father has a show at MOMA?"

"It's a group show. Jewish artists. I may want to interview you over the phone—I'm writing part of the catalogue."

"Great," Michael says, not wanting to louse his father up by saying *Ira Cooper? A Jew?*

And Gladstone, perhaps intuiting this, says, "Definitely Jewish. I see it in all of his work. There are all kinds of Jewish artists, Mr. Kuperman."

Excusing himself, Michael goes to see the young man with a pony tail and is very glad the wine hasn't run out.

January 16

Dear Dad,

Mazeltov on the show. Karen and I were really impressed. What a lot of wonderful work. And what a lot of persistence. We ought to talk—at *length* we ought to talk—about your work and how little I knew of it growing up. Sam Gladstone was telling me about your upcoming show at MOMA. My father the Jewish artist!

Let's talk.

Love,

Michael

January 19th

Michael,

Thanks for bothering to come down to a proletarian show like mine. What a patronizing prick you are! What did you think I was doing all those years?—jerking off? Big surprise!—*J e w i s h*. Why the hell not? Hey! There's Jews and Jews.

Eleanor sends her love. We're getting married. Can you believe it? You want to be best man?

Your Dad

You want to be best man! That question sits in Michael's shirt pocket all day. Gets folded, unfolded, folded. Midday, he reads the note into Deborah's voice mail. She's in Seattle, but since coming back from Brooklyn, they speak twice a day if only to make sure they're both okay.

"I don't believe it," she says instead of hello.

"I know. Don't you love all the defensive nastiness in the note? Just so he can ask . . . I'm going to do it, Deb. I'll be best man for him."

"God! I can see it now. Well, I *will* see it. I'm going to love this."

"Eleanor's *wonderful* for Dad. You know?"

"She sounds like a woman with a lot of class. I'm going to enjoy meeting her."

"Class! Don't you think it's ironic, *class* used in behalf of a proletarian artist?"

"You know what I mean, Michael. A lady who knows her way around."

"She does. You're right—she's getting him noticed after all these years. She couldn't have done that for him when Mom was alive. But now—she has the contacts. My mother—I suppose my mother has a grander perspective now. I suppose it's all right."

"You really mean that, don't you?"

Slade said they'd be protected. Still. Michael doesn't trust Ari
to go to basketball practice with another kid; he has Margaret take
him; he makes Karen call the minute she gets to a friend's house.
And he's always watching in the rear-view mirror, always checks
under the dash for a bomb, leaves an inconspicuous strip of Scotch
tape between hood and fender and checks that it's not been moved.
He looks in the trunk, examines the base of phones as Geoffrey
taught him. No one is permitted to open packages until he's vetted
them. He can hear in Deb's voice the toll it's taking on her. "Any
strange lawyers visiting you in Seattle?" he asks.

No reply. She fakes a laugh—a spurt of air from her nose—then
breathes heavily into the phone. The sound frightens him; it makes
him pick her up next day at Logan.

Weddings in America

On the Shabbat before a wedding, a groom no longer discourses
on Torah to the congregation. Not often, not in America. Michael
imagines his father talking Torah at a synagogue! While he's imagining this, a business meeting is taking place: Jonathan is leading
them through the changes from the same quarter a year ago,
finger on column A, finger on column M, eyes back and forth like
a tennis match or down a column like a minister reading scrip-
ture. Michael, oblivious, is grinning hard; Jonathan notices and
smiles back over his reading glasses. Michael's enjoying the imagined scene—his father on the bima: "Us Jews have always been a
pain in the ass. Look how we treated our own homeboy, Moses.
So you've got this fancy synagogue. What good is that without
heart and balls? You gotta make this whole lousy city a tabernacle!
You want to know what's out there? You should take a look at my
photographs. . . ."

Michael remembers his own wedding at the Mark Hopkins
in San Francisco. He played stooge for her family. What about his
own family? Belle Cooper was as much the *grande dame* as was
Roberta Schiff. Even his father! For once Ira Cooper was cowed
into submission. The best he could do was get drunk and sing YCL
songs from the thirties.

Michael played Jewish prince; Deborah, in a multi-thousand-dollar dress, played the princess. And, you know, what the hell, it was great, dressing up and playing the American aristocrat, commonplace oxymoron, knowing that when they returned from their honeymoon he'd be back at work for a community development corporation in Boston. This was just before he gave up community organizing and went to work with Jonathan and Steve and made his small fortune. It was like dressing up for a role, that wedding. Now that role is there, in the deep glow of the oiled walnut surface of this conference table. In fact, that wedding was the audition; now it's his daily performance.

If Jonathan asked a question, Michael could give him an answer. The table, pencil and spread sheets are present, but within dim shadows at the very top of his eyes is the banquet hall at the Mark Hopkins. Deborah's father, by then dead ten years, rules the head table; he's present in every toast, in the very elegance of the proceedings, down to the particular appetizers his wife and daughter chose for the occasion. A famous rabbi (his wife's life once saved by Dr. Schiff) reads a charming, funny talk for the occasion; a small orchestra plays Cole Porter and Irving Berlin, announced as "Dr. Schiff's favorites"; as wedding gifts Michael and Deborah receive from Deborah's mother and her aunt—really from a trust left by Dr. Schiff—a month at four-star hotels of their choice in Italy and France.

Deborah's uncle with the bushy eyebrows that lifted to a point invited them to use his thirty-foot sailboat, docked in Westport, for the summer.

The "wedding couple" also receive a set of bone china and complete silver service (they were listed at Tiffany's), and, oh yes, an old Jaguar roadster that lived with them as a family member until they were spending more and more money to keep it going—like a beloved dog that should be put to sleep but you haven't got the heart. Finally, when Karen was born and the car made no sense whatsoever, they put it on blocks, sprayed it with a preservative, covered it in a plastic shroud and left it in the mausoleum of a friend's barn in Lenox. It's still there, probably still worth most of what was paid for it new.

All that delicious phoniness! He could pretend to be marrying Katherine Hepburn in *Holiday* or *The Philadelphia Story*, while he kept the virtue—for a short while still—of helping people in Boston fight for health care, for legal services, for tenants' rights. But look at him from the outside and which was the pretense?

He didn't let himself in on a secret:

Why did he marry a Deborah? It was no mistake. Deborah was Jewish *but . . . not Jewish.* He grew up with an American ideal of beauty: small, precise features, long legs, blonde hair, elegance. "Good bones." What did that mean? It meant her face would become "handsome," wouldn't soften as she grew older. Oh, he knew what he was doing. What he didn't know was his shame of being a Jew that blended with his pride in being a Jew. His mother bragged, "Some Jew you've turned out. You look just like a *shagetz* in the movies." "That girl," Belle Cooper would whisper about someone at a party, "looks like she belongs in a shtetl. Look at those ankles. It'll take her five generations to make her a lady." Another girl—"you'd never know she was Jewish." This, said admiringly, was at the same time filled with hidden contempt for the subterfuge. Oh, she laughed at herself: "When you were a little boy, how many times a day I pushed your nose—like this—to make sure you'd have a nice nose!" And Deborah—cool, laid back, arrogant, in control. No effusions of feeling from Deborah or from her mother. All the cultural encodings of being Jewish, absent. And that was the point. Dancing at the Mark Hopkins, he didn't know he was in flight from the Jewish people. All the work and all the suffering to produce a secret anti-Semite!

It's Shabbat, Friday night, and Michael's staying home, not going to shul. It's Karen's turn to light the candles. Ari insists on turning out all the lights in the breakfast room, in the kitchen, in the hall and the living room and on the stairs, until there's only the street lights, lights of other houses, and, because it's past candle-lighting time, a pale gray sky over Brookline, over Boston, through the breakfast room windows. But tonight, borrowing from the Bolofskys, he's suggested a candle for each of them. Ari clumps them together in the center of the table so there's a bouquet of light, and when Karen lights them, he waves the magic light (that's how he thinks of it) towards himself with such force it nearly blows the candles out.

And this is Kuperman's fire.

It's not the burning bush. This fire of shalom, of Shabbos peace, will burn down, and in the morning there'll be just the brass candlesticks left. But next week, the same, and the next and the next, God willing, someone will light the candles. And so on for thousands of years. So in a sense it *is* a miracle, "a bush all aflame and yet the bush was not consumed."

And by this Shabbos light you see a different way. Faces have a depth and beauty that track lighting can't provide. You see with Shabbos eyes, see the vain and meretricious for what they are.

An Unexpected Merger

Max Ferguson is up before six the following Monday. He eases himself from Caroline Balisdell's satin bed and tiptoes—imagine two hundred seventy pounds on balls of feet, heels off the carpet—to the bathroom. Caroline opens an eye before he leaves. "I'll see you in a few days," he says. She doesn't answer; she pretends to slip back into sleep. He's amused; he leaves a one-word note: *Mmmm!*—knowing how it will irritate her to be perceived as a delicacy. The limo calls for him at 6:20, and he's at JFK an hour before the Concorde leaves at 8:00, with plenty of time to make calls to the Chemicorp subsidiary in London and the offices of the new dummy corporation that will accept the new shipments of chemicals.

Now he sits back at his ease, silver pot of coffee, coffee rising to his lips. The Concorde banks into the morning sun. With Cape Cod to their port side already thirty thousand feet below, the Concorde shivers through the shift to supersonic speed. It's as if the plane and his life have achieved a trembling orgasm, as if he owns that strip of expensive sand to his left, as if the plane, with its pilots and flight engineer, its steward and attendants and the food cart moving quickly toward him, with traffic controllers that pass the plane along and the leather he rests against, are all extensions of his will.

We see him ease back, let the leather enfold him. Through the window is the arc of Cape Cod. Caroline became frightened of him last night. Now, waking, she's wondering how to avoid a repeat. He knows this. It doesn't bother him at all. More than at any time he can remember, his life feels as if it has *come together* (although he'd never think in such a category; he'd say to himself, *Not bad, not bad. I've got the bastards now*), and the old humiliations are simply the sound barrier that he's just broken. . . .

At Charles De Gaulle, as the plane is about to land, he receives a message from a stewardess: He is M. Max Ferguson? Yes, that's right. M. Ferguson is not to take the flight for Marseilles; he will be met. A slip of paper. M. Reynard. Reynard himself? Just as well. It's already dark, and as darkness grows, his sense of accomplishment fades. A fine drizzle slants along the windows as the Concorde taxis to the gate.

As he leaves passport control, he catches a quiet nod. Ferguson, carrying his small leather overnight bag, follows the man at a distance along transparent corridors that seem to float in air, sky bridges from building to building; Ferguson finds a black Mercedes, driver in front, and in back—a glass partition between them—someone small, well dressed; this he sees at a glance. Suddenly Ferguson is frightened. The man who met him holds the door; Ferguson slides in next to Reynard.

"M. Reynard? Well, this *is* a surprise. A surprise and an honor. We meet at last."

"I happened to be in Paris. And this is so much more comfortable, isn't it, Mr. Ferguson? A few hours on the Autoroute. Besides, we have a number of things to talk about. May I pour you a drink? We have a well-stocked bar."

M. Reynard. Monsieur Le Fox. A French name, but Reynard speaks English with a peculiar accent, not French—Possibly Lebanese? Everything is subdued, delicate, about Reynard. Just as Ferguson has been informed. You wouldn't notice Reynard at a meeting except perhaps for the quality of his tailoring. He's a small man, his face narrow, sharp, his eyes very still, his voice low. He is sparing in speech. Simple, precise explanations. You have to listen attentively not to miss what he says. It's a trick; it forces the listener to lean towards him; literally puts the listener off balance.

"First," says M. Reynard, opening the leather-sheathed doors of the bar in front of them, "tell me about the questioning."

Max pours himself a bourbon and begins. Stops. "M. Reynard . . . before we start, I'd like to know where we stand. Tell me about *this* questioning. I feel I'm being interrogated."

"This enterprise," says Reynard, his tone quiet, flat, "is built on trust. Too many things have gone wrong with your part of the operation. I'm afraid I no longer trust you. Or that's not it precisely—I'm no longer sure I can trust you. But it comes to the same thing."

Max has no retort. His question was meant to elicit avowals of trust. At once, he's sweating. He sees an iron door near the old port in Marseilles, sees, feels his way down cement stairs to a cellar, then along a corridor to a room with heavy one-way mirrored wall. The floor, the other walls, are white. He remembers the screaming.

"We know you've been questioned. We know that shortly after, we received a corrupted disk. I'm not sure of you, Mr. Ferguson. I'm not sure we can trust your new sources. I'm not sure what you gave away to the FBI."

"I gave away nothing. But remember—Orion documents all named me as out of the loop. And the disk? I'm not the one who took that disk." Now Ferguson changes course. "But . . . if this is about our new source—I'm happy to name the new source and put you in contact, M. Reynard."

"Yes. Exactly. I want to hear about exactly this."

"You don't suppose I've informed anyone. Or that my source isn't real?"

"I want you to tell me," Reynard said simply, "precisely what you'll be doing for us. Where will the chemicals come from, what are the protocols, who knows what, who is to be in charge of the product?"

"I have all that for you right here," Max says, tapping his temple. "Now, M. Reynard. There *have* been problems. I've got them under control. With your help. I'm afraid we'd be best off to eliminate these men from Fusion. Greene, Kuperman—especially Kuperman. I suggested this to Mr. Murtaugh, but he was noncommittal. I'd like your opinion. As for the CD-ROM—well—I had nothing to do with that. You understand?"

"It came from Chemicorp. The material came from Chemicorp files."

"Through Planck. Through Planck and Kuperman. I had nothing to do with that."

"All right. That's under control. Now, tell me about your new sources of product."

By Dijon, the Mercedes at one hundred fifty kilometers an hour barely quivering, as he tries to explain everything, past the necessity for anything remaining that might be demanded through torture, Ferguson has laid out the new lines of communications, the cost of product, the protocols for order and shipment. By Lyon he's drunk too many bourbons and is beginning to slur his words, which are spilling out of him, as if information offered quickly enough can save him. He's named other illegal accounts, employees of his own who can be trusted, numbered bank accounts. By the time they're driving the back streets near the old port in Marseilles, he offers up the numbers and passwords to those accounts. The car stops. Max Ferguson is led out at a warehouse; he can hardly stand up he's shaking so badly. He has just pissed his pants. The man who met him at De Gaulle has to support him down a cement ramp.

"I / gave / away / nothing!" he calls back frantically.

The small man lowers the window of the car. "How can we be sure," he says quietly. "Look what you've given me tonight."

Ferguson doesn't recognize the door or the corridors through which he's led. He's brought to a small, cement block room with no windows; at the table in the center is a chair.

"Please sit," says the man we know as Geoffrey Slade. "That's right. Oh, don't pretend to be stupid," he says in a flat Midwestern accent. "Listen: two hours ago, the connecting flight to Marseilles landed. You *were* met, as you'd anticipated, here at Marseilles. Of course, you weren't on the flight. Think about *that.*" Geoffrey pauses for many seconds, then goes on. "But earlier, you see, a very fat man traveling under the name Max Ferguson was drinking too much—quite ostentatiously—in the Air France lounge at Charles De Gaulle. While waiting for the connecting flight to Marseilles. And he became sick, you see. A doctor examined him, and he was taken off in a wheelchair. He's probably better by now, the other Max Ferguson. He's at the Ritz. But it's time for him to call his associates, don't you agree? They're going to worry."

"*I'm* not going to call. You think I'm crazy?"

"Fine. Then this is what will happen. We'll take you to your associates right now. In a taxi. A few blocks from here. We'll drop you at the door and let you talk your way out. Would you like that?"

Max's eyes become slits of hate. "I *can't* call—they can trace the number."

"Yes. But Max Ferguson will be calling from the Ritz. That is, we can patch your call through Paris. Then, tomorrow, you'll be on the first morning flight to Marseilles. But . . . it's up to you, Max."

Now Geoffrey Slade picks up the phone from his side of the desk and puts it down in front of Max Ferguson. And he waits. Ferguson says nothing. He broods, statue of a malign Buddha. A minute goes by. "You're saying the call will look as if it's coming through that room in Paris?"

"Through the hotel switchboard. Oh, yes. Then you'll have to talk your own way out. Do you think you can manage that?" Geoffrey speaks collegially, as if they have a mutual problem.

"Possibly." Ferguson's tongue glosses his lips. "It depends on their prior sense of my usefulness. I was already uneasy. But I believe I'm still extremely useful to them—their arms business of course—"

"—But also the 'empty' chemical containers."

"Yes. Exactly. The containers. They're specially built, of course, and they can evade x-ray and other imaging systems, and the chemicals—"

"—make drugs difficult to detect. Yes."

"I'm a useful middleman. All right. I can tell them about an unfortunate drug interaction with alcohol at the airport. I think I'll manage."

Geoffrey nods sympathetically. "Just hit Memory and then number one."

"What other information are you going to want?" Ferguson says much later, bleary, needing sleep. Suit crumpled, hair fingered into a mess.

"We'll continue to debrief you. But it's more what we want you to do in the future. Look, Max—there will come a time, not more than a month, maybe two, from now—we'll need you to be part of a deal and tell us where and when a certain shipment will be coming in. You see, we know there's going to be something very big coming along."

"Yes."

"Yes. And when it comes, you'll be part of our plans—and then, I *guarantee*, you can disappear. Under a new name. You have no family. Your accounts will be switched. You'll be alive and able to start a new existence elsewhere. You'll be fairly wealthy. Why not? The alternative—let's be clear—is torture and death."

"Kevin Murtaugh is working for you?"

"Oh, no. We had to await our opportunity, Max. It's very simple. We know you fly the Concorde to Paris. Only the Concorde. We waited until reservations were made in your name. It was that simple."

"But suppose I'd met Reynard previously? Suppose I knew it wasn't Reynard? Suppose I wouldn't go along?"

Geoffrey shrugs. "We guessed you hadn't met. He meets almost no one. But if so—then, you see, we would have simply held you in an office at Charles De Gaulle—incommunicado. We would have explained your choices. So . . . why did we bother?—You think we played a trick just to get information? Well, yes, it did speed things up. But the real point, Max, is that essentially, this *wasn't* a trick. This was a creative fiction, a piece of theater. It was the *truth*, Max. We were playing out what would *really happen*. I wanted you to face the reality of your situation. It's exactly what *would* happen if we handed you to Reynard. Do you really think that if you told them the truth, they'd believe it? And—Max—oh, Max," he says, holding up his schoolteacher finger, "let's say they *did* believe—if they knew how we were breathing down your neck—*would* they want you around then? What would be your chances of survival? Not terribly high? Am I right? We wanted you to feel your situation, your terror. And now—well, now, with your assistance and a little luck, we can help you survive. Do we understand each other?"

Ferguson's eyes narrow into slits in the giant flesh of his face.

"Do we understand each other?"

". . . And indeed we *do* understand each other," Geoffrey Slade is telling Michael at a Starbucks on Beacon Street in Boston, middle of the following week. Cool jazz is playing. "We understand each other very well. There are things he doesn't know." Geoffrey smiles. "I told him we checked Concorde reservations—that that's how we found his flight."

"But actually. . . ."

"Actually—yes—we get copies of all electronic communications. I trust Ferguson not to do something stupid. He might run—but I've frozen his funds temporarily, you see, and he knows that. Or, rather, I've altered the account numbers and won't give them to him until we're done. Soon—a few weeks?—we'll be done."

"Then you'll let him go?"

"I'm not sure."

"Geoffrey, Ferguson's a monster."

"Yes. That's right. And specifically an accessory in two murder investigations."

"*You're going to let him get away with everything.*"

"Michael: what's important is we're unraveling the operation. I don't expect it, but *possibly* we'll take Reynard himself into custody. Ferguson may be needed to give evidence, but after that. . . ."

"I see. And those men who grabbed me. One was killed. What about the others? And who took them? Can you tell me anything?"

"Michael—you might have to live without getting that information. All right? Perhaps some day, I'll take you out on the Charles and make you fall in love with sculling, and maybe by then it will be possible. All right, Michael?"

"But are they still in the country? Are they alive?"

"They're no longer a threat. Okay? Ah, the weather's getting warmer, don't you think? I've always hated New England winters. Would you like another espresso?" And before Michael can say anything else, Slade presses his arm. "Here's what's far more important—Max Ferguson tells me that *no one is particularly interested in you, Michael.* Ferguson himself wanted you eliminated. He admits it. But no longer, I assure you. I made him see how counter-productive to his survival that would be. And Reynard—Reynard is not interested. Of course, we'll be keeping an eye on his communications just to make sure. But it seems the French think you and Jonathan are simply businessmen. They're sure it's Steve Planck who tried to disrupt their operations. Your feelings won't be hurt by that indifference, now will they?"

"Oh. Thank God." Michael closes his eyes and draws a deep breath. He has to cover his face—he's laughing but weeping, sobbing. Doesn't want the coffee drinkers to see. Geoffrey puts out a hand, squeezes his shoulder with his long, extraordinarily powerful fingers.

Michael nods. "I'm okay." Shrugging off Geoffrey's grip, he asks, "Who the hell were those soldiers? They *were* soldiers, weren't they? And what happened to the kidnappers?—that man with a Hungarian name—Kadar?"

Slade pays the check and they walk out of Starbucks and kitty-corner across the street into Boston Common. It's a chilly day, but children are on the backs of McCloskey's bronze ducklings. "One of those guys," Michael says, "had his head blown away. Slade? How do you get away with that in New York?—there'd be police all over the place."

"Let's just say, we had clearance, it was cleared very high up. All right?"

"But those men—are they alive? What happened to them?"

"Tell me—would it bother you terribly if they were simply flown out of the country?"

"Flown where?"

"Would it bother you terribly if somehow they never arrived at a destination?"

Michael thinks about this a minute. "Yes," he says finally. "It would bother me a lot. You're not God, Mr. Slade. You can't make people disappear like that."

Slade consults his watch. "I'm afraid *I* have to disappear, my dear man."

Michael goes off to call Deborah.

A Jewish Wedding

In a downstairs office of the large synagogue, unused on a Sunday, Ira Cooper is fussing with his bow tie. He's royally pissed at this lousy little black tie; it represents for Ira all the "fuggin' compromises" he's had to make for Eleanor's sake. *Don't laugh, sonny boy, this is no romantic comedy.* At the same time, the ire of the man is his insurance: I'm not defined by this crap. Michael smells his father's old rage, he knows it well. Out-*rage*-ous. Soon he'll start kicking loose objects. Then saying intolerable things to who-ever is close at hand. *Lord, guard my tongue from evil.* . . . When saying these words at the close of the Amidah, he often thinks of his father's tongue. And today—Ira knows he can get away with it because Eleanor, in another part of the synagogue with Susan, can't hear.

The way he's had to be handled all his life! Michael thinks. *The sugar-coating my mother used on him.* Like handling a nut case. Ira's pissed at this "big, fat synagogue—aach—you can smell the money. How can you stand this stuff? Can't you smell the *gelt* and the guilt? Sweatshops making dough so these big *machers* can pay off God with silver covers for the Torah scrolls! You happen to see the display cases upstairs, silver stuff from a million years ago?"

"Sure, Dad. It's a rich congregation. Is that so terrible?"

"This isn't Jewish. I'll bet the wedding is in English."

"Don't you *know*? Didn't you talk to the rabbi?"

"That's Eleanor's department. Hey—can you fix my damned tie?" He sticks up his turkey neck. Michael starts over. "I think it's funny, Dad, I think it's a riot, you want nothing to do with synagogues, with Judaism, then you get upset it's not traditional enough. The bow too tight?"

"What are you—my rabbi?" His neck twists in the collar. "The tie? Nah, it's fine. You can do up a bow tie like nobody's business. All that practice with your rich friends pays off."

"Why are you such a pissy bastard? Why are you so hostile to me? Look, Dad—*you* asked *me* to be best man."

"Ahh, 'best man' was Eleanor's idea."

"She put you up to it, huh?" Michael turns away to examine the copier, the computers. He scratches his scalp through his yarmulke. "Look, Dad, I won't be insulted if you ask one of your artist friends or labor friends. You can still do it. No big deal."

"Ah, bullshit. Bull-sheet. You're insulted already! Just don't mess up with the ring." He puts a hand on Michael's shoulder. "C'mon, Mike. Who the hell *can* I complain to if not to you?" Now he flings out his hand as if getting rid of something nasty. "I had to sign this . . . contract just now. A contract!"

"The *ketubah*. It's not part of the service?"

"Nah. Backroom stuff. Don't get me wrong, I'm nuts about her,
I always have been. No offense to your mother. But Eleanor's putting me through something here."

"It'll be okay, Dad. I'm glad to see you getting married to her."

"You!" Ira turns on him again. "The problem with you is you
want everything should be sweet and harmonious. Make nice, don't
fight. I've always been a fighter, Mikey. A club fighter. St. Nicholas
Arena over on the West Side, long gone now. Shit. *I'm* practically
long gone." The quaver in his voice—the very tone in which he
once made fun of Belle's *Yiddishe* theatrics.

A rap on the door. Michael turns from the arrogance and
self-pity.

"Go. Music's starting. She hired a three-piece band, like a
three-piece suit—there goes the schmaltz music to slide us down
the aisle."

They wait at the rear of the small sanctuary. The "three-piece
band" is actually cello, violin, flute, and they play something by
Mozart, a fragment, over and over, while the procession gets
ready and Eleanor comes upstairs. The sanctuary is full of artists
and union organizers, of Kerenbaums, and of Eleanor's friends.
Although in this generation they may not recognize one another,
many are here because of Jacob Goldstein—a father, a grandmother. They're part of Jacob's legacy. At the foot of the bima is a
restrained flower arrangement in whites and blues—delphiniums,
roses, iris, lilies. Michael, Edith (Eleanor's closest friend), Eleanor's
sister Sylvia, Michael's sister Susan (last week he spent twenty minutes on the phone pleading with her to come, Susan in audible
tears, asking: *What would Mom say?*)—all await marching orders.

Now, in step to the music, he leads Edith down the aisle,
holding the loose skin of her frail upper arm. He waits for his
father next to the young, beardless rabbi.

The music changes to a melody by Bloch. Michael catches
Jonathan's eye and closes his own, knowing Jonathan sympathizes.
As a favor, Jonathan and Jessica came down to New York, bribing
Marcus with a Knicks game last night. Tonight the Greenes and
the Kupermans will go to a show and a late supper afterwards. The
wedding guests will just have hors d'oeuvres and champagne in
the social hall—and go home. *With this bunch of alte kochers*, Ira

argued, *everybody's on a different food trip. This one can't eat salt, that one can't eat meat. Why make a big megillah and spend a million dollars?*

Michael wouldn't say this to his mother, but Eleanor looks beautiful. She's wearing a pale blue suit, the skirt long. Her hair is up in a chignon, she wears a veil. As she comes up the aisle towards Ira, Michael can see through the veil her long, bony, serious face. He welcomes her into the family.

She has her own family, of course, most younger than she is. And when the rabbi says (in Hebrew and in English) "The loving-beloved pair make joyful, O God—even as once in the Garden of Eden you made joyful your first man and woman. Blessed are you, Adonoi, who makes bride and groom joyful"—you can hear whispers. Well, sure, there's something funny about this. Can even God make Ira Cooper and Eleanor Kerenbaum blooming young bride and groom? But where does it say anything about age? Or about water under dams? Ira, for all his crankiness before, is smiling now, smiling the more for trying to maintain a serious expression. And Eleanor, her veil off her face, glows with a bride's delight.

Michael catches a wink from his father as he hands him the ring. The wink says, or Michael thinks it says, *How d'you like this costume, the whole get-up, don't I look like a dignified guy? We know better, but what the hell.* Michael also catches a grin from Karen, whose eyes—yes!—are shining.

He looks again. Eleanor *is* beautiful today. Ceremony, crunch of a wine glass under foot, and Michael's white-haired father grabs her around the waist and bends her back for a movie kiss, and the sanctuary breaks into applause.

Oh, not Deborah. No cheers from Deb. *We are not amused.* He raises his eyebrows at her. She raises hers, then furrows them. Thus, a complete communication in eyebrow words: *What's the matter, Deb? Are you too good for these people? Always Judgmental.*

Oh? And **who'**s *being judgmental? Why do you always imagine the worst about me? In fact, I'm amused.*

You and Queen Victoria.

They look away, he at his father as Errol Flynn, she at the gold leaf in the sanctuary.

Ari hears the wrap-up music and sees a receiving line form in back. He goes straight for the food—he's seen the two tables set up in the social hall downstairs. Deborah catches Karen's eye, points, looks at Ari, and nods; more wordless language: *Take care of Ari, would you mind, dear? I have to greet your grandfather and your . . . step-grandmother.* Deborah wants a chance to talk with Eleanor Kerenbaum. To check her out. It's the first time she's seen her, and this Eleanor is a great surprise. No little old lady, nor a face-lifted floozy, Eleanor looks calm and graceful, dignified and soft, and as the line moves along she hears the quiet but crisp voice of a woman of culture. So by the time she takes Eleanor's hand, the whole story in her head has changed. "My dear, I'm Michael's wife, Deborah Schiff. I can see how fortunate Ira is to have found you."

Eleanor closes her eyes in pleasure. "We'll talk later."

"Oh, yes," Deborah says, finally letting go her hand.

Ari has found the food. In the absence of a blessing, he makes his own: "Yessss!" and goes to town. Fingers were made before plates. Aha!—he finds the sturgeon, the only fish he likes. Oh—*loves!* He plucks slices of sturgeon like potato chips and is washing them down with Coke when Karen and Marcus find him. "Ari!"

"*Wha-at?*" high note, low note of a misunderstood, innocent child.

"You know exactly what, my dear brother. Don't put on an act." But *this* is an act, too. She's grateful to avoid the receiving line and the shmoozing.

So she just says, "You mind your manners."

"Be cool, Ari," Marcus says. To this Ari listens.

The musicians seat themselves, tune violin and cello to the flute, play a Gershwin tune. Karen knows that in a minute, the old people will be eating and dancing here. "Come on—let's go explore." Ari is faking karate kicks at Marcus, who drops suddenly, lifts Ari up over his back, and spins him. Karen shushes them.

Lots of rooms downstairs. Offices, classrooms, another small sanctuary, a fifty-person recital hall with upholstered seats set in an arc facing the baby grand. A Steinway! Karen steps up onto the low platform. "Why thank you," she says. "Thank you. And for my next performance—Ari, you want to be the audience? (Her real audience is, of course, Marcus)—I shall play the *Gymnopédie* #1 by Eric Satie." She sits, mimes flapping tails of an evening coat from under her, exercises her fingers to get the feel of the piano, and begins. It's three minutes long, one of the only pieces she knows by heart.

Ari sits up straight, doing his duty as audience. In the middle, the door opens, a boy has come in and stands in the back, listening. He's a descendent of Saul Kerenbaum, whom Jacob Goldstein brought to America. So the boy is here, is in existence at all, because of Jacob Goldstein. He's part of Jacob's legacy. Child of Eleanor's youngest niece, he's a junior at Hunter, and hopes to go to the Oberlin Conservatory or to Julliard when he graduates. A violinist. Luckily, Karen can't know that, or she'd be even more nervous than she suddenly is. But he's got a heavy swatch of perfectly black wavy hair that dips and sweeps across his forehead, and deep-set eyes in a long face, a strong mouth shaped by his being treated, unfortunately, like something of a prince.

She finishes the Satie and there's applause, and she camps a bow, but quickly, for she's embarrassed (although, she thinks, she played it well). "You with the wedding party?" she asks him.

He nods. "I'm Jacob Shulman."

"Karen Kuperman."

"Marcus Greene."

"So—the groom's your grandfather? Cool. The bride's my great-aunt. You play pretty well. I've got some music in the coat room. I've got my violin and sheet music, a Mozart sonata."

"For violin and piano? I'm not that good at sight-reading."

"A slow movement? Really slow."

"What are they doing upstairs?"

He shrugs. He's used to getting his own way. "I wouldn't ask if I didn't think you were really good."

She shrugs. She's used to not giving way.

"I'll get the music. Then if you can't, okay."

Ari says, "Do it, please do it, do it, c'mon Karen? You're great."

Marcus nods at her and smiles.

She's not that great, but in the KV 376, the andante movement doesn't ask for too much from the pianist. She looks at Marcus, and when he nods, she shrugs. She doesn't say yes, but she doesn't say no. Jacob gets the music, marked up from his practice, and they look it over together; she can smell his hair tonic. He can feel the warmth of her cheeks. And slowly, a few bars at a time, they play a little Mozart.

She doesn't excuse herself when she makes mistakes, just raises a finger and they start over. It's always harder for a pianist to sight-read. He knows the music and doesn't make many mistakes.

Soon she becomes breathless, keeping to tempo, supporting his flight.

Deborah and Michael are standing with plates in hand, arguing about their gift to Ira and Eleanor. What do you buy for an old father getting married? Michael has bought them a pair of original prints by Steiglitz. He knows Ira will crab, see something wrong with the choice, but what the hell. Deborah thinks it's coals to New-castle. *And* expensive. "All of a sudden you're against expensive?" he says to her curtly. She rolls her eyes: "God! Do you have to talk to me in Yiddish syntax?" She lifts herself into a stature John Singer Sargent would have loved to paint. Hopeless. They'll be like this at Karen's wedding, at the bris of her first baby, at Ari's graduations. Now they have a bite to eat, then walk off, champagne in hand, to bicker in private. And whispering, they argue all the way down the hall past classrooms until they hear, faintly, music: Mozart?—from doors at the foot of a staircase. The *AARON BLAUSTEIN RECITAL HALL* engraved in brass over the entrance. They peek through the window set into the door. Karen? Karen, Marcus, a strange boy, and Ari. So they go in.

Does Karen know they've come in? At once she stumbles, but lifts a finger and they repeat the measure successfully. Michael and Deborah take seats in the back. Deborah has forgotten all about the argument, the gift. She sits breathless, open-mouthed. Breath-less, because she's afraid that when breath comes, tears will come to her eyes. Well, and of course they do, like rain when the summer air feels full. The wedding didn't move her; *now* she's moved. To see Karen attempting, with a stranger, a sonata she hasn't played and doing it pretty competently, tenderly! Deborah kneads Michael's hand. And Michael, lately his heart has been breaking open every day, it's like running at high altitudes to open your lungs, until you could call him an athlete of heart, or you could say his heart is get-ting trained. In the Torah the mind is located in the heart, not the brain. So he has an experienced heart, a heart ready for expansions like this. Still, it's too much for him—it's Karen, it's Deborah—and his breath comes hot and big, heaving his chest. Deborah is smiling.

Michael's sister Susan has found them. Susan's wearing white—it's her own wedding dress, let out a little. Once she got talked into coming, Susan opened her heart and now, in white, she's squeezing hands, hugging; her eyes are permanently wet. She comes in, waits till a phrase is finished, says, "You guys? I'm sorry to stop the beautiful music. But they're cutting the cake in a minute. I've been looking all over."

Karen waves at her, lifts a finger, plays the last phrase once more, stands up and shakes hands with Jacob, who's wiping his bow and putting it into cloth, placing the violin in its case—frugal gestures of a pro. Michael, Deborah, Ari, Marcus applaud, and Susan hugs Karen and leads the way. As they follow her down the hall to the small social hall, Karen and Jacob talk about Mozart, and Jacob asks about Karen's favorite composers and does she go to music camp? But Karen stops, waits for Marcus. "That was amazing," Marcus says.

"Thanks." Karen locks arms with him.

They all walk in together while Ira is toasting Eleanor. "We've been buddies, Eleanor and me, a hell of a long time. I won't try to con you I met this lady last month. She's stuck by me, and believe you me I've given her plenty of reasons to run the other way. Now she's coming with me to Nigeria, to be my brains while I take pictures. Me, an old white guy, I can show what's been happening in the oil fields, show how Shell Oil is ripping off the country and paying off the strong guys, while the land is poisoned and the people are dying of cancer and anyone who protests is killed. But I got an American passport. I'm damn well gonna bring back pictures. Got a couple of magazines interested—or Eleanor does. So I may have another show in about six months, if I make it back in one piece. Now let's cut the cake and call it a wedding."

Ira sees Michael and Susan come in and waves them over. He winks, he rolls his eyes, he mugs. Now he poses with a big knife in front of a modest wedding cake. Flash cameras go off. Ira hates flash like poison but doesn't say a thing. Deborah, who's followed Michael to the front of the hall, takes Karen's hand and Ari's hand. She ignores, as well as she can, the Ken doll on the cake with his tiny camera, next to a Barbie with flour-whitened hair. Ira cuts, Eleanor serves.

Mazeltov. Michael watches his father strut his stuff. From generation to generation. Or in his father's case, is it to *degeneration*?—he laughs to himself. Suddenly laughter dams up and grief floods his chest—he thinks of his mother, and again he's ashamed to be taking part in his father's celebration.

More than that. It's not just the thought of his mother. Ashamed to be taking part in *any* celebration. Does it seems appropriate to celebrate? For listen: the murderers are still in business. Those who kill for money and power. Those who kill to feel like God. Those who torture and kill because they confuse the voices of politicians or religious hysterics for the voice of God. "You shall . . . break down their altars and dash in pieces their pillars, for you are a people holy to the Lord your God." And so, another *jihad*. Another.

Yet some of us survive to celebrate survival. Michael with the help of someone whose name isn't really Geoffrey Slade, has survived. All of us, Michael reminds himself, have survived by one miracle or another. Always, in surprising ways, people have helped; have hidden us, have fed us, have looked the other way. Mazeltov.

Then, too, a private celebration is taking place. Michael and Deborah glance at one another. Michael takes Ari's hand; he squeezes down the chain of Ari to Deborah to Karen. Michael remembers their own wedding in San Francisco. In spite of their bickering—and will that ever end?—he imagines he is marrying Deborah again, now, here. Secretly, he thinks, secretly, this becomes their wedding, too. We celebrate: it seems our marriage has survived.

Surely he can say Mazeltov, l'chayim. To recite the mourners' Kaddish, as he will for his mother these next months, he needs to be able to celebrate life. The Kaddish begins: *Let God's name be made great and holy in the world that was created as God willed.* If you mourn, don't you have to grieve for the loss of something beautiful? Can't we celebrate that there is something worth the mourning—a world created as God willed?